SOUTHERN LOVING

"Don't be afraid of me," Terry said.

"It isn't you I'm afraid of, only myself," Susannah whispered. Her glorious eyes were hidden by fluttering lashes. "Perhaps it's the fervor of war . . . men in uniform . . . looming danger and the future so uncertain, but I haven't been able to get you out of my thoughts, sir. Oh, Lieutenant! I'm never at a loss for words, but it is most difficult for a Southern lady to . . . I don't know how to say it. . . ."

"Your eyes tell it all," he answered. When she gazed up at him again, her faint flush spread from her high cheekbones to her slender throat. "Susannah, I need you in more ways than one."

She didn't move away when, very slowly, he bent his mouth to hers and just . . . tasted, affirming the willing softness of her lips. He yearned to bend her body to his, to hold her hard against him, thigh to thigh, discovering the warmth and lush density of her breasts. Without ending their kiss, Susannah moved against Terry into the circle of his arms and fulfilled some of his immediate yearnings.

He kissed and kissed her lips and her eyes as he held her against him, taking only her lips, handling and sampling her, his mouth and fingers inflaming her, until her breathy assertions and small cries told him she was ready.

JOYCE MYRUS

LOVE AND GLORY

ZEBRA BOOKS
KENSINGTON PUBLISHING CORP.

ZEBRA BOOKS

are published by

Kensington Publishing Corp.
475 Park Avenue South
New York, NY 10016

First Printing: March, 1993

Printed in the United States of America

Now is the judgement of this world.
Each man or woman is taking his or her measure. As it is taken, even so must it stand—it will be recorded.
The activities of war quicken into life every evil propensity as well as every good principle.

Hannah Ropes
Civil War Nurse 1862

Chapter One

Susannah Butler was certain her life was under control and she could see her future with a measure of clarity until two momentous events occurred and all hell broke loose. In April of 1861, the Union was dissolved when the Palmetto State, Susannah's own South Carolina, became the first to secede from the Union, the turning point in history that finally set off the American Civil War. A few days later, another first occurred as Susannah set her kelly-green eyes on Terrence Terhune Armstrong, an irresistible charmer, a magnificent ravisher, an *agent provocateur,* the spy who would cost her her heart and—more than likely it seemed to her a scant half a year later—her freedom as well, for some time to come.

By September, Susannah, herself accused of spying, had for some weeks been detained at her Washington residence, under house arrest, when Yankee authorities, concerned about the continuing flow of privy information to the South, removed her to the Old Capitol building. As she waited there in the grim anteroom for her interrogator, the notoriously cruel Napolean Baker, she passed the time writing, committing her thoughts and feelings to paper, a lifelong habit.

'This now-hellish place, once the seat of government of our young, hopeful republic, later became a boarding house, the very one in which South Carolina's greatest statesman, John Calhoun, lived and died. His spirit, still present here, gives me courage and determination even now that this aging structure has been turned into a military prison infested, I've heard, with informers, bedbugs and brave Secessionist fortitude. Its red brick facade may be faded and chipped, its windows barred with slats of wood, but within, Southern blood boils,' Susannah wrote, smiling to herself and drawing her cloak close about her.

Apparently, her reputation had preceded her to jail. She was greeted on her arrival there with cheers from Rebel prisoners she could not see, and with ceremony and deference by Superintendent Wood who, she granted, was something of a gentleman at least, despite being a Yankee.

"I am hoping, Superintendent, to be held in the west wing of the building, near the Rebel officers, after I am questioned. I've met this man, Baker, the State Department detective. I've been told he's a dastardly scoundrel not above using deplorable procedures to extract information from the prisoners he holds in solitary confinement in the Old Capitol Annex, Carroll Prison."

"He's a mean-eyed, taciturn man, Mrs. — Miss Butler, who does not say much to me but, be assured, I am aware of the honor of being your custodian. I *will* do what can be done . . . what is allowed . . . to make your stay here . . . tolerable."

"Thank you, sir," Susannah nodded, a humble gesture completely belied by her confident expression and coppery red hair that appeared to the Superintendent and his loitering officers a blazing banner of defiance. At that, ignoring them all, Susannah turned back to her scribblings, as she called her diary.

'I write in the hope that those who later peruse this little document will read between the lines, enabling me to yet do some good for my country. And if not? At the least, this narrative of imprudent behavior may save some other woman from the ruinous rewards of blind passion mistaken for true love.

'I had *some* excuse. You must understand that at twenty-six I had, not altogether unhappily, accepted my state of single blessedness. With no husband and babies to consume my time, I devoted some of my energies to our Low Country South Carolina plantation, the kennels and stables and that pleased my father. To please myself, I turned to books and the Suffragette Movement, not the usual pursuits of a Dixie belle of a prominent family. Also, I was a teacher. I had to keep that a secret from almost everyone because my father wouldn't have allowed it if he had known, and also because instructing slaves, or even free black people, to read and write, exactly what I was doing, was against the law.

'So, there I was, on the brink of permanent spinsterhood, not an altogether displeasing prospect to me, but also, perhaps, on the verge of prison as well, which would have been singularly disagreeable, I now know, when I received a proposal of marriage. It came from an old friend of my papa's, Will Chauvenet. When I said yes, after turning down a baker's dozen of men before him, I think Will was almost as surprised as I by my answer. I agreed mostly to satisfy Mamma and Papa, but also because I knew that Will, who shared my bookish proclivities, would be tolerant of my politics and keep my secrets. I have known Will all my life and I am truly fond of him. Our marriage would not have been one of mere convenience but rather the joining of two kindred spirits. Then, along came the War of Secession and that perfect specimen of a man and warrior, Lieutenant Armstrong.' Here she stopped writing and drifted into memory.

Terry Armstrong was the embodiment of physical manhood, Susannah had seen at once. He was tall and long-legged, six feet or more, slim in the waist, narrow in the hip and his mustaches

10

and shoulder-length hair were a rich, dark brown. He cut such a dashing figure that she was afraid he might be the one she had waited for and given up on ever finding, afraid because she did *not* want to upset her sensible plans by actually falling in love. By the time she first saw Armstrong, she had despaired of ever doing *that*. She no longer wanted the turmoil of love, she thought, especially not love from any damn Yankee.

That's what Susannah supposed Terry to be the April day in 1861 when they met. Six months later, waiting in the Old Capitol jail, it seemed to her that she had lived a lifetime since that day, and still, she did not know if her first supposition about Terry Armstrong was right or wrong. She still was not certain where his loyalties lay, with the Secessionist cause as he claimed, or with the Union. "The only thing I do know for a certainty," Susannah wrote, "is that I am in a terrible predicament now, because I went and fell in love as soon as I saw those flashing dark eyes of his, fool that I was.

'I must have been crazy or drunk, not with liquor but with war fever, like almost everyone else in the country, north and south. We were so relieved the shooting war had finally begun, we were wildly intoxicated with the excitement and jubilation—yes, *jubilation*—of the battle joined at last, God forgive us all.'

Amidst the high fervor and agitation of a truly

11

momentous occasion, one that was stirring and sad all at the same time, there *he* had been, Susannah remembered, her pen poised above the page, her expression distant. The man had been aloof from it all, lounging against a green willow tree, calm as you please, puffing on a pipe, detached and, somehow, alone in the crowd. Watching him, she conjectured he was one of the few Naval Academy instructors she'd not met.

It was a blue-sky April morning, the twenty first day of the month in eighteen and sixty-one, a Tuesday, one she would *never* forget while she drew breath, Susannah knew. Fort Sumter in Charleston Harbor had, only days before, fallen to Dixie and the State of Virginia, one of the holdouts of the Confederacy, had joined the Secession. The naval school at Annapolis in Maryland, a Union state of mixed political passions, was being moved farther north, to solidly pro-Union territory, for the duration of hostilities. That wouldn't be long, Southerners were sure. They were absolutely certain the Confederacy would rapidly win the day, after a battle or two up in Virginia or Kentucky, perhaps. The Federal Army was nothing but a rabble, they told themselves and each other, and they believed in their heart of hearts that Southerners would never, ever yield.

"And if half a whole year later it hasn't yet played out exactly as we predicted? Well, keep in mind that it's not all over, by no manner of means, nowise,' Susannah wrote, finishing her sentence with two exclamation points.

On that day upon which her thoughts dwelt, the *Constitution,* the great frigate of the 1812 war, nicknamed 'Old Ironsides,' was standing by to take the Yankee midshipmen up to Newport. The Stars and Stripes flying from her mast was stirred by brisk spring breezes. Even with most of her sails furled, the vessel was straining at anchor on Chesapeake Bay like a tethered swan beating her wings, wanting to be away among the fast-scudding clouds. On shore, parade bands blared out stirring martial music as the cadets and their instructors, half of them in tears, were marching together, wearing the same uniforms, under the same flag, for the last time before parting to don Confederate gray or Union blue. It was dreadful to Susannah to think that the next time those brave boys met, good friends all, they would actually be trying to kill each other. She was close to tears herself as she watched her somber father, Stephen Butler, splendid in the full dress apparel of a Commodore, shake the hand of each and every cadet who passed before him, even that of his own son.

Susannah's little brother, Simeon, the family's pride and darling, was one of the twenty Southern midshipmen resigning from the academy that day. The Commodore had been one of the founders of the Naval School at old Fort Severn in Annapolis fifteen years before, so it was an

13

affecting time for the Butler family, particularly for Simeon. "He was a fine, ruddy-faced innocent youth then, full of life and business!" Susannah said aloud, startling her guards, then lapsing back into silent thought. He, like the other midshipmen, despite their show of spit and polish, appeared to Susannah touchingly gallant and vulnerable and so very young. 'My brother, Simeon! Now,' she wrote, 'I can hardly think his name without a twisting of the heart and tightening of the throat. Oh, but I do get ahead of myself in the telling of this story.'

That day, in all the activity, there was a stillpoint, the manly figure of a naval lieutenant, which drew and held Susannah's glance. He turned in her direction, as if he had felt her eyes going over him, lingering on his profile, appreciating his fine broad shoulders. At once, he began to make his way toward her, slowly and obliquely, so that his destination wasn't obvious to any one other than Susannah.

But she knew, despite the distractions of music and tears and shouted commands, in all that kaleidoscopic chaos of marching men, snapping flags and restless, stamping and snorting horses—he had seen her, too.

The lieutenant moved slowly but with purpose through a crowd of ladies, and even then Susannah was already plagued with a premonition of jealousy as he cordially greeted several—Navy wives, mothers and sisters like Susannah and her mother, Catherine. They were all dressed in their best lustrous, belled gowns that day, twirling their parasols, giddy with excitement that was tempered only by vague forebodings of the war's likely cost in shattered lives and lost loves.

The politicians, too, were out in numbers for the occasion, mostly Lincoln's Yankee Republicans, swarming like horseflies and all a buzz. Some of them were dressed in black frock coats and stove pipe hats of the type favored by Old Abe and she noticed her lieutenant, as Susannah already thought of Terry, though she didn't yet know his name, stop to speak with one gray-templed sage, the Massachusetts Abolitionist, Senator Sumner, before continuing in her direction through an assembly of officers.

In contrast to the civilians, the military men were gorgeous and gaudy as butterflies, gilt-festooned, decorated with rows of ribbons and pendant silver and gold medals, with glittering swords and embroidered sashes at their waists.

But not Terry. Standing straight as an arrow, yet lithe and relaxed, he wore golden spurs with his dark blue uniform that was decorated only with brass buttons. He was lightly bearded, well-barbered, and from beneath his wide brimmed hat, that Susannah noted, was no military issue, dark hair fell to his shoulders. He had an austere, strong profile and he was uncommonly handsome, particularly when he flashed his shining smile, something he did often, each time he

15

paused to talk. Susannah grew most impatient to hear the voice that went with so impressive a form and winning manner.

She knew before he uttered a word to her that she had best take care to keep her reserve or she would be lost, totally.

She didn't want to deny this man anything he might require. It would have been nearly impossible for her to resist him, she realized, no matter how she tried, which she certainly did. Try. But she had too long wished with all her heart, in vain, for love. Like many other Southern girls, and not a few Northerners, too, she had been brought up to believe that a woman's true nature feeds on love, that love is its life. So, she had waited and *waited* for the overpowering sensation of true love, that strange spell which comes over a person only once in a lifetime, and the longer she had waited, the more she doubted it would ever come over *her*. She had already turned down some of the most gallant men of both Carolinas, finding shortcomings in every one, until she came to the conclusion that her head would always overrule her heart. So, trying to be level-headed and sensible about an admirable man, she accepted Will Chauvenet's proposal of marriage. Then, along came Terry and she did surely fall in love. Not a little, but in that sublime and yielding, immeasurable way that knows no bounds.

"May I call on you?" the lieutenant asked, finally reaching her side. His voice was rich and smooth and his diction was pure gentleman Yankee. Susannah was devastated.

"Sir, in normal times, I would not even bother to reply to a total stranger making such a request, but in the present circumstance, I feel obliged to respond in some way to a fellow soon to be facing battle. Aren't you going north with your students, Lieutenant?" she asked, pretending indifference though she was both happily startled by his straightforward request and crushed to be losing him, right off.

"Ma'am, they are not my students, and only Yankees are heading North now. I'm no Yankee. I'm from Galveston by way of New York and I'm here to help Commodore Butler build a Confederate States Navy."

"In that case, perhaps I will allow you to call," Susannah said calmly though feeling, to her annoyance, wildly elated.

"When and where will you be receiving?"

"At home, in Charleston."

"Ah, Charleston. The cradle of the Confederacy. Now that I know you'll be in that proud Rebel city, I'll be sure to ask old man Butler for a posting there."

He got his posting to Charleston, all right, Susannah mused, and now, the gossips were saying Terry Armstrong took advantage of her and broke her heart. There was a kernel of truth there, but even so, it was unfair to him to put it that way. She had been, she knew, as eager for his first kiss as he for hers, as impatient as he for everything that followed, if the truth be known. She was no child, but a grown woman. She *needed* a man, *that* man, she admitted now. Besides, it hadn't been up to her, really. Whomever, or whatever it was, gods, fates or furies—that decides about love and desire, had decided about Susannah Butler and Terrence Armstrong and that was that.

"And do you suppose 'old man Butler' will oblige you with the posting of your choice, Lieutenant . . . uh . . ." she had charmingly asked that first day, looking up into his fine dark gray eyes that were intelligent and warm and a shade forlorn, just enough to evoke a little tender concern.

"My name, Ma'am, is Terrence Terhune Armstrong, but I'm called Terry by friends of both sexes. Terry, at your service," he smiled, sweeping off his hat and, all at once, Susannah was the starry-eyed girl she'd once been, tall and leggy at sixteen, all dressed up and eager to go dreaming at her first cotillion, she reminisced, her head full of fluff and feathers and whimsical delusions.

Back then, she would envisage the mythical gods sitting around a table, perhaps sipping wine from golden goblets and dealing out destinies the

18

way mortals deal out cards for a game of whist. "Let's match up *these* two, and see what happens," she imagined one Greek god saying to the others as sketches were passed from hand to hand. Some lovers paired by providence were predestined to meet when they were fourteen or sixteen or twenty, was Susannah's assumption, while others didn't find each other until later, when their hopes of love had been all but relinquished. In her own view Susannah was, to put it bluntly, a spinster. Terry was a widower and the father of two little girls of five and thirteen. He thought he'd already lost the love of his life and she had given up on ever finding hers.

"We're close, the Commodore and I," Terry told her that first day. "I'm almost like a son to him, he says. You see, I've been invited to stay as a guest in his home during Confederate Navy strategy sessions. Luckily for me, he happens to reside in Charleston. I was only trying to impress a beautiful woman with my contacts in high places. I don't have to make a request — I've already got my assignment to your city," he grinned. "If I may call on you while I'm there, Commodore Butler will vouch for my integrity and I will be eternally grateful. I've been sorely missing my . . ." he hesitated for the briefest moment, ". . . my family in Galveston, Miss? . . ." He wanted Susannah's name. She was not about to give it.

"You're like a son to the Commodore?" she

19

interjected. "I, also, am well acquainted with him. I'll ask 'the old man' if you're respectable enough, Lieutenant Armstrong, to be allowed to call on a lady in her parlor. Perhaps we'll meet again, sir." She smiled coolly, dipped her parasol and strode off with purpose and also with great effort. She had no desire then, or ever, to quit Terry's company, but she was so elated he was to be billeted under her own roof, that she thought she might laugh right out loud with delight. Besides, her heart was throbbing so, she was afraid she'd give herself away and she dearly did want to see Terry Armstrong's handsome face when he discovered who she actually was, 'the old man's' one and only daughter, Susannah Butler.

Chapter Two

He couldn't help it. His expression, Terry knew, betrayed his total astonishment and delight at finding *her* ensconced in the Commodore's garden. She had been on his mind a lot in the past days. Her face, her voice, the sway of her belled skirt that had revealed a pretty ankle, the flounce of fiery curls down her back as she had walked away from him that April day, all had been with him like a vision of delight since he'd seen her at Annapolis. When out of the blue he'd asked permission to call, Susannah's very bonnet brim had trembled as if with an indignation of its own.

"Sir! Um, Lieutenant . . ." she amended, glancing quickly at the stripes on his sleeve and adding, before prancing off, "this is too solemn an occasion for flirtin' and fooling."

"I don't have time to court you properly or to mince words with the most beautiful female I have ever seen, south—or north—of the Mason-

Dixon Line," Terry called after her. In a full billow of belled skirts and crinoline, she swirled about to look at him for another long moment, one hand on the crown of her bonnet, the other set at her tiny, tight-laced waist, her shamrock green eyes incredulous.

Suddenly, Terry found himself staring into those same eyes again, staggered to find his elusive, exquisite lady before him, very much in the flesh. This time when she whirled about, it was to greet him and kindly but smugly laugh at his surprise. The sound, he thought, was musical, as if long fingers had swept the strings of a harp. He at once imagined the sensation of her elegant hands on his skin and he passionately desired this racy thoroughbred of a woman as he hadn't any other female in a very long time.

He had of course made conquests aplenty since losing his wife Abigail, but he hadn't much wanted any of them. It was to escape loneliness and a grief so wild and bleak he thought he might die of it, that he had returned to his old profligate habits. He had again become the "ladies' man" he was in his unwed, unruly youth.

It didn't help. He was lonelier still. His heart ached day and night, though he could, and did, seduce any woman who caught his eye and have her doing whatever he required after just a day or two of persistent attention. Susannah Butler was different. With her, it took less than an hour.

22

* * *

Terry had been briefed about the Commodore's beautiful daughter. She had been described to him as a woman of beguiling, buoyant disposition and resolute character, if untamed and impetuous. He had also been told that despite her flamboyance—she was a fearless, reckless horsewoman, for one thing—she'd been to one of the female academies and had a good head on her shoulders, so good in fact, she held herself superior, too smart by half, for any man who'd yet come courting her. That large group had included the wealthiest, most attractive gallants and planters of both the Carolinas, chivalrous southern gentlemen all. Terry took that as a personal challenge before he even suspected his Annapolis charmer, his dream girl, *was* Miss Butler. Now that he'd found them to be one and the same, he was almost certain she was just what he was looking for—a clever, gorgeous female with backbone and spirit enough to become his accomplice on a mission for his government. Either with or, if need be, without her realizing it, this woman could be an invaluable aide to him. He also understood, as soon as he heard her lovely laugh and recognized the longing look in her eyes, that sooner or later, if the two became colleagues, they would also become lovers. He had few doubts about her full cooperation on *that* score.

That first time Terry had seen Susannah, he had cause to hope his luck and his life were beginning to change. The first time he bedded her, the first time any man had, he knew he'd found a woman who could rescue him from despair, if their friendship prospered well. That was all Terry wanted, an alliance. He wasn't looking for more. When he lost his wife, he lost all concern for that idiocy men call love. He gave up his last prayer of finding an attachment of the kind that comes only to the fortunate, and only once in a lifetime. Yet, the first time that he and the vestal Susannah, as he thought of her, were alone together was an uncommon episode not only for her but for him as well.

Total strangers, they became instant lovers. Later, before deceit and betrayal made them foes, they had grown to be lovers *and* friends, co-workers, Terry presumed, in the same cause. But whether friends or enemies, Susannah and Terry were always lovers, though they did at times try to keep their distance. Even later, despite the rancor that grew between them, when they were alone together, neither could resist the other.

In retrospect, it would come to seem to Terry that Susannah was more ingenious than he gave her credit for being, that it was *she* who hoodwinked *him,* perhaps right from the start. Through it all though, she had never been false or coy when it came to passion. Terry liked that, but it did cause him to let down his guard. It happened this way with the Commodore's beautiful daughter and the handsome Lieutenant.

24

* * *

Late in April of 1861 he presented himself, satchel in hand, at the Butler town residence in Charleston, on the Battery at South Broad Street, the most fashionable part of the city. The tall old house of stuccoed brick stood with its shoulder to the street for privacy, facing south to catch the breeze off the water. As Terry stepped through the wrought iron gate and crossed the piazza, he saw there was a social gathering in the commodious garden, one of the finest in Charleston, a city of exceptional gardens. Most of the men and boys were in uniform and the women were as enchanting as the foliage — wisteria, roses, tamarisk and blazing azaleas that surrounded them in the garden. Miss Butler's back was to him when the Commodore, at his most garrulous, roared out an enthusiastic greeting. Then, with his hand resting on Terry's shoulder he said, "Susannah, is this your Lieutenant? Is this the bold young fellow you were inquiring about, Daughter?" With a silent cue Terry would in the future often see and come to love, Susannah daintily moved the fingers of her left hand to her lips to occasion a pause in the discussion going on about her. She peered intently at him as did the others in her circle.

"I'm not really sure if this *is* the man, Papa," she demurred. "Have we met before, sir?" she asked, her brows lifting like wings above green eyes sparkling with gaiety. She was very much enjoying her little hoax, of which Terry was the victim.

"Damn straight, we've met and you know it!" he inadvertently proclaimed, unable to hide his smile, an ear-to-ear grin she later told him it was. He took a step forward and planted his fists at his hips, a gesture, Susannah would also later tell him, she found slightly threatening and very attractive.

When she'd finally stopped laughing at him, he took her arm and led her a little distance from the others, across the deep lawn which stretched away to the sea wall.

"I must talk with you in private, Miss Butler, about a matter of great urgency," he said in a low voice.

"Mr. Armstrong, it's just possible I've waited twenty-six years for you, so now, you slow down a little and tell me, where on earth have you been?" she demanded with a low laugh. While she attended on his reply, the glow in her eyes changed from humorous to somber. Terry took his time before answering and used the opportunity to really study her at his leisure for the first time, but not the last.

She *was*, as he had been told by his informants and already discovered for himself, an unusual beauty—a tall, willowy, full-bodied, copper-haired, green-eyed young woman to delight all of a man's senses. Her pink lips were full, her rounded chin strong, her narrow nose freckled and her voice, like her laugh, was a throaty caress. She was also, he was about to discover all on his own, a passionate female who, she claimed at the time, had long been yearning for him and him alone.

"Waiting for me? I take it you're one of those believers in love at first sight . . . one man for one woman for life?" Terry laughed as the other guests began to move inside soon after his arrival. He offered Susannah his arm, presuming to claim her as a dinner companion. He got considerably more than the pleasant tête-à-tête he'd been expecting at the time.

"I think I am one of those believers, yes, but let's get to *your* urgent matters, Lieutenant, *before* dinner, shall we?" she asked. Instead of following the crowd, she led the way to a garden cottage some distance from the house. Hidden among palmettos, magnolias and fragrant opopanax trees, it was her special place, Susannah explained, where she went to read or think or talk with friends when privacy was required. No one would disturb them there. Ushering Terry inside, she shut and bolted the door. In the twilight's soft gloom, she lit a lamp, fumbling at the task, before she started talking. Terry thought she might never stop, but he didn't mind. He relished looking at her.

"These locofoco matches are supposed to ignite easily but I always have difficulty with them," she

27

explained in a quivery voice. "Now, sir, I asked Papa about you as I said I would. He has told me you are known to be, in certain circles, a rake and a rogue and a heartbreaker, but also, Papa said you are a loyal son of Dixie and, consequently, a gentleman, when circumstance requires. He welcomes you to his fireside and table because your work for the Confederacy is . . . vital. If I can be of help in some way to the cause and . . . to you, Papa says I *must*." When she raked back her copper curls, she made no attempt to hide the trembling of her slender hands. He caught them in his.

"Don't be afraid of me," he said. "Shall we talk now a while, or after . . . ?"

"After what, sir?" she inquired in a smaller voice.

"Dinner," he replied calmly with an open smile.

"I brought you here, Lieutenant, to talk, so . . . let me begin," she replied. "It isn't you I'm afraid of, only myself." Her glorious eyes were hidden by fluttering lashes long as palm fronds. "Perhaps it's the fervor of war . . . men in uniform . . . looming danger and the future so uncertain, but I haven't been able to get you out of my thoughts, sir. How are we to work together if . . . Oh, Lieutenant! I'm never at a loss for words, but it is most difficult for a Southern lady to . . . I don't know how to say it . . ." She was charmingly distressed and looked away, but she was not coquettish, or timid, not then, not ever.

"Your eyes tell it all," he answered, with not quite the easygoing aplomb he'd intended. When she gazed up at him again, her faint flush spread from her high cheekbones to her slender throat. "I want to kiss you, too," he said. "Susannah, I need you in more ways than one."

She didn't move away when, very slowly, he bent his mouth to hers and just . . . tasted, affirming the willing softness of her lips. He yearned to bend her body to his, to hold her hard against him, thigh to thigh, discovering the warmth and malleable lush density of her breasts. Without disjoining their kiss, she moved against Terry into the circle of his arms, and fulfilled some of his immediate yearnings which at once gave way to others more intense.

It was then he knew he had to gain a physical distance or risk dangerously confusing business with bliss when he felt her fingers, now deft, at his waist. Stepping back, smiling, she relieved him of his sabre, unsheathed and raised it before her. The brass hilt reflected lamplight as she brought the flat of the plated blade for an instant to her lips, an astoundingly provocative act, one Terry was to see and respond to many times again, one he would never forget.

He started then to undress her, too, his mouth touching not cool steel but silken, creamy skin. He kissed her hands each in turn, her brow, then her throat when she came into his arms and threw back her head, her tumbling hair almost

29

brushing the floor. Skillfully, eagerly he freed her breasts and as they protruded from her gown and the loosened bustier beneath, he mouthed them, nibbling at the peaks, putting her into a condition of breathless, shuddering pleasure. Stepping out of her hoops and crinolines, she let him lead her to a chair. Slowly, going down on one knee and looking deep into her eyes, he unlaced her boots. She herself removed her silken stockings, raising her petticoats as she did to reveal long golden legs. Terry was to be the first lover to possess and caress Susannah's sumptuous body.

When she stood again, the womanly amplitude of her swells and curves was concealed only by a filmy shift as she relieved Terry of his tunic and blouse.

"You learn quickly," he said, hoarse-voiced and there was that gesture, fingers to her lips to silence him, before she began tracing her hand, cooler and lovelier than he'd imagined it, over the harp of his ribs.

"Oh, the muscles ripple so!" she breathed before retreating behind him to press her lips to his shoulder blade and reach forward to undo his trousers. He helped and when he drew her to face him again, lifting the gauzy shift over her head, they both stood unclad, smiling, regarding and savoring each other, as much at their ease, despite racing hearts, as if they were in the Garden of Eden and not a Charleston garden cottage.

He was careful with her, and lingering. He

30

kissed and kissed her lips and her eyes and the shell curve of her ear as he held her against him and they stood stroking and fondling, skin to skin, thigh to thigh, her breasts warm against his chest, his hands claiming possession of her splendid abundance before she led him up a narrow set of stairs to a loft cot. She arched and stretched out to her full length like a languorous lioness, Terry thought, and he straddled her acquiescent body, the most perfect he ever had seen.

Even then, he held back, taking only her lips, handling and sampling her, his mouth and fingers inflaming her, probing moist furrows and sweet rises until her breathy assertions and small cries told him she was ready.

Chapter Three

"I wanted . . . just a kiss," Terry said. "Susannah, believe me," he persisted, "I never intended this to happen." Terry gazed at her, looking both pleased and troubled.

"I think I intended it," Susannah answered, not troubled, now that the deed was accomplished. "Terry, I'm not one for second thoughts and regrets, once I make a determination. Actually, I'm feeling . . . well, satisfied. With myself—and you," she said, her low voice smoky and warm.

That first combustible encounter had somewhat quelled the firestorm of their desire and they rested, awaiting a second wind and a second helping. They lay coiled on the narrow cot in the garden house, the same place where Susannah had passed many golden summer hours of her girlhood in sweet revery, daydreaming of her true love, with the hum of bees in the magnolia and jessamine all the music she needed. Being there with the real thing, Terry Armstrong, her body following the flex of his, the prickly old straw mattress beneath them felt bounteous and soft as goose down and feathers. She pressed her breasts to Terry's back, that was long and hard and muscled and beautiful, and she simply could not prevent her hand stroking it again and again from neck to firm swell of haunch. Susannah had never seen a man so perfect, nor one altogether disrobed. She was enveloped in the wonder of it all and glad she had waited for this man, the right one. "How shocked my beautiful and mannerly mamma would be," she mused. "Shocked, but not surprised, really."

"Why not surprised?" Terry asked, lifting an expressive brow as he turned to gaze down at her with pleasure.

" 'Susannah, dear,' Mamma's always sighing, usually when we are alone in her beautiful garden on a summer afternoon and as recently as this very day, 'Daughter, I deplore usin' the word spinster, which to my mind suits you not at all, but darlin', you *have* let the first flower of your girlhood come full blown, like a late rose of summer, saying "no" to one suitor after another, fine gentlemen, all.' I think it was the rose buds that set Mamma off today," Susannah laughed quietly. "That or our magnificent fig tree dropping its early ripening fruit on the brick walkway."

"Did you make exorbitant demands of these fine suitors of yours, Susannah, sending them off as if you were a fairy tale princess to win trea-

33

sures for you in the far corners of the world?" Terry asked.

"Oh, not all of them were so fine, I told Mamma, and I'm telling you. Some were just hell-raising fools concerned with nothing but their horses, dogs, and guns. *And* with their precious honor and virility, of course, being part of Southern chivalry as they've dubbed themselves. When I say such things to Mamma, who is luminous and delicate as a porcelain figurine, she closes her eyes and clasps her pale and long-fingered hands as if entreating the heavens for help. With her best efforts at parental sternness, not her strong suite, she said to me just today, 'Susannah, perhaps the Commodore is right. Susannah, perhaps too much book learning *is* a hindrance to marriage.' "

Terry, captivated by the soft southern caress of Susannah's inflection, by the way the tip of her tongue, like a kitten's, passed over her cupid's bow lips, by the saucy little light of independence in her green eyes, encouraged her to go on with her discourse.

"Is that what your father believes?" he asked.

"Papa often *does* say exactly that, sometimes with a wink, but not always. He *is* fond of proclaiming that he's not against education at all — except for females, because they are physically weak and naturally lightheaded. It's the Commodore's opinion that women must be accomplished just enough to make themselves the mothers of great men. He believes I am spoiled for domesticity by being overly educated, a serious fault in a belle, one which makes her too independent for her own good. So says my darlin' Papa."

"You got round him, obviously and now, you're spoiled for wedlock. Is that it?" Terry saw Susannah's lips pucker with determination and he kissed them. "How'd you do it?"

"When he refused to send me North to Catherine Beecher's Hartford Seminary to study some dead languages — Latin and Greek — and be influenced by Yankees, *he* said, Mamma worked out a compromise. She convinced Papa that to keep me out of trouble and groom me to be a good, dutiful Southern wife, the Patabsco Institute in Maryland was just the place. It *was* closer to home than New England but unbeknownst to Papa, some of the faculty had themselves studied with the northern education reformers and Suffragettes."

"So, one of the most powerful naval officers in the country is malleable in his wife's pale hands, at least when it comes to his exquisite daughter?"

"Mamma's is a deceptively fragile beauty. It always brings out the protective instincts of any man within a mile of her, especially Papa. Catherine Butler may be just five feet tall but she is every inch a magnificent Carolina lady, a *grande dame,* the perfect ornament for her husband. She's also a woman who sees to it her children get what they need. On the surface, she's

35

mild and moderate and agrees with Papa, but she always maneuvers to get her way—and mine."

"Are you like her, darlin'? Good at maneuvering . . . at getting your own way?"

"Mamma was brought up to be the ever-charming wife and to mask her actual sentiments, but in truth, she has an instinct for politics and a passionate concern for fairness and honor. I was brought up the same as my mamma. Fairness and honor are important to me, too, but I speak my mind about most things. Too many things, Mamma says."

"So I hear," Terry laughed.

"Also, I'm taller than she is. That's another difference," Susannah laughed, too, stretching her full length against Terry's hard frame.

"About six inches taller, I'd say," he responded running a measuring hand down the plains and rises of Susannah's silken back. "What else does your Mamma say?

"*She* says the real problem with me and marriage is, I am an utter romantic of the most passionate kind."

"Smart woman. She surely knows her own daughter, but why is that a problem?"

"All southern girls are romantics, of course, but I am worse than most, Mamma insists, or else I'd have taken some man's hand and name long ago. I have been holding out for perfection, a knight straight out of Sir Walter Scott's novels, Mamma says. 'Love's fine, Susannah,' she always admonishes, 'but if you can't make a love match, for heaven's sake make a good match. And *now* you've let another man get away, Will Chauvenet, the poor shattered man. You've had your chances, God knows, Susannah, and broken many a steady heart.' "

"Have you?" Terry asked, not laughing, his look almost forbidding.

"I never meant to, but it's true some of my disappointed swains might have made tolerable husbands, though for one reason or another, not for me. To get over their discouragement, a few ran off to sea or out to the border states. One of the most egotistical hotheads amongst them, Beverly Bland, who thinks himself irresistible to women, all women, accused me of being cold, not virtuously so, but frigidly chaste. I always supposed he was wrong about that but I had no way of knowing for a certainty, not until now. Now, I've proven the opposite, to myself, anyway." She waited for Terry's response with the gleam of a smile in her eyes.

"And to me. I've never had such convincing proof of warmheartedness. If you were fishing for compliments, you've caught one." Terry met her smile with his own.

"I am *glad* I waited so long for you, Terry Armstrong, for the pleasure you've just given me," she told him, sitting bolt upright. "I mean what I say. Even good as I was at imagining and conjecture, I could never have anticipated the exhilaration of it, the uproar in the blood, the . . . the triumph in the heart." In an outpouring of delight, she nuzzled Terry's ear and recognized the fragrances of Number Six Cologne—bergamot and musk and lemon—and also breathed in faint whiffs of starch and manly sweat clinging to his neck.

"Rub my shoulders?" he asked in a suddenly-dubious tone, as if expecting a refusal, Susannah supposed.

She was wrong. Terry wasn't at all unsure of her response, only his own. His hesitancy, he told himself had nothing whatever to do with the bubbling, responsive enchanting woman in his arms and everything to do with his wife, Abigail. It was she, and only she, no other woman, who had been allowed to preen and burnish his splendid physique with a fragrant unguent she herself made, of Georgia peach blossoms and lemon oil. That was but one of the secrets Susannah would uncover as she became aware of the several perplexities of Terry's hidden past.

Led to a cell in the Old Capitol prison to await the tardy Detective Baker, Susannah's thoughts again and again went back to the April evening when Terry first loved her. 'The air about us,' she wrote in her diary, 'was heavy with pollen and all nature was in riotous bloom. I was so elated to have come to full flower myself, I was unmindful

38

of Terry's true emotions and intentions. I was so pleased to have been saved from withering, virginal and unloved, on the vine, so impressed with my own generosity, with what I had so magnanimously done—given myself to a man—it didn't occur to me the lover I'd so favored with my charms could be preoccupied with anything *but* me. The very suggestion would have seemed preposterous. Well, I suppose 'tis good to live and learn, as Cervantes wrote.

'Now, I've done both—lived and learned. Back then, I could not deny the man anything, nor did I want to. It was of my own free will I joined the ranks of the Terry Armstrong Walking Wounded, a sizeable group. It would be a long time before I understood that, and it will be longer still, forever I'm afraid, before I mend. However, after I had just been taken, body and heart, by my first, and only love, I behaved as many another woman has before me, and many, many will after: Like a damn fool.'

That night, at the start of it all, Terry puffed on a pipe Susannah filled and lit for him. He liked that, she could tell, though he never said so. And she did massage his neck and shoulders as he asked and he liked that, too.

"Susannah," he said looking hard into her eyes, "finding you has been singular and . . . extraordinary . . . for me. You knew that without me

39

saying, didn't you?" He smiled and she nodded and smiled. She ran her fingers through his silky golden brown hair, enjoying the sensation and also the easy intimacy of being with a man, *this* man, just *this* way. He went on talking while stroking her breast as she leaned to him. "Neither of us are using the word 'love,' you notice?"

Not yet, Susannah said, but only to herself, nodding again, thinking how aboveboard, how honest he was. "For myself," Terry continued, "I must say this: it was . . . intense . . . deep, but . . . romantic love is not for me ever again, Susannah. I thought I'd found life-long love with Abigail, my wife and . . . what I found was love of a sort I won't ever recover from. It changes a man to lose what I had with her. I don't think I could chance it again. Susannah, do you . . . understand? I want you to understand."

"I appreciate that my situation would be grim if I were looking for love and marriage, because my competition would be a dead woman, a sainted angel. Fortunately, all I've been looking for is what I've found here with you tonight — passion and fulfilled desire," Susannah lied. "We *are* a full-grown pair of concurring adults, Terry, so don't look so . . . so worried," she added.

"It's a relief for me to know that, Susannah," he nodded.

Deeply touched, she flung back her hair with a toss of her head, an edgy habit, the way a fretful mare tosses her mane.

"When you do that with your hair and it catches the lamp light," Terry observed "you put me in mind of a little jennet filly I once used to own, of a lovely copper shade," he mused.

"Funny. Papa says almost exactly the same thing," she replied. "Only his mare was russet."

"Susannah, I . . . do you truly grasp my meaning, about loving, really loving, only once, and being lost forever after?"

"Oh, yes, yes! Of *course* I do," she whispered in an emotional voice, loving *him* terribly, *her* once, she knew without any doubt. She was aching to offer comfort and consolation, to take him to her breast as if he were a hurt child and try to make him happy, even just a little. She thought her swelling heart would burst with tenderness and pain and she thought, Oh, *I'll* save you, Terry Armstrong, if you'll only let me! You *will* love again, love me and be saved.

It was one of the few things she would look back on later with something like pride that she didn't say *that* aloud.

"I had to know you understood, so there'll be no misunderstandings later," he smiled, the pained little boy expression replaced by a grown man's look of raw desire. He set down the pipe and again drew her close, taking her mouth, his hands tracing down her spine, pressing her hips to his loins.

Arrows of passion, the most delicious pain ever imagined, darted all through Susannah, radiating

41

from the tips of her breasts and deep in her belly. Her arms went about his neck, her pliant body arched to his and he swelled against her, parting her legs, prying, piercing little by little, before the deeper thrusts buried him within her, where she so needed him.

Depleted again, Susannah and Terry slept.

The full moon was up when she awakened suddenly. Terry was fully dressed, sitting in a rocking chair, smoking, just watching her. Naked and abandoned to dreams, she at once felt vulnerable under the stare of those probing gray eyes. She sat up, perplexed, and pulled a quilt over her.

"Susannah, I'm going to ask you to marry me," Terry said and she managed to respond, dumbfounded as she was.

"When . . . are you going to . . . to ask me that?"

Chapter Four

"When are you going to ask me that?" Susannah wanted to know. "Also, why would you propose marriage, if not for? . . ." Here she hesitated ". . . if not for love, which you've just said isn't a possibility for you . . . for us?"

Terry had been watching her sleep. She was beautiful everywhere, in every position, from every angle, a beautiful woman with a copper mane and golden skin. Her face was heart shaped. So was her mouth. When her green cat's eyes opened wide suddenly, they took his breath away and he didn't answer until her avid expression and the urgent edge in her voice when she repeated her question strongly suggested that he had put his foot in his mouth and had better explain himself—fast.

"This powerful magnetism between us is really a bit of good luck Susannah, because I had another reason altogether for searching you out. Before I even knew your name, I knew . . . other things about you, knew I needed you." She looked up at that. "A short time later, before I ever saw your flaming curls or *amazing* eyes, I *had* been told your name and heard about your politics—that you were a Unionist, perhaps even a covert Abolitionist but, even so, a vehemently loyal daughter of Dixie. My country . . . *our* country, is at war. I'm on assignment. I've been sent here for a specific purpose, to seek help of a sort only you can give me."

"You were *sent* here to do . . . what you and I . . . just did? Because you need my . . . help? I thought you were assigned to Charleston to work with my father building a Confederate Navy. I thought . . . didn't you just say something about marriage, Lieutenant?!" Susannah, magnificently indignant, her eyes blazing, stood and hid her extraordinary body in the bedclothes which she flung about her in the style of an Indian princess donning a sari. "Well?" she said, so flushed and pretty, about to flare in anger, she again aroused Terry's hot desire. He never could resist proud, passionate southern women, like his wife and his mother. His daughters were on their way to being the same.

"I've misspoken and I beg your indulgence," he said with a touch of Texas in his speech. It came naturally to him when he was being most sincere and he knew ladies really liked it. Springing to his feet, he crossed the loft room of the cottage in three strides. "I have been alone for so long without benefit of genteel companionship and modulating feminine sensibility, I have become too blunt," he explained, and he was encouraged to see Susannah's wary eyes begin to soften. Ever true to the gallantry demanded of an honorable son of the South, he hastened to further ease her distress and clarify matters.

"What happened between us was . . ." he took her in his arms and kissed her hard on the mouth ". . . was just between us. It wasn't planned. It couldn't have been and it couldn't have been stopped. Nothing can ever take it away."

Susannah responded, she as needy of him again as he of her. When she reached up to caress his face and undo his collar, her makeshift wraps fell away, all her beauty again filling his practiced hands and appreciative eyes.

With great effort, he clasped both her hands in his and held his strongest impulses in check. Now was a time for commerce of another sort. There would be, if she agreed to the plan, ample opportunity—months—in which they could rollick. He went and fetched her hoops and petticoats and gown. He wanted her fully attired and less of an enticement to him, for the moment. He told her so with an appealing, apologetic smile.

"What I have to say is important to our cause, darlin'," he pleaded, and she began at once to dress.

Terry Armstrong had watched and assisted countless women disrobe, expressly for *his* plea-

45

sure, but observing and abetting Susannah Butler in her endeavors to cloak her loveliness was an unrivalled experience for him. He couldn't resist burying his face in her curls, lush and soft as napped velvet, before lifting them and tightly lacing her bustier as she requested. He gloried in the aroma of gardenia perfume that clung to her shoulders and then, of necessity, he stepped back, lit a pipe and just watched.

She brought to his mind the most divine of swimmers, the goddess Aphrodite, rising naked and perfect from the sea. Susannah's graceful arms emerged from wave after wave of frothy petticoats that billowed about her to settle at her slender waist. Then came hoops, a yellow silk gown with lace-edged fluted flounces, and an overdress of dotted Swiss. A man like Terry who had daughters, *and* an eye for the ladies, noticed all the details.

When Susannah was perfectly reassembled, her hair middle-parted, looping over her ears, curls decorously restrained in a coil at her nape, he took her arm and led her out to the garden, just to be on the safe side and avoid temptation.

Some of the guests were playing croquet by moonlight and young Simeon Butler was among them. He had of course discarded his United States Naval uniform. While waiting for his new Confederate Navy outfit, on which his mother's seamstress was sewing, he was attired in the apparel of the Citadel Cadet he'd been wearing before going up to Annapolis. It didn't do to be out of uniform altogether in such patriotic times. The boy waved and called. Susannah and Terry waved but kept their distance, meandering along a path toward the open space at the heart of the garden.

"Susannah," Terry began, "I have to tell you something about myself because you'll hear it soon enough from others. Your father has already hinted at the well-deserved reputation I enjoy as a ladies' man." Her expressive brows shot up questioningly but no word escaped her. She knew the compelling value of strategic silence and Terry went on. "What happened between us has nothing at all to do with my usual philandering. My feelings for you are genuine. Even so, they cannot hinder me in my duty to flag and country." He felt her stiffen and draw away.

"That's as it should be, sir. No woman of South Carolina would for a moment tolerate a coward. But I must tell *you,* Lieutenant, I have a reputation of my own, one I neither enjoy nor deserve, as a heart breaker." She spoke in a devil-may-care, almost teasing tone, to put him off his guard, to put a distance between them and gain the upper hand, Terry thought, deciding to quickly to put a stop to that parry.

"I was told by . . . certain informants and I have learned from personal exerience," he smiled, bringing her hand to his lips, "that men find you dazzling. I'm one who's been overcome," he said drawing her arm through his to sustain the tenderness they'd shared. "I know a lot more about you than that."

"Oh? Have you a dossier on me? How intriguing. Divulge all it contains before I perish of curiosity!" Again she strove, almost, but not quite, convincingly, for an air of amused nonchalance.

"Here's what I was told about you, Susannah Butler. You are the only daughter of an Up Country South Carolinian of Scotch-Irish derivation. The Commodore, an energetic officer, gentleman and patriot, is related to General Pierce Butler of Mexican War fame who later was governor of this state. Your gracious, hospitable mother, who speaks with the easy drawl of the Carolina Low Country, has the cultivated manners of the Colleton clan, one of the first aristocratic families in the state, English, holders then and still of a great tidewater plantation and of the largest of the Carolina rice-founded fortunes. You and your brother will inherit it all someday. You've already acquired the beauty and grace and artistic bent of one side, your mother's line, the energy and resolution of your father's, and the pride of both."

"I thank you, sir, for the compliments and for your interest in . . . well, in our family. But for all your hints of informants and schemes and official business, I can't help but wonder if you are not some kind of gigolo or fortune hunter, perchance? Nothing you've told me is privy information. Lieutenant, everything you've just recited is general knowledge. Who all have you been jabbering with?" she asked dismissively with a soft trill of a laugh, drawing closer to him again as they walked in step.

"One of my sources of information was States Rights Gist, a Charleston man. I made his acquaintance at the Harvard Law School."

"I know Stacey, of *course*. But none too well." She tossed her head. "His daddy, Senator Gist, was all for secession nearly thirty years ago."

"He must have been, to give such a name to his boy. Was the younger Gist smitten with you like every other loose male in Carolina? Was he one of the ardent, nervous, sweaty-faced boys who came wooing you, Susannah?"

She didn't answer and he went on talking about her, relying on his observation that most women are fascinated by nothing so much as themselves. Susannah, he had yet to learn, wasn't like most women.

"Your unmarried condition has long caused talk. 'Susannah Butler' it expounded 'is too proud . . . or too beautiful . . . or too spoiled, or all three, to give her hand and heart to any man.' " When Terry said that, careful as he was to use the most neutral tone, she drew their stroll to a halt and turned on him angrily.

"My condition? You make it sound like some ailment, the dropsey or the vapors," she snapped. As she went on to vent her long-smoldering an-

49

ger, her eyes took fire. "Oh, I know what the gossips say of me behind my back! They say I need a man, that I'm too outspoken and headstrong because I haven't a husband to keep me in check. If I did have, *they* say, I'd not ride so wild after fox and hounds nor read so many books nor . . . do some other things I do. But now, Lieutenant, I've *got* a man. I've got you," she laughed, vexation seeming to dissipate in charming humor. "I've got a man who took my virtue and then announced he was going to ask for my hand in marriage. The order of things may have been reversed but if I should agree to marry you, all their whispering will cease, will it not?"

"Not if you go on engaging in illegal behavior and keeping 'unsuitable' company."

"Such as who?"

"Such as Grace Ellison," Terry answered. This bombshell was meant to test Susannah's skill at dealing with the unexpected. Her competence was prodigious. She passed the examination with aplomb. Her rejoinder was so cool, she almost deceived Terry, no easy thing to do, he prided himself.

"Grace? But she's not 'company' or unsuitable. She's my hairdresser, silly. She comes to me every morning to *comb* my hair." Though Susannah made light of the matter, even offering me a charming little trill of her lovely laugh, Terry knew she was on her guard even as she chatted pleasantly on. "Grace has been everywhere, to the

50

best watering places — Drenon's Lick, in Kentucky, with her ladies to Saratoga and Newport. Southerners fleeing yellow fever in summer are well represented up there and the social competition between North and South is intense. Grace learned the art of dressing hair in the employ of a French countess — in France, I'll have you know. Grace is exceptionally talented."

"I could tell that just by looking at you, lovely. She is also a free woman of color and she does more than comb when she comes to visit you. You and Grace are teachers together. Your students slip into the garden cottage after dark and some of them eventually make their way to Cincinnati . . . to Boston . . . farther north to Canada, as contrabands. I know something not many others in Charleston do: Grace Ellison has been imprisoned for breaking the Fugitive Slave Law."

Susannah, going wary in the eyes and a lovely pink in the cheeks, sprang to her friend's defense.

"Grace simply tried to help the man she loves to reach freedom and safety. That is not a crime. In her place, I would do the same," Susannah proclaimed, no hint of frivolity in her manner now.

"Ah, so you countenance breaking the law in the name of love?" Terry queried, impressed by her opinion and by her forthrightness in proclaiming it.

Terry was not a man, like a good many others, who thought the weaker sex naturally lightheaded

51

or frail in body and mind. He *liked* women even though they often puzzled him. He had great respect for the feminine intellect and he could find something appealing or congenial in most any one of them, but it was beginning to seem that Susannah might be singular in his experience in more ways than one. She was not merely courageously outspoken and truthful *and* beautiful. She was also shamelessly, wonderfully wanton. She was too good to be true, Terry would tell himself, later. He should have known that, and been on his guard. But she'd disarmed him and he wasn't, not even after a glance at her then revealed that her green eyes had gone hard as glass.

Chapter Five

"Who sent you here?" Susannah asked, her glistening eyes narrowed with suspicion. Terry went on talking, fast.

"Before I answer that question, circumstance requires I put several of my own to you."

They had come to a wrought iron bench at the edge of a pond made black as midnight by cypress roots, crossed by a graceful white bridge and filled with silver moonlight. The setting was enchanted and the air, Terry reflected, was fragrant as a fresh-peeled Georgia peach. He found it hard to keep his mind on negotiations. He gestured Susannah to a seat, intending to put his boot on the bench beside her and loom over her as they talked. He wanted the advantage of the dominant position. She kept on walking.

"What 'circumstance' requires you to question *me?* What if I refuse to answer?" she wanted to know. "Or, what if my answers don't suit you? What then?"

There was a silence. Finally, with misgivings, Terry said, "If your responses are not what I've been led to expect, I'll take my leave of you. I'll be gone by daylight and nothing more will pass between us until this war is over, and then? . . ."

"Oh, just ask away, damn it, and let us have done with games," she interrupted with impressive hauteur before lapsing into a withering silence of the sort, Terry knew, that would usually get a southern belle anything she was after. It worked moderately well with him. Joined in a contest of nerves, he held out, but only about half as long as he had intended, all of two minutes.

"Susannah, I'll settle for knowing just one thing," he sighed, discarding the long roster of queries with which he'd been primed. "It troubles me to ask at all, but there's been other talk about you. When I explain, I hope you'll understand. Please don't take offense. I wouldn't want to wound you, not even a little, not in any way, not ever."

At the time, he really meant what he said and Susannah seemed to believe him. She laughed and came closer to him again and took his hand and looked into his eyes and right then, he would one day recall, he'd have believed anything she said, even if the devil himself had been sitting there on her shoulder darting his forked tongue and grinning like all get out.

"Are you a Unionist as I've heard said or are

54

you so loyal to the Confederacy you would sacrifice anything, give up all you have—home and land and the love of your family, even your life, for the future of your country?"

Susannah nodded with the solemnity of a wise child.

"I *was* a Unionist," she said. "Like many of us raised up south of the Mason-Dixon Line, sir, I did deeply believe the American Republic of States should remain united. Your own Governor of Texas Sam Houston, was and still is of that opinion. And so, too, was Colonel Robert E. Lee until his own State of Virginia finally joined what the Yankees are callin' the Rebellion. Me and Colonel Lee, many others, know where our greater loyalties must lie—where we live, with our families and with our states. We also know that the South will fight on for all it holds dear even if the rivers run with blood and the bleaching bones of our brothers are strewn over the mountain tops."

Terry was deeply affected by her words and her manner of speaking them, with determination and also with sadness and resignation as if, like the oracles of old, her heart and soul and very bones were infused with an ancient wisdom of the sorrows of war.

"But would you risk *your* life was my question, Susannah," he replied softly.

"There surely are some Southern women who despair of war but they keep their own councils.

They do not speak out. Those who *are* most outspoken seem almost frenzied, insisting that any man who hesitates to defend his family and the sacred soil of home should be *hanged* high as Haman. I suppose the same should done to any woman who does not stand behind her man and her country. I am sorely distressed you would have to question the allegiance of your future wife, Lieutenant," she blinked in mock dismay.

Terry shrugged, at a loss, distressed himself at the word 'wife' and something else to answer her with a quip. Either she was the most talented actress he had ever met, and he'd known many of the profession, or she was that other oddity, an absolutely forthright woman, of whom he'd known damn few. When he frowned in perplexity, her quick kiss, soft and sweet as summer rain, alleviated his doubts.

"I was suspicious," she went on, "that you were going to attempt to use me for some nefarious Yankee purpose. I will now give you an absolutely unequivocal answer to your question. Yes, I would risk all, even my life, for the Confederacy."

Terry credited Susannah's words. Anyone would have, he decided, as he revealed his ploy and her eyes grew round with wonder.

"Can you pretend, as I will, to 'go north,' to become a turncoat, to *seem* to abandon the South and accompany me to Washington and New York? Your past politics and your teaching activities and my northern education and Yankee father, God rest him, would bolster the sham," he explained. "It's no lark, no game, I'm asking you to play. We'll be scorned and detested, spit upon by friends and family, even by some of our foes who surely won't admire us for our apparent treachery even to the enemy. But, now listen, the information we could gather about troop movements and merchant shipping, the transportation of California gold, the location of Yankee whaling ships and war ships of the line, could be crucial to the success of our Confederate cause."

"Couldn't we tell *anyone* the truth?" she asked in a pleading tone as her eyes took on a look of excitement. "Father, or Brother or . . . ?"

"No one, and especially not Grace."

"Why involve Grace?"

"Well, travelling in the South, a Confederate lady must have a body servant. Then, after we get my girls and we all 'go north,' they will need a nurse-maid. That could be Grace, but she has got to believe in us. She may even help us inadvertently by overhearing gossip. Women—and their maids—talk a lot, often too much and give away all kind of secrets, including military ones."

"I don't think I can lie to Grace, even for the good of Dixie," Susannah shook her head sadly.

"This plan will work only if every detail seems actual. That's why . . ." Terry paused, "that's why I mentioned marriage. It would be expedi-

57

ent, you know—fitting and proper—for us to appear to be man and wife when we're entertaining, sharing staterooms at sea and suites at inns and hotels on our jaunts north and maybe even around the world. Our delightful experience today proves *that* will be no hardship." He kissed her, lightly. "This turn of personal events will strengthen the plan and, after what's happened between us already, who knows?" Terry asked, looking into Susannah's unflinching green eyes and brushing a strayed curl from her cheek. "We just might want to be together . . . a *long* time." He was carefully noncommittal.

"Do you want to marry me, Lieutenant—or appear to marry me?" she asked calmly and coldly. They were sitting side by side, hand in hand, on the bench by then. From a distance came the sound of laughter, the thump of croquet balls and scattered applause.

"I never intend to wed again," Terry said. He hadn't meant to admit that. In the circumstances, he realized at once, it wasn't really politic of him, but the words just slipped by him somehow, as if he couldn't just lie to this woman as he had to so many others. "But Susannah, news of a large wedding, *your* wedding, would be carried far and wide, north and south. That's sure to make our work all the easier. There's only one complication that comes to my mind. I heard you're betrothed to another. What Rebel soldier boy has won himself such a prize of Southern womanhood?"

58

"No Rebel and no boy, sir, but a *real* man, William Chauvenet. He *was* my fiance but even if he is a Yankee, he possesses some of the more admirable attributes of manhood," Susannah said with feeling. This man was using her, she decided, probably in more ways than one, him wanting her to merely *appear* married after what had just transpired between them.

Terry sensed the anger in her just then, but could in no way account for it and so assumed he was being overly sensitive. He hadn't been thinking clearly, he would later realize, because he was already feeling possessive of Susannah Butler, and jealous of her so-called 'real man.'

"So! Your poor fool of a fiance azzled out on you," he laughed a bit cruelly. *"I'll* uphold the honor of a jilted lady any time, 'specially if she's as beautiful as you," Terry said shortly.

"Sir! My honor needs no protecting," Susannah exclaimed, *really* angry now. "And if it did, I would not turn to a stranger, especially not to any smart-alecky spawn of Gulf pirates and Yankees. Papa told me about *you*, remember."

"You and poor Willy!" he snorted a false sympathetic laugh, shaking his head in disbelief, ignoring her jibe as he stood to slap his wide brimmed hat against his thigh.

"Will is modest, confident, brave and true. A man of fine address and elegant manners," she bristled. "He's calm and . . . and precise and gentleman enough to free me from our agreement

59

until the war's over. He understands full well the depth of my love for my family and home and for South Carolina."

The lady was protesting too much, Terry decided, though he was so shocked to find himself envious of Will, to his regret he let his actual feelings show.

"Chauvenet is too old, twenty years older than you at least, too studious, fastidious to a fault, altogether too starched for so lively and beautiful a young woman." When Susannah opened her perfect mouth to defend the man, Terry encircled her waist and pulled her to him. He took and kept her lips and fingered her breasts until he felt the tips rise and firm under his touch. Right then, he really didn't care what she was — Yankee, Reb, Suffragette, Abolitionist — whichever. "Marry me, marry me," he whispered. In spite of himself, his voice rumbled with emotion, "for the good of . . . the Confederacy."

"I could never revere any man, Yank or Reb, so rash as to tender a proposal of marriage to a near-total stranger merely because he needed an assistant spy and found the stranger's appearance to his liking. I must decline," Susannah proclaimed with bogus determination.

"So *that's* what you feel for Chauvenet. Reverence!" Terry glowered, arching a brow, not quite able to hide a relieved smile. She'd yet to speak the word love he noted. "I couldn't help but notice it wasn't an impassioned farewell you gave

60

him at Annapolis." Though Susannah's cheeks crimsoned, she didn't look away. On the contrary, she stared more intently into his eyes where a smile now lurked.

"Will did not break off our betrothal sir, because of lack of affection on either side, but because of conflicting loyalties, mine to the Confederacy, Mr. Chauvenet's to the Union. He exceeds all my standards of manhood and I harbor great fondness and respect for William," Susannah said. "William is . . ."

"There would be two or three things lacking in your marriage to Willy, darlin'. Fun's one."

"And the others?" Susannah couldn't prevent herself asking.

"Love. It's a word you haven't mentioned once. Passion's another." There was a weighty silence and then, Terry heard Susannah's low, conspiratorial, intimate laugh.

"How contradictory of you to say that, after asking me to engage not only in a loveless marriage but a mock one, actually. You just go right on now and tell me, Terry, how are we going to concoct it?"

"My good friend happens to be in town, Colonel Wigfall of Texas. He's an ordained minister, or so he claims, and a cooperative one, who'll do anything for Dixie. He'll tie a well . . . let's call it a slip knot for us."

"You think of everything, don't you, sir?" Susannah said, her head to one side, begrudging ad-

61

miration in her glorious eyes. "You know, Terry, seeing Will and I together for just a few minutes, you discerned what it took me months to admit to myself—I did not want to marry Mr. Chauvenet. When the war separated us, I was relieved to have regained my freedom, at least for a time. He and I may yet marry one day, but now was not our moment."

"No, the moment is *ours,* yours and mine, darlin'. You are a rare one, Susannah Butler, a woman lacking any talent for self-deceit. That's good, because I can speak straightforward to you as I would to a man. I can't offer you love and marriage of the sort you should want and surely deserve, not now at any rate." Terry added that last to counteract his earlier bluntness and give her hope. Egotistical fool that he must have been, he reasoned at a later date, he was sure she was already in love with him and that the prospect of their actually becoming man and wife some day would encourage her to help him. "I can promise you two or three things, if you'll agree to join forces with me."

"Those things are?" Susannah asked with some bemusement, pursing her lips, folding her arms across her bosom and tilting her chin assertively upward.

"Adventure, passion, and glory as few women ever experience," Terry grinned. "That's love of a kind, and better than most varieties of that particular malady. What's your answer?"

"It's yes, of course," Susannah said, leading Terry back toward the cottage. "I will join you. To serve the Confederacy, you understand. Besides, I never could resist a good adventure and a little glory to boot. You can tell me more about . . . the plan, later," she sighed. "Now I want the passion part of this deal."

So that's how it began with Susannah and Terry and how it would end neither one considered. That was something only the gods could know.

Cervantes wrote that love and war are the same thing, and stratagems and policy are as allowable in the one as in the other. Differently said, "All's fair in love and war." That's what Susannah and Terry were involved in, love on her part he strongly suspected, war on his, or so he thought, until the distinctions began to blur for them both.

Chapter Six

Susannah's single life, whether she was really married or not, was over. The whole of Charleston believed she was. Everyone saw her *wed* to her handsome, sunny sailor boy, a man, they all thought rightly, she really loved at long last. Of course, Terry, she thought, didn't know she loved him, and she was certain he didn't love her, — at least not yet, but he would, she vowed with complete confidence, before they had completed their work for the Confederacy.

There would come a day when Susannah would feel she had never been so happy as on the night of their 'wedding' ball, and she didn't expect to be that happy ever again, as when they had called their jubilee, which occasioned almost as wild a celebration as had the Ordinance of Secession issued by the People's Convention of the Palmetto State.

" 'The Union now subsisting between South Carolina and other States, under the name of the

'United States of America' is hereby dissolved.' Soon's that ordinance was passed," Susannah told Terry, "church bells pealed and cannons thundered. Bonfires were torched and Roman candles flared through the night. 'Damnation to the Yankees' was the most popular toast in the grog shops and taverns, which overflowed so that the wild celebrations and drunken revelries went on right in the streets of Charleston." Oh, we had such a lot to learn, Susannah later would sigh to herself, again and again, but not on that May the first as bells pealed for her and Terry too, and feelings were as high and wild and wonderful as on Secession night.

Their wedding levee was only a somewhat more sedate affair, even if the Scotch whiskey and claret and Spanish port flowed like water. Susannah noted that in her diary, while still waiting in the Old Capitol for her inquisition to begin.

'Papa had his wines and spirits shipped from England. His entire reserve was nearly exhausted by daylight of May the second. Commodore Butler wasn't ever one to stint, certainly not on his daughter's wedding day, though he might well have kept back some of his private stock had he known there would be so few shipments of any goods from England for many a year to come. We didn't expect the cowardly Yankee blockade of our Southern harbors, nor could we, in those early, optimistic days of war, have imagined the loss of the Carolina Sea Islands and the later siege and bombardment of Charleston that would destroy our beautiful city and its glorious gardens, my mamma's among them, which had been growing for more than a hundred years with the helping hands of several generations.

'We would be deprived of a lot more than wine and whiskey before long. When the blockade cut off our sugar, we used sorghum and honey. We drank 'coffee' so called, made of rye, wheat and sweet potatoes, dried and parched. We got white salt by digging up the dirt floors of our smoke-houses and purifying out the dripped, lost salt.

'But the earth would never give back our noble dead. The war would take the lives of so many of our sons and brothers and husbands, that a generation of Southern women were destined to live out their days in lonely spinsterhood.'

But celebrating that May Day night, Susannah had no inclination to morbid thoughts as she began to learn more about the handsome and charming stranger she had "married." One of the first things she discovered was that her husband—she *always* liked referring to Terry by that title—was as proficient at dancing as he was at . . . she blushed to think it, loving. Between waltzes, the band played Dixie. Boys waved the Lone Star flag of Texas and the Bonnie Blue flag

66

of the Rebellion with its one star for South Carolina, the first Confederate state, in the middle.

"Daughter, I'm just glad I lived long enough to see this day," Stephen Butler said when he and Susannah waltzed to Mr. Foster's popular song, *Beautiful Dreamer.* "Now, you're some *other* man's problem," the Commodore teased with a laugh that was as loud as a thunder clap, his jolly, jowly full face and balding pate turning crimson pink. Becoming serious as suddenly as he'd launched into jocularity, he added, "Susannah, you know you're the light of my life and, given my druthers, I would have preferred you marry a Carolina man, or even my Navy colleague and Yankee friend, Willie Chauvenet. If it wasn't for this war and your advanced age, I would never have agreed to so hasty a match, certainly not with any wild, cock-fighting, gambling Texas son of a damn Yankee merchant, and a damn pirate's descendent in the bargain. Now, if this Armstrong fellow doesn't treat you right, like royalty . . ."

"Tell me about the pirate, Papa," Susannah asked with intense curiosity, not missing a dance step. It was a slow waltz, luckily.

"On his mamma's side, Armstrong is the great, great grandson of Jean Lafitte, a marauding old sea wolf who got himself driven out of Barataria Bay and away from the Louisiana coast! Nowadays, the Armstrongs like to call him a buccaneer or a privateer, as if he had been engaged in a respectable calling. What Lafitte did was run a fleet of pirate ships off Galveston Island. That's one reason why Terry has got the sea in his blood. Another reason's Terry's daddy. He was a New England shipbuilder, a Yankee merchant who invested in Galveston commerce, real estate, too, to increase his fortune, which he sure did. Daughter, you have sat down in a honey tub — married a very wealthy young man."

"Well, so has he sat down in one. I thought he might have been after *my* inheritance," Susannah giggled. "I'm so glad to learn that's not true."

"You married a man knowing nothing about him and I know little more. I hope all his surprises are as agreeable as this one. Well, now you know he's moneyed and there's sea salt on both sides of *his* ancestry. Of course, there's me and my Cape Fear Scots fishermen brothers, so my grandsons will be born with sea legs, hey? Like your Uncle George and . . ."

"I know all about you and your relatives, Papa," she said, cutting off the subject of grandchildren. "It's Terry's lineage I want to hear more about."

But Commodore Butler never got in another word. Beverly Bland, a wedding guest, came bearing down on the father-daughter couple, his staggering approach and bleared eyes proclaiming his usual state of inebriation. He cut in with a little bow.

"Until tonight, Commodore Butler, I was not

68

. . . uh . . . not without hope . . ." Beverly hiccuped, swaying, looking close to tears. ". . . not without hope that you would one day think me worthy of your daughter."

"Bland, pshaw! Get yourself in hand, son. You're a disgrace to Carolina and the Confederacy, to say nothing of your righteous and patient mother," the Commodore bellowed before striding angrily off. He never suffered fools lightly.

If Susannah had not by then been holding Beverly up, he would have fallen flat on his face in the middle of the floor, tripping up the dancers. It would not be the first such occurrence for Bland, but much as she disrespected him, she had known him all her life and felt a residue of affection for the boy he'd been before his father passed, leaving large gaming debts behind. Beverly Bland went to the bad after selling off more than half his slaves to recoup his social position. Susannah just couldn't let him disgrace himself again, particularly not at her wedding, so she danced with the man, if one could call his treading on her toes dancing, and she let him berate her for marrying another man. He simpered on about loving her and only her.

"I am raising and supplying, at my own expense, a full company of volunteer soldiers in your honor, Miss Sue. I'll be fighting for you alone. It's to be called the Company of Charleston Yankee Killers. Simeon Butler said he'd sign up if he wasn't a seafaring man. Will you stitch us a battle flag, Susannah?" he implored.

She couldn't say no to his request.

"Yes, Beverly," she answered and he talked on, tipsy, rambling and ignored, about his desire to hear the din of battle and return victorious with her flag, be it and himself tattered and torn. Then something he said caught Susannah's attention.

"I am worried about you, Susannah. This Armstrong — he plays at being the chivalrous cavalier about town and ladies are trapped like bees in amber by his allure . . . but beneath that charmin' exterior, he's a rake and a rogue, a misogynist . . . something like that they call him, because he's all in a fury at the gentler sex, and at fate, for depriving him of love. When his wife left him, *he was hurt so deep,* he says, he'll never let another female into his heart. I had that information from a pathetic crushed flower, a fallen woman . . ." Bland snuffled. ". . . in a Washington bordello."

With an angry toss of her head, Susannah dismissed Bland's words out of hand.

"Stop this asinine talk this instant, Beverly Bland, repeating to me the slanderous talk of some disappointed trollop! Terry's already told me some about his wife. Abigail didn't *leave* him the way you imply. She passed on, poor soul."

"Funny. I thought . . . different. Are you sure you understood rightly? Well, I could have been

70

confused by what little Floride was saying." Beverly shook his head as if to clear a cloud from his eyes. "Susannah, my true love, you can lead a horse to water, but . . . well, you know what you can't make it do. My heart is broken over you, but my conscience is clear. I've told you about Armstrong. Remember that."

Susannah did remember when Bland's words came back to her later with something like the force of revelation. But at her wedding ball, she just gave 'that bad boy Beverly,' as she had always called him, a good talking to.

"Here you are, Mr. Bland, weeping to me about your broken heart *and* whining to Louly McCord, too, I know for a fact, so dry your crocodile tears, find another girl to sew you a battle flag and to fight for and listen to the promptings of your heart. I was obliged to follow the urgings of *my* heart to ease Terry Armstrong's loneliness and also to become a good mother to his half-orphaned girls. I knew I *had* to grasp my true destiny before it was too late. You'd be well-advised to do the same. Beverly, you aren't half as bad-looking as some."

She studied him a moment. He had a long narrow face, with eyes the color of watered whiskey, a soft chin and a pulpy, petulant mouth. He was pale as a ghost because he drank all night and then slept it off, never seeing the light of day nor it him. "Stop being drunk and offensive every chance you get!" Susannah ordered Bland,

71

nagging away like a shrew, she realized, but she just could not stop herself, that Beverly had her so exasperated. Luckily, her little brother rescued her by claiming the next dance.

Simeon, at twenty-two, wasn't little at all. He was of mid-height and broad shouldered with dark curling hair the same as his father's once had been. Simeon and his Papa were both addicted not to alcohol, but to the pleasures of the table. The Commodore could be described as corpulent, Simeon as burly. The boy had strong, pleasing features and the manner of a big, friendly puppy dog. All the girls just loved Susannah's little brother. She did, too. She tousled his curls.

"I hear you're smitten with Louly McCord," she said first thing, taking the offensive. Simeon was so like their Papa, she knew he, too, would be compelled to offer her counsel about handling her new husband. "So's Beverly Bland after Louly, Sim. Now, don't go getting into any duels over the girl, at least not until she's decided which one of you she'd want to survive." The boy looked his sister in the eye—they were near the same height—his eyes a darker gray-green than hers, all atwinkle with fun and playfulness.

"Where do you get your small talk, Susie, from Grace Ellison? Grace sometimes combs Louly, too, and Grace knows Louly's like you. She would never have one thing to do with Bland, either. The man's got a mean streak wide as a skunk's stripe. And he's a tar heel from *North*

72

Carolina."

Susannah noticed something telltale in Simeon's smile and stopped stock still to look at him in a special way she had.

Since he had been a little boy, *he* knew that a certain look of hers meant *she* knew he was trying to keep a secret from her. Him being so much younger, he was more like a child of her own than a brother and if there was one thing she could not abide, it was *him* keeping secrets from *her.*

"Oh, my sweet sister Sue, I must tell you something wonderful and . . . and important! You know, war makes a fellow think about the important things of life — heirs to carry on his name and the right woman to carry his heirs. For me, that's Louly. Always has been. So, Louly and me got *married!* We did it quietly, not like you and Terry, and we did it yesterday. Only her mamma and the Methodist minister, Mr. Sutcliffe, know what-all about it!" Simeon laughed and whirled his sister about fast as anything, trying to make her dizzy, but she could out-whirl any dance partner she'd ever had. Except Terry.

"They say all brides are beautiful," Terry smiled down at her when he had her in his arms again, "but you, *Miz* Armstrong, are the most perfect I've seen. This is a role you were born to play."

"There's another bride here today. Brother's gone and married Louly McCord. It's a secret,"

73

she whispered in Terry's ear. His guiding hand, as they danced, rested at her waist and he drew her closer to him.

"I waltzed Louly about a bit," he said. "She's a very lively girl, plain as a Quakeress' bonnet, but today, she's real pretty, somehow, with her warm, genuine smile. Now I understand why. I've known exceedingly beautiful women, like you, Susannah, like . . . others, to be vexatious at times. I think Simeon's done well."

When Terry mentioned beautiful women in a less than amiable way, Susannah thought about Beverly's Bland's comments. He'd said Terry Armstrong did not trust women and she started to worry a tad, until she looked into his soft and caressing, trusting gray eyes and she dismissed it all.

"Mamma won't think Simeon's done well. Mamma took a dislike to Louly soon as her darling boy took an interest in the girl. Mamma really is particular about her only son. She thinks Louly is real drab and she considers the McCords an insignificant lot of nobodies. She thinks the same of all South Carolina Up Country folk, except Papa. Mamma says they're all descended from felons and debtors, even Papa. He's the exception that proves Mamma's rule that nothing good comes from the north. Besides, she fell in love. Oh, and another thing about Louly. Her third brother Calvin, is a lawyer, Yale trained, and a strong Unionist. When he refused to join the ranks of our brave Southern soldiers, know

74

what folks did?"

"I can guess," Terry said, his expression impenetrable, his voice flat.

"I'll tell you even so. They gave Calvin a parcel of ruffled petticoats, for being a namby-pamby, then tossed him in Scudders Pond. He went north. Now, he lives in Philadelphia, betrothed to an Abolitionist's daughter. Calvin won't fight for South Carolina and the Confederacy. That surely doesn't help any with Mother's attitude about the McCords."

"It might be a help to us, though. We may want a reason to go into that Northern city without raising Yankee suspicion. A visit to a brother-in-law who happens to be a Unionist at that, is just the excuse we might need."

"Is that all you think about, Terry? Lying and spying?" Susannah asked with a light laugh. She didn't want him to think her question was a serious one. But he knew and commenced to waltz her out through the wide french doors to the garden, into the shadowed shelter of a weeping willow where he kissed her quite diligently.

"I do have a lot on my mind, Miz Armstrong," he murmured, "but nothing so pressing as . . ."

"As pressing *me?*" she sighed, clinging to him, pleased to have his full attention. Her voice, she heard, was soft with undisguised desire. The heavens broke apart just then and a sudden stab of lightning was followed at once by a deafening thunder clap and a rushing downpour of rain.

But they were kissing again and hardly noticed.

The fire of their desire always was unquenchable, their hunger for each other nothing short of voracious. Their hands played over each other. The wet, limpid fabric of their clothing clung to their shapely writhing bodies, bringing details of anatomy into clear relief, making the most sensitive, high-risen points and curving declivities more obvious and accessible. Terry slicked back his dripping, rain-darkened hair, then removed his jacket and wrapped it about Susannah's shoulders. Her delighted laugh at the futility of this gallant gesture was overpowered by another thunderclap as she undid his collar stud and stripped off his shirt, feasting her eyes on the sight of his water-glossed, shiny, hard-muscled chest, gleaming bronze in the lightning flares.

Terry didn't even bother to undo the fastenings of her wedding dress, but just tore the bodice from throat to waist, so that his wet lips could find the budded tips of her breasts while his tongue lapped raindrops.

They made their way through the downpour, gamboling from tree to tree, toward the garden cottage, stopping to kiss and laugh and caress as their glistening bodies emerged from their garments, which they left in little mounds all over Mrs. Butler's garden.

'I intended that to be the last time Terry and I

would share such easy pleasure,' Susannah wrote in her diary, 'the last time my affection and passion and body would be his for the taking, the last occasion, for the foreseeable future, on which we would share our mutual delight and satisfaction. If this strangely conceived marriage was going to work at all, and I wanted it to, more than anything, I would have to impel Terry Armstrong to fall in love with me, slow and sweet, in the old, honorable way, *and* marry me—again—of his own free will. My excuse, after our first few nights of immoderation, for keeping him from my bed, seemed obvious, to me anyway. The minister Wigfall, in Terry's eyes, was his cat's paw, his friend, our ally in deception. We weren't *really* married and so I decided it was unwise, perhaps dangerous, to continue mixing pleasure with our particularly chancy business. That's what I told Terry anyway, but I wondered at the time if he heard one word I said."

Chapter Seven

Naturally, Grace Ellison would not desert her dearest friend, Susannah Butler Armstrong, in time of trouble and though Mrs. Armstrong's — or Miss Butler's — as the case may be, jailers had not yet let the black woman speak to their prisoner hours after the arrest, Grace and the children, two of her own and Terry's pair of daughters, were determined to stand in front of that wretched Old Capitol prison forever and a day, if need be, until they got their way. The younger children whispered together and played touch tag and pitch penny and other street games while Venetia and Grace stood in silence, each plunged in thought, Grace's mind dwelling on the past six months, since Susannah had taken up with Terry Armstrong.

Grace Ellison thought about Susannah's wedding. The free black woman, who had been involved in all the preparations, took pride in the fact that she was free and independent, a hair comber much sought after by white ladies of the "better" classes. To no one, did such women, she knew, speak more freely of their joys and sorrows, than to the hairdresser who daily entered the privacy of their boudoirs and dressing rooms. Grace knew of all their tragedies, pleasures, and their sins.

When her favorite lady and dear friend, Susannah Butler, still the reigning unmarried belle of Charleston at twenty-six, was finally wed, to the relief but also to the concern of her family, on the first day of May in the momentous year of eighteen and sixty-one, Grace knew Susannah was really in love. With some reservations about the distinction between lust and love, the bride had said so to Grace. She needn't have. It was manifest. About the groom, Lieutenant Armstrong, a naval officer of the Confederacy, late of the United States Navy, Grace knew little except what her own sharp eyes and ears told her. He was a handsome, lean tall Texan who kept his own counsel. And his secrets. One of them, Grace was aware, was that he was in love, too, though he had told Susannah otherwise. Grace, a student of human nature, speculated the man didn't even know it himself.

There *was* some hearsay about him. It was bandied about that Armstrong had an undue fondness for the female sex and that he had drunk to the dregs the cup of dissipation. That Grace did not apprise Miss Susannah of this gossip at the time of the marriage would rest heavy on her heart months later, when tragedy struck, but on the day of the ceremony, Grace knew love had taken hold of her friend and she did not wish to taint Susannah's pure joy with what might well have been plain gibberish.

Though Miss Susannah and Mr. Terry, as Grace called them, had met a mere ten days before their nuptials, they seemed to her to know their own minds, and their hearts. There was a war commencing and they were wasting no time. Their wedding was arranged, with Grace's full participation, literally overnight. Even so, it was on the grandest scale. Mrs. Butler, the mother of the bride, informed Grace she would have it no other way for her only daughter.

Susannah wore her mother's gown of silvery *point de'Espagne* lace on which three seamstresses toiled a whole night, from dark to dawn, making the required alterations. The groom wore a uniform of Confederate gray with a double row of brass buttons and brass epaulets. There were twelve pretty bride's maids, their hair coiffed *a la Francaise* by Grace, and twelve groom's men, each pinned with a white satin rosette. The footmen, the servants, the horses and carriages, even the bride's own favorite saddle horse, Alcantara, all streamed white satin ribbons that fluttered gaily in the breeze as the party drove in a merry parade through the streets of Charleston after the service. It was performed in Mrs. Butler's glorious garden by the groom's friend, a so-called colonel and, in Grace's opinion, a most dubious man of God, with a fierce, scarred aging face, one L.C Wigfall, who claimed, perhaps falsely it was to develop, to be a minister as well. He had been a United States Senator from Texas. That was a known fact.

Colonel Wigfall had more recently become known as the Lion of Sumter. Without orders, during a lull in the Confederate bombardment of the fort in Charleston Harbor, he had several slaves row him out in a skiff and, standing in the small craft waving his sword, bawled out a demand for the Yankees to surrender their last stronghold in South Carolina. The Unionists supposed General Beauregard, who was in command of Charleston, had sent the Texas Colonel with official authority to bargain and, depleted of food and water, barely surviving in the rubble of the bombarded fort, they negotiated. Soon after, with military honors and a hundred gun salute to the American flag, the desolated fort was turned over to the Confederacy.

All in all, Wigfall's braggadocio performance, for such it was, was rather comic, though the fall of Sumter was not. The American flag had been lowered. The Yankees were outraged and energized. Mr. Lincoln called for seventy-five thousand volunteers and the South prepared to defend

81

itself against an army of invasion. About two weeks later, with Charlestonians, mostly fools in Grace's opinion, still congratulating themselves for triggering open warfare, there was a grand event at the Butler's.

When the wedding party returned to the house after its tour of the city, there was a gala supper waiting, prepared and served by an army of cooks and waiters. After came the levee.

The dancing lasted all night. Looking in through the ballroom curtains, Grace watched the Lieutenant and his lady move together with enchanted perfection. Terry's right arm was about Susannah, his white-gloved hand at her tiny waist. Grace saw Susannah's smiling, dazzling eyes, just visible over Terry's shoulder where the bride's hand rested like a graceful white dove on his darker uniform. The golden strands in her upswept mass of copper curls mingled with the gleam in his darker crown when he dipped his head to whisper something to her or brush his lips to her brow. The inclination of their bodies, the lovely curve of her long neck, the undisguised pleasure in her eyes, and his, left little doubt in Grace's mind they were *both* totally in love.

Miss Susannah was the most perfect bride she had ever seen and Grace had seen more than a few because she was so very skillful at her trade — her art — really, which she had learned in France in the service of the Countess Duras and her daughters. Grace was much in demand for daily combings and for balls and nuptials, jaunts to Saratoga and voyages abroad but, though she had combed many, many ladies, never had she been so fond of one, nor so close with any, as she was to Susannah Butler.

It was being said that Jeff Davis had personally given the Lieutenant leave so the couple could go honeymooning. That was only partly true. Terry was also looking over and rallying the Southern soldier-boy volunteers, most of them farmer's sons who had never been so much as five miles from home. Moreover, Terry Armstrong was preparing a report. He said it was for President Davis. Later, Grace came to suspect it was really for Mr. Lincoln. "Even if that was true, it didn't matter none," Grace protested aloud, surprising the children standing with her on a street corner in front of a jail, as the sun went down on Washington City. "That little dandy, the Northern General McKlellan, paid no attention to the information, if indeed he received any. The battle at Bull Run was a calamity for the Union, a horrid calamity."

It was still in the future on May 3, 1861 when Terry Armstrong, Susannah, and Grace left Charleston to travel overland to his home in Galveston to collect his little motherless children. Grace was elated to accompany them and care for Miss Susannah's lovely tresses. Besides, as she often said, hers was a naturally vagabond disposition. She was able to give in to the wanderlust because, though a woman of color, she was free.

"My father, your grandfather," Grace told her children over and over, because it was so important, "is one of Charleston's brown elite, a skilled leather worker who has long had his own harness and saddlery shop. He *earned* his freedom, then bought my mamma free when I was twelve. They both worked hard, *hard* and when I was fourteen years old, or thereabouts, they bought me. They could never pay the high price asked for your brother, my little mulatto boy, who was a strong and smart and winning child. Alexander is still a slave because his mother, me, was a slave when he was born.

"See, it was Mrs. Butler and the Commodore owned us all and many more, but though Susannah and I were close, *close* all our lives, my father, *your* grandfather, got no uncommon consideration from the Commodore when buying Mother or me, nor trying to get my Alexander. No."

Grace never had had any love for the Commodore, something he'd be startled to learn as would many another white slave holder who justified himself by supposing benevolent bondage was preferable, to a black person, to freedom. Grace always did care some about his compassionate wife, southern patrician though Catherine Butler was, and a believer in what she viewed as benevolent slavery. Most of all, Grace loved Susannah who taught her to hold her tongue and

84

control her fiery temper, thereby saving her life, most likely, Grace decided. Susannah also taught her to read. Miss Butler taught her oldest son his letters, too, though Alexander never did learn to curb his hot temperament.

When Susannah asked Grace to go travelling with her and her new husband through the Deep South to Texas, with the black woman posing as a bondwoman, Grace was afraid right at first that she could lose her hard-bought freedom. She declined to go, but the Lieutenant won her over.

"I thought then, and do still, that he is a fine and honorable man," she expounded to the silent children, "whatever he has or has not done in this war to aid the Confederate States or preserve the sacred Union, whichever. They were going to keep me ignorant of their work for the Confederacy, but Susannah refused to deceive me. You all remember that, always. She felt compelled to tell me what she thought at the time to be the truth. Mr. Terry agreed and gave Susannah her way as he 'most always did. He surely was convincing and well-spoken when he made clear to me I myself would not be aiding the Confederacy. That's how he persuaded me to become part of their travelling show." Grace shook her head sadly.

She had also thought, back then, that the journey might afford her an opportunity to aid the Union, which she had in mind to do in any way she could, favoring the North as she did, for obvious reasons, and for some less apparent.

Grace had a quest of her own—to find her husband who was still a slave, sold south by his masters, and to find her runaway, hunted son, Alexander.

"From Galveston, Susannah explained, we would all be 'going North' together, soon as we fetched Terry's children, you little girls. In New York City, we would part company, would go our separate ways and I would be under no obligation except to keep their secret. And I did keep it as I promised, though someone sure let the cat out of the bag."

Of course, Grace did not part company with Susannah in New York. She accompanied the Armstrongs to Washington where, not long after their arrival, a Yankee fellow named Pinkerton, calling himself a detective, came crashing through the front door, while Mr. Terry was busy escaping through the scullery window, leaving Miss Susannah to march up to the cannon's mouth and brazen it out without him.

Chapter Eight

The day after the wedding, Stephen Butler, wasting no time, sailed for Europe aboard the British packet *Trent*. His daughter Susannah actually wept when they said goodbye, which was unlike her and surprised them both.

"Daughter! Now, now, don't take on! I'll be home again perhaps before you will, and I'll be waiting here to welcome you with open arms. That's so, even if the Yankees do manage to blockade Charleston as they threaten. You know your old father. He'll get through," the Commodore huffed, fanning himself with his hat and looking to Mother—Mrs. Butler—for help. "Catherine, uh Catherine!" he exclaimed, "I think marriage has already had a curious effect on your daughter's temperament. This sensible female, this imperturbable young woman, has turned sentimental overnight!"

"I always said *your* daughter was levelheaded, even a trifle bullheaded, but also I said that beneath *my* daughter's composed exterior there beat the most romantic heart, the perfect target for Cupid's arrow, the eager victim of the *coup de foudre,*" Catherine Butler explained sweetly, if at unnecessary length. Often, Susannah knew her precious mamma used many words where few would do as well, but Catherine was adored and indulged by her family despite her loveable foibles.

She was perfectly dressed as always, as her husband liked, and her waist, tight laced, was but an inch larger than her daughter's. She wore a gossamer and cotton lawn hooped gown of a cool blue shade. It complimented her coiled crown of silver-touched hair which, over the years had dimmed from a golden flame to a lovely apricot hue. Slipping her arm through Susannah's and gesturing to Terry to step closer to them, she surveyed the small gathering at the dock from beneath her ruffled French parasol.

"If I tallied up all the occasions upon which I have stood dockside, bidding your father farewell, never knowing for how long, I would be the one crying," Susannah's mamma, being gently maternal, said. "You, my girl, should be all dreams and smiles, about to go off on your wedding trip with your handsome, winsome young man who, I'm certain, will prove himself a devoted husband, and a great warrior, a hero of the Confederacy."

"I intend to devote myself to your daughter's happiness and satisfaction, ma'am," Terry told Catherine. "Whatever is ailing her now, I'll tend to," he said seriously, looking at Susannah, then brushing a kiss on her brow. At that, Susannah extracted a lace handkerchief from her sleeve, anticipating another rivulet of tears.

"Look there, Susannah," Catherine said, tilting her fine chin to direct her daughter's gaze, attempting to distract her as she used to do when Susannah was a little girl. Now, it was her way of judging if what saddened the new bride was a matter of import or no more significant than the bruised knees and lost kittens of childhood. "It's the McCord girl. See there, that Louly, just running after our Simeon, as usual. If you want something to worry over, Stephen," Catherine Butler told her husband, "fret about your son and the McCords. If those Up Country dirt farmers and that Louly get a grip on him, he will never again dally in the halls of learning."

"Miss McCord is absolutely devoted to Simeon, I've noticed. That's a quality not to be undervalued in a wife . . . or future wife," Terry offered.

"Accept it, Catherine. Your son is off to war soon, Louly or no Louly." The Commodore nodded his great head for emphasis and dabbed at his pate with a handkerchief as the Captain of the British vessel *Trent,* James Moir, called his crew to attention. The Union Jack was run up the mast signifying he, the tide and time were ready for departure and would wait for no man, not even Commodore Butler, who then hefted his portmanteau, which contained important documents from the Confederate States government. His wife stepped close to him, allowing just a small sigh to

89

pass her lips. She would permit herself no show of emotion in public but their profound, if understated, constant love and affection was apparent in their every subtle gesture and small courtesy. Susannah had never realized so acutely before that what her mother and father had together was what *she* wanted and had been waiting for all her life.

Looking into Catherine's eyes, Stephen muttered, "We still do have some salt of our youth in us yet, hey Cath? Listen to me before I must leave you. Simeon's your boy, Cath, and no fool. He understands the value of an education for an officer and gentleman, but he will not sit idly by, poring over texts and let others fight his battles for him. Nor should he be expected to."

"I know, Stephen. I could not ask that of him but . . ."

"Only try to hold him here until he can serve under me, or with his new brother Terry, on a good fast ship. Make every effort to stop him from running off with the first patriotic passel of cavalry volunteers to march by him. Restless boys all over Dixie are already following unfit leaders into this war. Battle-tested officers can make the difference between . . ." Susannah was sure her father was going to say 'between life and death,' but for her mamma's sake, he stayed his tongue and substituted 'victory and defeat.' "Military discipline doesn't come easily to amateurs, eh, Terry, my boy?"

"No, sir!" Terry answered smartly with a glance at Susannah who, at the realization that she and her brother were both soon to be leaving home

90

and, worse, were both deceiving their parents, he about Louly, she about Terry, she was shaken by another little paroxysm of weeping, try as she might to get herself in hand. Catherine put her arm about her daughter's shoulders and gave her a steadying pat.

"If you'd been married even a few weeks, I might attribute your overemotional condition to a happy condition, but the brevity of the alliance rules out my delighted thoughts of an *accouchement.*"

"I mentioned to Susannah yesterday Catherine, that you and I feel the same — about being ready for our first grandson."

"Or granddaughter," Catherine said. Terry cleared his throat.

"I think what's disconcerting our Susannah," he said, "is the uncertain times and marrying on the eve of war." Susannah nodded, not trusting herself to speak, relieved Terry had taken over. Nothing seemed to unsettle him, she decided. The man was smooth as glass.

"Say goodbye to the Commodore now, you two. Then you, Terrence, take your wife for a gallop around the Battery. While you're at it, explain to her again how a few skirmishes in Virginia and Kentucky will put an end to all the commotion so you two can get on with your own lives," Mrs. Butler suggested to her new son-in-law.

Suggested, nothing. Directed, Susannah smoldered. Catherine Butler, no matter how delicately she spoke, always commanded. Because her daughter knew how sympathetic and generous she really was, she loved her nonetheless for her autocratic manner. It didn't bother her new husband at all, apparently. On the contrary he, too, seemed to find Catherine endearing and wise.

Terry and Cath Butler were both night hawks. Neither slept much and they had talked at length, after Susannah had fallen off last night, some about *her*.

"I think Mrs. Butler approves of me as a son-in-law," Terry reported to his bride in the morning. "She hands you into my care without misgivings for our trip to Galveston, she said."

At that Terry half-smiled, half-ogled his new wife across the breakfast table on the piazza and it was then that the seriousness of her situation came home to Susannah with renewed impact. She realized again that she was tied to a stranger, not inconceivably a menacing one, to whom she was irresistibly attracted and with whom she was going off across the country, leaving the security of home, family and friends.

Terry had returned to her bed with first light that morning, to take her straight from dreams to love. So softly and precisely did his body stir hers, his lips at her nape, his deft hands claiming and rousing her so deliciously, she responded without restraint, having neither the wits about her at that hour, nor the inclination to remind him of her edict of the previous night. That could wait until after some more love and sleep and a good meal.

They arose late and ravenous — for each other,

and then for food. The cook, Angie, obliged with a real Carolina breakfast of boiled rice, hashed turkey, roasted quails and a delicious variety of corn flour cakes. Terry was looking exceptionally attractive and relaxed in jodhpurs and an open shirt as Susannah watched him spread butter on a corn cake. He did it very precisely she observed, moving his knife from edge to edge like a careful workman painting a wall, neater than she had ever seen anyone do the job. He looked up, caught her watching and took her hand across the table. She let him because she needed to study him longer in the light of day. She was just beginning to learn about him, how he awakened and shaved and dressed, all very slow and easy. He liked a hot tub bath at night, a cold bucket in the morning, a dash of lime water or sandalwood oil on his neck after. Half-dressed, he had insisted on idling casually on the bed to watch her splash in her tub a while before he rose and slowly . . . slowly sponged her back and shoulders, watching water course over her breasts, following the route of the drops with his eyes . . . and finger tips.

"My own Venus rising perfect from the sea," he whispered when she stood in a shower of droplets and rainbow bubbles. He wrapped her in toweling and took her to bed again and it was wondrous what he could do to her, quickly, with a precise caress or a skimming touch as his mouth browsed her swells and hollows.

Starving for other nourishment, they didn't linger in bed, but the intense savory pleasure of their urgent morning mating was as inflaming, in a different way, as the other occasions when Terry had taken his time, and hers. What he had already done to her, to her love-starved responsive body had changed Susannah forever. And there was more rapture to come. She still had more wonders to experience, Terry promised. They were only just beginning.

He refused to let her call her body servant but helped her himself to dress, doing up all her lacings and ties and hooks, even brushing out her hair though when Grace arrived to do it up, he finally left the room, reluctantly yielding the moment to an expert.

And so they parted for the space of an hour, until they happily met again at table.

Angie the cook was a great baker. It was she who had made their wedding cake and brought each a tiny piece of it to breakfast along with her special persimmon beer. Though the confection had started out a full four feet tall, there was none left but what little she saved for the bridal couple, for luck.

"I'm glad Mister Armstrong is the one you been waiting for all along, Miss," Angie said shyly, barely looking at Terry. She preferred to be in the kitchen cooking, rather than out front serving, but for Susannah's wedding breakfast she had emerged from her stronghold to be sure all was perfectly done. It was her gift. She had another.

"I made you my benne brittle to take along," Angie said to Susannah, placing a wrapped parcel on the table. Then she was gone, all atwitter like a jittery squirrel, back to her sanctuary.

"Benne brittle?" Terry asked.

"You might call it sesame, in Texas. The seeds came from Africa. The blacks still grow them here in South Carolina. Angie boils them up with lemon juice and sugar, pours the molten mixture onto a marble slab, scores it in squares, lets it cool and then breaks it into pieces. It was my favorite sweet as a child. She must really like you, Lieutenant sir. She hasn't made any for me in years." Women all seemed to love Terry. He had already won over the three Susannah cared most about— Catherine, Grace and Angie.

"This will be a sweet, slow, agreeable journey, darlin'. Are you packed and ready, Susannah?" Terry asked, stretching luxuriously.

That moment, his mention of leaving, was the start of her emotional upset right there. Thinking, good Lord, what have I done? Susannah reclaimed her hand and stood abruptly, frightening an oriole that had made so bold as to steal crumbs of corn cake from the table.

"We'll see the Commodore sail and then, if we aren't off ourselves soon after, we won't even make Port Royal today. But I don't mind." Terry, too, rose and went to her side. She kept her back to him, disinclined to meet his eyes. "I think, Miz Armstrong, tonight we'll stop early, say at Beaufort. There's an inn there with good claret and *soft* feather beds. I know of lodgings like it for every night between here and Galveston and I am surely not rushing to reach there."

"You didn't listen to a thing I said last night, Terry Armstrong!"

"About . . . what? You said quite a number of things." He leered charmingly. She blushed.

"Just as I thought." She rolled her eyes heavenward and tried to move away from him as his arm went about her waist and entrapped her. "You didn't take me at my word. Listen now, please, sir. In the matter of our . . . relationship? From this time on, it will be strictly business."

"You don't mean you were serious about our honeymoon being over just when it's starting, before it's hardly begun, after just two nights of connubial bliss? They were, by the by, extraordinary nights, Susannah, as I've already told you at least once. You can't really want to end such . . . uh, compatibility?"

He was right. She didn't and the jagged texture of his voice, which suggested — and demanded — so very much, and stirred such positively lecherous feelings in her, didn't make it any easier. But even as she doubted her resolve and realized she would have to invoke all her will power to resist Terry, she began to distrust the thing called "love." Surely he was a well-made, handsome, deep-eyed man, and surely he did fire her passion but, was it love? Her heart said "yes" but her head, as usual in *affairs de coeur,* exhorted caution. If it was the genuine thing for her, she was in love alone and that would not do. Either she had to get him started really loving her or stop feeling anything for him. Simple as that, and whichever, it was best to stay out of his arms *and* his bed, for the time being. Susannah tried to be sincere about the reasons for, not rejecting him, precisely, but keeping him at a distance.

"Of course I *want* and desire you. I'd never . . . I just could never even have *imagined* such, . . . well . . . wonders as you've shown me, Terrence Armstrong, or the pleasure you and I have shared but . . . it's distracting, darn it! It's time for us to stop being lovers long enough to start becoming friends," she insisted in a small voice. "I mean, what comes too cheap and easy is undervalued."

"I value your directness, Susannah, and your spontaneity and the lack in you of feminine chicanery and subterfuge." He spoke softly and rationally and sounded *so* sincere, she almost relented. After all, she already knew how his lean hard body performed and moved to best serve hers and exactly the ways—some of them anyway, since it was true they had only just begun—hers pleasured his. But that was all she really knew. It wasn't nearly enough on which to construct a future and a life, which is what Susannah wanted with Terry—nothing less than forever.

"Frankly, I'd never have expected this of you, with your powerful intelligence," he went on, "straightforward and sensible as you are." He was frowning faintly, his brows knit above strong, determined features. "There's a rule in chess —*piece touchee, piece jouee*. If you touch a piece, you must play it. One thing you and I have done, is touch. Why not play out the game and see where our moves lead us? We're neither of us unworldly, nor all that young. You're nearly thirty."

"Twenty-six," she interrupted.

"Well, I *am* a few years your senior, five to be precise," he laughed "Susannah! We have something good started *and* we have a tough job to do together. I hoped we could make it agreeable for each other."

"Agreeable? That's what our trysts have been for you?" she chirped like a ruffled bird before taking herself to task and going cold and, she thought, expressionless as marble. "If you can't resist the temptation, if being restrained and meritorious in my company, day after day . . . night after night . . ." she linked the words slowly and suggestively, "is more than you are able to abide, you could 'azzle' out of this gambit," she offered with a smile, invoking the same word — azzle — he'd used to describe Will Chauvenet's behavior.

"Susannah, it's not too late for *you* to back out of the whole bargain. You could stay home and knit and sew for the troops and, if you've got the guts for it, nurse the wounded. There'll be plenty of them soon, who'll need you more than I do."

Terry rested one hand on her shoulder and raised her chin with the other so that she had to look directly into his depthless gray eyes that seemed to drink in her very heart and soul, as the morning sunlight drinks the dew. "If you and I were actually married, Miss Butler, it might be different. I'd not offer you this choice to 'azzle' out on me, but in the circumstance . . . ?"

He lifted a teasing brow as a smile tugged at his lips. He vanquished it. She was not about to back out and let him go free.

"Touche, Lt. Armstrong!" she said with an ineffectual effort at indifference. She had intended to engage in a little clever, disinterested repartee. Instead, she took his bait. She bristled with indignation because he didn't need her more than anything in the wide world and so she said, "You'll learn sir, that azzling is something I never do. I always live up to my commitments and I will this time, unless you feel you'll do a better job for the Confederacy spying with some other woman as your agreeable consort. Just say the word, and I *will* find another way to serve the South and no hard feelings."

Susannah was bluffing. No *way* he'd get rid of her so fast and easy. Terry flashed a fast, startling, white-toothed grin and his eyes got bright as beacon lights before he threw back his dark head and laughed with real mirth from deep down inside him somewhere, the first time Susannah had heard the full sound. It was infectious. She had to smile.

"Oh, my own Susannah!" he sighed in that purring seductive voice of his, the words "my own" sending shivers of joy down her spine, "if you can live close with me as peas grow in a pod, which you'll have to do, most of the time, to carry off our charade, and not . . . want . . . give . . . ask . . . touch, you can be damn sure I can, too. Anything you can do, Miz Armstrong, I can go you one better. Now, are you real, *real* sure this is the way you want to start your wedding trip?"

She nodded, smiling more broadly.

"Start it and end it," she said.

And so it was, amidst the uncertainty of war, their own battle lines were drawn.

And if they weakened and crossed them now and again? Well, they were only human, after all.

Chapter Nine

No mixing business and pleasure, Susannah declared. Terry felt she was throwing down a gauntlet and setting their stage for a dramatic clash of wills, if not for tragedy. If he kept his hands . . . lips and . . . all of him, off all of her tantalizing physical self, she would allow him to continue to enjoy her sparkling company and the Confederacy to benefit from her discernment and resourcefulness, both impressive. Otherwise, it was *adios amigo* and Godspeed.

She'd challenged him, doubtless supposing, he thought, he was so besotted with her, he would crawl for her favors. Crawl or run — to find a replacement. He did neither. He had never in his life refused a dare and began, instantly he had agreed to her impossible demand, to plot a way of honorably getting round her prohibitions and his promised compliance. The only way was to compel her to allow — better yet, to demand — exceptions to her own rules.

Two hours after the Commodore left Charleston, when Terry and his bride departed for Galveston, his plan to win her back into his arms, was formulated; he would have her slipping into his bed at night by stoking her passion in broad daylight. He would be as demonstrative and affectionate in public as propriety allowed. He would be discreetly indiscreet with his stolen kisses and hidden caresses so that by bedtime—there she'd be, primed, ready and wanting him.

The world thought Jeff Davis had personally given Terry Armstrong leave to take a wedding trip and that he and Susannah were travelling overland to collect his little girls before he went to sea to fight for the Confederacy. Actually, Terry's instructions from the Confederate President were to evaluate the green, eager volunteers in towns and cities he passed through on the way to Texas. Sub rosa, Terry was also to hand pick from among former shipmates he came upon, a complete fighting crew—from officers to powder monkeys—to man a special and extraordinarily important Confederate States vessel.

Susannah, his gorgeous, disaffected and, he grew to think, dissembling wife, appeared to travel on no instructions but those of her heart, which had turned cold to him, or so she pretended. Terry's doubts grew as he observed Susannah and her travelling companion, Grace Ellison, whispering and giggling and cooing together, as conspiring young women often did. He liked the burble of sound their voices made and rarely bothered to listen to their words as he rode mounted at a little distance from them. Grace, like Susannah, was also quick-witted and a beauty, a sloe-eyed, statuesque woman with warm sorrel hued skin. The two made a striking pair.

The new Mrs. Armstrong, prepared for any social occasion, toured the South with three large trunks filled with gowns—and a fortune in gold.

Word was strategically spread around, meant to be disseminated north and south, that Terry's father-in-law, Commodore Butler, had been dispatched to England to seek recognition of the Confederacy as an independent country.

"That'll put those Yankee pecksniffs in a huff and it's only a small part of the truth," Susannah gloated to Terry, well aware of the other, more auspicious purpose of her father's journey; to come to terms with a British shipyard for the secret construction of a screw steamer with full sail power, the fleetest, fastest fighting ship ever to ply the seven seas. The father carried the blueprint and specifications and the daughter the wherewithal—gold—to be delivered through Mexico to England, to pay for the vessel Terry was to staff and command. They were keeping Hull Number 203, the craft's code name, a real family project.

Most of the time, Grace drove the surrey, but befitting her bogus slave status, when the group neared a town or plantation, she walked or rode the tailgate of the buckboard carrying the luggage and supplies.

"I feel like Queen Elizabeth on her annual progress, visiting from one lord's castle to the next over all her domain," Susannah told Terry after several days' journey. They had been warmly received and munificently entertained not at inns but at some of the great estates of South Carolina and they had passed one night at Colleton, the Butler plantation, one of the largest and best run in the Carolinas. There, on the recessed entrance portico, between tall Doric columns of a massive mansion, built more than a century before, Susannah was indeed greeted like a loved queen by the household servants, many of whom had known her since her birth, and by one ancient, dark, toothless and revered old woman, presented to Terry simply as Aunt Bessie. Gnarled and crooked as her walking stick, Bessie had been nursemaid to Susannah's own mother when Catherine was a mere girl.

"You belong here," Terry told Susannah when they were enjoying French champagne in the domed drawing room where half round windows drew the eye to the blaze of color beyond. "This house, on the curving banks of the Ashely, really suits you, Susannah, surrounded as it is by these acres of terraced gardens blazing against the dark wild woods across the river."

"The first Colletons imported an English architect to lay out the estate and place the house. I'll show you through the labyrinth of garden paths later, after dinner, if you'd like."

"Once, you'd pass up dinner, to be alone whith me," Terry commented, sounding almost caustic as he allowed the wine to loosen his tongue. "Well, wither thou goest, ma'am—to bed or to the garden — I'll follow, of course." He refilled his glass and drained it. Susannah, observing him, sipped more slowly.

"That, Terry Armstrong, is what the biblical Ruth said to her *friend,* Naomi," Susannah smiled smugly.

Terry laughed. "That's what we — you and I — are becoming. Friends, right?"

"Exactly!" Susannah raised her glass to him, and her green eyes seemed to taunt him over the rim when she brought it to her full lips.

"Colleton is like you, Susannah: patrician . . . polished . . . civilized, and yet, set as it is, it doesn't let you forget the untamed wilderness beyond. Will this garden stroll be at all like our first?"

"I think it would be best to forego our walk this evening. Perhaps next time we're at Colleton I'll be feeling more . . . energetic," she smiled icily.

Susannah slept well that night beneath the cutwork testa of her single bed in her old room, still the same soft pink, as when she was a child, iced with white plaster molding, frothed with lace. Terry, in a sumptuous guest room at the far end of the opposite wing of the mansion, in a broad high feather bed layered with goose down pillows, a decanter of brandy on the night stand, slept hardly at all.

Susannah and Terry traveled on horseback most often, she riding side saddle, a requisite for any respectable southern lady. From time to time, to rest their mounts, they let them follow riderless, hitched to the back of the fringed surrey. When the couple availed themselves of its shade and privacy, the astute Grace had the discretion to leave them alone. Terry couldn't keep his physical distance from Susannah if he'd wanted to. They had to sit side by side, thigh to thigh and the occasional rut in the road gave him cover for a little more explicit contact. If his arm happened to be stretched across the bench back, that was useful. He consistently pretended not to notice as he subtly caressed her thigh or breast. When reaching behind them for the water flask, he let her feel his warm breath on her nape. She flushed and glowered at him from under her palm-frond lashes, her accusative green eyes, sunstruck, a clear, transparent green. Terry maintained an expression of angelic innocence, or as close as he could come to it. Sometimes, he even whistled *Lorena,* the most popular song of the day, or one of Stephen Foster's poignant, sentimental airs.

In hot dappled Southern sunlight, they passed through small towns and smaller crossroads, demarcated only by a general store or just a rough-hewn road sign and the crudely carved word, "Wentworth" or "Bluffton" or the name of some other sleepy little town.

"They could inter a vampire here, once they'd driven the stake through his heart, lonely as this place is," Susannah commented when they came at dusk one day upon a deserted, swampy stretch of cyprus bog where a signpost had "Savana" scratched on it. Though the air was thick as cotton and dishrag damp, Susannah shivered. As Terry responded to the opportunity, prompted by all his natural protective male instincts, to put a comforting arm about her, a rag-tag rabble of men meandered out of the woods and onto the road. Intentionally, Susannah moved even deeper into the protective circle of his arm and rested her head back a little on his shoulder. Then and there, Terry knew his strategy for reconquering Susannah was going to work.

"We're Virginia bound, General, sir," the group's leader informed Terry in a reedy, high-toned voice, saluting with the wrong hand. He was distinguishable from the rest of the men only by his more advanced age and by his extreme height and thinness.

"Is that you, Ben Speed?" Susannah asked, sitting bolt upright. The man came closer, looking like a blue tick hound dog on a scent, his long head moving from side to side. His keen black eyes lit up when Susannah sat forward out of the surrey's shadow. He nodded.

"Yup. It's me, ma'am," he answered pulling off his cap.

"Ben Franklin Speed, best tracker and sharpshooter in the Carolinas, meet . . ." she fluttered those lashes at Terry and hesitated. This was a test of her histrionics and intentions. ". . . meet my husband, Lt. Terry Armstrong, Confederate Navy," she smiled, reminding him of a pretty kitten who'd caught the canary—him. He found her adorable. He wanted to carnalize her on the a spot. Obviously, he did not.

107

"Well, I heard you caught you a husband, finally," Ben Speed said with a roguish smile before he gulped, pretending to have made a social gaffe though it was apparent to all Susannah could have just about any man she'd ever wanted. Terry liked Ben Speed's humor. Susannah, unfazed by the man, clambered down and the farm boys gathered round her slowly, looking at her shyly.

Her beauty, Terry had already seen, awed the most urbane men. These hayseeds, rambling down a Carolina back road in search of a railroad track, were just glad to be out from between the plow shafts and marching off to an adventure called war. They were vanquished straightaway by Susannah's natural attributes and fashionable elegance. She promptly put them at ease.

"I see you all are carrying some *seb punce* chickens, from home, *cuzns,*" she said. Mos' kil *bud* don't make soup, but one or two of them will. Join us for supper?" She was speaking the Gullah dialect, used mostly by Low Country blacks, and familiar to all who lived there, including the ploughboy soldiers. They at once agreed in a chorus of affirmative replies and began with relief to set up camp after unburdening themselves of their many pounds of equipment.

One exhausted lad had been launched from home toting a saddle, a horse blanket, bridle and curry comb. Also a coffeepot, a twenty-pound ham, five pounds of sugar and the same weight of coffee. He had shirts, pants, socks and drawers all in allotments of six, two blankets, a jacket, mud boots and a Remington revolver. The others were similarly encumbered and they had progressed only seven or so miles since dawn.

On that hot evening, as they all gathered around the cook fire, they talked of what might lie ahead for them all.

"When a fellow's time comes, down he goes," Ben Speed nodded, his peeled eye focused off in the distance as though he saw something out in the darkness the rest of them could not. He reminded Terry of a lean gray wolf, grizzled, seasoned, always on guard. "Every bullet has its billet, it's said, but I do not expect to be killed. All men that go into fights are not killed. Why should I not be one to escape? And if I fall, what more glorious death could I wish for?" A murmur of agreement ran round the circle of boys. Susannah, moving closer to Terry, watched them with worried eyes and rapt attention.

"Plague take all them Yankees," a boy said. He couldn't have been a day past fifteen.

"I hope a bullet or a bayonet will pierce the heart of every northern soldier that invades the south," added another, perhaps all of twenty. Ben Speed spat into the fire.

"When you come up close to 'em, it'll be like you're seein' your own selves in the looking glass," he snarled affectionately, " 'cept they'll be wearing blue and talking funny. Drink up your ration of spirits, you brave young sons of the South, and then, go off to dreamland. I'm already tired of playing nursemaid to the lot of you and we been together but one day."

Susannah slept in the buckboard that night, Terry beneath it. He tried to climb in with her after she'd walked with him, hand in hand, under flickering stars that seemed big and close as candle flames. Her cascading hair already undone, she kissed him once, long and deep, her lithe body pressed to his, her firm-tipped breasts uplifted as her arms enfolded his neck. Terry fiercely ached for her as he had yearned for no one as long as he could remember, but he let her go at her first request. Beneath the buckboard, he tossed in dire need of her. He did not close an eye *that* night. He doubted she did either, though he derived little comfort from that thought.

Next morning when they waved the boys off, pointing them toward the Sea Island coast of Carolina, enough supplies were left behind to outfit another entire company or two and they also left Benjamin Franklin Speed. Their lightened load was increased only by the weight of written orders from Terry to report to General Beauregard's officer in charge at Beaufort.

"The islands will need defending men, vulnerable as they are to assault from the sea. You show those bully Yankees some Southern steel, hear?" Terry directed, never thinking Beaufort would fall as soon as it did, and at such great cost in lives to both sides.

Though Ben Speed had never been to sea, Terry, with Susannah's help convinced him to become a warrant officer and chief gunner on a vessel not yet built. That was after he and Terry had done some early morning target shooting. Probably, he agreed

110

as Susannah had said, Speed *was* the best shot in South Carolina and, not unlikely, south of the Mason Dixon Line.

"What's the man's trade?" Terry asked Susannah. "Buffalo hunter, farmer, fur trapper? . . ." They had saddled up and were moving out of camp. Terry was in a great hurry to reach Savannah, Georgia to spend a night in a fine hotel. With some good food and enough wine and candlelight, he was confident Susannah would join him in a hot tub and a soft bed.

"Ben F. Speed has done a variety of things," Susannah answered, looking at a monarch butterfly that had settled like a fluttering jewel on the black velvet lapel of her riding habit. "He's from North Carolina, like my papa. He used to fish the banks off Cape Fear with the Butler brothers. He went west for a while, then came back to guide emigrants going out to the Colorado gold fields. He did best at trapping raccoon and mink in the Great Dismal Swamp up on the Virginia border. Ben Speed knows that swamp, every square mile of it, probably better than any other white man alive. There *are* black runaways, some of them turned footpads and highwaymen, who can disappear into the Dismal so even Ben can't find them, probably."

"What's he do now? I mean, before he decided to lead boys into battle?" Terry asked looking at Susannah as she did at the butterfly, with quiet delight.

Susannah in the morning, he thought, was a joy to behold. When her face was still flushed with sleep, her just-opened eyes, glinting green slits, were

111

provocatively heavy-lidded and her movements were languid and luxurious. Long, curly, wildly tousled hair lent her the elemental aspect of a wood nymph. Soon, too soon for his liking, she was wide-eyed and coiffed and brimming with eagerness for the adventures the new day would bring. After coffee, all she would have before the midday meal, she was bubbling like a mountain spring with energy. Her green eyes, still narrowed, now against the light of the morning sky, missed nothing — not the faintest movement of breeze or wildlife in the trees, not distant herons on a cypress lake, not even the common milkweed and resurrection fern growing at the side of a pond or road stead. His very civilized and stylish Eastern aristocrat, Terry found, had a rustic's soul and he took pleasure in a recurrent fantasy of absconding with her to some Blue Ridge Mountain aerie and just letting the South, the North, the world be damned. They'd be gone for a time . . . a fairly *long* time, but not forever because love, he'd learned, for one reason or another, is never forever.

But he and Susannah both had their principles and had made their commitments to a noble cause. Neither could shrink from duty, and so there would be no running off, not yet, Terry knew.

"To my knowledge," Susannah interrupted his reverie to answer his all but forgotten question, "the last paid work for hire Ben Speed performed . . ." Her white Turkish Barb Alcantara, skittered sideways just then. Lucky. Terry's musings were turning licentious as he rode beside her. She kept her elegant seat and patted the animal's neck with a gloved hand that calmed him at once.

" 'An Arab horse, a stately stag, a barb/New broke . . .' " Terry quoted.

"He was the gift of a Levantine Bey of my father's acquaintance," she replied. Alcantara, a small stallion lacking only a golden horn, mimicked a mythical unicorn as his modern mistress did a wood sprite. ". . . the last actual job Ben had was — *is* — slave catcher," she added. Terry was stunned but he said nothing.

Susannah put Alcantara into a fast trot, leaving him behind — but not for long.

Chapter Ten

"See, Miz Armstrong, there's something about this man you married up with," Ben Speed said to Susannah one night after they had been traveling awhile together. "He prevailed upon me to sightsee with him."

"There's something about him, alright," Susannah agreed with a laugh. "He prevailed on me, too. How did he convince *you?*" she asked remembering, with a small blush unseen in the dark by Ben, how she had been won over.

"I said to him, 'General, if fate should break my stride during our rambles, will you take me home to be laid to rest in the Great Dismal?'

" 'That's Lieutenant,' he corrected me 'and yes Ben, I will do as you ask, unless we're out to sea.' I said 'fair enough, General.' I thought he deserved the rank. I wanted to go with him. You know, Miz Armstrong, I'm a loner, usually. Where I was raised up, same place as your pa, folks say, 'Drink your whiskey with clear spring water, in the shade' and also, 'Never live near enough to your neighbor to hear his dog bark.' I have heeded those maxims, 'specially the second, yet someway, I always get to know my fellow sufferers, as my pa called the rest of humanity, all their trials and triumphs. My surmise is, people favor talkin' to a near-silent man like me. Like I usually am. Not like right now. Now, I feel the urge to talk."

" 'Bout what? Go on, talk," Susannah invited.

"Take this black woman traveling with us, Miss Susannah."

"What about Grace?" Susannah asked. "She's my best friend Ben, so don't go saying anything to slight her."

"Me? Slight her?" Ben asked with incredulity, whether mock or real, Susannah couldn't tell in the scant light of a lantern at their campsite on a Gulf beach.

"Listen," he went on, "Grace has light brown, summer-colored skin. I like that. And she's neat in her dress and pretty in the face. She come to me one night. She says she has some money, would I work for her. Yes, I said. I have worked for blacks before. Free ones. Men. Never a female. Slave owners, black ones and white ones, hire me to find their contrabands. I'll track runaways for a black or a white owner for the same money so why not for Grace, long as she can pay? Susannah . . ." Ben hesitated. "Do you mind me calling you by your given name, now you're wed? That's what I've always called you." She shook her head.

115

"Of course I don't mind. Go on about Grace," she prompted.

"I have seen a right smart of the world since first leavin' home an' I have divined to my own satisfaction that people are more alike than different. There's many wouldn't agree, but that is no care of mine. I said I would work for Grace. She said thank you kindly, she'd mull it over, let me know.

" 'Stay with me a while?' I asked her as she turned to go. She knew what I meant and, now you're a married woman, you do, too," Ben said.

"When did this happen, with you and Grace?" Susannah pressed, agitated. "She didn't say . . ."

"Nothing happened. She answered me, real lofty like, 'I'll stay with you in the sweet bye and bye,' meaning never. This transpired when we was camped at the edge of that cotton field, remember, white as snow in full moonlight? There were lit cotton clouds on high, floating over. You and the General — Terrence — were inside a grand house, eating and plotting with some Tallahassee bigwigs.

"In plenty places I been, what I left behind me was not even a memory, just the blue in a baby's eyes." Ben lapsed into a silence then, while he censored his thoughts. Married or not, Susannah *was* a woman, a lady at that. I do like putting my work-hard hands on a woman's tender skin, he thought but did not say aloud. "Some ladies like me to . . . like me, too," he went on, but to this day, I have never found a woman, nor any living thing, I would want to walk through this world with me. Except my old yellow dog Bobby, and it broke my heart when

116

he died. I got me other dogs, but I had learned a lesson. Now, I keep my heart's distance. It's strictly business between us, theirs and mine, tracking. That's what it's going to be with Grace and me, business. I didn't care all that much nor really expect different. Just thought I'd try, though." Another silence descended. Susannah waited patiently.

"You be careful," Ben had said to Grace. "You don't want a man's apples, don't go shakin' his tree, coming to him in moonlight. Who you think you might want me to find?" He had spit out a chaw and took another plug of tobacco.

"My husband," she answered. "And my boy. Maybe. I have not convinced myself to put a slave catcher on them. I don't know can I trust you."

"I'd be finding 'em for you, no one else, if you the one payin'," Ben had shrugged. He liked her. He said so. "I like you Grace. I know you. We both have made our way by our own sweat and toil. My father was one of them brought over from Ireland to dig the rice beds. Black slaves were of too high a value for such killing work. Tell me about . . ."

"My husband?" Grace asked. "My Marcus was owned by the Blands of Charleston. I tried to help Marcus escape to Canada with me and our two young ones. We were apprehended in Cincinnati, in the state of Ohio, a *free* state, but they credited the Fugitive Slave Act. We got sent back across the bridge to Kentucky where I passed four months in prison refusing, that while, to admit to any wrong." Grace had squatted down a few feet from Ben, her

117

dress and arms wrapped about her knees and he had wanted the woman more than he had admitted to Susannah, or to himself.

"They let *me* go, but by then, Beverly Bland had sold my Marcus south. I like to have died, my heart was so sorely wounded. My strength of will was gone and my anger was consuming my own self." There was such an awful pain and sadness in Grace's pretty face, Ben looked away.

"Why'd they let you go?" he asked. She hesitated and sighed deeply.

"Listen and you'll learn. Susannah saved me then. She arranged for me to go away to France with her friend, Mrs. McCord. You know her, Speed, a delicate, devout little Up Country woman, and her daughter Louly. Though they are simple folk, Mrs. McCord wanted her daughter to learn some good taste and have advantages, so she took her to the Continent. I stayed behind in France after they left for home and it was there I learned my trade. I was treated well by the French ladies. Though their husbands were of a jealous temper and ate a great deal of garlic, compared to some hellions I've encountered in Carolina, they were most refined. I recovered my spirit in a foreign land and I regained my gumption. I resolved to come back and find my manly and beautiful Marcus no matter what, *and* my runaway boy, Alexander, if the Lord was willing, which I hoped He would be on the way to Galveston. Maybe He sent me you."

"Yup," Ben answered. "Lost your only child, too?"

"No. Susannah sent my two youngest children, Marcus's son and daughter, to Maryland, to a teacher who had instructed her. Susannah profoundly admires Miss Daisy Ballard who is a Northern-educated abolitionist, suffragette *and* prohibitionist." Grace had paused, Ben recalled, probably to let all the big words sink into him. He had spat again, this time in anger.

"I am called 'poor white' and I have never owned a slave, Grace, and never will. But I hold Abolitionists to be fit subjects for Hell," Ben said in a soft dangerous voice. "I believe their souls are destined for those lakes of fire and brimstone because they are tryin' to bring down Dixie by taking away the rights of the states and the people in 'em." Ben had no feeling about the Bloomers, women who wanted to vote, like men. He had never seen such a creature, nor did he care to. He skipped that subject and said, "Prohibition." He had said the word and nothing else because he did not know exactly what it meant, or understand why anyone would be talking about whiskey, for gawd's sake, instead of drinking it. He had come by then to think it was some part of the Yankee plot against the South. Grace put her own meaning to Ben's one-word reply. He found that folks often did do that with his lean responses.

"Yes, Miss Ballard is a good person, Ben," Grace said. "There's a sizeable number of upright women like her, wanting no luxuries for themselves, who are strong in their beliefs and tireless in their work."

"She is, or was anyways, 'till this war started,

breaking the law, harboring contrabands," he answered.

"Slave catcher, we were breaking no laws!" Grace hissed out. "Not that Miss Ballard or Susannah would have scrupled to do so. Understand, though Marcus is bound, his children are free because *I* am and was free when I bore them."

Ben, in his laconic way, had been shocked by her answer and her manner when delivering it. "You kin to William Ellison, the cotton gin maker in the High Hills of the Santee? He owns sixty slaves or more. I worked for him once or twice."

"He's the richest free man of color in South Carolina. But I will claim no slave holder kin to me. Oh, Mr. Speed . . ." Ben had seen, as Grace rose swiftly, that she had a look of fear in her face, of a sort he'd seen often before. "By imparting my secret to you, that I am a free woman, I have put my liberty at risk. I pray you, say nothing to anyone else." He knew why she was so scared. There was strong feeling in the South that no person of color should remain free. Many of the emancipated had already fled Charleston, sailed off to Haiti or somewhere in Africa called Liberia.

"I wouldn't hurt you, Grace," Ben said. When he nodded, she knew that was so. She knew his nod was as good as his handshake or his X on a lawyer's paper. She hurried off then, leaving him to wonder alone, as usual, about the ways of the world.

"What are you pondering on so hard, Ben?" Susannah finally asked, recalling him to the present.

"How a solitary sort like me has got his self in so close with Grace and you and Terrence," so close Ben thought and didn't say, that you're all telling me your secrets, with words, or without 'em.

"Probably, I joined with you all because Terrence is a man's man. He speaks direct but with a touch of the poet. He struck a chord in me, with his talk of ships. He said ships are like beautiful women, some willful and challenging, some compliant to the gentlest command."

"Which sort did he prefer?" Susannah asked.

"He didn't say," Ben replied. "What he said was, the briny wild sea was a part of the world I'd yet to explore. He got right to the soul of me when he talked of sunsets and calms, and squalls that come on bringing squadrons of clouds over the waves, and then long lines of rain like silver lances."

"You are not the only one Terry Armstrong touches deeply, Ben Speed," Susannah sighed.

"Terrence knows folks everywhere, don't he?"

"Specially women," Susannah commented dryly.

"I have noticed as we been traveling south, how men greet him with true fondness and pleasure, and look at him with respect. There's always a few who display ill-hid envy . . ." Ben kept his next thoughts to himself. That's partly because of *her,* Susannah there, a girl so fresh and lovely, a man might think to die for her.

But there was something curious about Terrence and Susannah, Ben ruminated. They were touching and talking and laughing and funning all day, but still, it was like there was a wall between them. They were wild in love. Any fool a could see it. That was not the trouble. It was like as if each was holding something back from the other *and* each was wanting exactly what the other wasn't giving.

"Ben," Terry called as he came riding up along side the woodsman next day." You knew Susannah when she was a child. Tell me something about that." He seemed very determined and serious. Ben nodded wondering if he should refer to her, in front of her husband, as Miz Susannah or Miz Armstrong. He fixed on just Susannah.

"I've known her since she'd was real little and ran about barefoot with my dog, Bobby. They took to napping together in the heat of the day, General, in the hayloft of the barn at the Colleton plantation, with about twenty cats and kittens sleeping all about them." Ben decided to tell his friend Terrence about the time one of those gangly kittens caught himself a Carolina chickadee.

"There was a particular long, scrawny black and white cat that was a good hunter.

"Sounds like you," Terry teased. "Go on."

"That cat mauled a fledgling bird, but did not kill it. Susannah nursed that bird. Hovered over it, fed it by hand. Bugs. Chickadees are fearless, friendly little things, and they make good cage birds, real amusing when they go swinging and climbing. Susannah Butler saved this one I tell about, cured it, but let it go, hurried it into the air, back to freedom. She listened ever after for his six note call. Whatever

chickadee was trilling, she always said it was hers."
Terry smiled at that.

"She'll be a good mother to my children, I imagine," he said. Ben nodded, wondering why Terrence hadn't thought about that *before* he married the girl, not after.

A day or so later, it was Susannah who asked Ben to ride a while with her in the surrey. She had the reins in her gloved hands, her toes resting on the dashboard. On her golden copper head, was a peaked soldier's cap with a scarf draped over and covering her neck.

"It's called a havelock," she said, "after some English general who fought in the desert." Terry rode up and trotted along beside them a minute.

"She's an original, isn't she, Ben?" he asked proudly. He put his hand on her shoulder, then rode off.

"Yup," Ben said but Terry didn't hear him. Susannah did.

"Ben, you've always known I do things my own way, right?" Ben nodded. "I never have intended to fit into a story other people had all written for me."

"What other people?" Ben asked, not exactly sure what she was getting at.

"Oh, my mother, my father, my . . . husband, whoever *he* was going to be. I had every intention of living my life to fit a story of my own creating."

"Yup," Ben said. He thought he knew what she was getting at now. She wanted to do what she wanted to do, not what anyone else wanted. He felt the same. It wasn't what she was getting at, though.

"That was until I met my . . . the General." She winked at Ben. "Then, all I wanted was what every woman does—a hearth and a home and children with the man she loves. It's an old, *old* story, of course, even if my version is a bit peculiar. But, I'm worried, Ben. Terry's young daughters are part of his wife. Seeing them could rekindle his need for their mother. He may feel untrue to Abigail. He *adored* her, you know. What if I can't compete with her memory for his love, or theirs?

"He adores you now. What's Grace think?" Ben was puzzled.

"Grace says to let the dead sleep. It's a live woman I should be thinking about, the one who's been raising those girls. *His* mother, not theirs. I've heard she's a magnificent, formidable woman. When we leave with her granddaughters, she'll be entirely alone on her windswept spit of Galveston Island. She might want to keep those girls with her."

"They ain't hers to keep," Ben said. "They're his." Ben knew there was a lot more to it than that, but it was all that came to him to say because that was the first he'd ever known Susannah Butler to doubt herself. The Susannah *he* knew would compete with Juliet for Romeo, she was usually that sure of herself.

There were other things Ben did not understand about the Armstrongs, specially not with them both talking about babies and mothering and such. They rode so close you could not get a thread of spider

124

silk between them. They'd be all day talking, thick as thieves, sometimes writing things down in a book she had, like a diary, with a green velvet cover and a golden clasp. *She* kept the key on a ribbon round her neck and *he* had a preference for retrieving it. Ben wasn't snooping but he just could not help but notice that or their sighs and smiles and touching hands. After a whole day of that sort of thing, Ben supposed, a man and woman would be all riled up, but then, come night, most the time, they'd go their separate ways, not off together when they were on the trail. Nor did they climb the stairs together, Grace had reported, when they were guests at the great mansion where Susannah or Terrence or both of them were acquainted with the wild young gentlemen who were champing at the bit to fight Yankees, spinning out dreams of valor and victory.

Chapter Eleven

"My wife prefers her own *private* accommodations Josephine, but with so many guests under your roof, perhaps she'd agree to share a room with me tonight." Terry took Susannah's hand and almost smiled at her, one corner of his sensuous mouth curling up a smidgeon. That happened, Susannah had learned, when he thought he'd got one up on her and wanted to make certain she knew it. Now, she winked at him, to acknowledge his little victory. Josephine Izzard, proprietress of Oglethorpe Hall, looked from Terry to Susannah and back again making no secret of her curiosity about the couple.

"Your husband and I, Mrs. Armstrong, are good friends of long standing. You were such a perfectly lovely bride! As a guest at your wedding, my dear, I was so well cared for at Charleston, I will not have you discomfited in the least on your first visit to Oglethorpe Hall. I'll see to it you have your own rooms — and Terry his, of course." When she patted his hand, Susannah knew the woman's intentions were at best, suspect.

This Mrs. Izzard was no beauty, Susannah noted. She had ordinary brown hair, a sharp-featured, cunning little face and prominent teeth. But Susannah knew none of that mattered; what she had been told by Grace, her foremost source of gossip, was true. There *was* a radiance about Mrs. Izzard who was said to have a certain allure, a talent for attracting men. Grace's own source had been a servant to Mrs. Senator Clay of Alabama, who had passed on this tidbit, among others, during the wedding, and Grace in turn reluctantly passed it to Susannah as the travelers drove up the long approach to Oglethorpe Hall.

"I often have the feeling you keep a huge store of gossip which you dole out to me bit by bit only as necessary," Susannah complained, looking decidedly miffed as the surrey, followed by the wagon load of luggage and their mounted entourage, came to a halt at the entrance to the Florida panhandle mansion of the Izzards. "Anything else I should know *right now?*" Grace nodded.

"This Josie always had a weak spot for Mr. Terry, I was told."

"As have half the other women south of the Mason-Dixon Line. Well? Out with it Grace, for pity sake. Here she comes," Susannah urged, fixing a smile of greeting on her lips

"Terry Armstrong and Miz Izzard, then the barmaid, Josie O'Malley, were known to be 'carrying

127

on' up in Washington not so long ago, before Josephine was wed to Oglethorpe Izzard. He is a man ten years younger than she is, Susannah."

"And besides, he's the scion and only heir of the powerful Izzards of Pensacola. They have recently acquired great wealth raising cattle and selling lumber," Susannah whispered hurriedly. "This marriage caused quite a scandal. The woman fascinates me. Mrs. Izzard!" Susannah, getting down, had greeted her hostess. "Such a pleasure to see you again!" That pleasure evaporated, though, when Josie made her continuing interest in Terry quite clear.

"My husband and I must have adjoining suites," Susannah smiled, first at Mrs. Izzard, then up at Terry. "If that's not possible, Miz Izzard . . ."

"Josie, dear. Call me, Josie," she was interrupted. "I'm afraid I just do not have connecting rooms to offer you. In fact," now *she* smiled at Terry, "I haven't even rooms on the same floor so . . . but my dear, are you transporting a king's ransom in those cases?" Josie exclaimed as servants, unloading Susannah's luggage, struggled under the weight of the gold in her trunks.

"Gifts for Terry's mother and the girls," Susannah answered quickly. "Well, Josie, my husband and I will certainly manage, for a night or two, in *one* room if need be," Susannah pronounced, envisioning herself peering out of her comfortable bed, through the mosquito netting, at Lieutenant Armstrong asleep on a chaise, his long legs extending over the end. Josie looked rankled. Terry, his expression impassive, nodded his handsome head and put an arm round Susannah's waist.

"We'll suffer through, Josie. After all, you *are* accommodating half the officials of the Confederate government for the meeting here at Oglethorpe tonight. We must all make some sacrifices. Right darlin'?" he asked Susannah. She didn't know if Josie saw her elbow jab Terry's ribs. Certainly, he gave no sign of anything untoward until he exhaled with a faked whooshing sound, toying with her, after Josephine Izzard showed them upstairs and, gazing cow-eyed back over her shoulder, reluctantly left them.

"So, one more of your mistresses has been held at bay by me," Susannah proclaimed with satisfaction, removing the pins from her hair and shaking loose her copper mane.

"I warned you about me, didn't I?" Terry shrugged, grinning. As he had predicted, he knew a great many women, all of whom were drawn to him like bees to honey. Susannah couldn't really blame them, except those like Josephine Izzard who actually flaunted themselves, making clear their availability, even though she, his wife, was right there at his side.

"Your Josie Izzard is the worst yet," Susannah proclaimed. "There is, of course, and likely always will be, the celebrated Southern belle—the charming and fashionable flirt, a lightheaded creature who is able to pick out a few rudimentary tunes on the piano and speak a smattering of the French language when required. Most of these so called belles are ornaments, coquettish teases. By pure dint of personality, or beauty, or both, though not necessarily, she gathers a coterie of devoted admirers. We all know that some young, and not so young, men will follow her everywhere and hang upon her every word. This, the participants think, makes them part of the old tradition of the steadfast knight and his virtuous lady. But I thought more of you than that, Terry Armstrong."

"Well, from the start, I *said* . . ." he began, folding his long frame into a straight backed chair, settling in for what he knew by now to expect — the rest of Susannah's lecture.

"Besides single girls, there are married belles, you no doubt know sir, women who have never stopped encouraging admirers, who go on bantering, flirting and sometimes heartbreaking. For most married charmers, it's a continuation of an innocent game of whisper and giggle and sigh. For others, like your Josie, it's more than a game."

"*My* Josie?" Terry rolled his eyes at the wainscotted ceiling. "She was never that, and now she's wed and so am I supposedly there's no question of. . . ."

"Marriage matters not one whit to a really dedicated belle. Certain experienced women are amenable to more than talk and Josephine Izzard, it's said, is one of those. If you, Terry, discouraged such conduct in her, or in any female, it hasn't been apparent to me. If anything, you appear to truly enjoy and invite the company of women—*all* women. You listen with *such* attention to what they say, however insipid. You take note of the smallest details of their attire and coiffure, fans and parasols. With your wonderful, sincere smile and direct dark-eyed gaze, you ask after their offspring and kin you've not seen in years. You admire their infants and you're more than courteous and attentive when introduced to gosling girls, some of whom are charmed speechless by you . . . your flattery. Others, the baby belles, follow you about batting their lashes, vying for your glance and smile . . ."

"Enough!" Terry roared, only partly in jest. He crossed the room and put his hands on Susannah's shoulders. "If you're that jealous, I'll keep my mouth shut and my eyes closed and you can lead me about like a dog on a chain!"

Susannah drew herself up tall and met his eyes.

"Jealousy has nothing to do with this, discretion all," she replied, taking control of herself. "Do whatever you wish, but with some prudence. I simply won't be shamed by having those . . . those vain, simpering women, who suppose I am your devoted little wife, thinking they have outwitted me, sir."

"So that's your complaint! When it comes to vanity, you're the saucepan calling the kettle black, Miss Butler," Terry said with a cool laugh, before he kissed her. "And you're lying. You just gave yourself away. You are jealous," he said before striding out of the room.

Susannah was truly disappointed to see him go.

So, on their first evening in Pensacola, looking out for her own best interests, she never took her eyes off Terry. At the same time, to keep him on his toes, she herself played the belle, a pastime she had mastered to perfection ages ago, and which bored her totally. Even so, she *was* very good when she wanted to be, she admitted to herself, and she had her usual success that evening, even with the former Senator from Mississippi, who had become the President of the Confederacy.

Jefferson Davis was reputed to be a cold, arrogant, fastidious man. At the ball in his honor, he coolly played the courtier to perfection, claiming two dances with Susannah, one of which they sat out, sipping from silver claret cups and talking.

"You, my dear, are what we are fighting for. Your reputation as a consummate example of Southern womanhood does not do you justice, Mrs. Armstrong. The Lieutenant is to be envied," Mr. Davis said. Over an enormous crinoline, she was wearing her lime green watered silk, trimmed with gold lace, and her mother's emeralds, a marriage gift. Susannah *knew* she looked *fine*. Demurely, she thanked Mr. Davis kindly for the compliment and went on to a subject that interested her more.

"Sir," she began, "I know you to be a graduate

of West Point and a hero of the Mexican War."
Davis nodded in stuffy agreement. "How do you
expect the fighting will go? Where will the first
battles be joined, how many men . . . ?" He
frowned a little.

"Miz Armstrong, a woman has no more place
discussing war and politics than being in an army
camp or on a battlefield. I know Commodore Butler shares my opinion. I will say this, because I
respect your intelligence and cherish our bold
dream of a new Cotton Confederacy. We plan to
lure the Federals guarding Washington out from
behind their barricades and into Virginia, at least
as far as Bull Run Creek, and catch them there.
Mark me, Mrs. Armstrong, Washington will yet be
the capital of the Confederacy."

"My mother says the city is no fit capital, just
some unfinished Greek temples set in the wilderness among sloughs called streets. As for women
and politics, my husband would not agree with
you, though my father would, Mr. President.
Ornamental ladies and silly chatter are a more acceptable combination, to you and the Commodore, so if you will, do please tell me, is it true
that when you quitted Washington the social scene
was a shambles?"

"The place is dominated by a rabble of back-
woodsmen and uncouth Westerners. Washington is
overrun with free soilers, Republicans and appall-
ing Bloomers, and the office of President of the
United States is not any longer a fit one for a

133

gentleman to hold." Jeff Davis shook his head, his lips curling in haughty disgust. "I doubt Abe Lincoln had ever donned a pair of white kid gloves before his inauguration. The man's a rube. He talks in parables and lacks any gift of eloquence. His eccentric wife is indescribable.

"Mrs. Davis and I and our true countrymen left the city in a hurry. Our houses are dark, our blooded horses gone from the streets. In the chaos of high-piled baggage wagons rattling though the town, I left behind my little Japanese dog. It broke my wife's heart, losing him." Mr Davis squared his shoulders as Susannah was about to defend Amelia Bloomer and her pants for ladies when the orchestra began to tune a quadrille, and she looked about to find Terry at her elbow.

"The Japanese ambassadors of the Tycoonate visited Washington not long ago," he said, insinuating himself into the conversation. "They caused a sensation, don't you agree Mr. Davis, with their fans and embroidered robes? You'll be interested to know, Susannah, they wear *two* swords and give away little dogs as gifts wherever they travel."

"You mean the Shogunate, darling. Tycoon is just a title," Susannah corrected Terry, thinking with satisfaction, *now* who's jealous? "Will the Orientals deal with the Confederacy, do you suppose, Mr. President? Are many foreigners and Northerners sympathetic to our cause, sir?" she asked.

"You and your husband will yourselves soon

134

have the answer to that question, Mrs. Armstrong, and you will be able to inform me of our support among Yankees as your father will of the proclivities of the British who desperately need our cotton." Jeff Davis paused and looking directly at her said, "I will ask a personal favor of you, for Mrs. Davis' sake. See if you can find that canine when you reach Washington and bring it to her at Richmond. Lieutenant, please refill our claret cups, sir," Davis asked. Watching Terry saunter off again, he said to Susannah, "I have a particular fondness for your husband, and sympathy. We both lost beloved first wives, he his Abigail after too few years, myself Zach Taylor's darling daughter, after only three months of wedded bliss. But Terry and I have again both found excellent women to walk at our sides."

"Where *is* Mrs. Davis, sir?" Susannah asked, looking about.

"In Richmond. *She* would not set foot in *this* house. Nor would any other lady of her circle. They find Josie O'Malley Izzard vulgar. The woman is a tavern keeper's daughter. Terry should have told you."

"I'd have attended her soiree even so, sir. As you know, for me, this is more than a social occasion. I feel I'm a soldier on duty in the service of the Confederacy." Jefferson Davis smiled and nodded sagely as Susannah noticed Terry leading out that Izzard woman for a dance. Mr. Davis offered his arm.

There were other dance partners for Terry and for Susannah before the evening ended. All of hers fell in love in that special Southern, romantic but temporary I'd-give-my-life-for-you-this-minute — but perhaps-not-in-an-hour-from-now way. It was to be expected. It was a required part of the entertainment. The same was true of Terry and his partners. By the time he claimed his one waltz with Susannah, the last of the evening, they were both wrought up and exhilarated by their teasing, by their social successes and not a little jealousy, which had consequences Susannah had not foreseen.

"Why isn't Mrs. Davis and her coterie here tonight?" she asked Terry. He twirled her about.

"Because Oglethorpe Izzard married his experienced and seductive mistress, who was also the mistress, at the time, of a dozen others," he replied.

"Yours, Terry? She seems very, very fond of you," Susannah had to ask, though striving for a tone of indifference. Terry had been right, he realized, she *had* been jealous. But now she was silently gloating. She'd shown Terry Armstrong that his Josie Izzard had nothing on *her* when it came to flirting, despite her years of experience and her dozen lovers. "Well, was she yours?" Susannah prodded.

"Gentlemen don't kiss and tell, Susannah," he answered with his white flare of a smile, before he kissed her, right on the mouth, right there in front

136

of everyone, eliminating the formal dancer's distance between them by pulling her close and bending her back as her lips parted to his. She had so missed the touch and taste and warmth of him, so yearned to be in his arms, she never wanted to let go. So, she kissed him right back and would have gone on kissing him if the music hadn't dwindled away. They surfaced for air to find themselves alone in the middle of the ballroom, surrounded by a gaping circle of observers, some smiling, some not.

"My salts, my smelling salts before I faint away!" an antiquated, shocked old woman called in a surprisingly strong voice, breaking the silence. Others cheered, some younger girls giggled and one fellow, with mischievous blue eyes, wanting to know if it was some new sort of dance they were doing, asked to cut in. Terry firmly and not quite politely refused him.

"See what you've made me do, Miz Armstrong, darlin'?" he whispered to Susannah. "Overstep the bounds of propriety."

"What I made you do?" she asked playfully. She did not care a straw about shocked elders and propriety just then. "How did I?"

"By tempting and tantalizing every man in the room, me included, you caused me to forget my good manners," he grinned. "For days, weeks, you've been whetting my appetite, then denying me my spousal rights."

"Your *what* rights?" she laughed. "Are you ignoring reality or changing your notions of love and marriage?"

Terry never answered because the music began again. Susannah's hands rested lightly on his shoulders, his hands encircled her waist. They looked into each other's eyes, filled with yearning, as he waltzed her about faster and faster until she was breathless and flushed and laughing with exultation.

They hardly made the sanctuary of their room before pent passion broke over them like a wild storm. They kissed again, this time almost violently, murmuring, bruising each other's lips as Susannah tried still to resist the forces of desire and keep Terry at arms length, at least. She pushed him away and loosed her gloves, finger by finger, first one of one hand, then the other in precise fashion, drawing each glove off, slowly. She undid her hair, withdrawing jewelled clasps and tortoise shell combs — slowly, carefully replacing each in her jewel case. When she shook down a cascade of curls, she caught sight of Terry in the looking glass. He was at the window, just watching her, an unlit cigar clenched in his teeth. Their eyes met and, like a bird flying into a sandstorm, she knew she could not fight him, or herself any longer. She kicked off her silk dancing slippers, opened the fastenings down the front of her dress most efficiently, slipping her arms from the sleeves, dropping gown and crinolines in one gesture and stepping out of her cage to stand, trembling with desire, in her pantalettes and bustier, fumbling at the back of her neck with the clasp on her emeralds in which her hair had become entangled.

She was about to lose control and break the strand, sending the jewels flying to the four corners of the room when she looked at Terry again. He still had not moved.

"Help me, *please,*" she asked, three little words imparting more than she'd intended. With his wonderful little twitch of a smile, Terry came to her, discarding his jacket half way across the room, then his cravat, collar and shirt, so that when she stepped into his embrace, she could caress his bare chest with her hands and lips and, soon, with the firm-budded tips of her breasts.

When she woke next morning, Terry was sleeping beside her, not on any chaise longue. She was still wearing her emerald necklace and one earring. That was all.

She resolved to *try* to do better the next time the heat of passion addled her heart and brain and overwhelmed her errant flesh but, for the first time in her life, Susannah began to wonder if females were not called the weaker sex for good reason.

Chapter Twelve

Susannah was in love, and thought she would have given all on earth to have children of her own. She needed to be a mother and she hoped Terry, despite the peculiarities of their union, would some day give her a baby, or even more than one. As soon as she saw his girls, she became *their* mother in her heart. She resolved to be a good one. Her greatest obstacle, as Grace had foreseen, was going to be Terry's mother.

Susannah had her first view of Adella Lafitte Armstrong and of her stepdaughters, the elder Mrs. Armstrong's granddaughters, from a considerable distance, through a nautical spyglass.

After a train and coach trip through north Florida and into Alabama, with troop-recruiting stops in Tallahassee and along the Gulf Coast panhandle, they had taken sail from New Orleans. The city was in Confederate hands, a situation that would change before the year had passed. At that interval, the travelers were still able to board a vessel flying the Confederate Stars and Bars, the flag that replaced the Bonnie Blue as the South's official banner, and approach Galveston from the sea. The island rode low in the water like a foundering whale.

When still a distance off shore, Susannah focused on the Armstrong women, waiting on the wharf. She isolated each in turn in the magnifying circle of the glass and was able to dwell on precise details which, when meeting someone for the first time, face to face, often elude the naked, busy eye.

The little girls stood immobile, strangely so she thought, for such young children, not even tapping their toes with impatience to see their father, nor craning their necks to look about them. They were dressed in matching, starched white pinafores and spotless white, high laced shoes. There was a long yellow braid, be-ribboned in red, dangling over each squared shoulder, the plaits woven so tightly Susannah could see the fine hairs at the girls' temples pulling taut. There was not a wrinkle between them, nor a smile. Her heart lurched.

Their grandmother, too, was motionless, her piercing dark eyes so fixed on the approaching ship, Susannah had an uncanny feeling the woman knew she was being scrutinized and did not at all approve. Adella Armstrong had a deter-

141

mined, unsmiling mouth, drawn thin. Though her brow was clear as a girl's, her hair, done in one thick braid that was coiled on her head like a crown, was steely gray. There were fine etchings around her eyes, that Susannah would have called smile lines on some other face, but crows feet on that bleak, striking visage. There were also more distinct vertical lines, perhaps engraved by sun and wind, perhaps by sorrow, marking the woman's gaunt face from cheek bones to jaw bones. Susannah's first impression was of a fading, bitter beauty.

The round-faced five year old, Baby Saidee, had hazel eyes soft as a new foaled colt's and as curious and defenseless as a kitten's. Her older sister, like their grandmother, appeared to be an austere, restrained disdainful creature. Unlike Adella, though, Venetia, at thirteen had a budding, not a withered loveliness.

"Which of the girls looks most like her mother, like Abigail?" Susannah asked Terry, deciding to face at least one of her challenges headlong. Lowering the spyglass when she got no answer, she saw him pacing the deck, looking not landward and homeward, but out to sea as though he, like the fisher hawk circling above them, would fly far away, if only he could. Susannah exchanged meaningful looks with Grace, to whom she passed the spyglass.

"That little motherless baby child there is love-starved," Grace pronounced. "They all three are. All three. The other two, the woman and the bigger girl, are trying to hide their privations behind haughty eyes."

"Grace, you always were good at getting straight to the truth of a thing," Susannah marvelled.

"*Isla de las Culibras,* the Spanish called Galveston, Island of Snakes. Lots of 'em here. Also, the place was once named *Malhado,* misfortune," Ben informed the women. "I'd just as soon not stay long." Speed, still a sort of greenish sickly color in the face, had survived his first ocean voyage, barely. It had taken until the third and final day on the water for him to find his sea legs, get his stomach settled and come up on deck to observe the approach to Galveston.

When they docked and the ship was secured, the children did not run, Susannah noted, to their handsome father as he descended the gangway before anyone else. Oh, they wanted to. She could see them struggling to control every muscle and sinew in their young bodies to prevent themselves from rushing to Terry and hurling themselves into his arms. They did not budge an inch until Adella Armstrong freed them with a nod. Not until they saw an almost imperceptible lowering of her chin did they spring forward with exclamations of delight, like the young gulls that were darting and dipping at evening over Galves-

143

ton Bay. Terry went down on one knee with outstretched arms.

Susannah was feeling tender, almost teary, as she watched him with his children. His sad and joyful gray eyes went over each of them hungrily, gratefully, before he crushed them to his heart, lowering his head. He held them as if he never would let them go. Obviously, Susannah was happy to see, he adored them and had missed them sorely in the year since he'd last visited Galveston. Even so, a distancing reserve almost at once replaced his open demonstration of love.

The aloofness of manner, the dark mood which had descended on him during their last night at sea before docking at Galveston, was evident when, grasping each child by the hand, he stood and walked toward Adella who had not moved one step in his direction. It was then Susannah began to understand at least one cause of the change in him as they had neared his home place.

"Mrs. Armstrong," Captain Kells of the sloop *Helen,* greeted her, "I can say of the Lieutenant, as Lord Byron said of Don Juan,
'He was the mildest mannered man
That ever scuttled ship' or cut a throat.' "
Jon Kells, a mannerly, handsome young Virginian, with a sheaf of wheaten brown hair and

round bright blue eyes, was master of one of only seventeen small vessels that made up the Confederate Navy, no match then for the Yankee's two hundred warships. It was his first command.

On the *Helen*'s second night out of New Orleans, he and Susannah waited for the other officers and Terry to join them in the cabin. She sipped a claret and the captain, strong for the South in all things, a Tennessee whiskey. The May air on the Gulf still held a faint chill and Susannah had wrapped a black, fringed cashmere shawl about her shoulders over her dinner gown of rustling green taffeta.

"I don't know which interests me more, sir, your description of my husband as a cutthroat or as a Don Juan," she laughed, teasing the earnest fellow. "Tell me, do you suggest he suffers from a want of scruples?"

Kells, blinking and squaring his shoulders, was taken aback.

"I hasten to assure you I meant no such thing, Madam. I sailed with Terry Armstrong in the US *Columbia* as part of the Africa Squadron. He is a man for whom I harbor nothing but admiration. He's is a *great* sailor, Mrs. Armstrong with an instinct for the sea akin to a fish's. I've never known another like him for hitching a ride on the Blue God—the Gulf Stream, or for safely clearing Hatteras, the cape of storms, the graveyard of

145

the Atlantic, off Diamond Shoals. The only ships he's scuttled as far as I know, were flying the skull and cross bones or should have been — pirates. I hope he'll soon be scuttling Yankee craft with the same dispatch.

"As for his way with the ladies," Kells almost stammered, "I never meant *he* was a Don Juan sort. There's no finer man, none more gallant and . . . now your wed . . . married and . . ." Kells fumbled for words. "He loved his wife . . . his *first* wife I mean, Miss Abigail, as much as. . . . and . . . uh, not that I mean he doesn't feel the same for you as her but. . . ."

The poor man was digging himself in deeper and deeper and, though the mention of Abigail brought Susannah down a bit, she felt obliged to relieve his distress.

"I was only toying with you, Captain," she smiled. "I, too, admire my husband inordinately."

"You can't tease our Captain Kells, Susannah. This otherwise excellent fellow lacks a sense of humor," Terry explained, ducking his head to step through the bulkhead passage into the wardroom. "When do we make landfall at Galveston, sir?" he asked Kells.

As always, Susannah was more than pleased to see Terry. Flushed now with warmth, she put aside her cashmere shawl and moved quickly to take his arm. They had been separated for barely thirty minutes, but anyone watching them might have thought it had been hours, days, weeks. Susannah didn't care. She had given over totally to love. She openly adored the agility of Terry's pleasure-bestowing body which, by then, she had given up even trying to resist. His smile had become sun and moon and stars to her, all dawning at once, the sound of his voice an elixir of love.

"Tomorrow afternoon," Kells replied to Terry's question, "we'll sight the island and disembark soon after."

"Ah, my ravishing bride," Terry said to Susannah as she came to his side. "We must all enjoy her elaborate display of feminine subtlety and artifice now, while we may, Captain Kells. It won't be long before we will all be alone, as men always are, facing our enemy, Yankees out for blood." His choice of words, the tone of his voice, the unfamiliar desolated look in his eyes let Susannah know, in that moment, something had changed between them and she was hurt to the heart. Later, she would realize, the transformation had been coming on for a while, as they had approached Galveston.

Terry was never less than charming, and always brilliant in conversation but he was also increasingly detached, spontaneously responsive only to small children, stray dogs, beggars, and Susannah—particularly when she was unclothed. In that condition, she was a beggar of sorts herself, stripped of her armor of finery and nakedly, urgently needing his touch just as a morning glory needs the dew. Despite all her proclamations of chastity, since her fall at Oglethorpe, not more than two nights had passed in succession that they did not find each other in the dark. Sometimes, they could not even wait for the shield of night and would go off, away from the others into the woods or fields to love each other amidst the wild columbine and meadow beauty, jacks in the pulpit, and Queen Anne's lace.

Spring is called the loving season and it certainly was just that for Susannah and Terry. They were feeling warmhearted, lazy, and sensual. The air about them thrummed with cicada calls and the hot breeze was almost too indolent to stir a loblolly leaf. So, she gave up all resistance. The approaching summer and Terry were her twin delights in that year of eighteen and sixty-one, but the honeymoon did not last as long as she would have hoped, that is, forever.

Adella Lafitte Armstrong greeted her son with a parsimonious smile. To Susannah she offered no smile, no word of greeting, just a searching look and a cool hand, and that only briefly before she drew the girls close to her, one to her right, the other left, and placed a hand on each sun-warmed golden head.

"My wife and I have come for my children, Mother," Terry said, giving her a quick peck on the cheek.

"Have you?" Adella said. "Your wife, you say?" She looked at Terry with a fast sharp glance. "While I live, these girls will never be subjected to a stepmother's ill-use."

"I could never maltreat any child of Terry's, nor any child at all!" Susannah exclaimed, unprepared for the woman's venom.

"Easily said. You'll have to prove that to me, and to them . . ." she drew the children closer to her, "before I let them go. The world abounds with little Cinderellas."

"Mother!" Terry began, "you have no right to say such things and we . . ."

Susannah placed a calming hand on Terry's arm.

"Darling, you have every right to take your children from here. I don't *have* to prove anything to your mother, but I will, *and* to Venetia and Saidee, too. Mrs. Armstrong, if the girls want to leave here with us, if I win their trust, and yours, will you be willing to let them go?" Susannah asked, extending a hand herself now to each child's shoulder.

Her eyes met Mrs. Armstrong's, which said even more explicitly than her words had, "You will *never* take them from me," and Susannah believed then that she and Adella Lafitte Armstrong were destined to enmity, just as she and Terry were fated to love.

But at least their rivalry was out in the open. That's the way Susannah liked to do things and she intended to engage in this contest on her terms, not in an underhanded and devious manner that would cause the children distress.

A tug of war had begun and everyone, including the girls, knew it.

Chapter Thirteen

"Your heart must be dry as dust, Miz Lafitte, ma'am, to treat your son and his wife as you are doing," Susannah overheard Grace say as she strode past Adella Armstrong's room. It was their third day on Galveston and she was on her way to keep an appointment with the girls and their father to take a skiff out on Galveston Bay before supper. Curious, Susannah stopped to eavesdrop. Her mother-in-law disliked the name Adella and asked to be addressed as Lafitte. Grace complied. Susannah had yet to address the woman as anything.

"And you Grace, are brazen to criticize *me*, to my face," Lafitte responded in her low, bruised-sounding, whiskey voice that perfectly suited her jaded face. Both were beautifully worn, worldly and very intriguing. In other circumstances, Susannah speculated, she would have befriended Lafitte as Grace was doing. Just listening, she knew Grace had already won a measure of Lafitte's affection, if not trust, by coddling and comforting the vain woman who had too long been living alone with two grieving little girls on her wind-swept acres of wild lowlands, miles from town, out along Old South Road. Lafitte must have been desperately lonely for adult feminine companionship, and masculine company as well.

"That's our way, Miz Lafitte, Miz Susannah's and mine," Grace said, "to be forthright. When I was young, I was insolent, always in trouble, till Susannah Butler helped me govern my temper and tongue."

"You mean she taught you to catch flies with honey, Grace?" Lafitte snapped.

"Catch nothing, ma'am. I'm only honest, like Susannah. But I can be too truthful on occasion, and that's hurtful sometimes. Susannah is more . . . well, kind and sympathetic. She *loves* children, and she loves your son."

"I have noticed all that, thank you, Grace," Lafitte answered, enunciating her words with exaggerated clarity.

"Well, why you treatin' 'em hard like you are then?" Grace blurted, so annoyed she forgot her high-toned diction, so diligently learned from Susannah.

Though Terry had tried repeatedly to reach out to his mother, they had exchanged not more than ten words in three days and Susannah didn't even exist in the older woman's eyes, not since their meeting at the wharf.

"I do not trust first impressions, Grace, and in this matter of your mistress and my son, you are speaking out of turn and from ignorance. To me, it is of no moment if all you say of Susannah Butler is correct. She will have to prove herself to *me*."

"Now, didn't she say she'd try to do exactly that? Old woman, are you going to give her the chance?" Grace was near boiling point.

"My son has not recovered from the loss of his Abigail. Right after she . . . it happened, Terry swore he would not ever wed again, that he would feel untrue to Abigail. What changed his mind, I don't know," Lafitte grumbled,

"Love, of course," was Grace's reply. Susannah wanted to rush in and hug her. "They fell in love in the spring and they knew it right off. We all knew it."

"Spring is the loving season, Grace. Fall is the cure. Why, just looking at the little girls was too painful for Terry to bear. That's why he left them here in my care when their mother died and hasn't been back here in more than a year. He fled to sea, to New York, to the arms of loose women and hussies—anywhere, to try and forget. And then he up and marries in a matter of days? No, no, Grace, I can't credit any of it."

"Miss Susannah is not a hussy!" Grace said, and there was an exclamation from Lafitte. The comber, Susannah reasoned, must have given the woman's hair a little extra twist. Grace's famous

153

temper was rising dangerously and Lafitte, who apparently knew it, was goading her, just to see what would happen. Clearly, Lafitte had a really cantankerous streak.

"Susannah loves Terry." Grace insisted.

"Oh, you needn't tell me that. It's apparent. But, is he a man in love? No, he is not. You see how downcast *he* is, being here, where he and Abigail were so happy together? His judgment is still impaired but mine is not, and I will be damned before I let a desperate, headstrong woman use my grandbabies to work her wiles on their father's heart."

There was a quiver of righteous indignation in Lafitte's voice that made her sound simon-pure, as though *she,* at least, believed what she was saying. Whether or not it was the whole truth was another matter, but Susannah knew then, in her heart, that she had to befriend Adella Lafitte Armstrong somehow, if only to truly win over her son. She just had to find the right way to go about it.

"Oh now, Miz Lafitte, you have yourself all in a conniption fit for no cause. I don't know nothing about Abigail, but I'm telling you Susannah would never hurt those children. The last thing Susannah is is conniving. You could learn that for yourself, ma'am, if you gave her half a chance."

"I couldn't help eavesdropping," Susannah said, stepping into the room, which was as aus-

tere as its occupant. It was fitted with a simple
four poster slat bed, a threadbare quilt, a table
and single ladderback wooden chair, all of the
same northern white pine. The one eccentricity
was a tall cheval looking glass elaborately framed
in ormolu-gilded wood, its claw feet detailed with
precisely carved hairs, its sphinx-faced phinials
hollow eyed.

"See that, Miz Lafitte? Susannah *is* an upright
lady," Grace declared, rolling her eyes at her
friend over Lafitte's head. "She could have hung
back there outside the door listening, but did
she? No, she did not. Now, don't you look
good?"

Guests were expected and Grace was doing Lafitte's hair before dinner. Today it was in a
French roll. Last night, Grace had created a
crowning chignon, held in place by scarab-embel-
lished gold and silver pins. With her cosmetic
talents and stored wealth of gossipy, harmless
stories about folks who were strangers to Lafitte,
the hairdresser had promptly achieved a privi-
leged position in the woman's boudoir and had,
as she'd promised, kept her busy and entertained
for hours on end while Susannah got to know the
little girls.

"Grace, please leave us now," Susannah said.
"It's time the two Mizs Armstrongs got better
acquainted. Time's a'wasting. I've been here three
days and there's only one more to go and I am
not going without those girls!" Or without hear-

155

ing your son say he loves me right out loud, she thought. Susannah knew she surely did have a lot to accomplish in just the brief time left her at Maison Rouge.

They had left the harbor and turned their backs on the remote and trackless waterways of Buffalo Bayou and treacherous Galveston Bay to follow South Road in the direction of San Luis Pass which, not long before, had been a gap in the narrow barrier island. Through it, the sea had poured into the bay and out again with the tide, until a recent hurricane sealed the breach.

Lafitte Armstrong's house, which she built on its lonely site after her husband's passing, was named for the mansion of her pirate forbearer whose ghost still wandered the island, seen mostly by drunkards and fortune hunters with shovels, digging for buried treasure in the dark. The residence was, as Jean Lafitte's armed stronghold had been, painted barn red—blood red, though as she had first approached it through starlit evening fog, it had seemed to Susannah a mirage floating in a purple haze. There was no light burning, not even a single lantern in the dark to signal journey's end. Slaves, servants and children, Terry had explained, were expected, like Lafitte, to retire at dusk.

But that night at Maison Rouge, and the next few following, were going to be different. When the small entourage of wagons and carriages drew to a stop at the dim house, its front door flew open and a single candle was lighted in the dark. From that first, another and another and another took fire until many smiling faces, black ones and white, were illuminated in fifty or more small, warm dancing flames. Without hesitation, grinning broadly, Terry got down from the carriage and handed Saidee, who was asleep on his shoulder, her downy baby curls against his cheek, to a tall, broad ebony woman, who was grinning as generously as he.

"Good to see you smilin', good to see you," she sang out as Terry helped Susannah, then Venetia, down. Lafitte refused his hand.

"Jack," Lafitte barked, "whatever this buffoonery has cost me in candles, you will repay. Now, get to earning your salt and come help me out of this rig," she ordered an elderly black who came forward to lead the carriage to a mounting block.

"We've fixed up a feast for the boy, Miz Lafitte, but no part of it come from your larder. We fished shrimp and sea trout, blue crab and oysters waitin' for you all to come. We throwed our own chickens in the pot, and some greens and beans. Mr. Terry always loved a good party, ain't that right?"

"He loves his chili gravy, too, and sour dough rolls. I made you some," the big woman, Annie, said, still grinning.

"Don't you two tell *me* what Mr. Terry loves or doesn't!" Susannah heard Lafitte complaining as

157

Jack, carrying a lantern and leading her carriage, disappeared into the darkness.

"Hurry on back here, Jack, I want you and Annie to meet my . . ." Terry took Susannah's hand and smiled at her ". . . meet Miss Susannah from the Carolinas, my wife."

The party that night was the best Susannah had ever attended, the food the greatest she'd ever tasted, the people the finest, the children the dearest, the music the sprightliest. On their second night, things got better still. That's when she learned to dance the Texas two-step shuffle, the double shuffle, and how to "cut the pigeon's wing." As they say in south Texas, the splinters did fly.

"She dances Texan like she was raised up in this state," she heard one of her partners tell Terry when he handed her off to Joe John Riley. Jack, standing in the doorway of the barn, had gestured to Terry and Susannah heard him say, "You best come with me, Mr. Terry. Something I must show you now and . . ." The rest of what was said was drowned in a flood of music and Susannah did not hear the black man add, "I been waitin', holding off, Mr. Terry, so's not to ruin your homecoming but, jes' come along with me, sir."

Her new dance partner valiantly huffed and puffed his way through a strenuous double step. The small, squarely-built, dark-haired Irishman had grown rich, he breathlessly explained, on the

158

Galveston *Strand*.

"The *Strand's* the street facing the harbor where you made a landfall. It's the Wall Street of the Southwest . . ." he caught his breath for a shoot-the-shoot, a demanding dance maneuver. "Fortunes being made there . . . shipping . . . insurance . . . banking . . . Whew, ain't' this some *fandango,* though?" he wheezed. The music, which was provided by one man playing fiddle, another banging rhythm on a clevis and pin, a metal plow part, stopped and Riley stood mopping his brow.

"Doesn't the climate here suit you, Mr. Riley?" Susannah asked, looking about for Terry. She wandered toward the wide open doors and Riley followed along.

"I am getting downright rich so I sure can't complain. When it comes to climate, you gotta take what you get in Texas. Lucky for me I'm a hell of a lot better at predicting cotton prices than weather here, but it's only fools and strangers that try to do that, predict weather in the Lone Star State. What we call Texas northers come sweeping down on you sharp and cold as a witch's teat, pardon me ma'am." Riley's already red face, crimsoned more deeply at the indelicacy. "Sometimes there's a few black clouds before the rain breaks, or the hail, but not always though so don't count on clouds. A sudden puff of rising wind and — wham! We're in a near gale. It can blow for days — two, three, four — the mer-

159

cury drops fifty degrees sometimes. 'Course, here on the coastal prairie near the Gulf, it's hurricanes we get most. Like the night Abigail Armstrong drowned."

"We get hurricanes in the Carolinas, and . . . what was that you said, Mr. Riley?"

"About Texas northers?"

"About Abigail Armstrong, Mr. Riley."

"You don't know? Well, I'm not surprised you don't. Terry could not talk about it then, when it happened, and likely he never will be able to. Abigail disappeared during a bad Gulf hurricane. She wasn't never found."

"I see," Susannah said just as Terry returned looking drained and afflicted as if, she thought, he'd just seen a ghost. Until that moment, she had actually allowed herself to believe things might be working out well between them.

On their first night on Galveston Island, after the great fish and chili feast there was an exchange of news with the hands—who'd married, been born and died in the year since Terry had left, how many tons of cotton had been harvested from Armstrong lands, how many Armstrong ships, deep-loaded with the produce of the land, had sailed for England and France. Terry seemed content, even happy to be home.

"I've done it, Susannah," he said as they walked along the bay shore of the island later.

160

"I've come back *here* and . . . the world hasn't disintegrated, yet."

"Is that what you expected?" she asked. She wriggled out of her dancing shoes and left them on the sand. A few steps farther on, Terry stepped out of his boots.

"No. I expected I might."

"You? Fall apart? Oh, Terry, is it still so bad?" she asked, taking his hand, surprised that he'd not only revealed his feelings but actually admitted to a weakness.

"In a way it's bad. Not the way you think. Not as I expected. Now, I feel the past might be loosening its hold on me. You've helped me there, Susannah, more than I can say just yet." He took a firmer grip of her hand. The water lapped at their ankles. The moon was sailing through a rushing navy blue sky, threading its way through rifts in clouds, falling all around them — touching Susannah's lips and hair and breasts and it seemed she could feel the universe swirling about them. Her heart swelled with the joy of it all — the magical night, the man who really might be getting ready to love her, the children they had, those to be born. Susannah was sure she had actual cause to hope that night.

She broke away from Terry, gathered up her skirts and ran, fast as she could, her heart pounding, half-laughing, half-crying until she couldn't take another step and then she just flung up her arms to return the moon's embrace.

161

"Touch me with magic, moon!" she called out, and Terry was right there to do what the moon couldn't, really. "Oh, Terry, touch me . . . touch me in moonlight," she sighed as his hand cupped her face and his lips took hers. They sank to their knees, their hands at each other's clothing, so needing each other, they were in a state of disarray when their bodies joined in the moonlight.

His sweet and tender regard for her, and his carnal command of her body seemed infinite there on the beach with the soft lapping of the bay about them and, later, all night long, to the pounding of the surf that reached them in their room at the top of the sleeping house where the world stood still for them that night. She loved him and he loved her truly. Susannah *knew* that, felt it in every nuance of Terry's long hard body touching hers, in every taut muscle, in the gentle touch of his lips and fingers on her skin. And she sensed it every time he sighed her name. He never did say "I love you," the words she yearned so to hear, but she was sure then she would — someday. Susannah wanted that day to come before they left Galveston.

"Oh, Terrence Armstrong!" she sighed on opening her eyes the morning after the barn dance and looking into his that were dark with distress. Either he was already wide awake at dawn, or he'd not slept at all. "Oh, don't grieve so! Riley told me about the hurricane and what happened to Abigail. If she was never properly laid to rest, that makes her loss all the harder to bear."

"It's this house, the memories here, the . . . misfortunes," he muttered. "Let it be." No words of comfort came to Susannah just at once. Obviously, Terry was thinking of Abigail and all she could think to do was comfort him — wordlessly. Her body moved to his. She stretched long as she could at his side, then rolled to lie against him, half over him, trying to search his eyes with her own. He turned away.

"I might never be what Abigail was to you but, please . . . let me be . . . *something*, long as we have to be together anyway," she said, her voice soft. His eyes closed. She saw his throat working as he swallowed. Terry wasn't over her yet, and likely never will be, exactly what he told her from the start, she thought, just as Lafitte said. She'd been a self-deluded fool to think she could reach him.

"Don't ever repeat that to me, never again!" he rasped and she felt her heart break. He virtually had said, "don't bother trying, *you* can't even begin to replace *her.*"

"Do you want me darlin', right now?" she asked, falling back on the one sure way she *knew* she could always reach him. Rolling onto her stomach, she pressed her lips to the soft, warm

163

place between his right shoulder and ear and his hand began to travel her back from nape to thighs. She parted them and he found the hot damp center of her with his fine hands, found her ready lips with his, drew her over him so that she bestrode his narrow hips. He held back, not entering her, not until she asked . . . implored . . . and then, she felt his hard, deep, desperate thrust and cried out at the profligacy of passionate pleasure he gave, and went on riding him high until he rolled to loom over her, penetrating deep and hard, deeper and harder, more passionately, his heat unquenchable, his desire more desperate than ever before.

"Is it *me,* Terry you're making love to, thinking of, feeling here in your bed and in your arms?" she asked. "Is it?" Had she, would she ever, become something more to him than a delicious diversion, as he called her, more than a pleasing consort to help him escape his tormenting memories at least for the time it took to satisfy his passions? There were no answers for Susannah, not just then.

Chapter Fourteen

Adella Lafitte Armstrong reluctantly agreed to a walk with her new daughter-in-law, Susannah, whose presence in Galveston and in her son's life she did not, to say the least, welcome. It was too soon, after Abigail. Yesterday's misfortunes don't disappear all that quickly, if ever. Lafitte knew that from first hand experience.

She did recognize however, that this Susannah her son Terry had brought home was a ravishingly lovely creature, tall and graceful and her coloring was superb. But that was not all. She was strong-willed, not a good quality in a wife for Lafitte's son. There could be but one strong, opinionated female in a family. *That*, Lafitte insisted, was she and no other. She set the tone, she made the rules for the children to follow, and she gave the orders. The lady from Carolina would have to be brought to heel.

Susannah, however, was no feeble April fool,

Lafitte ruminated. The young woman was polished and shrewd and supremely confident.

"You remind me of myself, before age robbed me of my looks and gradually turned me invisible," Lafitte told Susannah, who didn't answer at once. She was distracted, watching Terry and the girls who romped on ahead. Rather, Baby Saidee, playful as a puppy, romped with Terry. Venetia, Lafitte took note, was her subdued, ladylike self. My son and Susannah, she thought, had spent many hours with the children since they'd arrived, a lot more time than they had spent with *me*. Lafitte had not spied on them exactly, but watched from a distance, seeing that Venetia, like her father, had usually said little, just held tightly to his hand. Baby Saidee, from what she had observed, prattled on with Susannah without lapse.

"I'm speaking to you, Susannah. Pay attention," Lafitte demanded.

"Your dress is a beautiful claret color, Mrs. Armstrong," Susannah said as they walked. "You're still a handsome woman with an elegant sense of style."

"Kersey," Lafitte corrected. "The shade of my dress is kersey. Men *used* to come after me like boys running to a fire. Not any more."

"Oh, I can see the young beauty lurking there, trapped behind your aging eyes. Perhaps you'd not be so discontent if you let her go," Susannah said, just like that, straight out, not mitigating

166

the effect of her words at all, Lafitte was shocked to hear. "I think a woman able to accept the seasons of her life with composure, if not pleasure, will be . . . happier," Susannah said. Lafitte barely controlled her tongue and her temper.

"It will happen to you," she taunted. "Men will show merely polite attention, and there will be many things, you'll realize, that you will never do again. I used to swim West Bay. It's a mean piece of water, but even so, I could swim it. No more."

"There are Charleston belles of a certain age who are still surrounded by admirers. Some are women who never were very pretty, but always witty, clever, interesting . . . kind. Now, my mother, among other things, takes deep pleasure in her gardens. A glorious garden, Mother says, is a kind of immortality, like grandchildren. Flowers die. Gardens, like dreams, never do."

"Besides her flowers, Mrs. Butler still has the Commodore, your father," Lafitte answered sarcastically. "*You* give her grandchildren and leave mine alone. They are all I have left, now that you have Terry." The woman scowled, grabbing up a crooked stick and swinging it vigorously as they strode along toward the Gulf side of the barrier island, more or less following a sandy path that was overrun in places, with tangled underbrush.

"Why live your life solely through others? It's not fair. It can be a burden to children, knowing they're your whole happiness. I think one should look to the future, theirs and yours." As Lafitte

167

prepared to put this bold Susannah in her place for lecturing *her,* Terry and the girls turned to walk back toward them. Susannah waved. "You could marry again," she said to Lafitte, "as your son has done."

"Don't talk bosh. I will never take another man's name," Lafitte protested and Susannah darted a fast glance of pure exasperation in her direction.

"Ah ha! I saw that look, Susannah. You didn't think I'd catch you looking at me with daggers, but I did! You are obliged to show me respect." This frontal assault was ignored by Susannah.

"What's troubling Venetia? She's a sorrowing child. Hardly even childlike at all."

"Not that it's your affair," Lafitte answered, "but, just as the child seemed to be accepting her mother's . . . leaving, she fell into melancholia. I gave her a book, about having good thoughts and coming of age as a young woman. *Purity and Truth, What a Young Girl Should Know.* It is purported to explain what gentle women are too reticent to teach their daughters directly. There are sections, chapters called 'Twilight Talks'—'What it is to Become a Woman,' 'Millions of Fish Eggs Never Become Fish,' 'If All Children Were Good Now, The Men and Women of the Future Would Be Good,' and so on for twenty or thirty chapters. Dr. Kinnicut said it was absolutely safe to put into the hands of a child."

"I see," Susannah said. That was all, but her

voice carried reproach. Lafitte was losing patience.

"My granddaughter is growing into a beauty, perhaps not a classic one like you—she *is* a bit awkward—but a beauty nonetheless. That is the crucial matter of any girl's life, because women hold power only through men," she told Susannah. "If Venetia would only realize it, her spirits would rise." Susannah looked at Lafitte with disbelief for a long moment, speechless.

"You're wrong. There's more to being a woman than standing about looking beautiful," she finally said, very emphatically. At that contradiction, Lafitte had had just about enough of her forthright companion.

"No one disagrees with *me*, not openly. Abigail dared not, her daughters do not and you will not. Is that understood?" Susannah, appalled, did not answer. "Why have you come here? Lafitte demanded. "You will never take Abigail's place. She was the perfect wife for my son. She fit into this family as if born to it, not like you, you . . . brazen thing."

"Damn Abigail! She was just an ordinary mortal woman, like me," Susannah exploded.

"Oh, don't you flatter yourself. She was nothing like you. Ask Terry and you'll find out!" Lafitte taunted as Susannah turned on her boot heel and went off at a run, very fleet, even on sand. Lafitte did *not* call after her, not even when her own boot toe caught in a runner vine and she fell, sprawling. Unhurt but blinded with frustration and anger, Lafitte scrambled to her knees and thrashed out at the underbrush, striking again and again with the warped stick she'd been carrying. It was a terrible mistake.

Never in her life had Lafitte *chosen* to ask anyone for help, and she particularly did not want to call out to her son's unflinching, cruel, and critical wife. Her call, more a scream, was involuntary, wrung from her stiffening lips by the searing pain of a rattler bite on her right cheek. The nerves of her face started to go numb even as she kept on clubbing the snake who bit again, the second time on her arm.

The wind was up, whistling, laden with the surf's roar and carrying the strident calls of the fisher crows skimming the bay. The wind took Lafitte's single cry in the wrong direction. No one would hear her, she realized, even if she had been capable of calling out again. Before the world went dark, as if looking through the wrong end of a spy glass, she saw Susannah overtake the others, throw her arms about Terry's neck and kiss him, give Venetia a bear hug, then gather up Baby Saidee and swing her about.

When Susannah spun in Lafitte's direction, she abruptly stopped, set down the child and broke into a run again, back in the direction from which she had come, in Lafitte's direction, the stricken woman saw, as she fell, and just as she had always heard it would, her whole life began

170

to pass before her dimming eyes. She did not much like what she saw.

One of the first things Lafitte actually did see when she opened her eyes was Terry's concerned face, then beside it, Susannah's. Once aware that she wasn't dead yet, Lafitte knew it had to be that young woman's doing and tried to say thank you. No sound came from her throat.

She had been aware for a while she was alive. She had just lain in her bed with her eyes shut tight, in no way showing she was awake, listening to them all, particularly her grandchildren, talking.

"Lafitte is going to be her gritty old self again soon, you'll see," Terry was reassuring the girls.

"She's not going to go, the way mother did?" Venetia asked. For the first time, Lafitte heard the hurt and dread in her voice. Maybe that was because it was the first time she'd ever listened to the child, she mused.

"Susannah got the snake's poison out of your Grandma. Lafitte will be fine," Terry repeated.

"How did she, Da? How did the poison get out?" Saidee asked. Without looking, just listening to her sweet little voice, Lafitte visualized the child's big, round, trusting eyes, and she was *glad* she was alive.

"Susannah made a cut on grandma's cheek where the snake bit. Susannah did that with a broken piece of scallop shell, and then, she

171

sucked the poison out. It was a difficult thing to do, and it could have been dangerous. Susannah is very . . . brave." Terry's voice was mellow and loving. Lafitte *heard* that for herself. She kept her eyes closed and went on, not listening, but *hearing*.

"Tell about Pecos Bill, Da," Saidee asked with a yawn. Terry used to tell them about Bill at bedtime, before he went away. He laughed now, clearly happy the baby remembered.

"You mean the Pecos Bill who fell ofn' a westering wagon? That one? The one's mam and pap had eighteen young 'uns and didn't notice they'd lost Bill, who got raised by up coyotes and scared the rattlesnakes into the cactus?"

"That's the one, Da!" Saidee chirped, clapping her hands.

"Okay. That's the same Pecos Bill who invented tarantulas because he needed pets to keep him company on the desert, the Pecos Bill who saddled up mountain lions instead of horses to ride, *and* rode a cyclone across three states, one that levelled mountains, uprooted forests and made the Texas panhandle.

"Bill had a true love, Slue-Foot Sue. *His* Sue could ride any four-footed critter with hoofs and, on their weddingday, against all advice—she was stubborn like my Sue—she rode Pecos Bill's bronc, a horse name of Widow Maker. That devil bucked so long, four days, and so high, Sue had to duck her head to keep from having it bumped

172

on the moon."

"When will Lafitte wake up?" Venetia asked in her soft-voiced, shy way. Pecos Bill had never been her favorite.

"Perhaps not for hours, perhaps any minute. Why don't you run and get the book she gave you, Venetia, about growing up?" Susannah suggested. Lafitte almost opened her eyes then because there was a troublesome silence. "What's wrong, Venetia? Don't you like the book?"

"Some yes, some not," the child answered apologetically as if she was obliged to be pleased with anything anyone gave her. That's *my* fault, Lafitte marvelled.

"Run get it anyway, will you please, Tia? I'll read from it," Terry said. Tia was a pet name he hadn't used since Venetia was a baby and the girl rushed off to do as he asked. When she returned, Terry opened the book at random and began to read.

" 'You feel very sorry for the little baby fish that are orphaned before they are born, and, indeed they need your sympathy. Many of the eggs will be destroyed before they are hatched and many of the little baby fish will be eaten up by other fish . . . This is a good thing for us, for one fish lays thousands, even millions, of eggs . . . they would fill the rivers so full . . . that it would be a very serious thing.' " Terry stopped reading. "Girls, come sit close to me while we read."

"Me, too?" Susannah asked with her little laugh.

"Darlin', there's not *quite* enough room in this one rocking chair I brought from the porch. You do the next part, okay?" he asked and Susannah took up where he had stopped reading. There was more about fish, and about frogs, flowers, seeds, worms, birds and nests, and chickens. Bored, Lafitte was about to announce herself, when storks came up. According to the author, Mrs. Mary Wood-Allen, MD, they did not bring babies. Humans came from a special little room in a mother's body.

" 'You would like to know if I knew you were there . . ." Susannah read. "Yes, I knew, though for a long time I had to wait patiently for you to let me know . . . Then one day I felt a little movement, just as if you had knocked with your tiny hand on the wall of your little room, "Mother, I am here." . . . and I would reply, "Good morning, little one . . .' "

"Did my mamma say that, 'little one' like in the book?" Baby Saidee asked.

"She did," Terry said with gruff affection. "Oh, she surely did."

"Will *you* say it to your baby, Susannah?" Venetia's candid question surprised her grandmother.

"Well . . . one day, perhaps," was the restrained answer. There was a catch in Susannah's voice that so startled Lafitte, she had to have a

174

look at them all. She opened her eyes to find her son and his wife lost in each other's eyes but not so lost that the girls were excluded from the circle of love. In the few days they had all been together, that foursome was becoming a family and, though she was not within that glowing inner ring, Lafitte, too, had a stake in it. She tried to sit up, to tell them that, to say, "don't forget me, *please*."

"Mother, don't talk, listen," Terry cautioned hurrying to the bedside then. "Doc Kinnicut's here, down getting coffee. He's seen to you. Susannah saved your life."

"Thank you," Lafitte actually managed to say, croaking out the words this time. She tried to move. She could not raise her head and when she brought her hand up, she found one side of her face swathed in bandages. "Rattler," she coughed. "My fault it struck. I struck it . . . first. Everything . . . Abigail . . . all my fault." With incomprehension, Susannah actually smiled at her.

Terry did not smile. He just stared down through narrowed eyes.

Chapter Fifteen

Terry Armstrong was in trouble.

He was falling in love with Susannah Butler and he did not want to be in love with her, or anyone, not in a world where nothing seemed to last, not on his way to war, not on a secret spying mission, not ever.

He had for some time, from the start, been trying to convince himself as, apparently, he had convinced Susannah, that what the two had found together was blazing passion. And that was just splendid, he would repeat and rephrase and reiterate, but it was just the easy part, not to be confused with love. He only *wanted* her, he told Susannah, and tried to tell his heart. Since their overnight stay at Oglethorpe, neither had been listening. She was too perfect.

Terry was having a damnable time holding sway over his feelings. The more into love he got, the harder he fought against himself and the more distance he tried to keep between him and the object of his ungovernable affections. He wasn't often successful at doing that, even after he abandoned his strategy of flirting and trifling with her in the light of day. About the same time, Susannah had begun regularly inviting him to her bed after dark and never once did he have the inclination, or strength, to pass her open door.

The first chink in her armor had shown after her social triumph at Ogelthorpe, where she had thwarted Josie Izzard's plans for Terry, and charmed President Davis himself, who paid her chivalrous court. After that night, any little thing—Terry's inviting smile or a secret come-hither touch, particularly when combined with a fine glass of brandy—would do the trick. Spirits, Terry discovered, went straight to Susannah's head and her heart and warmed her lovely body to a fine heat before he even had touched her. After Ogelthorpe, she gave up altogether on her celibacy idea and, by the time they took ship for the cruise to Galveston, they were literally *all* wrapped up in each other most of the time.

At Maison Rouge it got worse—or better, depending on his mood—when memories came swirling about Terry like autumn leaves on a chilly wind and he was in dire need of the warming diversion of Susannah's ingenious hands that inflamed the uncoiling spring of his passion. Her soothing voice, always a bit raspy, became more so when she was being seductive, murmuring

177

softly as her lips roamed over his skin and her tongue did . . . amazing things.

Besides all that, he *liked* this woman and so, Terry could see, not surprisingly, did his children. That his mother did not care for Susannah was not surprising to Terry either, and should have been all the confirmation he needed that he was not only in love—but with the right woman. Still, he held out, or tried to, even after Susannah had saved Lafitte's life.

"Here you are," Terry heard her voice in the thick darkness of that windblown overcast night. She found him on the veranda. He had not lit a lamp. It was late. The house behind them was finally quiet, Lafitte medicated, the children and the servants asleep, the doctor gone. "Are you brooding out here all alone?" Susannah asked, feeling her way toward him, depositing herself in his lap.

"No," he answered. "I'm thinking about my next move."

"I'm for moving up to bed," she giggled. He pretended to ignore that.

"I must leave here tomorrow or the next day at the latest, while I can still get through the Yankee blockade. Where's your book of numbers?"

"Oh, that kind of move, a spy move. The book's safe in my luggage, locked tight as a lady's diary should be. The key is here, hanging about my neck." Her head had dropped to his shoulder and his hand, resting at the curve of her

178

waist, slid up over the swell of her breasts, to delve and discover the key, warmed and safe between them. She sighed and kissed him. He kissed her, too, then, abruptly stood, setting her down in the rocking chair. He couldn't see the features of her face in the dark or her expression, just the outline of her bowed head. He heard the creak of the rocking chair, then her voice.

"What do you mean *'I'* must leave tomorrow?' What about me?"

"I've rethought the matter. I already told you, this would be the most outrageous thing you'll ever in your life be asked do, act as if you're betraying everything and everyone you care about. I can't go on insisting you do that. Stay here with the girls. Wait here for me. When it's all over . . ." he slammed his fist into the wall.

"Stay here? With *your* mother?" Susannah laughed coldly. "Listen to me, Terry Armstrong, if you want to get rid of me, say so. I'll just go . . . home. Where I'm loved. If you want, I'll take the children away from this sad place. I'm not so stupid as to pound my head on a brick wall, or to try to come between a man and his mother and his dead wife's damn ghost! I told Lafitte earlier today and now I'm telling you, Abigail was just a flesh and blood *woman,* like me, and if she loved you, she'd want you to be happy, to go on . . ."

"Abigail? Like you?" Terry said roughly. "Oh, no, no!"

"Some people agree, without so much as a word spoken, between them, to leave certain doors closed. You and I have been doing that about lots of things, especially about Abigail. Your mama was the one who said I should ask you about her, Terry, ask you what your wife was really like. But you know what? I do not give a damn or even a hoot in hell. You just keep on living with your demons. I won't!"

Terry heard the empty chair, rocking wildly, thump the wall twice and knew Susannah was gone into the thick blackness of that clouded, moonless night, vanished into the rising wind, lost amidst the flailing trees and he felt his heart shredding in his chest. "Don't . . . don't leave me!" he howled, overwhelmed by a sensation that he had lived through exactly the same moment once before.

When he plunged blindly off the porch and began to run, his heart pounding in his ears, visions of riptides, rocks, rattlers and other fatal terrors flooding his mind, he knew it wasn't *deja vu*. It all *had* happened the same way once before. On the tragic night Abigail had fled from him, a Texas norther had struck Galveston Island and now, he had to find Susannah fast, before he lost her too—forever.

He charged off heedlessly down the same beach path they all had walked earlier that day, where Lafitte had been struck by the rattler, the same one Abigail had taken on her last

180

night in the world.

Though he didn't remember lighting it, Terry had had the wits about him, at least, to take a lantern. Holding it high, he came crashing out of the underbrush and crested the low dunes, calling at the top of his voice, the wind blowing full in his face stealing away his breath as he hurtled toward the sea-roar and distant hint of white, roiling ocean foam that reflected what little natural light there was that stormy night.

The next thing he knew, he was in surf up to his hips, the sputtering lantern held above his head, and he kept calling and calling, with the Gulf mud sucking him down, when he felt something in the water behind him that tried to drag him back up onto the beach.

He fought his demons then, with all the strength in him and he was winning the struggle, resisting, towing whatever had a hold on him farther from the shore to drown it, once and for all, for good when a wall of water crashed over him. Terry lost his footing and went down in the cross currents as the undertow took its deadly grip.

Only his companion of the storm saved him from slipping away forever by grasping his belt and holding on fast. Susannah had found Terry.

"No!! Let loose of me!" he roared out. "I have to find her . . . save her . . . Susannah," he bellowed, "Susannah, I love you! Don't leave me . . . don't!"

Somehow, the lantern, before it fell hissing into

the waves, struck his head hard, knocking him, as Susannah would say later, not unconscious, just silly enough to let himself be half-led, half-dragged, staggering up the incline toward the beach.

"All my life, I've hurt what I tried to love, Susannah. I'm *afraid* to love you." Actually, he was almost afraid even to look full at her.

"I'll chance it if you will," she whispered, "and I'll change it. Love me, Terry." They had made their way back to the house, clinging to each other, kissing, touching in the dark, through the maelstrom of the sudden summer storm and stood, soaked, in a shivering, loving embrace beneath the overhang of the porch, listening to the roar of rain and wind. Susannah went to change and to get towels and a blanket for Terry while he peeled off most of his clothing.

"Listen to me now," he said as she reappeared, gliding across the porch in beautiful dishabille, a white satin *peignoir* replicating the softness of her skin to which it clung. She handed him a towel and stood still, two feet from him.

"I'm listening," she said.

"As a boy, I had a stallion, a golden palomino splendid as your Alcantara. I tested him too hard, I took him over hurdles too high until, one time, I heard the crack of his leg breaking, before he went down under me. I had to shoot him."

182

Terry could just barely see her sorrowful face in the dark. "Can you know how guilt-struck and pained I was? Wait, there's more. Listen to me now," he told Susannah, who was about to speak. "I've trained a few good bird dogs in my life, but the very best was Hal, a pointer I raised from a three month pup. Smartest dog I ever knew, all character and *class,* never a false point from Hal. He would range at my side, head up testing the air for a scent of game and then, he'd freeze into the most noble pose, head and tail high. The other dogs would always honor his point, even the young rowdy ones, as if they knew *here* was something *right.* There's nothing quite like the feeling."

"I know," Susannah said. "What happened to? . . ."

"I lent Hal to a drunk. Drunk shot him. Susannah, I lost my horse . . . my dog . . . my wife, walked away from my girls . . . and I didn't want to love you because . . . I was afraid I'd lose you, too." Terry sat in the rocking chair with his head in his hands and Susannah dabbed at his wet hair, then massaged his neck and shoulders.

"Oh Terry! I knew I was seeing *awful* things in your eyes I couldn't have put there. Who *was* Abigail? How did she hurt you so?"

"She left me. She was bound to, one way or another. Abigail was on her way to run off with Arthur Roswell the night she . . . drowned. If I had agreed to take her away from here as she'd asked . . . it all might have been different."

"What happened? You were so in love, so . . ."

"We were that, all right. I came back to Texas from school up north and lost my heart to a lovely child-woman just turned sixteen. She was too young and she was fragile and vulnerable in her emotions. I was away from Maison Rouge a lot of the time, out to sea in an Armstrong ship, off hunting, riding, gambling, cock fighting, drinking and raising hell most of the time I was ashore."

"You were proving your southern manhood as you were expected to do," Susannah said with a vexed little sigh. "And your wife was supposed to be sweetly virtuous, restrained and pure, at home."

"She languished, isolated here without me," Terry went on, his voice strained, "so Lafitte took charge—of Abigail's children *and* Abigail's life. On the night she died, my wife had begged me to take her and the girls away from Maison Rouge to live in town. When I hesitated, she disappeared into the storm."

"She tried to love you. You wouldn't let her. Let *me!*" When Susannah said that, Terry drew her to him, encircled her hips and hid his face against her sleek body.

"The day you and I arrived here, during the dancing, Jack called me outside to show me a gold ring tied tight in a scrap of cloth. He'd found it washed up on the shore months ago,

184

Abigail's wedding ring. I didn't take proper care of her. I never will forgive myself."

There was a gentle, sad smile, a sympathetic one on Susannah's lips. She understood his turmoil. She said, "You know, Terry, better than most people, that a sailor can't change the wind, only the sails. No one can change the past, only affect the future. It wasn't your fault alone. Let it go, love. Try to. All this while, I've felt like a bird beating its wings against a closed window. Open it for me. Now, *our* moon is waxing, our star rising. I'll help you now, you'll see."

"I love you, Susannah," he said, finding her emerald eyes swimming in tears. "I think I might never have meant that before. I think I didn't even know what it meant."

They went to bed and just held each other and touched a lot and talked all night.

"There's just one word for this—it's love," Susannah said.

"You know, I've been faithful to you since our eyes first met, that day at Annapolis," Terry told her.

"All that time? A whole month and a half?" she laughed softly.

"Your eyes were blinding mine that day."

"It was love, dancing in them."

"I always have been drawn to rushing water, fine wine, and proud southern women."

185

They talked of the lure of distant train whistles and the taste of wild blueberries, of old friendships, and childish things.

Susannah told how she and her clique of little girls would go into the woods on nutting parties on Indian summer days and she was always elected Little Brown Squirrel because she filled her basket first. Terry told her how he had made squirt guns from bamboo, slab canoes and lampwick torches for night fishing.

"See, we are doing it now, the hard part — getting to be friends," Susannah smiled.

"We already knew a fair lot about the easy stuff, though we have some yet to try, and some to try again and again because it keeps getting better and better," Terry answered. "Ready to improve on a real good thing?"

"Almost ready, almost," Susannah laughed. "I like hearing your voice too much to silence it just yet, so . . . keep on talkin' to me, love, just a little longer."

Terry did. And they didn't give way to soaring passion until an exuberant burst of song invaded their solitude. He thought it was the last call of a night hawk, a chuck-will's-widow, on its way home to its nest. Susannah said it was the first andante note of a Wilson's thrush, greeting the new day.

Chapter Sixteen

Terry Armstrong loved Susannah. That made her think that there could be a happy ending for them, after all. Not only did he love her, but she had a hold over her domineering mother-in-law. Lafitte now owed Susannah—her life—and the younger woman meant to collect on the debt, not in kind, but in kindness.

Weak as she was from the snake poison, the doctor restricted Lafitte's physical activity to coming down the stairs and sitting in a chair in the shade—that was it, for months to come. But she was feisty and Susannah credited her for that.

"Know who's coming to stay a while when you all have gone and deserted me?" Lafitte asked her.

"We are not deserting you," Susannah answered. "We have important business at hand."

"Eugenie Lavender, my friend from Corpus is coming here. She and her husband came to Texas

187

from France not ten years ago. She was already acclaimed as an artist over there but she liked the colors of Texas. When she ran out of the supply of paints she brought with her, she made new ones from herbs and leaves and flowers. Another of my old friends will soon be here, but I suspect he needs my help more than I do his. Sam is coming on, more to see Terry than me, I conjecture."

"Corpus?" Susannah asked, and "Sam?" as she went on spooning custard into her mother-in-law's mouth. Lafitte hated being dependent but unless she was fed she'd not have eaten. She and Susannah were settled under a great spreading flame tree in back of Maison Rouge, both women wearing flour sack aprons. Beside them were laden tables, groaning with what Lafitte called the good things of life. Another social gathering was about to begin at Maison Rouge, a farewell party, this time.

Nearby, Terry was busy hanging a rope and barrel swing, showing the girls how to make certain useful knots and splices. In deep concentration, they were putting their heads together, two yellow, one golden brown, over the project. They were intent and happy, in a seventh heaven of their own and Susannah took quiet joy in watching them. If Lafitte took any notice, she didn't show it, but Susannah had come to realize the woman always was more interested in herself than in anything else.

"Corpus *Christi*, girl. Sam *Houston*. If you are planning on becoming a Texan, you have a lot to learn," she lectured Susannah.

188

"That remains to be worked out, about Texas. Open," Susannah ordered, the spoon poised. Lafitte kept chattering instead.

"Sam is an old, *old* friend. He and my husband, Mr. Armstrong senior, hoped to turn the Texas Gulf Coast into a new Mediterranean. Galveston was going to be their Manhattan of the South, a new Wall Street built on King Cotton, not solid rock, the damn fools. They didn't consider the hurricanes, the floods or the yellow fever."

"Oh, you're acquainted with Governor Houston?" Susannah asked, curious, but also because she knew Lafitte wanted her to ask. This time, she delivered two fast spoonfuls of custard before she got her answer.

"Former President of the Texas Republic, *and* former Senator when we joined the Union *and now,* former Governor of Texas, Sam Houston. He was voted out of office when he wouldn't sign the Texas Order of Secession. The man's always been a Unionist and he's always been stubborn. Know what? I'd have waited forever for Sam, if only I'd known he'd come into my life." When Lafitte made that pronouncement, without any warning, Susannah nearly dropped the spoon. As it was, a great glob of pudding landed in Lafitte's lap.

"I *thought* I was in love with Terry's father, Mr. Armstrong, when I accepted his proposal. He was a good lookin' well-off northerner from New York City, of an old reputable family. I think *he* loved the *idea* of me, my passionate pirate blood and my heritage of wild Louisiana French Cajun uh . . .

189

zest. You know about that?" Lafitte asked. Susannah nodded.

"Some. The Commodore mentioned your . . ."

"My great grandfather, Jean Lafitte, came to this island and called it Campeachy, French for camp site or some such. Other pirates and privateers flocked here after him, mostly riffraff, scavenging birds of prey and passage, Indian squaws and loose women—prostitutes. Jean Lafitte had a thousand followers before he was done for. He caused to have built a combination house and fortress, *Maison Rouge,* with canon muzzles protruding from the upstairs windows. This was a *thriving* old place in Jean's day. A lot of carousing went on here—at the slave marts, gambling halls, saloons. Lafitte's sea raids on Spanish ships brought him tons of spoils and filled his warehouses to overflowing though all I ever inherited from him was a brace of flintlock pistols. He was a great success at his vocation, pirating, as my husband was at his, different kinds of pirating—banking, real estate, shipping. My husband was a brilliant man but . . . cold. He was all business, not much emotion. To him, Lafitte was just another *very* successful trader. Jean was a hero of Mr. Armstrong's and so, Mr. Armstrong wanted me to bear him progeny, six or seven offspring he wanted, mostly boys. I feel I fulfilled my connubial obligation by giving him one remarkable son, my . . . *our* Terry," Lafitte corrected herself with a sly smile. "But, as often happens, embers die where once there was a fire. Mr. Armstrong and I never ignited a real hot

190

blaze, anyway. He was not a . . . sensual man."

"Terry takes after your side of the family, then. I mean he is *warm* and ardent," Susannah suggested and Lafitte hurriedly gulped down a mouth full of junket.

"Miss Abigail Austin would have agreed with you about that. Oh, dear," Lafitte said, pretending discomfort. "If I was a nice woman, I wouldn't have gone into the past — Terry's past — that way. But you know by now, Susannah, I am a *wicked* woman," she tittered. There was a streak of humorous perversity in her Susannah was getting to almost like.

"If you're trying to shock me, you'll have to do better than that," she laughed. "And who's wicked? Not you, Lafitte. *Really?* Tell me about it, about you and Sam." Susannah insisted feeling as if they were two girls giggling over their flirtations. At that moment, the remarkable, sensual man Susannah was always ready to be wicked with was pushing his daughter Venetia in the swing and the child laughed irrepressibly every time she soared high toward the leaves. It was a good sound to hear. Baby Saidee clung to her father's leg, demanding her turn. Susannah's heart turned over, watching them. And Lafitte? She was so delighted to be asked about Governor Houston, she glowed.

"When I first met Sam, long ago, I'd already been wed a while, but I was strongly drawn to him. I was an extraordinary looking woman in those days, and he was a tall, handsome vigorous specimen of a man who showed up here in Texas battered by scandal and with a badly broken heart. He had a mysterious past. He had been living for years in The Oklahoma Territory with a Cherokee tribe that adopted him when he was a boy growing up in Tennessee. Sam was Governor of Tennessee, and resigned when his wife left him and ran home to her mamma. Neither he nor she ever *have* said why, or who was at fault.

"Well, as for me and him, it took Samuel longer than it took me to recognize what was going on between us, but when he did, there never was anything like it, not for me nor Sam, not before or after. It was the real love everyone wants and not everyone ever gets. Sam . . ." Lafitte actually crooned the name, "that man unleashed passions in me I could never have dreamed of."

Susannah was not inclined to tell about the effect Terry had on her and so remained quiet. Lafitte refused more pudding as her eyes drifted closed and she went on with her story.

"Because of what had happened in his life before, with his wife, Sam would not let me leave Mr. Armstrong to be with him. Said he would not have me if I did." Lafitte's lips drew into a thin hard line. She was silent so long, Susannah thought she must have fallen asleep. But Lafitte surprised her, as usual. When those dark eyes fluttered open, they had a forlorn, distant look as though she were still sifting through those embers of long-cold wildfires.

"Here he comes now, along the wagon road," Lafitte said and Susannah looked up to see a long, bowed, white haired old man arriving on an even older, more dejected-looking cavalry horse. "Oh, Sam," Lafitte murmured, "where has the time gone? Where have we gone? Somewhere inside me, I'm still that wild in love young woman you knew long ago but . . . who are you?

"Susannah, Sam and I talked some about our dreams. I gave him all I had to give, but I think I never *really* knew him, except in one way." There was a silence soon broken by Lafitte's crisp cackle. "But you know? I didn't care then, and I don't now. That old man you see is the best of my youth, Susannah. Remember us, later."

It was hard to kiss right when both participants in the activity were wearing ten gallon hats, but Susannah had to go and touch Terry right then, to raise her hand to his tanned cheek, lean to his hard body, reaffirming his warmth and strength and love. Lafitte's confessions had made her sad.

"What's wrong?" Terry asked. "Did Mother get to you again, darlin'?"

"Not the way you think," Susannah answered, giving Saidee, now in the swing, a little push. "Terry, I don't ever want to lose you," she said.

"You won't while I'm still drawing breath. Love has taken hold of me. I *need* to walk through the world with you from this time on. We have an unknowable future to face soon, a complicated, dangerous time ahead of us before we settle down to living and loving. Always remember this moment, darlin', right now, all of us together in this time and place. And always remember I love you, even if . . . if you come to suppose you have cause to doubt me. Promise."

Terry's jaw was set, his handsome face fixed in an expression of strong determination. Of course Susannah promised. There was no reason, then, not to.

"Marry me *now*," he asked eagerly as if the idea had just come to him. His velvet gray eyes searched her face, his hands gripped her shoulders. "I want to hear you whisper 'I will' and I want to shout it, for truth and good and always this time."

It was then and there that Susannah made a mistake, a dreadful one. At that moment, when she and Terry truly belonged to each other, when there was nothing between them except trust and love and passion, she *hesitated*. And she saw a look of doubt flit over his face, a shade of foreboding in his eyes which, she supposed, he himself wasn't even aware of. But damage had been done she was afraid, and tried to remedy it.

"Oh, Terry love," she said, "they all suppose we *are* married. There would be such a lot to explain. Why get everyone all riled up and confused, the girls especially, just now when we're about to leave?"

And so, speaking those few needless words and quelling others like "yes I will marry you right now," Susannah planted seeds of mistrust that would grow into a jungle of suspicion. What they had found together would become enmeshed in tendrils of lies and deception, and their love would be strangled by betrayal.

"So 'Old Coffin-head' almost got you, Adella." Sam Houston called Lafitte that—Adella. No one else was allowed to."For the information of the other Mrs. Armstrong, Terry's lovely lady from South Carolina, 'Old Coffin-head' is a mythical giant rattler, Susannah. He usually is found in the east Texas piney woods, though he travels far and wide in the imaginations of all Texans. His den is near a tree that's haunted by some poor ghost who keeps on complaining she's buried too close to her husband's offensive relations."

This feeble, lonely and defeated old fellow, Sam Houston, was still an impressive figure of a man, Susannah decided. Some of the young frontier hero, and a lot of the politician's charm, was still evident. He made a particular effort to charm all the ladies, from Baby Saidee on up to a rickety, ninety-two year old neighbor, a preacher's widow, Ellen Glenn, who still loved her whiskey and pipe of tobacco. Terry, Susannah noticed, was drinking tea of the same shade as the whiskey he was liberally pouring for almost everyone else.

" 'I love everything that's old: old friends, old times, old manners, old books, old whiskey,' " old Sam expounded. "Know who said that, Adella?"

"One of the eighteenth century English poets said that, Sam. I earned my degree you'll recall, from the Texas Women's Institute. I am a Mistress of Polite Literature."

"Lafitte, you are an amazing woman. I've always said that," Eugenie Lavender winked at Susannah, who was charmed by her accent and her style, layers of many-colored, many-pocketed aprons gathered up over a black homespun skirt worn with an eyelet blouse and a red straw bonnet. The effect, not easy to achieve, was of a very devil-may-care chic. "Your daughter-in-law, Lafitte, has the beauty of a painting, of a Pre-Raphaelite red head you know? Texas is so colorful with the Indian paintbrush growing and the verbena. Susannah, *ma petite,* you come from South Carolina, oui? That is where the wild *impatiens,* the touch-me-not, grows. That plant makes a very fine orange dye. Was it there, too, that Eliza Lucas of Antigua, who married a Carolina Pinkney, began the cultivation of the indigo plant for its color and dye? That is an important export, non?"

"Madagascar rice and Antigua indigo brought a wealth of gold to Carolina, but after the Revolution, cotton became more important — everywhere. Eliza Lucas Pinkney was a great woman, Madam, for more reasons than one. She was not typical of the fictional heroines of her time, timid, shrinking violets. She ran a great landed estate, grew rice, cultured silk, raised two sons alone, after her husband passed. She had great character and ability *and* humor. George Washington was her friend and admirer."

"Indigo's all well and fine," Lafitte protested, "but the maguey — for its pulque and mescal, good medicines — blooms only every twenty years here in

Texas, like me. Samuel, is it twenty years for us, again?"

"I don't know about you, Adella, but I am bound for the land of the sweet bye and bye before long," Houston answered her mildly. "Do you all realize there are sixty-four million dollars worth of slaves in Texas, each one of them expecting the United States Government to free 'im and give 'im forty acres and a mule?" Sam asked no one in particular.

"Geography will protect Texas from the Yankees. Except for a coastal skirmish or two, a tussle over Galveston Port, Mist-tair le Governor, this state will come through untouched," Monsieur Lavender proclaimed.

"Twenty-five thousand blacks were taken from South Carolina by the British during the American Revolution and sold at great profit in the Indies." It was Grace who interjected that information. Susannah had not seen much of her in the past few days, engrossed as she had been with Terry and his daughters while Grace had spent most of her time in the quarters.

"Your hairdresser is speaking out of turn again, Susannah," Lafitte complained, half-heartedly.

"There are thirty-one stage coach lines in Texas now, charging ten cents a mile all across the state," Sam was saying. "That's because we caught Santa Ana after the Alamo slaughter, that libertine opium a-dict. I told them, the men there, the Alamo was a death trap, to get out. A hu'nerd and eighty-nine men disagreed with me and died there and Santa Ana sent a poor little girl, not twenty-one, carrying her infant and the grim news. We got him, fooled him by running. It took me a mite longer than some would have liked, but in the end, there was Santa Ana, tryin' to sneak off in a private's uniform, asking for his opium and begging me to be generous to the vanquished after . . . the Alamo. Well, in the end, he agreed to cut Texas loose from Mexico and that was the start of the Texas Republic."

"Sam, you say you ain't long for this world?" Lafitte grumbled. "Of course you're not, if you go on living in the past like you're doing, like Alexander the Great. He was often in his cups, too, at the end, but at least he had a woman at his side and the music of a lyre lulling him.

'Soothed with sound, the king grew vain,
Fought all his battles o'er again,
And thrice he routed all his foes,
And thrice he slew the slain.

"That's you, my old Sam."

"Alexander wasn't half my age, Adella. Course he had girls and music.

'Bacchus, ever fair and young,
Drinking joys did first ordain.
Bacchus' blessings are a treasure,
Drinking is the soldier's pleasure . . .

Sweet is pleasure after pain,' " was Sam's rejoinder. "I have always lived by that verse, but I still know what's going on, Adella. The so called Texas 'radicals' — good Union men, like me — will be sending more than two thousand troops

198

to fight for the North," Sam proclaimed.

Terry looked at Susannah. She made a mental note of the number to write in her book.

"I wish you and Terry as perfect a union as is ever permitted to humanity," old Mrs. Glenn was saying.

"More than ten years ago, Galveston voted tax money for free public schools . . ."

"Ice cream socials and tent revivals are the way for young people in isolated places to meet . . ."

"*Matachines* are dances going back before the Spanish came here. It's an Aztec dance they do on December 12th. The only music comes from a rattling nut, a gourd, they get from Mexico, and the leather sandals of the dancers who are got up real grotesque in feathers, reeds and beads. There's no other sound . . ."

Susannah's head was spinning with numbers, contending voices and brandy. She did not see Terry and suddenly needed to find him.

"I know Jeff Davis," Sam said. "Four years ago, 1856 I think, a cargo of camels with Arab and Egyptian handlers got here from Tunis and Constantinople by order of the United States Secretary of Transportation. That's what Jefferson Davis, himself, was then. These camels, nasty beasts, were supposed to make travel to California easier. See any camels now?"

"April of '42, I put out the first paper in Texas, *The Galveston News*," another guest, a Mr. Bangs, informed Susannah. "My only advert that first day was placed by a Mr. Beauchamps. He begged leave to inform the public, and his friends in general, that he had engaged the Saloon at the Exchange Hotel, for the purpose of giving lessons in dancing, teaching waltzing, and all the fashionable dances in vogue in Europe. Ask Terry about me. You ask him."

"I will, sir," Susannah replied, standing. "Right now." But Terry and Sam had gone off into a huddle and were speaking earnestly together.

". . . and Texas crops will feed the Confederacy despite any sea blockade, if . . ." she heard Sam saying as she approached the two men.

"Well, where are *you* going?" Lafitte called after her and then Susannah heard her exclaim, "Land sakes, who on God's green earth is *that?*"

Ben Speed, who had been waiting in town for their horses to arrive from New Orleans on the next boat, was leading them, Alcantara dancing in front, around the house toward the stables. Ben's long, grizzled face cracked into a smile when he saw the gathering and the tables full of food, though he went on cursing the horses in very colorful style in his high, reedy voice.

"Oh, that's Benjamin Franklin Speed. He signed on to go to sea with your son," Susannah answered Lafitte's question, starting toward the man.

"Give Ben Speed the attic room at the top of the stairs," Lafitte commanded.

"I sleep under the sky, thank you kindly, ma'am," Ben said politely.

"Under the sky? Not another primitive," Lafitte

MORE PASSION AND ADVENTURE AWAIT... YOUR TRIP TO A BIG ADVENTUROUS WORLD BEGINS WHEN YOU ACCEPT YOUR FIRST 4 NOVELS ABSOLUTELY *FREE* (AN $18.00 VALUE)

Accept your Free gift and start to experience more of the passion and adventure you like in a historical romance novel. Each Zebra novel is filled with proud men, spirited women and tempestuous love that you'll remember long after you turn the last page.

Zebra Historical Romances are the finest novels of their kind. They are written by authors who really know how to weave tales of romance and adventure in the historical settings you love. You'll feel like you've actually gone back in time with the thrilling stories that each Zebra novel offers.

GET YOUR FREE GIFT WITH THE START OF YOUR HOME SUBSCRIPTION

Our readers tell us that these books sell out very fast in book stores and often they miss the newest titles. So Zebra has made arrangements for you to receive the four newest novels published each month.

You'll be guaranteed that you'll never miss a title, and home delivery is so convenient. And to show you just how easy it is to get Zebra Historical Romances, we'll send you your first 4 books absolutely FREE! Our gift to you just for trying our home subscription service.

BIG SAVINGS AND FREE HOME DELIVERY

Each month, you'll receive the four newest titles as soon as they are published. You'll probably receive them even before the bookstores do. What's more, you may preview these exciting novels free for 10 days. If you like them as much as we think you will, just pay the low preferred subscriber's price of just $3.75 each. *You'll save $3.00 each month off the publisher's price.* AND, your savings are even greater because there are never any shipping, handling or other hidden charges—FREE Home Delivery. Of course you can return any shipment within 10 days for full credit, no questions asked. There is no minimum number of books you must buy.

4 FREE BOOKS

TO GET YOUR 4 FREE BOOKS WORTH $18.00 — MAIL IN THE FREE BOOK CERTIFICATE T O D A Y

Fill in the Free Book Certificate below, and we'll send your FREE BOOKS to you as soon as we receive it.

If the certificate is missing below, write to: Zebra Home Subscription Service, Inc., P.O. Box 5214, 120 Brighton Road, Clifton, New Jersey 07015-5214.

FREE BOOK CERTIFICATE
4 FREE BOOKS

ZEBRA HOME SUBSCRIPTION SERVICE, INC.

YES! Please start my subscription to Zebra Historical Romances and send me my first 4 books absolutely FREE. I understand that each month I may preview four new Zebra Historical Romances free for 10 days. If I'm not satisfied with them, I may return the four books within 10 days and owe nothing. Otherwise, I will pay the low preferred subscriber's price of just $3.75 each; a total of $15.00, *a savings off the publisher's price of $3.00.* I may return any shipment and I may cancel this subscription at any time. There is no obligation to buy any shipment and there are no shipping, handling or other hidden charges. Regardless of what I decide, the four free books are mine to keep.

NAME

ADDRESS   APT

CITY   STATE   ZIP
(   )
TELEPHONE

SIGNATURE   (if under 18, parent or guardian must sign)

Terms, offer and prices subject to change without notice. Subscription subject to acceptance by Zebra Books. Zebra Books reserves the right to reject any order or cancel any subscription.

snorted. He looked at her bemusedly with his big soft hound dog eyes.

"Yes'm," Ben said in his singsong way. "Uh, Grace? Grace, you'd best come on with me now. I got to say something to you, and if'n . . ." Susannah saw Grace go pale and when she took her friend's hand, it was clammy.

"That slave catcher can always wrench my heart and stir up an old, old fear," Grace whispered to Susannah. To Ben she said, "If what, Speed?"

" . . . if you want to see Marcus this side of the grave. These others can meet you down at dockside at dawn, in Galveston City. You all are slated to sail on the morning tide. Marcus is too."

Chapter Seventeen

"Ring the bells of morning!" Grace said to Susannah. "Lord . . . maybe this time my prayer will be answered, this time it *will* happen. 'It is not good that man should be alone,' the Good Book tells."

After some mistaken or baseless reports of Marcus's whereabouts, and one near meeting, missed by a day, just part of a day, Grace was afraid to wish too hard this time. "I do hope to see my man one time again. This might be my last chance. Tomorrow we all are sailing away north and he's sailing off to somewhere else."

It was agreed that Governor Houston and the Lavenders would come east to Galveston Port before noon, bringing the girls and the trunks, because Susannah and Terry went along with Grace and Ben. They insisted on that. Grace was glad and comforted. They knew love and the fear of its loss, and well understood how overwrought Grace was, with hope and dread. Though inside she was frenzied and yearning, on the surface she was her controlled self, a little tough, a little guarded. She kept up that false front by telling herself it wasn't ever going to happen, she and Marcus getting together, meeting again and, at the same time, she was terrified Marcus would be gone again before she could see him . . . touch him . . . hear his voice.

"Lieutenant Armstrong," she challenged Terry in an antagonistic, jittery voice. "To pay for rebuilding *Maison Rouge,* when it got burned down by the American Navy, your blood kin, Jean Lafitte, collected all the blacks at his Campeachy, the free ones and the slaves, and sold them in New Orleans."

"I know. There's no way I can repair that damage, Grace, but I'm going to buy Marcus free, now," he said. She started to cry.

"Grace, about Marcus?" Ben began, "this time I am going on the word of a free black, a Haiti man, one of the crew of a Yankee whaler. He tells of a Marcus from the South Caroline Low Country who's signed on with 'em. It might could be your Marcus, a tall, well-spoke, smart man. It could be some other. This whaling ship come into the Gulf of Mexico to deliver oil to the Yankee craft readying to blockade Galveston, also to sign on some hands. Marcus Smart, as they're calling him, a runaway, is one of the new men." Ben, who was dangling his legs off the tailgate of the buckboard, turned around to give Grace a disputatious look.

"Now, you know, Grace, I could get me a big bounty for Marcus from his master, if I snatch that slave off the gangplank of a Yankee vessel. But

203

Grace, Rebel as I be to my bones, I could not do that to you."

"Well, hallelujah, slave catcher! That'll maybe buy you one less day in purgatory," Grace lashed out. "You'll be finding yourself speeding straight to hell today, you threaten Marcus," she added. Well aware as she was of being rash and reckless, talking as she was to a backwoods Southerner, she was beside herself with worry and unable to hold her tongue. Susannah set aside the pretty book she was always writing and sketching in, put her arm about Grace's shoulder and held on tight. Then she started talking in her smooth, low voice, the one Grace had heard her use before to quiet an unbroken stallion or an unruly retriever pup with promising blood lines — and Grace.

"You know the flower the French lady, Eugenie Lavender, talked of, the wild *impatiens?* Some call it jewel-weed because the dangling flowers look like pendant earrings. It's got another name, touch-me-not, because its seed pods explode at the slightest graze and burst open and let go a barrage. That's like you, Grace. You have held on so tight for so long that now, you're like the *impatiens*. Anything touches you, you erupt like a volcano and lash out. Hold on, Grace darling, hold on just a little longer — maybe."

"And if it's very much longer . . . forever? How will I bear it? How would you?" Grace felt a tremor run through Susannah.

"I'd hold on forever, for my love's sake, and try to be strong for the young ones. That doesn't mean I'd succeed but I *would* want to." She looked to Terry.

204

His possessive, loving eyes caressed her. His face was drawn—with worry and solicitude.

"Grace," Terry said, his voice thick and laden with feeling, "your children need you. Susannah was the one who showed me how children thirst and hunger for love. With or without Marcus, you'll do right by yours. If we can help . . ." Both Terry and Susannah went silent, thinking about losing each other, Grace supposed, and about the war, and she started crying again.

"Oh, I am being buffeted by a terrible perplexity of emotions!" she said haltingly.

West of the outskirts of Galveston City, in a little bandstand square, the travelers ran into a hindrance, a crowd of people jamming the road with wagons, children and dogs and mules. Grace thought she would die of nerves. She wanted to push everyone out of the way, but of course she couldn't and they had to slow down. She fidgeted while Ben chewed his tobacco a lot faster than usual and Susannah and Terry sat close as they could get, talking low. Grace listened. She had nothing else to do.

"You and that adamant old Unionist, Samuel Houston, were thick as thieves, Terry. What about?" Susannah asked.

"Sam was reminding me Jeff Davis fought in Mexico with him. Sam said that despite the West Point training, Davis is a poor military strategist. Sam also said Kentucky can't be held by the North, not with the number of Rebs answering the call for volunteers. They . . . *we* will quickly take Kentucky. Sam believes, same as this military man Sherman, another

205

West Pointer, that the war will be a long, cruel and bitter fight. It's going to be hard for both sides to supply and feed and clothe their troops. Oh, and Susannah? Sam says stay clear of newspaper people, like that man Bangs you met up at Maison Rouge. They publish anything, even war secrets the enemy will be free to read, whichever side you're on, whoever the enemy is."

"You and Sam are on different sides in this fight. Why was he advising you, Terry?" Susannah wore her endearing, puzzled expression, the one that wrinkled her freckled nose and narrowed her green eyes to pretty little green gems.

"The governor has always had a paternal interest in me, Susannah. Sam's been around Lafitte and me all my life. He was the one took me hunting . . . fishing . . . carousing—the first time. I think I saw more of him than I did of my father."

Susannah did not pursue that line of talk. Among her other attributes, was a sensitivity to delicate subjects. Either she was showing great discretion that day, or she had become distracted when, in the early evening on their way to the Galveston Harbor, they came upon a cavalry company of volunteers, three hundred strong, forming up to march off to war and defend the Rebel capitol, Richmond, in Virginia.

The road was crowded because the Johnny Rebs were getting a big send-off. It would have been disrespectful to push on through, with the Stars and Bars waving, so Grace and her intense, hurrying escort were obliged to stop.

There were patriotic speeches, long ones, one

made by a pretty belle who presented a Confederate battle flag, different than the tars and bars, of red and blue displaying the St. Andrews Cross and thirteen white stars for the Confederate states.

"Brave boys, you are heroes, every one! Accept from your mothers and sisters this banner, woven by our delicate hands and when it floats before you on the battlefield, be inspired with courage to defend your country's honor and glory against a heartless foe." She had a strong, carrying voice and did not readily relinquish the stage to the sergeant at arms who came forward to accept the banner.

"Ain't he a long-winded, misbegotten son of a gun!" Grace complained to her companions, at her wits end. "The tide waits for no man and the ship Marcus is on, if it *is* him, will sail before I can get to him!"

"Oh, dear, dear ladies!!" that big, overemotional sergeant trumpeted, "our pulses throb with feeling as we accept this proud emblem of our country, showing the same blue as your eyes, the red of your lips, the purity, in its white band, of your fair cheeks. To him whose fate it is to fall in battle, this moment will be a cheering remembrance and he will bless you as his life and spirit take to the air. Those of us who return will bear this banner home in triumph, tattered and torn though it may be. Mars, the god of war hears our vow that no stain, save our own blood, will ever besmirch this flag, no matter how fierce the carnage, how terrible the smoke and glare and din of battle . . ."

The volunteers were escorted by a fife, a drum, and a bugle that burst into 'The Girl I Left Behind Me,' as the men were presented with an excessive number of frying pans and a wagon load of bandages besides a barrel of beer. Girls festooned the men with floral wreaths and kissed them indiscriminately with no thought to their station in life, something the Carolinians had never before known to occur among southern females of wealth and social standing. There was to be plenty of kissing and tippling and feasting all along the way for this Texas company that would be among the first, though no one knew it then, to undergo the baptism fire at Manassas.

"I'm going to walk to Galveston," Grace announced. "I mean, run!"

Susannah lost patience too, at that point. As the beer keg was being tapped, she stood up in the buckboard, brought the back of her hand to her brow and very dramatically, with a great long ooh! swooned into Terry's ready arms. He placed her gently on the seat and kissed her lips and Grace saw her left eye open just a mite as he climbed down to lead their wagon through the festivities.

"Pardon us! Look out, there, please," Terry shouted. "Clear the way folks, my wife has taken a faint! It's this excitement . . . her condition . . . too much . . . too much for her. Let us pass on through now, please. Thank you, thank you kindly." He took the lead horse by the bridle, and guided it through the crowd, in the direction of Galveston City, still miles off. When Grace heard Susannah, who'd just done such a good job of clowning, swallow a real sob, she was shocked.

"Lord girl, what all is the matter?" Grace asked. Susannah sat bolt upright.

"I can't help but think of our brave boys at Charleston and wish I was there to . . . to help send them off. Oh, Terry, I'm sure my little brother will not remain idle at home, waiting for a ship, when such stirring events are unfolding about him. Terry, if any harm should come to Simeon . . ." She buried her face in her hands. Terry didn't say a word, just climbed back in the wagon, took her in his arms and handed the reins to Ben Speed.

"Now's the time to live up to your name, man. Get Grace to the docks with real speed on time.

Grace saw Marcus through Terry Armstrong's spyglass.

It was four o'clock on a remarkable morning. The universe was lit by the moon setting in the west, and by the sun's rays bleaching the eastern horizon. Marcus leaned at the rail of a ship at anchor some hundreds of yards off shore. The *Eagle,* out of Sag Harbor, was waiting for the tide.

Grace thought the cry loosed from her throat must have moved heaven and earth and all between, because it moved Marcus, far off as he was. She saw him lift his dark head, heard the defiant roar of his heart-stopping voice. She watched him climb up on the rail and plunge over the side of the ship, his body cutting the water like a sabre.

And then, she cried out again, just before she

fainted away, "Oh, my Lord, help him, please! That man will sink like a sack of rocks. He can't swim a stroke!"

Grace came to herself looking into a pair of soft brown eyes, Marcus's eyes, full of love and pain and loss and yearning. She felt herself held by his two strong arms, propped against the bulwark of his chest.

"Where are my babies?" was the first thing he asked. There was a new scar on his cheek, another across his chest. She traced each with a loving hand, experiencing herself the pain that put them there.

"Your children are safe up north," she answered, "with a Abolitionist school teacher, Daisy Ballard."

"And Alexander?" Marcus, still waterlogged, gasped, brushing the hair from her brow.

"I don't know for sure. Ben Speed says he'll look."

"The slave catcher, Speed? This him?" Marcus flared. Ben stepped closer, gun and shackles in hand.

"I could catch you, now. When you jumped off that Yankee whaler you were a free man, but soon as you set foot on Confederate soil, you were my fair game. I'd do right well on your hide, *Smart*. But I ain't catching you, am I?" Ben said, spitting a chaw of tobacco. "I won't catch Alexander either — if I find him."

"I'd cut your damn throat, Ben," Terry Armstrong said real soft and sinister. No one could have doubted him. Marcus said nothing, just looked at Ben with raw hate.

"Grace, I been hidin' out along Buffalo Bayou,

near Houston City. It's a remote and trackless place. The waterways are traitorous, shallow, tidal but the manhunters and their dogs come even there, so where you suppose young Alexander can be hiding safe?"

"In the Great Dismal Swamp of North Carolina," Ben Speed said. "Ay, Smart, don't try to play dunce with me. You know there's a settlement of runaways been in there for two . . . three generations. There's a thousand black folk cowering like beasts in a lair, at Culpeper Island."

"They got bacon, salt fish, molasses, whiskey and courage. They are never going on the auction block again. You set foot in there, slave catcher, you are a dead man. Am I right, Grace?" Marcus asked. She could hear the ancient anger reverberating in his deep voice. She could feel it rumbling in his chest.

"Ain't my life my lookout, Smart?" Ben shrugged.

"Only if you still got in mind to let me go a free man on the *Eagle* . . ." Marcus scowled.

"Don't go. Stay with me," Grace said quietly, knowing the answer before she even asked.

"Stay here, in slave country?" he asked, incredulous.

"We're going North in a few hours," Terry said. "Come with us. I'll buy you free, Marcus."

"Thank you, sir. But for all the love I hold for Grace, I can't accept your generosity. I have to fight this war the only way they'll let me. I can't get in the army. Army won't give a black man a gun, so I'm going to sea to hunt whale and bring oil to the Union.

"Grace, we tried for Canada once and failed. Get there now, if you can, and wait for me."

211

"Wait how long? Forever, Marcus?" Grace asked. "I have been alone and waiting a long time now." She didn't look at him. "I am going to fight this fight *my* way, like you. One day, perhaps we'll find each other again. I'll wait, but not in Canada."

"Wait forever," he said. And then he was gone as if she'd not touched him, seen him, heard his voice. He left a shell in her hand, a small conch. It was a token of freedom for slaves. 'By the sea we came, by the sea we shall go — free.'

"I've heard it said that cranes are the souls of soldiers killed in battle, flying to heaven. I hope we don't see a whole lot more of them before too long," Grace said, watching a pair of the birds take wing. Susannah was sketching the harbor from offshore as she and Grace stood on the deck of the ship taking them away from Galveston on the evening tide. "Who saved Marcus from drowning?"

"It was Terry who got Marcus out of the water," Susannah replied, turning a page.

The whaler *Eagle,* with Marcus aboard, was long gone by then, but where it had been anchored Grace saw a golden glow and a mile-wide gap in the universe.

Chapter Eighteen

Allen Pinkerton, according to his official report, introduced himself to Susannah Butler Armstrong on the evening of 22 October in eighteen and sixty-one, on her own doorstep as she returned home to her house on Lafayette Square in Washington. Or maybe it was September, a note in the margin said, referring the reader to Pinkerton's original notes on the case. Following is *The First Pinkerton Report on the Hostile Female Operative Known as Susie Shadow.*

'Using my alias, Major Allen, I arrested her as a spy. She had been living in Washington for a couple months when I put the woman under house arrest, just at first. There were the two little girls to think of. Also, I was setting a trap. She was my bait. There were a number of southern sympathizers—copperheads—in Washington. I'd snare any politico or officer of the Union Army who came to call on Susie Shadow, the beautiful Mrs. Armstrong, bearing gifts of flowers and information.

'Among her regular callers was General Charles Stone, the officer responsible for the fiasco at Ball Bluff the day before I made my move on Susie. The newspapers were calling Stone inept and saying he was sympathetic to the South. I was calling him a traitor. The Rebels were ready and waiting for him, *our* man, fully expecting the Union attack on Leesburg in Virginia. They drove our men back against the steep bluff on the river. Seven hundred drowned. A goodly number of others were killed and wounded. Colonel Baker, a friend of Mr. Lincoln, was killed. The president was seen to shed tears.

Before the battle at Manassas Junction that ended at a sluggish, muddy little creek by the name of Bull Run, *someone* had provided the Rebel General Beauregard with drawings of our capitol city's fortifications, even with notes of Mr. Lincoln's cabinet meetings. That's what caused the Union route earlier, at Manassas, in July.

But even as we were escorting Mrs. Armstrong in through her own front door, someone, likely her husband, was leaving by a rear window. That suited me. I let him go for reasons of my own, but those children foiled my plans to use their step-mamma as a decoy. The older one, a pretty young rebel girl, wriggled out between Secret Agent Lemon's legs, knocking him right off his pins.

"Blast and drat!" Lemon grunted, flat on his back on the front walkway. Then he said something like "oof" when the smaller girl chased after her sister and stepped on his stomach. It would have been hard for her to avoid doing that. Lemon is a sizable man with a big belly. He took up the whole path, lying there.

Before we could haul the girls back inside, with their mother encouraging them and saying to my men, 'Unhand those darling children, you damned cowardly poltroons!' the darlings were swinging on the front gate and shouting out loud that their mother had been arrested.

I don't know how many informants they warned off. We got two callers who stopped by later that night, that's all, small fish. By then we had finished searching the house—beds, wardrobes, the desk in the library—and sent away for cipher decoding some incompletely burned scraps of paper still in the stove, along with a heavily notated copy of Philps *Guide Book to Washington*. If Mrs. Armstrong kept a diary, as I had been told, we did not find it that day.

End of First Official Report.
Detective A. Pinkerton re: Susie Shadow.

His prisoner was the most magnificent example Pinkerton had seen of the Southern womanhood the Rebs were fighting for. She had big and defiant, lively green eyes that could strike terror — or love — in any man, he thought, maybe both at once. And her swirling red hair with streaks of gold was a sign of her high spirit, passion, and independence.

Susannah didn't deny she was spying for Dixie. Caught, she was *proud*. In fact, to Pinkerton's bafflement he'd been prevented by higher-ups from arresting her weeks before, when she had shouted out the truth to a wounded Rebel prisoner at the Union Hotel Hospital, where she had been working. Southerners taken at the Manassas battle were marched to General Mansfield's headquarters, those that could march. The others were at the Union.

"Please name your accomplices," Pinkerton asked, taking a small pad and a pencil from his pocket and setting a chair at the table. Susannah stood. They were in the parlor and could hear the other men searching about the house. Grace took the children to the kitchen, where they were guarded by Lemon who was not keen about that assignment.

"I am a Confederate to the marrow. I won't answer that question, no matter what you do to me, Mr. Pinkerton," Susannah said. "But will you tell me, sir, if my brother . . . Is he . . . alive or dead?"

It surprised the detective that she knew who he was, his real name.

"How did you know my name?" he asked. He ignored her question about Simeon for his own reasons. Pinkerton had many reasons for the things he did or did not do, and it was just as well if he kept them to himself. His plots were sometimes incomprehensible to his associates.

"Your accent, Mr. Pinkerton, gives you away. Your Scottish inflection is very distinctive. I can't say more than that of my knowledge of you and your nefarious activities. Honor prohibits," Susannah said. "Do tell me, Mr. Pinkerton, how you've chosen such a noble profession? What on earth have you done to deserve the tough and enviable job of arresting gentle women and small children?"

She was mocking him, Pinkerton realized.

"These days, I go after spies, Mrs. Armstrong, of any age or either sex. Train robbers used to be my quarry. By trade, I'm a cooper. I made good barrels when I first came to America from Glasgow, and set up shop in Dundee, Illinois. I quite haphazardly stumbled upon a gang of counterfeiters, got elected county sheriff because of it, and then I joined the Chicago police as their first detective. Also, I then formed my own agency of private sleuths."

"How exciting for you. Do go on, sir," Susannah said. She was looking at the man with a lofty self-satisfied expression, because she'd gotten him talking when *he* was the one who was supposed to be asking her questions. They both knew it, but Pinkerton had his reasons. He wanted her calm, off guard, before he pulled his ace of hearts from his sleeve. He was maneuvering to surprise her into letting information slip.

"There was a plot to kill Mr. Lincoln when he was on his way to Washington. They said he would never get through Baltimore alive to be inaugurated," Pinkerton went on conversationally, putting his notebook aside. "I was hired by the President's supporters in Illinois and also by Mr. Sam Felton, owner of the Philadelphia, Baltimore, and Washington Railroad, to protect the president-elect. I put my operatives, dressed as track workers, between Susquehanna and Baltimore. The assassins were thwarted by me and my associates," Pinkerton said proudly.

He lit a cigar and exhaled slowly. Blue smoke circled the oil lamps. He was appreciative of the fact that Susannah didn't cough falsely, as many genteel women did, to ambiguously object to cigars in the house. She just waited. She was, he was discovering, an expert at the use of the strategic silence. "I had my people in Baltimore then and I've got them behind Confederate lines now. Also, several men . . . and women, are crossing the front, going right into Richmond and coming back with all sorts of invaluable details. Mrs. Armstrong, I think you are very closely acquainted with at least one of them, likely two. I have yet to check out one . . ." He flipped through his pad ". . . Grace Ellison, a woman in your employ."

Pinkerton, who wanted to jolt Susannah by implying her husband and her housekeeper were in his service, succeeded. Her eyes flared with anger before they went as frosty as an ice-coated window pane.

"Sir, I'll not even discuss Grace's loyalty to me, but tell me, why *did* you let my husband go tonight?

You heard him at the window, just as I did, making his exit."

"One in the hand, Mrs. Armstrong. You know the proverb." She was soft and pretty and lost-looking, and it troubled Pinkerton to pressure her. But it was his job, he reminded himself, and he was determined to press on.

"You could easily have had two under arrest," she said.

"One in the bush suits my plans, particularly if that one is Terry Armstrong, *Major* Terry Armstrong, United States War Department."

"That sir, is just his *modus operandi*. My husband is loyal to Dixie, Pinkerton, and far more clever than you will ever be, at serving his country! Only a bald-faced cowardly blackguard would cast such dastardly aspersions behind a man's back, when he cannot demand satisfaction!" Pinkerton, a little to his own surprise, had actually tricked Susannah into defending her husband by giving away his dodge. She must really have believed it, or really wanted to, and Pinkerton realized his question probably activated a seed of doubt already sewn in her mind. That suited his objective, because he had doubts about Armstrong's true loyalties himself.

"Thank you, Mrs. Armstrong," he said in a patronizing tone. "I knew you were too proud to allow that slur on your family to go unchallenged. That's one thing, the most important, I hoped to pry from your very lips. There *is* more you could tell me now that I'd be interested in hearing. I know you could."

Susannah went ghostly pale and swayed on her

feet, and Pinkerton prepared to soften her fall when she dropped in a faint. That was not her style, however.

"Now, *you* tell me about Simeon Butler, sir. Does he . . . draw breath still?" Her hands were clasped at her bosom as if in prayer. The detective just looked at *her* this time, saying not a word, as long as he could meet her eyes. Then he stood and turned his back.

"You loathsome man! You won't tell me if my brother is dead or alive and . . . you tricked me into betraying my . . . husband! But you won't ever catch Terry, not . . . Oh, my God, I've really given him away," she whispered, sinking to a chair and hiding her face in her hands. Pinkerton noticed they were small and smooth and pale and he felt swelling sympathy for her.

"Mrs. Armstrong, you are not in control of your tongue under the strain of detention and my calculating, merciless questioning. It's not your fault. War is not a woman's game. 'Then gently scan your brother man,/Still gentler sister woman;/Though they may gang a kennin wrang,/To step aside is human.' The Scot, my countryman Robert Burns, wrote that.

"I don't understand a word of it," she snapped, looking up at him with bemused irritation.

"It means we all make mistakes. Don't blame yourself." She hurled a vase at the man. The water soaked his blue uniform. The flowers, lilies, flew all over. One landed on his shoulder. He slipped it into his pocket. He saved it for years.

* * *

Pinkerton had his treasured captive fed on pigs feet and gingerbread, which some of his other upper-crust prisoners — Rebel officers and spies — refused. They ordered in their meals, with wine, from Willard's Hotel.

"Not *this* lady," he reported to his associates at the War Department. " 'I will accept nothing our regular prisoners, our brave boys, are not provided,' she proclaims. I admire her. I didn't bother to tell her that most of the Johnny Rebs we have captive are lucky to get maggoty gruel and thin stew once a day."

Pinkerton never got another jot of information out of Susannah and what she *had* told him, about Major Terrence Armstrong, being a double spy, was of no interest or use to the War Department.

After a week or so, Susannah was confined to her room when her house was turned into a women's prison where Pinkerton also held a Mrs. Phillips, a Miss Onderdonk and two others, one, Zelda Poole, his own operative. Zelda, an obvious tattletale, learned nothing from her jail mates. Information was still getting out to the Rebs, and the detective was forced to move them all, Mrs. Armstrong included, to the Old Capitol Jail.

Chapter Nineteen

'How did I get myself arrested and put here in the Old Capitol Prison?' Susannah wrote on the rough sheets that would become part of her diary. 'It was foreordained the minute I saw Terry, of course, but from the time we sailed from Galveston Harbor, I was rushing headlong toward the moment when Pinkerton accosted me on my own doorstep.'

For Terry and Susannah, the return trip to Charleston was a second honeymoon. They got out of their bunk late and retired early, as soon as the children did. They traveled by sea in an armed Dixie privateer—there was virtually no Confederate Navy—riding the sailors' Blue God, the Gulf Stream, north along the Dixie shore line.

They made love in the torpid, humid, sensual heat of the Gulf in early summer, their bodies smooth and moist, gliding together, his hard, contoured muscles to her supple ones, his tanned skin contrasting with her paler shade. There was no stopping them, no satiation.

Susannah would be awakened in the small hours every morning, after earlier hours of love which gave way to contented sleep, to find herself in an exquisite affliction of pleasure, as Terry, gathering her to him again enfolded her in his strong arms, their bodies fitting perfectly, their passion so utterly complete, nothing else existed in the world, but the two of them, together.

The closer they traveled to Charleston, the more intense things became, though to look at them in daylight, no one would have been aware of their delicious desperation. They were attentive parents. Mornings, they walked the deck with Saidee and Venetia, talking, watching the flying fish and gulls and the crew at work. In the afternoons, after everyone had napped, they all four sat on the shaded side of the ship playing whist or euchre. And always, there were Terry's eyes, like dark banked fires, lazily moving over Susannah.

"This is different, love, than our trip *to* Galveston, isn't it?" he asked. It was late. No one but the watch, and Susannah and Terry, were on deck.

"I wanted to extract the love from your stubborn heart by keeping you at arms' length, making you ache for me," Susannah answered, slipping her hand into his that rested on the rail. He turned to face her, leaning back against the polished brass, his face lit by lantern light. There were no stars.

"And I had determined the only way to win you was to keep close, closer than arms' length, to you . . . toy with you, pet and fondle you, like this . . ." His lips found hers, then covered her eyes . . . her throat with kisses. "I played with you all day so that at dusk . . . you'd have a burning *need* of me . . . would come to me as a supplicant and . . . give . . . all."

"Who won?" Susannah asked in a whisper, undoing his collar stud.

"Both," he answered pensively, his opulent, seductive mouth compressing. "So far." She looked up, her head at an interrogative tilt. "If anything should happen to me . . ." Susannah raised her finger tips to her lips to silence him, then pressed her lips to his before he could go on.

"Don't, please," she whispered. "Tomorrow, when we step ashore, who knows what we'll find, what to expect? Tonight is ours, it belongs to us. Let's do anything but talk of war, of losing each other. Let's count stars, pace the deck, shoot darts in the ward room, sing songs or . . . go, um, to our cabin?"

"All of those, in good time. First, tonight, I need to look at you, hear your voice, touch your face . . ." He did, tenderly bringing his hand to her brow. "Summer was expressly made just so you could wear that dress. Walk for me, Susannah."

She smiled and walked away, but not very far,

looking over her shoulder until he beckoned her to turn and come back to him. She ran. Into his open arms.

" 'And such sweet girls! — I mean, such graceful
    ladies,
Their very walk would make your bosom swell;
I can't describe it, though so much it strike,
Nor liken it — I never saw the like . . ." Terry
recited.

"Girls? Ladies?" she laughed. "There's to be but one singular female in your life from now on, sir."

"I was just saying some lines from *Don Juan*. You wouldn't have me tamper with great poetry, would you? I'm only trying to express what I feel about you, the same as *he* — Byron — did about the ladies of Cadiz; I never saw the like of you, love. Now, talk for me in your honied voice that can . . . drive me . . . wild, sometimes . . . all the time."

"I'll talk if you'll go on holding me this way," she answered, not wanting him ever to let her go. She had been made uneasy by yet another reference — Captain Kells was first — to that fictional seducer, *Don Juan*.

"You've got a deal," he said, drawing her closer. His back was to the ship's rail again and she fitted her body to his solid length and herself recited,

"Farewell ungrateful Traytor!
Farewell my perju'r Swain!
Let never injur'd Creature

Believe a Man again.
The Pleasure of Possessing
Surpasses all Expressing,
But t's too short a Blessing
And Love too long a Pain.' "

"I don't care for that," Terry scowled, turning his face to the sea. The helmsman rang two bells and the forward watch replied. Then all was still again. Susannah put her arms about Terry now, resting against the bulwark of his long back. He was truly angry. She could feel the tension in him.

"I think you're the same as all the women I've ever known, like an exotic foreign language I'll never really understand," he said, seething.

"You told me when we first talked of our mission that you'd not ever risk love again, nor ever marry. You were afraid, then. Now, I am. The pleasure you give me is so great, it's close to pain," Susannah said haltingly.

"But I *have* asked you to be my *wife*, damn it, and you turned me down. You can't measure in silver the way I love you." She glimpsed his hard profile. He was intense and smoldering.

" 'The starlight of heaven above us shall quiver/ As our souls flow in one down eternity's river.' I can't recall any more of that poem. Like it better?" Susannah asked him gently as though addressing an offended child.

"Better," he shrugged.

226

"Now, you talk to me, Terry Armstrong. Say anything."

He drew her to his side so that they were both looking out at the ink-dark sea, and his arms went about her waist.

"Lafitte and my father hardly spoke to each other for twenty years. It was burdensome to a child. I loved them both. I was torn. I developed a habit of brooding silence, following their example I suppose. Then, there was Sam Houston, my idol, friend to both my mother and father, and good to me.

"Houston City, was named after him, of course, after he became the hero of the San Jacinto battle that freed Texas from Mexico. The city was founded by New Yorkers, the Allen brothers, John Harrison, and Mr. Armstrong, as Lafitte always called my father. Those men were all clever real estate promoters. They picked the spot, because a decisive battle had been fought along Buffalo Bayou. They drew up a street map before there was even a plank road to Galveston, no less a single street. They advertised Houston City in newspapers all over the United States when there was nothing there but mud, mosquitos, Indians and alligators. People were lured into coming and then made the best of it when they got there, made a town. Eventually they got the Galveston Houston and Henderson railway to run the fifty miles down to the Gulf coast. But Houston is no great city and never will be unless they dig a deep draft channel so ocean going vessels can reach the place. And there'll always be too much rain, floods, fires."

"And Sam?" Susannah asked. "Tell me about Sam himself."

"Sam's a real frontiersman but not a loner like Ben Speed. He's a very congenial fellow, a politician, a lawyer, a really persuasive talker. One thing he didn't talk about was women. Firstly, he's a gentleman and secondly, he had his own troubles on that score. So . . . thinking I was emulating Sam, I taught myself to be glib and silver-tongued, but I was also secretive about real important things, sometimes false."

"All surface, no heart? Was that the problem with you and Abigail? Not . . . conversing?" Susannah asked. Terry nodded.

"Partly. Plenty of heart, no words, no sense. It took you to get me to bare my heart, and soul."

"And I was twenty-six years old and afraid I never would adore—really love—any man. So now, my darling and my dear, that I have found you, *that* fear has been replaced by another, which is, if anything, worse. How will I live if I lose you?"

"You will survive whatever you have to, Susannah, and raise up my girls. Your courage will get you through. In war, nothing—no one's life—is certain. At the least, I expect I'll be going away from you all, Susannah, for a time. You know I have a job to do." He had taken her in his arms again, and kissed her in a way that was both ten-

228

der and desperate before they began walking, arm in arm.

"I'll be waiting, no matter how long you're gone, Terry. I don't fear time, long as I know that after the storms of winter, spring will come again. So, love, where are you planning on going without *me?*" she asked lightly. They had been getting too somber and now that she had his pledge of love — again, she wanted to cheer things up. There would be a necessity soon enough for seriousness.

"When we reach Washington, you're to remain there. Where I'll be sent, I don't know yet, but I will have to pass through Yankee lines regularly, to report to Jeff Davis and his generals in Richmond." Terry lit a cigar given to him at dinner by the captain. He cradled the light in his muscular hand. "Tell me," he said through a puff of smoke, "where do you keep your little book hidden? It could be an incriminating document, north or south, if we get into a scrape."

"In my small carpet bag, among the flimsies. Of course, you know where to find the key," Susannah giggled.

"I got in mind to do just that, Susannah, soon's I finish this smoke and we've done everything that was on your list: count stars, pace the deck, shoot darts in the ward room, sing songs and then," he grinned wickedly like a naughty little boy, his eyes alight, "go to our cabin."

The moon had risen. It was two days scant of full, fat and round so they couldn't count stars, their glittering little lights absorbed by a greater radiance. So they went on to the next activity on their list and sang *The Yellow Rose of Texas*. They sounded really *fine*. Their voices, Susannah's contralto, Terry's low tenor, reverberated in a particularly perfect and beautiful way, like everything else they did together. They went on to mingle voices on *Greensleeves, Barbara Allen* and *Lorena* — all songs, they both realized, of lost love and betrayal. They were getting better and better at the harmonies and didn't care to stop but chose different sorts of tunes — *Dixie, Listen to the Mockingbird* and *Home Sweet Home*. This last prompted the man on forward watch to break out his mouth organ and, misty-eyed with emotion, accompany them. When Venetia, inclined to bad dreams, called out in her sleep, they bid him goodnight and hurried to her, but she had fallen back into a sound sleep.

"Will it ever be so good as this for us again, Terry?" Susannah whispered, taking his hand across the child's recumbent form. "I have a . . . a premonition of loss. I'm scared."

"Darlin' Susannah," he smiled, "there's some things just keep getting better. You and me are one of them."

In their bunk that night, Susannah told him more than once he was right about that.

The Yankee blockade was not yet in place when they entered Charleston Harbor, and so their landing was unimpeded. Catherine Butler, who had been signaled by pennant that they were on board, was already at the dock waiting to greet them, looking dainty and impeccable, as always. As the gangway was set in place, Susannah could see, as Catherine waved and threw kisses, her mother's pleasure at their return. But Susannah saw something else, new worry lines on Catherine's brow, a distress in her eyes.

"Susannah, Simeon's gone, marched off to fight in Virginia with the University Greys." That was all she said before turning her beautiful smile on Baby Saidee and Venetia. But it was then Susannah realized just how terrible a blow their defection to the North would be to her mother, who was already separated from her son. For the first time since Terry had recruited her and she had promised her help, Susannah had doubts about whether she could keep her word and her commitment.

Chapter Twenty

"Dears, our Simeon has not had patience to wait for a ship. He has marched off to fight in Virginia, as the Commodore thought he might," Catherine Butler told Terry, dismay showing in her eyes. "As the wife of a seafaring man, I'd rather he took his chances with felon winds than Yankee infantry." That was all she said on the matter before turning her magnetic smile on Baby Saidee and Venetia. "Terry, my fine friend, what a grand gift you have brought me. I've been waiting for grandchildren ever so long."

"Catherine," he smiled his best lady-killer smile reflexively, merely out of habit, because she was *so* attractive and kind. "I can't imagine anyone keeping so lovely a woman waiting for anything."

"If my mamma were younger and free, I think, Terry Armstrong, you would have fallen headlong in love with her, instead of me," Susannah laughed.

"Younger? Heck, as it is, I *am* a little in love with Mrs. Butler," Terry winked but the words caught in his throat, and he felt his heart sink at the prospect of taking Susannah away, to spy. The pretense of their "going north" Terry saw, was going to be very hard on Catherine Butler.

"Whose grandmother are you?" Baby Saidee wanted to know.

"Well, darling child, yours of course," Catherine laughed.

"But we have one already, in Texas. *She* can be Venetia's" the innocent tot answered. "You'll be mine."

"You can have two at once, two grand-mothers," Grace explained. "I suppose you're happy to see me, Miz Butler. You're looking perfect as usual, but not as perfect as when *I* do your combing."

"No one is your equal," Catherine said as she hugged Grace to her. "What of Marcus? Did you find Marcus and? . . ." she asked. Grace, her smile quivery, nodded. Catherine hugged her again.

"Where he is right now, I don't know, but I saw him, Miz Butler. I touched him. Perhaps I will see him again in this life."

"Be of good faith, Grace," Catherine said, pressing the woman's hand. Then the children captured her attention totally and she theirs. Wearing a bell-hooped summer gown of tissue

233

faille cotton in a pale blue shade, and a fresh-flower-laden deep brimmed bonnet, she was a charming, if not an especially grandmotherly, vision as she placed a tissue-wrapped gift into each child's hand. Saidee's big eyes got bigger. Even reserved, shy, and guarded Venetia was obviously pleased. She took to the lady straight off, just as he had, her father was pleased to see.

"These children love your daughter, too, Catherine, and did, right from the start, soon as she took them skinny dipping in the Gulf. They got a touch too much of the sun, nothing dreadful, just bothersome, a faint pinking of the skin. But my mother, their Granny Armstrong made as much of it as she could, tsking and clucking."

"I'm sure Susannah soothed them all over with apple blossom unguent," Catherine smiled, holding Venetia's hand in hers, that was lace gloved.

"Any word from the Commodore?" Terry asked, ushering the group of delightfully chattering, pretty females toward a waiting barouche.

"His ship spoke another three days out of port. His letter said he was suffering a savage attack of the gout and that he was trying to convince several officers of the Royal Navy to take leave and work for us, for the Confederacy."

234

"The whole world knows the Union will have command of the sea, but their blockades won't be in place until Autumn. The Confederacy's naval hopes are vested in sleek sail steamers that will be able to outrun the blockaders to neutral islands — Bermuda, the Bahamas, and the Danish West Indies," Terry told her. "You know the Commodore's overseeing the construction of one such ship." She nodded.

"Right now, while it can still be done, Rebel privateers, like the vessel that brought us back to Charleston, paid in spoils if there are any, and in letters of marque by the Richmond government, are already going after the Yankee merchant fleet."

"It has been in decline for years," Catherine nodded. "At any rate, our raids are also part of a plan, the Commodore said, to get Lloyd's, the maritime insurance company in London, to raise the rates for Yankees. *That* will interfere with Union commerce by forcing New England ships into port or to sail under foreign flags, will it not Terry?" Catherine asked. In the carriage, she held Saidee on her lap.

"Yes'm," Terry answered, not saying that he was itching to get to sea and try his hand at a little commerce raiding himself. But he had work to do before his fun would begin.

And there *was* Susannah. Every night.

235

* * *

For the next week, Catherine and Susannah showed off the girls to Charleston society. They called on Pinckneys and Brutons and Pointsetts and Rhetts and more, Terry's daughters all dressed up in frocks Catherine had copied for them by her seamstresses from Paris fashion dolls. Their hair, loosed from the restraints of Lafitte's austere and simple braids, was done in fashionable corkscrew cornsilk yellow curls, by Grace of course. They had green and pink and white dresses, in taffeta, in dimity, in organdy, with huge silk bows. Baby Saidee's were high-waisted, her sister's scoop waisted, befitting her advanced age of thirteen. They were given lace half-gloves, ivory satin slippers, floral halos with ribbon streamers, sun bonnets, parasols. Catherine, who doted on their every word, never ran out of fairy tales, and stories—about her son Simeon, about Susannah as a girl, about their father's wedding to her daughter, which always sent Terry, feeling uneasy, quickly out of earshot. Never had the Armstrong girls been so lavished with material things, and attention. Susannah and Terry agreed it was just what they needed, for the moment, at least.

While his favorite females socialized, the Lieutenant conferred with some of Charleston's more powerful citizens to discuss military matters while liberally serving out what was left of the

Commodore's Kentucky bourbon and imported clarets.

"I'll burn my house to the ground, and everything in it, before any Yankee bastard sets foot inside," John Heywood ranted.

"We don't expect things to come to such a pass, Heywood," Terry told the portly, irate aristocrat, "though the Yankees may be able to shut you down here in Charleston port. They know our daring seamen in swift little runners right now are darting in and out of here, loaded with cotton for Nassau, coming back with rifles."

"Any Yankee sets foot in Charleston is going end up stiff in Southern dust." It was Beverly Bland, blustering and sword rattling, who offered that hollow threat. He was, as he had been weeks before, Terry noted, just about to leave for Virginia.

"One thing we have got, gentlemen, is our palmetto. It makes the best logs, for fortifications. The spongy wood doesn't splinter when bullets fly," Reynolds Clark explained. The pragmatic Low Country planter followed the direction of Terry's wandering gaze out the open library window to the garden to discover Susannah, who was looking almost like a child herself with her hair in a braid, a white smock over her gown. She was playing tag with the girls and several other visiting children, one of whom was a boy of thirteen in a cadet's uniform, who made an obvious effort to make Venetia his special prey. They were all fleet and agile and clever at their game. Bright sunlight and dappled shade fell on happy, carefree young faces, full of spirit. Their laughter was infectious. Susannah, tagged, saw Terry watching and waved him a kiss.

"Armstrong!" Dundee Laing barked, recalling Terry to business. A crooked, dyspeptic old fellow, once a well-known orator, Laing liked the sound of his own voice. "It's for just such moments, such charming scenes as is set outside this very window, that we will prevail in preserving our own southern way of life. Lovers of liberty long ago sniffed the tainted winds of tyranny blowing from the north."

"True, Mr. Laing," Terry nodded.

"We have a habit of self-government here, from Colonial times. Hell man, long ago as 1827 the South Carolina War Hawks of the 1812 combat, John Calhoun, Langdon Cheeves, David Williams, William Lowndes joined with Henry Clay of Kentucky to talk of seceding. Where is Commodore Butler's humidor, son? I crave a cigar."

"We had that habit of independence right from the start, from 1663, when King Charles gave the land of the Carolinas to eight of his loyal Lords Proprietors. A few years later, Dr. Henry Woodward came up here from an English settlement in Barbados and became one of the founders of Charles Town. He helped see to it that the religious freedom part was written into the charter. We—they—took in dissenters. They tolerated 'em in from other colonies—Baptists having a bad time in Maine, French Hugenots, Quakers, even Catholics and some Jews who had helped finance the first explorations of this beautiful state of ours.

"Sure," Laing said nipping the end off his cigar with his teeth. "The Methodist circuit rider, Francis Asbury, came by here around 1730 and called Charleston the seat of Satan, dissipation and folly. 'Cause we were rich in rice and slaves."

"In 1776 this was a right prosperous part of the world," Matthew Williams lectured Terry. "Fill my glass son, and I'll tell you more. Don't stint on that good whiskey, that's it," Williams smiled holding his glass to the window to let sunlight pour through the amber fluid. "That's it. Now, where was I?"

"Talking about prosperity in South Carolina in. . . ." Terry supplied.

"Oh, yeah. See, we had the most interesting, civilized social life in America right here. Carolinians were livin' like English gentlemen while Indians were still roamin' a little to the west of here, boy. Then, like now, we had our estates and our houses in Charles Town, with fine furnishings and of course our English gardens. There were English tutors for our sons, and they and even some of our girls were sent abroad to be finished, in England, of course. With it all, we fought mad King George for freedom alongside the other colonies and we are not about to be giving up that freedom now, dag nab it!"

"You've a great tradition to defend, sir," Terry agreed, "but now, the point of all this talk is to get practical about defending it. There are more volunteers ready here in Charleston right now than we can process. They all have to be mustered in by the Confederate government, and equipped. That takes money and time."

"The ladies *are* busy making uniforms, even bullets. Society leaders are raising funds putting on fairs and amateur theatricals. We have bread to feed our people, gold in our vaults, cotton in our storehouses and the fighting blood of Moultrie and Marion in our veins. We will prevail."

Terry listened to those grandiloquent old fire-eaters simply to be polite. He had heard all the bombast before. It was the military experts, the West Pointers, even the disciplined young cadets of the military schools, he was more interested in hearing and later that night, at dinner, he and Susannah entertained General Beaugregard's Charleston staff.

"There is talk, Lieutenant, of the Yankees preparing a flotilla of old whaling ships, soon to sail out of New Bedford, in Massachusetts, laden with rocks taken from New England farmers' stone walls. Sunk in the mouth of Charleston Harbor, the 'Stone Fleet' is intended to block entrance to our port." Chief of Staff Logan Lord was a small, blond, blue-eyed, fierce looking man who reminded Susannah of a fighting pit bull dog. She looked along the table at two rows of pretty pastel gowns alternating with gray uniforms aglow with shiny brass buttons and epaulets behind glinting stemmed wine glasses of Irish Waterford crystal and candles in silver sticks softly lighting eager, confident faces.

"So, they are *really* plannin' on a blockade?" she asked. "It's not . . . *right*. It *is* downright craven, making war on civilians and women and children. More claret? More Claret, Ralph please, for Chief Stuart," she directed the white-gloved butler.

"We will have huge Drummond lights, ma'am, which burn incandescent lime, to illuminate our fortifications and ward off night attacks. We have 'Greek-fire,' which has been used to good effect since Byzantine times. It's an explosive that burns wet. It will be laid by to counter the North's monstrous big cannon. Our informers tell us a very big gun is being mounted on piles driven into sixteen feet of our Carolina swamp,

241

off shore. This so-called 'Swamp Angel' is capable of hurling a two-hundred pound shot over a distance of five miles to bombard Charleston."

"Bombard . . . Charleston? Our beautiful city?" Catherine appeared deeply dismayed and personally offended. "You mean the damn Yankees do not intend to fight fairly, gentlemen?"

Dr. St. Julien Ravenel cleared his throat and a respectful silence fell among the two dozen individuals at the dining table. The butler and the serving maid stopped in mid-gesture, to leave a plate hovering in the air, a glass half-filled.

"Madam," Ravenel said, "I will counter that monster cannon with my new invention, a craft capable of slipping in and out of Charleston harbor virtually unseen," he said to Catherine, who smiled tentatively. "When you see President Davis at Richmond, Lieutenant Armstrong as I've been told you will be doing within the next few days, please tell him of my device, now being built. It is a boat sir, which lies so low in the water, there will only be ten inches of freeboard. She will sneak up on Union ships, carrying a hundred pounds of powder in a bomb—a torpedo, I call it—on a projectile shaft. My torpedo will be delivered beneath the water line to sink large Yankee war ships."

"Have you heard of the 'fish boat,' Dr. Ravenel?" Terry inquired as the gentlemen retired to the library, the ladies to the drawing room.

"That the same as the 'David' so called after the biblical hero, because it's small but powerful? Robert Fulton already tried to construct an underwater craft boat without real success," Ravenel noted, on the defensive.

Terry nodded, puffing a cigar to light as the other men, an elite group of officers, did the same.

"A submarine, yes, being built at Mobile Bay. This is a modern version. I managed to get a look at it on our way from Texas. It's forty feet of galvanized iron, cigar shaped, with a propeller and crank turned by a crew of seven inside it. It will be able to submerge totally and set its torpedo under the hull of the enemy."

"A damn lot good she'll do us, in Mobile. Now Dr. Ravenel's invention will be right here to . . ."

"The *Hunley*, the submarine's actual name," Terry interrupted Major Arlesby a bearded, bespectacled man who had seen action in the Mexican War. "Is to be brought here, where she'll really be needed, by train, as soon as she's ready."

Susannah, gay and vivacious, but also very attentive at dinner, had entered the library with a tray of coffee, her excuse to listen to the men's talk so that later she could write everything down in her little book as Terry had instructed, in the event, he explained, anything slipped his mind. She had also done sketches of the Confederate coast from Texas and Florida north to Port Royal and Charleston. What she hadn't heard herself, Terry dictated to her later, before they retired.

Watching her concentrate, writing diligently, the nib of her pen scratching as she bent over the dressing table, leaning into the soft light of a lamp, he was enraptured by her, again. Her red hair was unfurled, the color in her face high, her dressing gown loosely draped about her voluptuous body so that the cleavage of her high breasts was visible to him, just as her smooth legs, bared to mid-thigh. All combined to urge him to get business done, fast. She always shut the book with a decisive snap, locked it and looked at him with a sweet and tender, very enticing small smile and he knew it was time. He waited for her to come to him, only because her advance across the room was so . . . *perfect*. Her dressing gown would be allowed to fall open and slip low on her silken shoulders, fully exposing her breasts, the incurve of her slender waist, the swell of her thighs as she moved toward him with a sway of her hips that Terry could best describe as scandalous.

Sometimes, he stood to strip off his clothes as he watched her, meeting her halfway to become part of her, thrust deep inside her standing, before they even made it to bed. Other times, he just waited for her to get all the way to him. Then, his head thrown back, he let her explore, touching him, satisfying herself that he did surely want her at least as much as she did him. Her hands and lips and tongue worked at him superbly as she helped him to disrobe, very slowly. And then he would take her to bed, and take her, just as slowly, as she moaned softly, her body accepting his unconditionally, taking him deep, prolonging the pleasure interminably.

How could he leave her? Terry asked himself, every morning.

"Marry me *now*," he asked Susannah every other day. "We can go quietly to your Minister Sutcliffe and be bound forever in eyes of man and God."

"What? And have the good man Sutcliffe think me a wicked woman for, um, being with you all this time—unwed?" she protested lightly.

"I want to make an honest woman of you, Susannah. Let me return your gift of love. You set me free from the past and you made a good man of me. I don't want to lose you . . . leave you . . . until I know you're mine for all time. That's married. To me." Terry argued.

"Well then, if I don't want you to leave me

unwed, sir, why *should* I marry you and risk waking up alone?" she gently teased. "When all this is over, Terry, the war, our spying . . . well then, if we still both feel the same . . ."

With a sweep of his arm, Terry cleared her dressing table of all its bottles and pots and jars and then kicked a hole through her dressing screen. She came out from behind it and hurled herself into his arms, her mouth finding his, wide and hungry.

They left Charleston the next morning, exhausted and deeply content, though their parting from Catherine was anything but easy.

"If you two must go gallivanting off to Richmond, at least leave the children with me," she implored. "It's safe and quiet here, life is good here and always will be I do hope. The girls know me, and Grace can . . ."

"They all three are coming with us, Mamma," Susannah said. Terry let her do most of the talking.

"Grace? Oh for pity's sake, Daughter! Are you that vain? Can't you live without your comber for a few days? I may not be able to and I want her for myself," Catherine laughed, her effort at jesting falling flat. She didn't want to lose them all at once.

"Mamma, I have to tell you a piece of news,"

Susannah said somberly. In her dark traveling dress with white collar and cuffs and bonnet, she was exceptionally lovely, and agitated. "Mamma, listen. Louly's having a baby," she blurted.

"That wisp of a girl? That innocent child? Oh, I'm . . . flabbergasted." Catherine's eyes opened wide and she clasped her hands. "Can it be! Her poor, poor pious mother. Oh, it's the times, everything changing. I do declare I feel for poor Miz McCord!"

"Mrs. McCord is singing with joy, Mamma. Louly's married to a fine young man who has gone off to war."

Catherine threw up her hands then, in surprise, and blinked repeatedly, starting to pace back and forth across the red Turkey rug in her drawing room.

"Well, at least Simeon is safe from her, the immoral woman, though I never thought Louly McCord would toss over my son for anyone else. He'll be crushed, but he'll get over it. It's all for the better. Well, you two, tell me at once, who married little Louly and fathered her baby?"

"It *is* your son, Simeon, Catherine," Terry answered when Susannah couldn't bring herself to. Catherine kept pacing.

"Oh, how startling—I mean, Louly . . . and who? I'm sorry, Terry. What did you say?"

"They're married, Simeon and Louly.

Mamma, Simeon is grown now. So is Louly."

"My son and . . . Louly? Married?" Catherine sat down. "Of course," she said, all at once composed, in command of herself and the situation. She was, Terry marveled, a most admirable, seasoned woman. "Children grow and go their own ways, Susannah," Catherine said. "I know that. They follow their hearts but they needn't have kept this a secret, not from *us*. Oh dear me, I suppose Louly never will speak to me, after the way I've treated her."

"Mother . . ." Susannah said, "listen to us for a . . ."

"Susannah? Do you know what? I *am* glad. I need Louly and her baby. My son is gone away, you're going with your girls and Terry. The South, my whole world, could be shattering. I know, whatever happens, our lives will never be the same again. Father and I need all of you, but more than anything, right now, it's Louly's baby—Simeon's—that will help us believe there really is a future."

"Mamma, Louly is here. Louly is here, now, to see you. I'm going. I must. I'm leaving two letters, one for you to open in exactly three weeks. The other must not be opened unless . . . something happens to me. Hear me, Mamma?"

"Yes, of course, Susannah dear," Catherine said, absently putting both envelopes on the mantel. "I've been so cold to Louly, and . . .

248

short-sighted. All that shallow meanness about social position and . . ."

"Mamma, we'll all be together again, Lord willing. Remember that, no matter what." Susannah turned and fled. Terry gave Catherine a long hug as Louly quietly entered the room.

"Take care of her Louly, and of yourself," Terry said, turning on his heel to follow Susannah.

The next time they heard from Catherine Butler it was to notify her daughter, through her lawyer, that Susannah was disowned, disavowed, and forbidden to cross her ancestral doorstep again.

Chapter Twenty-one

Suddenly, nothing was clear to Grace any more and, even worse, there was no one who could explain matters to her. The Lieutenant, if that's what he really was—there was some doubt—had vanished and his wife, which Susannah apparently wasn't—there was doubt about that, too—was in a Yankee prison. What it all seemed to come down to was that Terry and his "wife" and *her* "bondslave" were all impostors in their roles. Terry was no Rebel, maybe, and Susannah was it seemed no more a wife than Grace was a slave.

Things unravelled fast, as soon as that "dreadful Pinkerton man," as Grace called the detective, appeared on their doorstep. Now, he had taken Susannah away and Grace and the four children—two of hers, two of theirs had been standing vigil for hours. They were sad, tired and hungry when "that Pinkerton man" finally came out of the Old Capitol Jail to say that Susannah would be looked after and to take the little ones home.

"We are not leaving here till we see her with our very own eyes," Grace responded, omitting the 'sir' that was expected in the circumstance. Her dislike of the man was obvious. He pursed his lips, looked back at the prison over his shoulder and beckoned Grace to follow him.

"Can you keep those two she-devil, agitating wee Rebel lassies under control?" he asked warily, looking askance at Venetia and Saidee, who stuck out her tongue.

"Be a lady now, and apologize to Mr. Pinkerton, Saidee, if you want to see Susannah," Grace winked at the child, who curtsied and pouted but said not a word.

"That's *Detective* Pinkerton and I've been promised army rank soon. Now, when I take you inside, there's to be no talking, no signalling, just looking. You'll see she's unharmed and you'll leave. Is that clear?"

"Sure is," said Grace, nodding meaningfully at Venetia and guiding the younger children along like a mother hen.

Susannah was about to be removed from the jail anteroom as her little group of partisans were shown in and Pinkerton reminded them all there were to be no words exchanged.

"Now, you see she is looking her usual bonnie bright self," Pinkerton nodded as Susannah went down on her knees and opened her arms to the children, grasping Venetia's hand, encircling the other three, who began loudly wailing as they had been coached, and shedding copious crocodile tears.

251

"Y'all let my Susannah come on home to my pa, now," Baby Saidee sniffled, starting toward Detective Lemon, who spilled his coffee on a stack of very official papers while escaping her, and the room, mumbling "arrest that female person . . . arrest them all . . . as spies!" In the confusion, Susannah passed two script-covered pages to Grace.

"Grace, children . . . listen fast," she said. "We were all just used by Lieutenant, or Major or maybe Captain, Armstrong, as cover for his spy work. The man's actual rank is open to question and so are his loyalties. Grace, it seems he was actually spying for the Union, not the Confederacy you'll be pleased to learn. Scoundrels are what they are, all Yankees, jeopardizing the safety of small children and taking women into custody," Susannah flared as a pair of mortified young soldiers flanked her and removed her from the anteroom.

"Hear that? All of you and *Miss* Butler, were just part of Armstrong's plan. Go on home now, Grace, and don't come back here. It won't do Miss Butler any good at all," Pinkerton said with mean pleasure showing the downcast little group out of the jail.

And so it was that Grace found herself the only one left to care for two lonely children who were not her own, along *with* her own, Esther and Enoch.

Grace didn't mind. She loved the Armstrong

girls, forsaken as they were. She had seen many a family ripped apart, root and branch. She understood how dreadful it was to lose a mother, or a child, to be torn away from all familiar surroundings. These Armstrong children, pale as ivory, were as blameless for the troubles of this world, she knew, as were all the precious black infants, abandoned as worthless along roadsteads and railroad tracks, grabbed from the arms of their young mothers by slavers. Those poor girls were being fed so they could pick cotton and not be giving any of their strength to loving their babies.

"We are luckier than most, Esther," Grace said back home later, whispering very softly, to the sleeping child in her lap as she rocked their chair steadily. "When we left Charleston four . . . five months ago, baby, in early May, it was sweet spring, and Susannah, Terry and me were three optimists. Now, Miss Susannah thinks Mr. Terry and me were on the same side all along, the Yankee side, and that she was being hoodwinked by him. I don't know if he lied to her, to me, or to us both, but whatever is the truth, I forgive him because he was the one who found your brother, my runaway son, Alexander." Grace sighed deeply. "I wish Alex was here with us now. But he's not and it can't be helped. It just can't be, Esther."

Terry, using some of his widespread connections, had the boy, Alexander, taken north to Massachusetts to train with a company of black volunteers who might not ever be permitted to take up arms to fight for their own freedom. But for the moment at least, thanks to Terry, he was safe.

Everywhere Grace had been in the company of Terry Armstrong, he'd had welcoming friends, serious ones, not gladhanders. His friends were the kind who would lay down their lives for Terry and for his sake, take charge of Alex. Terry was modest when Grace asked him how it was he had generous, trusted comrades, North *and* South, which was remarkable in such times.

"Men who ship before the mast are much alike in some ways, Grace," he explained, "a special breed apart."

"Well, be that as it may," Grace told Terry, "I thank you and those other sailors more than I can say, for getting my son safely away from the slave south, though I'm not exactly clear how you did it."

They had gone out of Charleston fast as cannon shot, not even stopping at night, just changing horses, running north, not for Richmond as they had told Catherine, Terry explained, but for the Norfolk Navy Yard, that was in Confederate hands. He had naval affairs to attend to. There was a captured Yankee frigate, the *Merrimack,* being converted into the first ironclad ship the country, north and south, would ever see.

But speeding as he was, Terry did stop the carriage at the fringe of the Great Dismal Swamp.

"Where's Ben the slave catcher at, now that I need him?" Grace had asked in a deriding way.

"You recall, Ben suffers from the sea sickness. He's coming overland, collecting the men I signed up to crew for me. *I'll* find Alex now," Terry answered, "if he's in there. Sit tight, you all."

And they did just that, sit, staring ahead down the ditch towpath they had been racing along, until the carriage had been pulled to a halt.

"Would you mind saying why are we waitin' here in this dark eerie place, Lieutenant Armstrong?" Grace finally asked irritably. She was on edge. "I want to find Alexander, not linger here."

"Are you going in that swamp alone, Grace?" Terry asked her and she shook her head 'no.'

"That's best. I wouldn't either, because you never know what you might find, wandering in a place like the Great Dismal."

"Are you trying to frighten Grace?" Susannah asked as Venetia cuddled closer to her.

"Sailors like me can be superstitious at times, you know. There are some places on this earth we avoid like the plague," Terry insisted. "And always have."

"Where?" Grace wanted to know.

"Oh . . ." he began, looking up at the overhang of trees and moss, pausing to think, "well, for one example, the ancient druid lore tells of a secret oracle shrine on the Isle de Saint, off Finistere, a place known to seafarers for centuries because of all the ships that wreck on the rocks there. The story tells of nine fearful beldams who live on the island, brewing up storms and peering into the future."

"What's a beldam?" Venetia asked suspiciously. "Is it like a witch?" Terry pondered a moment.

"More like a hag," he answered and Grace couldn't tell if he was being serious or bedeviling them, to keep their minds off just waiting. "Many living things change shape, you know, from one sort of creature to another. Some of the Norse gods put on falcon mantles so they could fly and there were Norwegian berserkers, the bear men. In battle they went into fits of frenzy, howling, foaming, biting through their shields. *That* would strike paralyzing fear into their foes. Then, too, there's the marauding evening wolf of Norway . . ."

"What happens here in *this* place?" one of the children wanted to know.

"I don't know about right here, Venetia. But don't you worry. You're safe with me. Do you want to know about France? I'll tell you about France. At the edge of a certain deep, haunted pond, at the full moon, some half-grown boys of the Normandy countryside were—-maybe still are—compelled to gather, strip off their clothes and dive into the icy water. After their swim, the boys find wolf pelts left on the bank of the cold pond by a wizard werewolf, a demon. As soon as the boys dress in the animal skins, they no longer are really human."

"Well . . . what are they, then?" Susannah asked as Saidee climbed into her lap and hid her face in a carriage robe.

"They become . . ." Terry growled low and hesitated, for effect, "bond slaves of *Satan,* depraved and terrible, who go wandering about plundering the countryside. Sometimes, they hide in waiting for some unlucky prey—a doe and her fawn, little rabbits with pink twitching noses, wandering house cats and barn cats out hunting after those little rabbits. . . . want to know what a werewolf's favorite kill is?" His transfixed audience nodded, except Venetia, who wasn't so sure she wanted to know.

"Tipplers—men meandering their drunken way home from the village tavern in the dark of small moonless morning hours."

"What do they do, Da, the wolfs?" Saidee asked with large eyes, peering over the blanket.

"When a staggering sot comes their way, the werewolves leap out of the underbrush howling, to attack, pillage and plunder."

"What do they want, Da?"

"Blood!" Terry croaked, and all his listeners shrank back when he set up a long, barking wolf-ish howl. Then he had to soothe the spooked carriage horses before continuing.

"Did the wolf boys ever . . . go home again, Father?" Venetia whispered. "I mean, they couldn't help it, could they, they couldn't stop their thoughts or stop doing . . . what they did?

Did they ever get caught?"

"Just before dawn, the werewolf boys cast off their enchanted envelopes of animal skin and plunged back into the same pool to resume normal shape. But sometimes, one of them might have been hurt running with the pack, or had gotten wounded by a brave hunter with a good tracking wolf hound. Next day, after the poor victims were found, the peasants of the area would search every house for a boy with an injured shoulder or leg or face, wherever the hunter reported he had struck a werewolf. And if they found such a boy . . ." Terry paused.

"Can't a girl be one of them?" Saidee asked at the same time Venetia said, "What? What if they found him?" Everyone was caught up by Terry's demons, listening intently for his answers, which never came. At that tense moment, Susannah shrieked and Grace came close to fainting at the sight of what at first glance was as good a stand in for a demon as any one of them could have concocted in her head.

An old, *old* black man, with white hair and a long white-fringed beard, materialized at the side of the carriage as if out of thin air. He was wrapped in an old shredding blanket, wearing tattered breeches and shabby boots and he carried a gun, a rifle he cradled like a baby in his arms.

Chapter Twenty-two

"Osman!" Terry said with a great grin, getting down. The old man shook Terry's hand in both of his own and looked hard into his eyes. They hugged and pounded each other on the back. "Meet my family, Osman," Terry said and the man, flashing a near toothless smile, glanced furtively at the occupants of the carriage before the two men disappeared together into the vines and underbrush.

Susannah, holding a pistol, knew enough not to stir or make any sound and somehow, Grace and the little girls knew that, too, because they were waiting exactly as he had left them when Terry came back an hour later, not with his friend Osman, but with Alexander.

The boy had spent the past two years living at Cullpepper Island, a shingle-maker's camp in the cedar swamp. Slaves, sent there to make shingles for their masters, passed on some of their work, and food, to runaways who worked beside them.

"Mamma," Alex told Grace, too shy then to even look at anyone else, "I met a man, been in there, been in the Dismal for twenty years. Had plenty of whiskey, but he never even seen a woman once, all that time."

"Why were you there, in that place?" Venetia asked softly and Grace answered for her tongue-tied son.

"My firstborn is owned and posted as a runaway, by the Butlers, even though his father, who is not my Marcus, is free and white." She and Susannah exchanged glances over that.

"And now," Terry explained, sensing something unsaid, "we're going to smuggle Alexander north, hidden under blankets, until we cross the Potomac River into Maryland. That's not far."

Just across the river, he disappeared into a small cottage and when he emerged, Lieutenant Armstrong had changed his rank and his Stripes, from gray to blue, for the first time, but not the last. He had donned the uniform of a Union Naval Captain.

"There's still a need for caution, for Alexander's sake," Terry explained. "There are more than a few Confederate sympathizers in this state, but I think we'll find the same is true in New York City, even in the nation's capitol at Washington."

* * *

260

"God never made me for a maiden lady school teacher," Daisy Ballard quipped, "not if there's men like *him* wandering loose in the world." She meant Terry Armstrong, of course. He gave her his warm crooked little smile, Susannah noticed.

"Pleased to make your acquaintance, too, ma'am, I'm sure," Terry said, breaking into an all out grin when Susannah introduced them. "I've heard a lot about you, what an influence you've had on my wife's thinking."

"Susannah was one of my very best students. She had a natural aptitude for Latin. And politics," Daisy twinkled. "If I've ever seen political promise, you've got it, but say, how about Latin? Have you studied Latin, Captain? Would you like to?"

"Jealousy is the jaundice of the soul," Susannah laughed. *"You* taught me that, Daisy, so don't go making eyes at my man. If you took your little nose out of your books, you could find one of your own." The two women laughed and hugged and then, almost at once, at Terry's insistent urging, said a sad goodbye as soon as Grace's two young children, who had been in her charge, were packed to leave for the dash north.

Daisy Ballard got down on her knees in the dust and hugged Esther first, then Enoch and gifted them with a Bible and a copy of *The New England Primer.*

261

" 'My Book and Heart/Must never part,' " she quoted from the primer. "Remember that, you two. Oh, Gracey!" she said to their mother, "I am going to miss them awfully. You all come back and see me, hear?" Miss Ballard called after them, "or it could be, I'll come on up north and surprise you all!"

"Isn't she a pretty thing—blond and little, with her brown eyes and that short nose, turned up like it is?" Venetia commented. Grace, holding her babies hard to her, agreed.

"I just cannot understand why no man has claimed her," she said.

"Daisy banters, but really, she thinks marriage is another form of servitude, Grace. She has her principles," Susannah explained.

"I do not agree, about marriage and servitude, but Miss Daisy's mistaken opinion is not my lookout. I have all three of my children with me now, thanks to her and to uh, the Captain, is it now? Terry, preoccupied, nodded. "And we are going north, to freedom, together."

"Where are you thinking of settling, Grace?" Susannah asked, almost teary, sentimental and affected by the sight of Grace and the children, reunited.

"Just at first, we'll go on to Ontario as Marcus wanted, where he'll be able to find us, but after . . . Well, I have been saving my earnings and I went and bought us a house to live in, children," Grace beamed. "I, myself, own a little piece of dirt, a patch of land with a shack on it, in Cincinnati. Know what's most amazing to me? I also own an actual tree, growing on that little lot, right out of God's earth!"

"We haven't made it to Canada or Cincinnati yet, have we Esther?" Grace crooned to the sleeping child as she placed the small girl into bed and pulled up a light coverlet. "And where my son Alexander is now, or where your daddy Marcus has got to, I do not know, but I came close enough to see them, and touch them both. It hurts dreadful the way I miss them. But also, I *know* now, we will get to our place in Ohio one day and that gives me hope."

Grace couldn't help wishing Susannah had some of that left — hope. Now, it seemed to Grace, her friend had nothing but anger in her heart. And Terry Armstrong, too, was in a terrible wrath when Grace opened a back door to his tapping.

"I've been denounced as a spy for the North *and* South by my own loving so-called wife, which I am now surely glad she is not!" he had said in a mean tone of voice Grace had never heard before. "I kept on asking her to marry me and she kept turning me down, lucky for me. Did you get to see her at the prison, Grace? Is she . . . tolerably well? Did she say . . . anything about . . . me?"

"She couldn't talk to me hardly at all about you or anything, except to say Yankees are scoundrels who lie about love and you might be the worst of a bad lot. But there's something going on here that's not just . . . *right*. I have got a feeling there's some mistake that's come between you two." Grace stood looking at Terry quizzically.

"I knew soon as she blurted out for all to hear she was a Rebel spy, it was only a matter of time before she betrayed me, too, but I hoped I was wrong and I . . . waited."

"Waited for what?" Grace's eyes narrowed. "Did *you* turn her in, get her arrested?"

"My only mistake was trying to work with a woman, a beautiful one, and falling in love with her," he said with a white flash of a chilling smile. "I'll never do that again, Grace."

"Never love a woman, or trust one?"

"Both. Neither. Oh blast, I don't know what I mean!" He slammed his left fist into his right hand and his eyes got darker.

"She loved you, too. Lack of love is not at the root of your trouble. One of you two is way off the mark about something somehow and that maybe-minster, Wigfall, who she talked with long and serious in the garden before your maybe-nuptials, could shed some light on this

264

matter but he is far from Washington, of course."

"It's nothing to do with him. Now, I'm going up to sneak a glance at my own children for a minute or two. When I'll see them, or you, again, I can't say." Grace listened to Terry's light tread on the steps and then heard the creak of springs as he sat on the edge of one of the little beds in the blue room. Picturing him with his girls, she was glad she hadn't told him what Susannah did say, on the morning they took her off to the Old Capitol.

"Terry Armstrong is a damn Yankee! I must have met that man on damnation's road because the devil owns him!" she blurted as Grace brought in her breakfast tray to the room Susannah wasn't allowed to leave.

"If that's so," Grace had replied, "any friend of the Devil's a friend to me. Terry has been nothing but good as gold to me and mine."

"It was never love between Terry and me, just pagan passion we shared," Susannah insisted. Grace had rolled her eyes in exasperation.

"At least be honest with your own self, Susannah, if not with me. You are a mortal woman who would have run through fire and water for that man. You'd have followed Terry Armstrong beyond the night, across the day, to hell and gone no matter what, and you still would, in love as you are. That's what I think but, after all that's happened, it's hard to be certain about anything in this world, especially not about love."

"I don't see him going through anything for me, now I'm a prisoner. Grace, you should have stayed up there in New York, if all you're going to do is lecture me," Susannah sighed as Grace removed the picked-over tray.

New York City was crawling with copperheads, Confederate sympathizers, who detested Mr. Lincoln. Even the mayor, a man named Wood, was one of them, Grace had been shocked to discover. Others though, thought the whole business was a national disgrace and recruiting stations were drawing crowds all over that amazing city. Grace would like to have seen more of it, especially the neighborhood, street after street of it, where free black people reside, but she would have to go back another time to do that. She decided not to remain there but to stay with Susannah right to the bitter — or sweet — end of the war and turmoil and Susannah and Terry, still starry-eyed together, were in a race to get on to Washington. Consequently, on her one day in New York, while Susannah and Terry, now known as Major Armstrong of the Union Army, were out at the harbor, Grace took the children to Mr. Barnum's Gallery of

Wonders. On the way there, they had passed a photograph in a shop of window, of the President without a beard. His appearance, Grace thought, was much improved by the subtraction. She saw that for herself when they had been in Washington barely a week.

On a terrible hot day in July, at the height of the first real battle of the war, at a place called Manassas, she observed Mr. Lincoln hurrying through the city's puddled streets on the way to his residence. He was wearing a gray suit, not his usual black. In one bony hand he held a fist full of dispatches. With the other he was mopping his brow with a red handkerchief. He reminded Grace of nothing so much as a great blue heron fishing a stream.

"Susannah once told me her private theory of love," Terry said with subdued distress when he returned to the kitchen. Grace poured him a whiskey as he slumped into a chair.

"It seems there are matchmakers in her imagination, a pantheon of love gods who meet to match up men and women. If it's early, and they're fresh on the job, the pairings these matchmakers come up with are sensible and love comes kindly to the couples they join. Later, when the gods get weary and less keen for the work, it's then, Susannah says, they frame world-without-end bargains which should never have been made in heaven, or in hell—like her's and mine, she'd say now." He dropped his head in hands.

"Here," Grace sighed. "She slipped this paper in my hand at the prison. You might's well have it," Grace said with a helpless shrug. Terry carefully unfolded the pieces of shop paper Susannah had been given by Pinkerton. Going to a lamp, he skimmed the words, his eyes moving rapidly side to side down the pages.

"Damn! Listen to this—'I write in the hope that those who later peruse this little document will read between the lines, enabling me to yet do some good for my country. And if not? At the least, this narrative of imprudent behavior may save some other woman from the ruinous rewards of blind passion mistaken for true love,'" Terry read aloud before crushing the pages and flinging them into a corner. "I have the real diary, Grace, and a very incriminating piece of work it is. I took it to help her, to keep it out of Pinkerton's hands. I'm sorry I even went to the trouble."

"Before all this trouble, just a few weeks ago," Grace recalled, "you two couldn't get enough of each other. You spent all your waking, and sleeping time together, and quite a lot of it Susannah was sketching and writing. She got good drawings of the secret ironclad boat the Rebs are

268

working on at Norfolk, and the one, also supposed to be a secret, being built by the Yankees in New York harbor. She was always very careful to get every little detail, too. Terry Armstrong, what do you really have in mind to do with that damning little diary?"

Chapter Twenty-three

The Armstrong party reached Washington City on the sixteenth of July and took charge of a town house in sight of the President's residence, on fashionable Lafayette Square. Susannah found her new home charming, with a small, though decent, library and Axminster carpets in most of the rooms that, though not as fine as Aubusson rugs, were acceptable to her. She was particularly delighted by the melodian in the parlor.

Washington City was a surprise to her. When she had last visited there with her father, it had been a sleepy country village, more precisely, she had thought, a frontier town lacking Charleston's culture and solidity. By 1861, though still mostly a rugged place where pigs freely roamed the streets, the capitol had become an armed camp and there was no difficulty accommodating the friendly invasion of troops that had poured in to defend the city.

The Seventh New York, known as the kid

glove regiment of that state, the wealthiest and best equipped unit in the country, had been quartered in the Rotunda of the Capitol, in the crimson and gold hall of Representatives. The men fell into formation every evening to march down onto the avenue to dine at Willard's Hotel and other fashionable inns and eateries, so well-off they never had to rely on the standard army rations of bacon and beans, as the less affluent militias were forced to do.

The dome had not yet been set in place on the Capitol when they arrived and was left off, for ventilation. The Eighth Massachusetts was also installed there along with the Sixth Rhode Island and the boisterous men held mock congressional sessions to the accompaniment of tramping feet and banging drums. The First Rhode Island, put up in the Patent Office, had brought a laundress from home and drying shirts and skivvies dangled the marble balustrades and display cases.

Troop ships swarmed at Annapolis to unload more men who entrained at the rail junction there to avoid passing through the hostile city of Baltimore where Rebel opinion prevailed.

As more and more men arrived to garrison Washington against expected attack, soldiers were billeted in every nook and cranny of the Union capitol. Dragoons slept in warehouses, militias in government bureaus, troopers in court houses. The Garibaldi Guard, a unit composed entirely of foreigners—Italians, Swiss, Spaniards, Hungarian and others—recruited on the streets of New York, marched into Washington in their red blouses, French style with loaves of bread spiked on their bayonets. A rowdy troupe of New York City volunteer firemen, all large contentious men, were uniformed in the colorful full pants and fez headgear of Algerian Zouaves. After encamping as ordered near the Insane Asylum, the Fire Zouaves, as the unit was called, armed with footlong knives, stormed about the town frightening old ladies and demanding to take on Jeff Davis at once. And all the while, marching bands blared on the White House lawn, military choruses sang at the least excuse and the great, large cast iron Dahlgren cannon was fired repeatedly in salute to new arrivals.

At first, Washington's cheering citizens, who greeted every train load of arriving volunteers, were pleased to awake to reveille and drop off to sleep at night to the sound of taps. After a short while, so many soldiers were drilling, bugling, drumming and shooting off their weapons all over the rough, unfinished, tumultuous town, polite civilians were discomfited, and by the time Susannah and Terry arrived, the men were gradually moved out to bivouac in the Virginia countryside.

Susannah, eager to get into the thick of things and do her part for her own cause, entertained at

272

home on her second evening in Washington. A Union move into Virginia was imminent, Terry informed her. The Confederate General Beauregard was already poised at Manassas, not far from Washington, with twenty-two thousand men ready to repel the Yankees and chase them right back to, and through the Yankee city. Terry and Susannah were to try and determine if more men would be needed to hurl back the Union attack and take the town. Other Confederate spies were also set to the same task so that information could be compared and combined to determine Southern strategy.

At the Armstrong dinner table that night, among a dozen Union officers and their wives, was the esteemed Winfield Scott himself, the aged hero of the Spanish War. The Union General, who had haughty eyes and a puckered, pompous little mouth, was clearly over-the-hill, a smiling, sparkling Susannah determined as the man kissed her proffered hand. Scott was tall and very heavy, more than three-hundred pounds, and had to be helped out of any chair he settled in, a chore Captain Armstrong gladly performed that evening, gaining the immense old man's appreciation.

"I agree with the English philosopher Hobbes, when he said that war is the natural state of man, but not civil war," Scott held forth. Susannah sat not at the foot of the table, the usual position of a hostess, but at Terry's right hand, the place of honor, an arrangement he preferred and insisted upon. While they amused and diverted and subtly probed some of the most influential men in Washington, more than one or two of the ladies there, Susannah realized, noting their veiled eyes and smothered sighs, were among that regiment she had come to think of as the Terry Armstrong Walking Wounded. If she had had even the slightest inkling that she would, before long, join their ranks, she might have been less blithe, but that night she *was* the one seated beside him and he toyed with her as he always did. It was a game they played, to see how precisely, and secretly, he could touch and fondle her, and she him, without either giving any noticeable sign of rising desire to the earnest company surrounding them.

"Nations are like dogs. The weaker must put his tail between his legs and sneak away when trouble brews," General Scott pronounced. He had eaten and imbibed prodigiously and, between the meat course and dessert, rumbling and patting his lips, took the limelight. "These traitorous Rebels will do just that, turn tail, before long. Major General McDowell right now is at Centerville with thirty-five thousand men." Susannah felt Terry's hand, that was resting upon her knee, grip firmly and they exchanged meaningful glances.

"Will that force advance soon, General?" she inquired, trapping Terry's hand between her thighs.

"Mr. Horace Greeley's *New York Tribune,* the most influential newspaper in the Union, is urging us 'On To Richmond' in blaring headlines. A foray must soon be essayed, Mrs. Armstrong, if for no other reason then as a sop to the press, but I'd prefer to hold off a while. Most of our men are green," he rumbled. "Some officers of the North and South are trained professionals, West Pointers, but most of them have been elected by their undisciplined men in what amount to popularity contests and nothing is done sharp, there's no proper discipline. The men don't march. They take offense when told by police to go to their campgrounds, and they fall off to sleep on watch. My only solace comes in knowing the Rebels are as green and, if anything, even less inclined to follow orders than our side. But tell me, Mrs. Armstrong, what has brought you, a southerner, to our camp?"

"I believe in the Union, sir," she answered quickly and, she hoped, convincingly. "My father has been a United States naval officer most of his life, loyally serving his country. I was taught to do the same. Though the Commodore and I have painfully parted ways now, I hope for our family, as I do for our country, the breach will soon be closed."

"There are a great many southern sympathizers here in Washington . . . all over the north, so have a care about confiding your sentiments to too many people, my dear. You may not always receive a kind rejoinder. I sure do wish your father, like you and your husband, had come with us. We need men like Commodore Butler.

"Armstrong, this is a splendid woman you've wed — astute, and such superb high coloring," the general said to Terry, charmed by Susannah's blush, which had little to do with his compliments or the heat of the room.

She was wearing a dinner dress that offered a discreet hint of cleavage. It was fashioned of the most fragile, gossamer gauze, trimmed with white clematis and honeysuckle of a scarlet shade, which intensified her rosy flush.

Though the ladies at the table had all dressed for dinner, the men were in uniform, the prevailing American fashion, and made hardly any distinction between day and evening apparel. They wore black swallow tail suits and brightly colored neck cloths, unlike Englishmen who had gone over exclusively to white neck cloths for dinner.

"How do you find Washington, my dear?" the general asked Susannah.

"Well it is . . ." she cleared her throat as Terry moved his chair closer to hers and took her hand beneath the table, to move it over his lap, "Washington is very . . . busy, even bustling, General,

276

what with all the vendors on the streets, and the hotels and rooming houses filled to capacity. It's a very different city than it was when I first came here with my father some years ago. Then, it was just another sleepy little southern town."

"Northerners do find this place slow and lazy but in reality, people here inhale politics with the air they breathe. It's a city mad for gossip, and corruption of every kind prevails." The jaded speaker was a sleek, dark-haired, sharp-featured young woman, Mrs. Napoleon Baker, Gilda Baker, earned a look of disapproval from General Scott. Terry motioned Susannah to lean close to him so that he could whisper in her ear.

"You should keep in mind this is not the gallant South, not genteel Charleston. This place is a hotbed of power and sex. Don't play the belle here. Don't go beau-catching or some fellow will forget you're mine and take you up on your implied offer."

"But flirting is a southern woman's best tool, Terry. I mean, if you expect me to pluck gems of information from highly placed northerners, that *is* the most effective way for me to go about it." She was only half-jesting and he took her very seriously. His look darkened.

"You are bound to me by silken cords of love and we would be tied by law, if only you'd agree to it. Well?" Terry demanded. She shook her head 'no' and extracted her foot from her slipper before letting her silk-stockinged toe glide up along his leg. Now *he* cleared his throat.

"Charles Dickens visited Washington City about twenty years ago. He described it as a place of 'spacious avenues, that begin nothing, and lead nowhere; streets, mile long, that only want houses . . . a city of magnificent intentions.' Not very much has changed, has it?" Terry asked the party, shifting in his chair as the table was cleared and places laid for the last course, trifle, and a Carolina confection of pitted, crushed, sun dried, sugared, jellied and rolled peaches, which kept perfectly packed tight in tin boxes. Susannah never traveled without 'peach leather' and it was always the sensation of the evening.

"I've not been here to Washington in two years," Gilda Baker said, licking her lips and leaning forward to rest her chin on the heel of her hand, her elbow on the table. In her smooth, tightly bound hair, she was wearing a tiara of pearls large as grapes. "Let me warn you, my dear Mrs. Armstrong, as I hear you're settling in here, the place is a mud puddle in winter, dry as dust, as you no doubt have noticed, in summer, a cow-pen and pigsty all year round. The canal running through the city emits the foul odors of dead cats and dogs, and occasionally of a human derelict . . ."

"I haven't had a complete tour of the town,

278

but surely you exaggerate, Mrs. Baker?" Susannah asked. Actually, she fully agreed with the woman but used the opportunity to console General Scott who appeared to take Gilda Baker's criticism personally.

"Why such a sour expression, Scotty?" Gilda exclaimed. "I speak the truth. Ask anyone here if I exaggerate, except our unsuspecting and unseasoned hostess, of course. I do believe our own Captain Armstrong was in Washington when last I was. He'll substantiate every single word I say, won't you, Terry darling?" When Gilda smiled at him, he winked and nodded at her and Susannah felt a coil of jealousy unwind in her heart.

Chapter Twenty-four

"I should know better than to contradict *you,* Gilda but . . ." Terry answered with a studied coolness that was, Susannah realized, not his usual tone when addressing a female, particularly a striking one, which Gilda was in a severe, faintly sinister way with her sleek, sharp features and warped smile.

"But nothing, Terry darling," Gilda crooned. "Crime and poverty were very much in evidence in 1859, riot and bloodshed were everyday events, unoffending persons were shot, stabbed, and otherwise maltreated in the streets. Assaults by children were especially troublesome. Things have not improved."

"Citizens went about armed, then as now," her husband, Napoleon Baker confirmed. A middle-aged man of unexceptional appearance except for a long knife scar on his neck below his left ear, Baker had brown hair dusted with gray, narrow shoulders, and dull brown eyes that lit at odd moments in the conversation, such as when someone mentioned the notorious Dan Sickles.

"Speaking of armed citizens, Congressman Sickles is back in town. Can you fathom it?" Mrs. Colonel Ames asked. *"That* man showing his face here again?"

"Who ees theese Cycles?" another guest, J.J Selz, inquired. A European of imprecise provenance, he sometimes claimed France as his native land, at other times Russia or Sardinia, he professed to have been one of the few surviving members of the infamous Light Brigade during the Crimean War. Most of the four hundred men of that unit did not emerge from the jaws of death, yet many Europeans, claiming to have been part of the Brigade, had come to Washington, drawn by the chance of finding adventure and perhaps fame in yet another war.

"Sickles was a Congressman from New York, a brawler and shady Tammany politician known for his own philandering," Colonel Ames explained. "He is, Monsieur, famous all over our country, made a veritable luminary by newsmen, after he killed his wife's lover in broad daylight right outside on Lafayette Square here in Washington."

"Madame Cycles must have been some woman. Oo was her lovair?" Selz asked.

"A federal District Attorney, Barton Scott Key, the son of Francis Scott Key who is responsible for our national anthem. Do you know, Juan . . . uh Jeanne 'The Star Spangled Banner?' " Gilda asked. The man nodded. "The younger Key was a close friend of his killer. Both men were known about town as rakes. But of course," Gilda half-smiled, "Washington is full of them, men on the loose, away from their wives. Isn't it so, Terry darling?" she pointedly asked. Susannah, seemingly deliberate and aloof, but with anger welling, fixed her green gaze upon the woman.

"Sickles' wife was only nineteen, a notable beauty just half her husband's age, Mr. Selz," Terry answered, whistling faintly between his teeth when Susannah's searching, caressing foot came to rest at a sensitive place.

"Indiscreet, by God, the pair of them, and brash!" Napoleon Baker pounded the table and Susannah, disconcerted, sat up straight as a broom, abruptly ending her tactile exploration of Terry's anatomy. But the man hadn't discovered their intimate diversion, he was addressing the subject of Key and Mrs. Sickles."There were—are—numerous bordellos frequented by men in high public positions, officers of the army and navy, Governors of States, lawyers, doctors. Why did the man bother with Emmy Sickles?"

"What a romantic you are, Napoleon," his wife said, rolling her eyes heavenward. "Some men are more . . . discriminating than you are, perhaps? Do you think that might be one reason for Key's

282

preference? Do you think they could have been in love?" Mrs. Baker asked Mr. Baker.

Not a happy couple, Susannah thought, looking from one to the other. "Would you commit murder for me, Napoleon, if I took up with . . ." Gilda looked about the table, "Juan, or Tom Ames . . . or . . . Terry Armstrong?" Baker frowned and equivocated, not answering directly.

"I recall reading in *Harper's* magazine, when the Sickles trial was on, that as terrible as homicide is, it is a method that, on the whole, is the most effectual revenge of an outraged husband," he said.

"The courts, and the country, agreed, as we all know," Susannah said. "Sickles went um, scot-free, if you'll forgive the pun. That same magazine commentary also remarked that in the same situation, the French, unlike us, would merely yawn at the dalliance, and an Englishman would sue." Maxwell Hood, a Justice Department lawyer seated beside her nodded, laughing.

"In Sickles case it helped that the defendant was also a good friend of former President Buchanan. His was the first acquittal ever on the grounds of temporary insanity, the first time, I believe, that defense was ever used." General Scott, feeling ignored, harrumphed, then gestured to Terry to heave him out of his chair. Several other men also leaped to assist, fortunately.

"Sickles was a national hero—until he took

back the adulterous fallen female. How could he?" Scott grunted with authentic disbelief. "It's one thing for a man to defend his honor, even if murder is the method, but quite another for a woman—a *wife and mother*—to commit adultery." With that, the old mountain lumbered off toward the smoking room, followed by the other gentlemen present.

As she was taking her leave later that night, Gilda Baker took Susannah aside. "I feel, as a woman, I must warn you about Terry Armstrong," she began, smoothing her shining dark hair. "He may be handsome, wealthy and charming beyond words, a veritable lion of Washington and New York society, but be careful. Your lanky Yankee may have you fooled. It's being speculated in some circles that he's a Rebel spy and . . ." her smile was fleeting ". . . that you may be one as well. Either that, or he's using you for his own ends, or that you are using and exploiting him."

"Land sakes, Miz Baker, that about covers everything but the truth!" Susannah feigned surprise in an exaggerated Carolina drawl which, she was learning, led some Yankees to think her giddy. "You cain't be raght about *my* own darlin' Terry." Seething inside, she nonetheless bid Mrs. Baker a sugary if abrupt, goodnight.

Terry was waiting for her upstairs, half-undressed, shirtless, shoeless, his black suspenders criss-crossing his splendidly muscled back, his trousers hugging his narrow hips.

"What's wrong, darlin'?" he asked as soon as she entered the room carrying on a silver tray a bottle of claret and two glasses.

"That woman . . ." she began.

"It meant nothing. To either of us, or at least not to me anyway. It was years ago." He looked hapless and helpless and chagrined. Susannah just looked straight at him, and fended him off when he came to take her in his arms. "Susannah, don't tell me you're jealous? Of her?"

"Oh, of course not. That's not what's bothering me," she lied. "Gilda said you're a Confederate spy, or that I am. People know."

"And you said?"

"Land sakes, or something equally silly, and then I said goodnight."

"Perfect. Nappy Baker is a thief—and a detective, ambitious in both roles. Set a thief to catch a thief, the War Department decided. Baker works with a Scotsman, Allen Pinkerton. They're always theorizing. Now . . . forget about them." He turned and walked away from Susannah as, with pleasure, she watched his long muscles move and shift under his smooth bronze-tan skin. When he faced her again, looking more serious than she had ever seen him before, he held an envelope in his right hand.

"Is that my mamma's script I recognize?" she asked, and reached out for it.

"Susannah, this is going to be the hardest part," Terry warned her, his eyes soft.

She held the sealed letter in her own hand while they drank a glass of wine. Then, bracing herself, she opened the envelope carefully so that it didn't rip or tear and then found she couldn't look hard at it the first time. She only glanced, skimming.

"Mamma thought I was leaving those letters to surprise her, to tell her we were expecting a baby, Terry. Now that I've 'gone north' I'm disowned and banished, and . . . Mamma's heart is crushed." Susannah felt tears welling up. "I'm not surprised, but . . . oh, Terry," she whispered, letting the tears slip, "she burned the second letter, the one she was supposed to save and read if anything happened to me, the letter that explained it all and . . . now she . . . they may never know . . . the truth."

"She'll know because you yourself are going to tell her when the time comes. I won't let anything happen to you, darlin'." Terry went to Susannah and scooped her up in his arms and she took comfort from his warmth and strength and silence.

He just held her, all night long, sheltering her

from the world, consoling her for the loss of love, for her separation from everyone on earth she most loved — except him.

In the morning at first light, she felt an immeasurable, heart-swelling desire for a different sort of touch from Terry, a hunger for his masterful, hard body claiming hers, for the taste of him, the sound of whispered love words in her ear, for the sublime power of the deep piston thrusts that could make her forget there was anything or anyone else in the world but the two of them, alone.

Just as he had known the night before, he knew in that blue summer dawn exactly what she needed and he gave her what she craved from him. He loved her then, feral-wild and strong with an abandon and mastery that was both pitiless and tender and she responded to his body, his greedy mouth and precise, possessive hands, loving him, grateful and forever indebted to him for the ecstasy he gave, that changed her immutably, then and there and for all time.

Terry's all-encompassing kindness inflamed a new greater love in Susannah, and she granted herself leave then to really *need* him, to yield more, in every way — heart, body and soul, and he made her his own, again and again and forever.

Their reckless generosity brought them to a peak of passion that indelibly stamped their fate together, that branded his heart and tested the heights and depths of Susannah's love. Susannah could not say enough, do enough, give enough and, giving all, she yearned to bestow greater gifts of blissful licentiousness and shining love.

Only weeks later, she held the memory of that time as the dearest thing she owned, when it came to seem there would not ever be another time like it for Susannah, not with Terry or any man.

"I have a job for you to do today, darlin'. You'll feel a bit less troubled and grieving about Catherine when you've done something more for the Confederate cause than take notes and sketch." Terry said this to Susannah over slow, sweet cups of coffee, after the girls had left the breakfast table and gone off on their own pursuits. "You're going to cross the Long Bridge over the Potomac and take a message to Fairfax for General Beauregard."

Chapter Twenty-five

In mid-morning on July nineteenth, Susannah and Venetia set out on a drive in a light, two-wheeled runabout, a sprightly gig, pulled by a vain and pretty dappled gray mare. They were the very picture of two sisters on their way to grandmother's house, with a basket of goodies, which was exactly what they were pretending to be. Their "grandma" lived on the far side of the river, south of the Union lines, through which they had to pass to reach Confederate territory.

"I can't let you by, ladies," a sergeant protested when they reined up at his outpost on the border road.

"His Irish brogue is thick as clotted cream," Susannah said softly to Venetia. "He's not young and probably not inclined to put up with frivolity." Just as she had been instructed by her father, Venetia gave a crestfallen look. Susannah sighed volubly. Both, like simple country girls,

289

were plainly dressed in dark cotton frocks, high-laced shoes and unadorned poke bonnets. Susannah's hair was coiled up out of sight, Venetia's done in neat braids. They were the picture of pink-cheeked innocence faced with despair.

"Oh sergeant," Susannah said, "this war is already doing dreadful harm. Our old grannie is a woman well advanced in years, not in good health, and she dotes on our monthly visits. We're all she has, now that our brother . . ." Susannah pulled a handkerchief out of her sleeve. ". . . has gone for a soldier. Think if your granny was Mary Kate O'Dwyer down there waiting . . . wondering."

"Sir, Granny has the rheumatism bad. Have we come all the way from Pennsylvania, only to be stopped here, in sight of her cottage?" Venetia said sadly. They both were speaking with a Pennsylvania intonation, to hide their southern accents, and with this man, at least, their efforts seemed to be working.

"Sorry, missies. I have me orders," he answered setting his jaw but also looking off down the road. "Which cottage you mean?"

"You can just see the roof from here," Venetia pointed. There was a wisp of smoke rising from a distant chimney. Close by, someone was whistling "Yankee Doodle."

"It's dangerous, ladies. There are troop movements under way. Rules are rules." He crossed his arms over his chest, looking more like a bulldog every moment.

"Perhaps you could find it in your heart to take a basket of things to Mrs. O'Dwyer? Sugar cakes, meat pies, a few bottles of stout. You could tell her . . . oh, sergeant couldn't you make just this one exception? We shan't stay long." Susannah could see his eyes begin to shift and he shuffled his large feet.

"Stout? How many bottles of stout?" he asked, squinting down his broad nose at them as other men gathered to watch the disturbance.

"Why, is this not the valiant Sixty-ninth New York Brigade?" Susannah inquired, knowing precisely who they were. She had been well primed by Terry and besides, their emerald colors were flying. "Are you the very men who stood up for Ireland against the Prince of Wales when that dubious monarch visited your city?" The sergeant was nodding but not yet smiling.

"Tommy Corcoran refused to let us parade our colors in *that* one's honor. They were going to court-martial our Tommy but then this war come about and they pardoned him so he could lead us into battle against Dixie."

"Where is your Colonel Corcoran? It would be an honor to meet such a man. Please Sergeant, bring me to him, I beg of you. *He* would not deny Mary Kate O'Dwyer the comfort of her only living kin. *He* would not keep us from the poor old woman's house and hearth." The other men began to mutter at the sergeant, and to laugh and shout out imprecations.

"Go on, Michael, look the other way!"

"These ain't the enemy, man!"

"I'll go wid 'em, see they don't make no trouble . . . Okay, Mike?" There was a laugh all round at that remark and then, the men snapped to attention.

"Sergeant Dempsey! What have we here?" a mounted officer demanded as he drew up beside ladies' gig. He was a weary looking man with a very narrow face and long mustaches drooping nearly to his chin.

"Sir! This lady is an admirer of yours. She asks for the pleasure of making your acquaintance, sir!"

"Are you no other than *the* Colonel Tommy Corcoran himself?" Susannah smiled.

"My pleasure. Drive all the way out here, did you, to the end of the Aqueduct to see me?" Corcoran asked mildly.

"They come to see their old grandmother, sir, Mary Kate O'Dwyer whose chimney you can see just yonder. They come from Pennsylvania." The sergeant had become their champion.

"Not in that little rig they did not." Corcoran looked them over.

"We borrowed it in the city, Colonel," Venetia explained. "Our surrey lost a wheel." Susannah

292

was pleased with the girl's performance and presence of mind.

"And, from who did you borrow it, may I make so bold as to inquire?" Corcoran, less suspicious, asked the child.

"From Mrs. Baker, Mrs. Napoleon Baker. Do you know her, Colonel?" Susannah responded. He nodded.

"I know her, and her husband and her dappled gray mare as well. I'll give you a two hour pass *and* an escort. Sergeant Dempsey, you go with them."

"I think the sergeant needs help, Colonel Corcoran."

"Well, do you now? I suppose you'd like me to give you the job, Private Quinlivin, instead of sending Mr. Dempsey?"

"Yes, sir," the boy answered, grinning right at Venetia. He may have been all of seventeen, with dark hair and very fair skin. His uniform was too large and his cap askew but there was a scapegrace, skinny charm about him, like an eight-month old kitten on his way to becoming a fighting tomcat.

Both men rode escort, Dempsey and Quinlivin, mounted on rather good cavalry horses. Susannah left Venetia outside the cottage, settled under a tree, chatting happily with her two protectors. She herself disappeared inside the small house where a riding costume was laid out, ready and waiting. She tore off her modest dress, kicked off the high shoes which seemed to take an eternity to unlace, then let her hair flow free. From its coils tumbled a tiny velvet pouch containing a map and two dispatches, both in code, one addressed to President Davis, the other to General Beauregard. These she concealed in her bosom where her diary key, which she had left behind in the event of capture, was usually hidden. She slipped out a rear window and, crouching, made her way to the barn out back where an extraordinary Virginia thoroughbred waited, ready and saddled.

"Granny?" Susannah whispered. "Mary Kate! Where are you?"

"You just go on now," ordered the tall, stick-thin, ancient woman with a grizzled hair on her prominent chin. She had tottered out of the shadows and took Susannah's soft hand in her scaly and wrinkled hand. "May the road rise to meet you, dearie," she whispered. "Oh, and pleased to meet you I'm sure."

"Dempsey fell asleep in the sun after drinking a bottle of stout," Venetia later told Susannah, "and Tommy Quinlivin was too polite to invite himself along when I went inside to visit. Mary Kate was nice, she gave me buttermilk and I took some out to Tommy. She may be all right as someone else's granny, but I'm glad she's not mine." The girl was flushed with the excitement of the adventure, and something more her companion couldn't help but notice. "Well, *tell* all, Susannah!" she insisted.

"I rode like the very devil for Fairfax, and back, to make the time limit. I gave the dispatches to a Major who is to pass them along."

"You *were* late by twenty-five minutes, but Susannah, I could hardly believe my eyes when you came out of the cottage. I wondered if you'd really been gone, you looked so calm. Even the buttons on your dress were done up just as they were, the second one half-undone and your bonnet was at the exact same angle as when you went in! *Now* can you hint at what was in the dispatches?"

"Your father's description of the Union Army in the field, which he went out to visit. Suffice it to say that fortifications are poor and Brigadier-General McDowell has yet to secure a really accurate map of Virginia. However, along with the dispatches was a diagram showing the route of the Union advance to Manassas. This first real battle of the war that's now brewing well may be the last. Oh, I *wish* I was in Dixie, darlin'. Now, you tell all. What's *your* report? I just know you have one."

"Tommy Quinlivin is a three-month volunteer, like most of the Sixty Ninth. They all have put in their time already and want to go home. Not Tommy. He wants to fight. He's coming to find me, soon's the war is over. I don't know how he ever will. He thinks I live in Pennsylvania."

"And?" Susannah prompted.

"That's all," Venetia said, looking down and Susannah, not wanting to pry, asked no more questions on the subject.

Terry greeted them with warm delight and relief and gave them great bear hugs and kisses when they arrived at the house on Lafayette Square. He had been waiting on the parlor window seat with Baby Saidee in his lap, the two counting passing carriages.

"I shouldn't have let you go," he told Susannah, looking into her eyes. She saw the worry and relief in his eyes. "I can't . . . take it, worrying over you two."

"It went perfectly, love," she smiled, beginning to feel the tension now that the job was done.

"She never turned an eyelash, Pa," Venetia reported. "Susannah is *so* composed."

"And my accomplice is a superb little actress with a good head on her shoulders. We're a team, aren't we, Venetia?" Susannah asked, hugging the girl. "Tell us, Saidee my dove, what happened here while we were gone?"

"While you were gone, we watched men putting wire up every place." There had for days been huge rolls of insulated wire parked all over the city streets.

"The new telegraph," Terry smiled at Saidee, his head resting on her golden curls, "will connect the War Department with the Navy Yard and the Arsenal."

Venetia nodded. "They even are running the wires across the bridges into Virginia, Pa."

"And the cattle for feeding the troops? The ones grazing around that place half-built?" Saidee asked, perking with excitement. "They all fell into the Canal and some of them drowned before they were driven out again. Pa and me went to watch and Pa helped!" Saidee was describing the beef herd put to pasture around the unfinished stump of what would be the Washington Monument.

"There was more excitement at home than where we were, it seems," Susannah laughed as the girls went off to the kitchen. Once they were alone, she and Terry came together and into each other's arms. He crushed her to him and took her mouth. She clung to him, and her arms went about him and the fit was perfect.

"I gave the dispatches to Major Jenks," she said. Terry poured her a glass of sherry. "On the way to "grandma's" we passed neat little villages of army tents. Cook fires were burning, men were singing, strumming banjos, talking together

297

all so peaceful and . . . I had a premonition of something . . . terrible coming for us. And Terry, I saw Beverly Bland in Fairfax. He's a sleuth, too, now, I learned, probably because it's a safer job than standing up to face the enemy."

"If he ever falls into the hands of Napoleon Baker, he'll wish he had faced the 'Swamp Angel' cannon straight on. Did he see you too, darlin'?"

She nodded. "He told me . . ." Susannah hesitated. She took a big swallow of sherry that was warm and lovely going down. Then, her whiskey courage up, she blurted out, fast, "Well, he said that no matter what everyone else in the Confederate spy service supposes, you are really a two-timing Yankee bastard. They are keeping you dawdling about here in Washington so you can easily cross the lines on the pretense of delivering information to the South and then take note of Confederate fortifications and such."

"Did you believe him?" Terry asked, looking hard at Susannah. His hand, that was raising a glass to his lips, stopping short of its destination.

"No. But . . ."

"Ah. There *is* a 'but,' a doubt in your mind. Speak it, Susannah, now." He drained his glass of whiskey. Sherry never was his kind of drink.

"They already had most of the information I risked my life to deliver."

"Most is not all, is it? " His face had gone dark, with what she thought was anger.

"I'm sorry. Terry, I'm sorry. I never really doubted you, only . . . Forgive me? It's been a trying day."

"Forgive you for what? For using your head instead of your heart?" he said in a rough, low voice and then, she knew that what she saw in his eyes wasn't anger. It was pain. She had hurt him, and she felt horrible. She flew to him and kissed him — his eyes and brow and lips and throat.

"Bland said something else, love," she whispered. "He said Simeon was in an advance Confederate company. My little brother will be among the first to face the enemy. When's it to begin, Terry?"

"In a way, it has begun. Because of your dispatches, and some others, the Confederate Army will fall back from Fairfax tonight, to regroup and wait for more divisions to bring their numbers up to Yankee strength. The Union brigades are advancing as if on their way to a clambake, one newsman told me. You can't get a hack for hire or a saddle horse, not even a mule in all of Washington tonight because parties of civilians, on horseback and in carriages, are following along to see the fight and watch the Rebels run for Richmond."

"So," Susannah said as they mounted the stairs, "the Civil War, it seems, is going to be a gay holiday outing and we are all invited to the festivities." A steaming tub, to which she had been looking forward for hours, was waiting for her. Terry helped her out of her clothes and she sank appreciatively into the soothing hot water.

"Tomorrow, when we join the crowd of onlookers, I expect we'll see something very different than they're expecting to see," he frowned.

They sat up late that night, curled together on the window seat. Later, the moon blazed bright through the mosquito netting around their bed. Tired as Susannah was, it took a long, long time for sleep to find her.

Chapter Twenty-six

There was not a decent saddle horse left in town by the time Susannah and Terry left Washington City. The day before, the European cooks at Willard's Hotel were inundated with orders for picnic hampers, to be taken out to Virginia by observers of the war.

When Terry and Susannah reached the hill at Centerville in mid-afternoon, a few people, were already leaving for home, certain of a Yankee victory, misinformation they carried back to Washington. Carriages were lined up as at a race, some ladies observing the action through mother-of-pearl opera glasses. Dust rose through the air, along with the sound of firing rifles and the shouts of men. Susannah was sick with worry and she felt even worse when Terry announced he was going to the field.

"I just cannot not sit here and watch like a damn bump on a log when men are risking their lives. Darlin' you told me yourself no fiery woman of

South Carolina would tolerate a coward for a . . . husband and I am going to be yours, come hell or high water." He winked and kissed her quick. "I'll be okay because you love me, I swear it," he added as she almost wished she could take back her words about southern belles and cowardly lovers, but of course, she could not and never would.

"Terry, it's impossible for a tried and true actual Southern woman to respect a coward who is a disgrace to his manhood and his name but I wish . . . I wish I could be like Daisy Ballard and be above all this fervor and passion and romantic southern chivalry but . . ."

"I'm not in love with the scholarly, untouchable Miss Ballard. It's you, my proud, wild southern beauty, who's got my heart."

"I know which side you'll be fighting for, but what uniform will you wear? Yankee blue will be safer to start out in," Susannah said, knowing full well Terry would be donning Confederate gray.

And so, hard as it was to fathom, loving that man as she did, Susannah let him go. It was impossible for the patriot in her to even try to hold him back.

She let him go and for hours did not leave the place at which they parted, afraid he'd not be able to find her if he needed her.

The fighting went on, and on. Quite late, when the battle began to shift and she could neither see nor hear much, and was undecided about what to do or where to turn, she caught sight of a slight

302

figure in tattered, grimy Union blue. He wasn't cowering exactly, but crouching against a large tree.

"Jimmy Quinlivin!" she called out, "if you're going to disgrace your damn uniform, take it off — right now!" Susannah walked toward him, brandishing her buggy whip.

"Colonel Corcoran's gone missing or taken prisoner!" the boy cried out on recognizing her. "The men are scattered. I told your Venetia I'd fight for her, and not run . . . but . . ." The boy was close to tears and Susannah's heart was close to breaking. He could have been her little brother. Simeon might be lying dead right then, or wounded, on some Virginia field. And then another cold hand of fear gripped her throat. Terry, too, might be down there, calling out for her. She hugged Jimmy close to her. When she spoke again, her voice was a hoarse whisper.

"Give me your uniform, Jimmy, *please*," she asked.

"Wait exactly right here for me, understand?" she ordered, leaving him in his skivvies as she unhitched one of the pair of her bay carriage horses and mounted, bare back, astride.

Reckless as she was, driven on by love, she had no fear in her bosom, though she was bound for the Confederate line wearing Jimmy's Yankee blue uniform.

Her mount was shot out from under her almost at once and then she crawled forward on her belly,

303

with dust in her face, feeling small, fully perceiving for the first time the vulnerability of a mere human body as the musket balls flew about her, pinging against tree limbs above, sending down showers of splinters. When she raised her head she saw cannon balls hopping through a field, like rabbits.

When she came to a small, apparently deserted, orchard where the grass had grown tall, she stopped to rest. Lying flat on her back, arms outstretched, her right hand touched something, a firm apple, newly fallen. Lying flat, biting into it, letting the juice drip down her face, Susannah thought no food or drink had ever before pleased her so as that crisp tart apple. The crunch of the first bite, the feel of the firm flesh of the fruit on her tongue convinced her she was alive, and wanted to be, for a long time to come.

"Them Billy Yanks is all dead men, not one of 'em even moanin' or lamentin'," she heard someone say in a familiar, welcome drawl. As she scrambled to her feet she heard the sound of many pistols being cocked, and then, she saw she was surrounded by a dozen soldiers all taking a bead on *her,* and the bodies of two dozen more, strewn all about the orchard.

"Dear Lord, I hope never to behold such a sight again," Susannah whispered. "Don't shoot me!" she called out. "I'm for the South . . . from the South . . . *South* Carolina." She found herself confronting a Virginia regiment of backwoods boys who promised, as they guided her back close

304

to the Yankee line, they would keep a lookout for her husband and her baby brother.

Amazingly, Susannah found Jimmy Quinlivin precisely where she had left him and they made their silent way back to Washington together. They did not reach the Long Bridge until nearly midnight. They were both still silent, stunned by all they had seen that day,

Passionately as she believed in the Confederacy, Susannah's heart ached for those "damn Yankees," as they *ran* in terror amidst the crush of fleeing, and wrecked carriages, panicked horses and horrified civilians. Susannah relinquished her carriage, now drawn by only one horse to carry the wounded, but other spectators, enraged at what they took to be the cowardice of the military men, purposely blocked the roads to slow the retreat. Several politicians, in their linen summer afternoon coats were taken prisoner by Rebels and forced to shiver through the night in open fields or dank barns, as the temperature dropped drastically.

Back in Washington, one and all were castigating the volunteer officers and disparaging the dedication of the three-months men. When Susannah and Jimmy got to the streets of the city, by hitching a ride with a racing teamster, they were filled with people awaiting news of the battle's outcome. Even as the air grew chill and a steady rain began to fall, the crowds swelled through the night, many people standing outside Willard's, taking comfort from the glare of lights. Susannah herself saw more than one high-ranking officer gallop up, dismount on the run and dash inside for the consolation of a glass or two or three of whiskey.

And then, in the dreary dawn, the grimy, defeated Army, the fighting men themselves, footsore and straggling, came stumbling like zombies through the mud and rain, hardly a company in proper military order. Officers arrived asleep on horseback and men fell, slumped against curbstones and doorways, exhausted.

"Soldier, can we buy you a drink?" Jimmy asked as he tackled a large figure, pale and bleary-eyed with exhaustion, none other than Sergeant Joe Dempsey.

"This city is doomed, doomed! The Rebs are hot on us. Laddy, I am making straight for the railway station and you best come with me. My three month is up and God bless me, I've had war enough to last me the rest of me life."

Susannah asked the weeping sergeant home for breakfast and a bath, and as he and Jimmy, who was near collapse, were both gratefully accepting her invitation, Confederate prisoners marched by on their way to incarceration in the Old Capitol Prison. Her gallant southern boys, to Susannah's fury, were being spat upon, assailed with mud clods and taunts and angry curses and she froze, unable to move. She already knew that she was not the only Southern sympathizer in Washington, but as she stood looking at the boys in gray, hoping against hope to see Terry or Simeon, someone in the surrounding crowd shouted out a cheer for Dixie. She was thrilled, and when the fellow was chased down the street by a pack of Union soldiers with drawn guns, it was only Dempsey's grasp on her arm that kept her from going to her hero's defense. It was fortunate because before she dashed off, one of the Rebels called out to her.

"Miz Butler! Ah, Miz Butler, your brother has fallen at Bull Run Creek!" She broke free of Dempsey then ran to follow the cheerless group of prisoners, recognizing a school friend of Simeon's among them, Cyrus Etheridge.

"Fell? Fell . . . killed or . . . wounded?" she implored, but the boy wasn't sure, and begged her forgiveness for his ignorance. "Don't worry, don't worry Cyrus," she said, pressing a fistful of dollars, enfolded in a scented lace handkerchief, into his hand. "Greenbacks. Always useful," she told him. "I'll try to visit you later. Be strong now," she called as he was hauled off by one of the marines guarding the prisoners.

"I'm going now," she told her two escorts, "to find my brother alive or . . ."

"Not again, you ain't goin' to that bloody damn war! You was there once already today and what good did it do you?" Jimmy exclaimed. "Don't let her sergeant. She was almost kilt already today."

"I'll be taking you home now, Mrs. Armstrong.

Then I'll be going off to learn what I can about
. . . your men. One's a Yank and one's Reb, that
it?" Susannah nodded. What else *could* she do, she
wondered?

"Have a care, Mr. Dempsey," she told him as he
mounted up. "And . . . thank you." She had given
him a good meal and a stiff drink, but even though
he'd had no sleep after thirty-six hours on the
march, he insisted on riding out. "Have a care" was
not all Susannah wanted to say to the big man, but
it was all that she could manage at the time. She
had it in her mind to say that civilized people
ought not go around killing each other, that there
must be some better way, but she just watched him
round the corner and stood looking after him, at
the fog that swirled where he had been moments
before.

Soldiers, wandering the streets, begged for food
and drink all the next day and the women of Washington stood in the rain handing out sandwiches
and coffee, Susannah among them.

"I'm going to kill me some Rebs," she had heard
a bald-faced boy brag the morning before as he
had loped past her house with his comrades,
headed for the battle.

"God is for the right, for the Union," said another, who had worn a distinctive emblem, a blue
silk scarf embellished with red roses, the gift of his
lady, no doubt, tied about his brow.

Susannah recognized that soldier again when, in

308

the early afternoon the day after the Union defeat, he was wheeled through the city right past her, his face wrapped in a bloody handkerchief of the same crimson shade as the red roses still encircling his brow.

Late one night soon after, she was awakened from a dream, half-asleep, lonely in her bed. There was a single thud of the brass door knocker. Sure that it was Terry coming home to her, she raced downstairs without a wrapper, just in her nightgown, a candle held high in her hand. Grace and the children were right behind her when she tore open the door to find . . . no one.

When a figure in uniform emerged from the fog a few feet away and came trudging toward her, she thought she was seeing a specter, but then it spoke her name.

"I had to be sure it was . . . safe . . . it was really you," the man said haltingly.

"Good God, Will Chauvenet, how badly are you hurt?" she asked.

"Oh, fair to middling," he said before his eyes rolled up and he crumpled at her feet.

Two days later, Will was recovered enough from a bone-shattering shoulder wound to sit up in bed. He was able swallow some crackers, crushed to crumbs and mixed with wine, whiskey, brown sugar and water, which was what the doctor ordered as a tonic for a wounded man weak from loss of blood.

"I was dispatched west to take charge of naval operations on the Mississippi River. I couldn't help joining the fight at Bull Run," Will told Susannah and she told him that sounded like someone else she knew. Will wanted to get on his way at once. She would allow him to do no such thing.

Leaving Will and the children in Grace's care, and sending Dempsey and Quinlivin back to their regiment, Susannah went the very next day to the Washington Infirmary to volunteer to nurse the wounded, Yanks or Rebs, she didn't care, but she was not greeted with open arms. Instead, she was sent off to be approved by the chief nurse, the daunting Miss Dorothea Dix.

A fierce New England woman she had done good works in the prisons and mad houses of Massachusetts before coming to Washington to offer her know-how to the Union. She was made Superintendent of Nursing and given the authority to accept or reject any volunteer as she saw fit. Miss Dix interviewed each and every one herself. Conscientious though she was, she was also arbitrary, opinionated, severe and capricious, and her requirements were stringent. One had to be able to read, write and cook, be of the highest moral character, plain in dress and — preferably devoid of any physical attraction. *That* almost became Susannah's stumbling block.

Miss Dix turned away many volunteers and

310

would have certainly have rejected Mrs. Armstrong if the beautiful volunteer had not been forewarned. Susannah arrived at the nursing administrator's office for scrutiny in her plain dark, shapeless country frock, her hair hidden beneath a bonnet and with thick-lensed wire rimmed spectacles on her nose which, she hoped, would somewhat dull the color of her eyes.

"Remove your glasses, please Miss . . ." Dorothea Dix studied a sheet of paper on her desk, on which Susannah had written a description of herself. She looked up and asked, *"Mrs.* Armstrong? Where's your husband? Has he given his permission for you to work among unclothed men?"

"I don't know where he is, ma'am," Susannah answered. "I do know he would . . . support me in my resolution to be of use."

Mrs. Dix glared.

"Good grief, you sound like a Southerner, *and* a Suffragette," she almost snarled.

"Yes, ma'am," Susannah said, trying not to show her own annoyance as the woman peered critically at her. "My interests in the Suffragette movement, in politics and teaching, are not the usual preoccupations of southern womanhood, but mine nonetheless."

"Please stand up," Miss Dix ordered with such authority that, angry as Susannah now was, and sure of being turned away, she sprang to her feet and stood at attention.

311

"You are too pretty for this work, Mrs. Armstrong," she declared.

"I can't help that, can I?" Susannah, exasperated, demanded. "It's not fair of you to use that as a reason to prevent me from . . ."

"But," the great Dix trumpeted, "you are also self-contained, outspoken and write a neat, clear hand. And you're quick. You can be my assistant."

"I want to work with the wounded and ill, Miss Dix," Susannah answered.

"You're looking for your husband is what you mean, isn't it?" The women removed their spectacles and glowered at each other. Miss Dix sat back in her chair. "Florence Nightingale has written that nursing is a noble profession," she said, "for those unable to wield a weapon in the field. Nursing is *not* a vocation to take up for political purposes — to prove women's 'rights' — or for other petty personal reasons. Sit down, Mrs. Armstrong."

"I'm a defector from the land of Southern Chivalry and slavery. My husband and brother are missing. I am disowned and have lost forever the comfort of my parents' love. I know what it means to be lonely. I wish to give what care and comfort I can to brave boys far from home, most of them for the first time probably, I think. Of *course,* I have some personal reasons for volunteering but I'm sure you do too, Miss Dix."

Susannah was given a choice. She could work with Hannah Ropes, a head nurse in one of the city

312

hospitals, or with Clara Barton, who went out to serve in the camps and bivouacs.

"Clara *was* horribly, painfully shy. She has had several nervous attacks, total mental collapses, which incapacitated her for months on end. But, like you, Mrs. Armstrong, she writes a beautiful hand and was given a position in the Patent Office here in our nation's capital. The quiet mousey little clerk from New England met the Sixth Massachusetts at the train depot when they arrived in April—and her whole life changed."

"That happens," Susannah offered. Miss Dix frowned.

"Next day, when the men were quartered in the Senate chamber, Clara brought them thread, needles, handkerchiefs and other small necessities of life, and she read aloud to them from the *Worcester Spy*, a Massachusetts newspaper. Now, she advertises for supplies of all kinds in the *Spy*. Boxes are streaming into the city. Clara somehow sidestepped the usual regulations and her own timidity, and managed to secure a wagon and driver to take her to the fighting. At Bull Run she fed and nursed the wounded with preserves and coffee and bread soaked in wine. You, Mrs Armstrong, are hired. I think it's your willful streak that won me over."

"Thank you, Miss Dix," Susannah smiled upon leaving, probably a mistake, she realized. She had good teeth. "Oh . . . I think we both know that I *could,* if I chose to, wield a weapon in the field and likely, so could you."

313

Because of the children, she decided to work close to home, with Hannah Ropes, another of those courageous New England biddies of remarkable character, a woman who described herself as "a homely hen with wings of an eagle."

Chapter Twenty-seven

The first thing Susannah saw on setting her slim booted foot in Union Hospital at Georgetown, was Mr. Vincent Collier, who had been dispatched by the YMCA, to pass out bibles and tracts to soldiers and others in need of comfort or redemption. He was sorely needed in Washington, inundated as it was with both categories of persons. Just inside the entry way of Union hospital, Mr. Collier was kneeling in prayer beside a mortally injured man and Susannah felt an impulse to turn and run, thinking she might find Terry or Simeon, or both, requiring Mr. Collier's final ministrations.

But of course, she would not, could not flee, especially not after she raised her eyes and looked beyond her nose. The sight of other injured men and boys who still could benefit from *her* sort of help touched her heart.

The Union Hospital, an old Georgetown hotel, was a sorry structure of narrow hallways, small windows and decaying woodwork. These undesirable quarters made so inadequate a hospital, few officers of either side were sent there, only enlisted men — Yankees and Rebel prisoners. She would not be likely to find Terry at the Union, Susannah knew, but she might come upon her brother who had joined up as a private soldier.

Many patrician Southern gentlemen, the natural officer class, it was believed, went into the ranks to fight beside their trusted friends and equals. Better to be a private among blue bloods than a captain of rustics, was their thinking.

Matron Hannah Ropes, a woman of deep maternal tenderness, was in charge of nurses at the Union Hospital. She greeted her new attendant hurriedly but gratefully, and offered to make inquiries of other nurses and doctors in the Washington area, about Mrs. Armstrong's husband and brother.

"Think of all our patients as your brothers, Mrs. Armstrong, as I think of them as my sons, and you will do inestimable good with a smiling face and a gentle hand. Many of our men, particularly those from Maine and Michigan, have succumbed to the climate, not to their wounds. It's hot as blazes for them in this fetid city, and I needn't tell you the place is humming with mosquitos. In this damp, we are all perpetually drenched and wiping our brows, but I know you'll do your best. Welcome to the Union Hospital." With that, Matron Ropes set Susannah to changing dressings. "Read this, at your leisure, of course," the matron said with gentle sarcasm, slipping a book into Susannah's pocket, Florence Nightingale's *Notes on Nursing: What it Is and What it Is Not*. The novice nurse did read the book, at home, lonely in her bed, on the nights when sleep eluded her despite her bone-aching weariness.

Susannah learned from Miss Nightingale, who had done noble service during the Crimean War, that, though every woman is at times a nurse, no one could learn the art and craft and skill from merely a book, only from practice in hospital wards. And even there, all one could really do, was aid in the process of healing by keeping the air fresh, the linens clean and the patient in the best condition for nature to act. Susannah tried. And she learned.

With husband and brother ever on her mind, she went about her duties from six in the morning until well past gaslight. Her work day began with building fires and adding blankets in some wards, throwing windows wide open for the fresh air that Miss Nightingale, who had never been to Washington in summer, insisted was so important to the recovery of health and strength. The nurses had to cajole and joke and tease to get some of "our big babies" as Susannah's co-worker, Miss Alcott, called them, to eat army bread and drink muddy coffee, and to get others washed and freshened and smiling even a little.

Dr. Hargrove Haight, a surgeon of small skill and great talk, was Hannah Ropes' nemesis, Susannah soon learned. He was indifferent to pain, belittled the value of the matron's kindness to the patients' cure, and performed more surgery than was necessary. A poor private with harrowing wounds fascinated Dr. Haight, while an officer with a mere scratch did not. Though he never had a merciful word for any ordinary soldier, Haight's manner was servile with the occasional officer who came to the Union Hospital in error and was soon transferred to a better facility. And as for the nurses, the doctor thought they were all his fair prey and in addition to their other chores—they all, no matter how well they fit Miss Dix's criteria for plainness—had to constantly fend off his advances. His crass and self-centered behavior only emphasized the sacrifice and courage of the brave fighting men in Susannah's care.

The first time one of her patients, a man she nursed for some time, departed this life, she was bereft. Able Ross had lain for more than two weeks, among many other men, in what had been the hotel ballroom in happier days.

"Thank you, Miss," Able Ross said to Susannah one day, his chest swelling with labored breath. "I . . . must be marching on." Those were his last words, and she was shattered. Matron Ropes and Miss Alcott tried to comfort her with not much success.

"He went with manly dignity," Louisa said. "For the good of the others here, *you* must say Godspeed to Able now. Let the empty tenement of this

318

finest of soldiers be taken away from here now."

"Until the end, he was never capable of uttering more than one word at a time," Susannah said, "and he tried so *hard* to tell me . . . something. He gripped my wrist not two hours ago and now, he is gone."

"The angels came and took him," Matron added, "and you, Susannah have worked hand in hand with them. Now, Able is in their charge. Take that comfort at least."

Beneath his pillow was a much folded and smudged pastel sketch, a likeness, of his wife and two small children. Susannah cut a lock of his hair to send home to them and went off and wept, privately.

That same night, late, on her way home from the hospital, a woman followed Susannah's carriage from the corner of Lafayette Square to the house.

"Miss Butler, Miss Butler, if you be her, give me a moment, please!" the woman said as Susannah placed a hand on the front gate. The girl, not twenty years old, was shaken by a cough and a tight, gasping sound and in the lantern light Susannah saw that she had the oddly beautiful glow of the consumptive. The illness had a bizarre effect on its fading victims. Some became, for a time, ravishingly lovely, dissolute, even wanton. This woman's eyes were glazed, her cheeks flushed with fever. She shivered and pulled a cheap cloak of thin

319

shoddy about her shoulders. She seemed about to collapse and Susannah took her arm to support her, waiting.

"My name is Maggie Crandell," the girl said as if expecting it to mean something to Susannah and it did stir an elusive echo in Susannah's mind, one she could not grasp. "Your father was most kind to my mother, and me, though . . ."

"Yes, yes! When was that?" Susannah asked eagerly, impatient for news of home. Most of the letters she had sent to her mother on the truce boats that traveled between Washington and Dixie came back unopened, and she hoped this woman was bringing her news from Charleston. "Are they . . . safe and well at home? Has Father returned from abroad?"

"I've had nothing to do with Captain Butler since I was born. I don't even remember him."

"Commodore Butler. He's been a Commodore for some time," Susannah pointlessly corrected the child, just out of habit. She had no use for such information.

"You see, my mother, Margaret, was left destitute when my father died at sea aboard the *Somes.* I never knew my father or yours, Miss Butler." Miss Crandell swayed on her feet and Susannah remembered who she — or rather, who her mother — was.

"Come in, do please," she invited and they were met in the vestibule by Venetia who saw to their guest while Susannah removed her gloves and bon-

320

net. She ordered a light supper to be served and went to the parlor, where a fire had been lit despite the heat of Washington in August. Maggie Crandell was shaking with fever and Susannah settled her on a divan among soft feather pillows and draped a shawl over her. When she removed the girl's boots, she saw the soles were worn to holes.

As the cook brought a tray, Susannah dropped wearily into an armchair, ready to hear Maggie's tale of woe which, from the look of the girl she knew the story would be, when she heard a sound at the gate at the unlikely hour of eleven. Her heart began to thunder as she raced out of the room with a gasp of hope to throw open the door to — Jimmy Quinlivin.

"Sorry I ain't someone else," he shrugged, and trembling, she hugged him before leading him to the parlor.

Maggie had fallen into a restless doze and Venetia greeted Jimmy, who had become her first persistent admirer, with her fingers to her lips, a gesture she had unknowingly taken from Susannah.

"Who is that lovely girl?" Jimmy whispered, and Venetia's brow lifted.

"That's Maggie Crandell," Susannah told him. "Her father sailed on the maiden voyage of the training brig *Somes* years and years ago. Her mother became acquainted then, with *my* father. In a way, Robert Crandell is as much to be credited as Stephen Butler for the founding of the Naval

Academy. Maggie Crandell, sleeping there, paid a high price for the school."

"How could she, Mrs. Armstrong? She's young, hardly older than me," Jimmy said.

"Because in those days, when there was no navy academy, officers were trained in 'the school of the ship,' in working vessels. Boys aboard studied the mathematics and literature besides seamanship. The teaching of academics, what there was of it, was left to a schoolmaster hired aboard, often one who was poorly suited for the job, a nere-do-well running away from something or someone ashore. Working officers, who attended to running the ship, had little time for the boys, raw recruits, who got in the way more than anything else. Back then, too, grog was still doled out aboard all ships, military and merchantmen, to all hands, old salts and youngsters alike.

"There was clamor from Temperance workers, starting in the early 1840s. They objected to youngsters training in such unsavory surroundings and, moreover, receiving alcoholic spirits besides. So, the *Somes* was built. She was a tiny ship good for nothing but training officers and apprentice seamen, such as Maggie's father. The *Somes* was a poor ship, a toy, shallow of draft, slender of hull, a design experiment that failed. She was fancy, low and fast and too small for the hundred odd men who sailed in her on the first cruise. She was also unusually difficult to handle. At the best, sailing is always dangerous work. Sails are wild and massive,

322

anchors are heavy, the behavior of cable and chain unpredictable. And of course, there's sea and wind.

"A horrible episode occurred aboard the *Somes*. A ghastly crime perpetrated on the foredeck led to the founding of Navy School that was—is—run, like West Point, by the government."

"What happened on the *Somes?*" Venetia asked, almost as if she didn't really want to know.

"Murder," Susannah answered. "Of three crewmen by the captain. His insane justification was mutiny. The three men—boys—were hung for mutiny and plotting piracy. One of them was Maggie's young father. Another, a bad boy but certainly no pirate or mutineer, was Philip Spencer, a son of the United State Secretary of War then, John Canfield Spencer."

Venetia gasped and clapped her hand to her mouth.

"How old were they?" she asked, all agog.

"Seventeen and eighteen. It still makes my blood boil, my feelings are so strong on the subject," Susannah proclaimed.

"Strong? Oh, yes, I recall . . ." Maggie roused herself long enough to take a sip of soup and then was out again. Susannah decided she must be put to bed—at once. Grace went to prepare the guest room before going to fetch the doctor.

"Well, after that . . . outrage, my papa, Commodore Butler, and Commander Franklin Buchanan, were charged with inspiring midshipmen with the ideals of honor, patriotism and rectitude, and with the sea savvy required of men staffing a good navy. Mr Chauvenet upstairs taught academics, his strong suit."

"Will's pretty smart, I have to say," Jimmy told us. "He said he'd give me schooling, after the war."

"You're lucky. Will is a *brilliant* teacher. He'd done so well coaching senior midshipmen for their lieutenant's exam they wanted him at the Annapolis Naval School."

"What did Spencer do to get himself and two others hanged?" Grace asked, returning to the parlor. "The Doc's on his way," she reported.

"It was said Philip Spencer was a difficult child. He was slovenly. He drank to excess and always had a big cigar in his teeth. Most offensive to his elders, he would take orders from no one. He had twice been thrown out of the navy before his father sent the boy to sea again, for his own good, on the *Somes*. Spencer was a misfit there just as everywhere, an officer-candidate who took up with enlisted men, an unforgivable breach of the naval code. He fraternized. He gave the crew food and smokes and spirits and, it was suspected, drugs of some kind. The boy had always been moody and he became more so after a visit ashore at Liberia where he could have come into possession of some evil substance which affected his mind. But the master of the *Somes*, Ralph Mackenzie, was also unbalanced in his own way, and unsuited to the job. No matter what crime, if any, had been done aboard, he did not have the legal or moral right to hang any man without a court martial. But though Spencer's father was well-connected socially, Mackenzie, was better connected politically. He got *his* court martial, and he got away with murder. My father tried to be of help to Margaret Spencer, but her life was a shambles after that. She didn't long survive her husband."

"Oh, Venetia Armstrong!" Jimmy exclaimed, suddenly leaping to his feet. "It all happened long ago. Don't cry!" The restrained girl was more and more often allowing her true feelings to show and this time she had burst into tears as she was adjusting the shawl placed over Maggie, who then awoke.

"Oh, Strong . . . Mr . . . Armstrong. They said I must tell you . . . something." A puzzled look came across her face, then the light of a smile. "I remember. They said I must tell you he is at . . ."

Susannah was on her feet and starting for the door. "Where is he? Where?" she demanded. Maggie cowered at the immoderate response and Susannah went to her. Taking herself in hand, she asked with all the patience she could muster, "Dear Maggie, please, *please* tell me, where is Lieutenant Armstrong? Who sent you to find me? Did he? Did he?"

Venetia made Susannah wait for the carriage to be brought round, otherwise, she would have run all the way.

Chapter Twenty-eight

Six men had been brought to the Union that evening, about the time Susannah's relief came on duty. When she hurriedly left there to wander and search the hallways and wards of other hospitals on her way home, she had not been told of the new men transported from a field hospital where they had remained since the Bull Run campaign weeks before.

While still waiting on a stretcher on a hallway floor for a bed to be prepared, one of the Johnny Rebs spoke to Maggie Crandell. The girl was doing the same thing that Susannah and many others were—apprehensively but eagerly searching row upon row of spectral faces in the hospitals and white tent villages of the city, hoping against hope to set eyes upon a certain cherished visage of husband or son or brother or, as in Susannah's situation, which was not a unique one, on more than one beloved face.

"Susannah Butler . . . get Susannah, please ma'am," the rebel soldier said to Maggie, repeating his words twice, before he lost consciousness again. She had queried Matron Ropes because the name 'Butler' meant a lot to her and, ill as she was, Maggie made her way across the city reaching Lafayette Square at about the same time Susannah did herself.

Back at the Union late that night, in a scarcely contained frenzy of seesawing emotions, Susannah's heart-swelling hope alternating with despair, she went tip-toeing frantically from bed to bed with a lantern in her upraised hand, with Grace at her side, Jimmy in their wake. She had yet to find Terry when there was but one last room left to visit, a dank, small one in the basement of the building. It had a single high window with broken panes and was used only when no other space was available. With rising dread, Susannah pushed open the door and stepped inside.

In the shifting yellow circle of light cast by the swaying lantern, amidst ominous leaping shadows, she saw at once the room was bare but for two iron bedsteads, both empty, thin mattresses and threadbare blankets folded.

"Terry's gone, Grace," she said in a toneless voice. "He died alone, without me, without knowing how much I love him and need him, without knowing . . . many things I should have told him, things he had a right to know."

"What the devil are you doing here at this hour, Mrs. Armstrong? Looking for me?" Hargrove Haight leered, appearing in the doorway with one of the younger night nurses, a Miss Brumgart, in tow.

"Have we lost any patients tonight, Doctor Haight?" Susannah asked coldly. When he nodded, she would have dropped the light if Jimmy hadn't taken it from her.

"Two of the new admissions are graveyard dead, Mrs. Armstrong. Now, if you'll excuse us, we need this room . . . to prepare it, of course. "

"Well, who were they, sir, the men who passed?" Grace inquired. "Speak their names."

"Who? How the devil should I know? They rarely come to me knowing themselves who they are or what their names, and this last lot was very poorly, just wounded Johnny Rebels, not the highest priority of a field hospital staff. Not my highest priority either."

"Mistakes *are* made. I'm looking for my husband, a Union officer. I was told he was brought here this evening. Have you treated a tall, slender handsome man, with hair of a . . . of a fine dark brown and eyes of gray, so deep, so . . . ?" Haight looked away from Susannah.

"Fine dark brown hair? Oh, Nurse Armstrong,

you know better than most the condition of the men who come here from the field, untended to, unwashed, insensible with pain after the jouncing of the ambulance wagons. One man, apparently an officer, *was* removed from here, barely alive. Matron might be of help to you, with the details."

Grace and Susannah, following Jimmy, abandoned the squalid little room to Haight and Brumgart.

"Susannah!" Louisa called in a whispered shout as she came running toward them from the opposite end of the hallway. "We sent a rider off to your house to tell you . . ." Susannah's left hand came to her lips. She didn't want to hear what she expected Louisa to say. Instead, she said it herself.

"He's . . . gone."

"Oh no, no!" Louisa said emphatically and shook her head. "Come! Come with me right now."

The sun was risen and most of the men were awake to greet it and the nurses as they swept into the ballroom ward. Two visitors were already there, Rose Green and Nancy Phillips, ladies of strong and outspoken Confederate sympathies, "unlike me, the undercover spy," Susannah thought, "known everywhere as the turncoat." Notified of the presence of new Southern wounded *they* had arrived with hampers of food

329

and flowers and clothing, and they glared at Susannah with contempt as she approached the bed to which Louisa and, now, Matron Ropes also, were steering her.

"Oh my Lord, oh . . ." she gasped. "It's Simeon! Oh Sim, Sim, it's me, Susannah," she said, approaching his bed. Her brother's pained green eyes fixed on her and lit with rage before he turned his face away. "Simeon! Please, don't behave so to me. I've come to care for you, to take you home."

"Nurse," he spoke with effort to Louisa who stepped forward. "Nurse, please get this traitorous female away from me." The two visiting ladies in the room looked at Susannah with scorn and outrage.

"Leave the boy alone," Nan Phillips said. "You will make things worse, agitating him so."

"We'll see to him," Mrs. Green snapped.

On Susannah's first day in Washington the same Mrs. Green had cursed her quietly and spit upon her as they passed in the street and Susannah was tempted now to tell her to mind her own damn business, that she was no lady, just a nasty gutter snipe, but she held her tongue and turned her attention back to her brother.

"You're a traitor, Susannah, a Judas. You broke Mamma's heart, and Papa's . . . and mine. Go *on* now." Simeon would not look at her but she saw pain and melancholy in his eyes.

"I am your sister, same as I ever was," she insisted. He did not answer, at first.

"Nothing is the same as it ever was and never will be again," he managed to say, and then turned his pain etched face away from his sister. Not until then did she realize what he had sacrificed for their beloved Confederacy: his left leg and the use of his left arm which he could move only by shifting it with his right hand.

"Simeon, I am no Yankee," Susannah said, unable to stop herself. She *had* to say it. "Oh, Brother, I'm no traitor but a spy for Dixie, believe me!" His eyes remained closed but his lids flickered. "Simeon, I rode south through the lines with a map for General Beauregard of the planned Yankee advance to Manassas. You know who won that battle, of course." When his eyes fluttered open, they were awash with tears. He smiled through them looking exactly like the little boy he'd been, not very long ago. Now, weak as he was, dosed with laudanum, and mourning, Susannah knew, the changes in his lithe young body and the loss of his innocent youth, he loosed a real Rebel yell and the men close about them, all Rebels, too, joined in, those who could, before they broke into cheers.

Rose Green, ever her grandiose and dramatic self, flung her arms about Susannah. Word went round the ballroom ward like wildfire spreading on a dry prairie and Susannah saw Nurse

Brumgart look at her with indignation, then hurry off, to report the spy, no doubt.

Why she was not arrested on the spot Susannah didn't understand and would not until, weeks later, she *was* taken into custody.

"God, Susannah, I should have known," Simeon said. "Susannah, promise you'll take me home to die beneath southern skies? Bury me beneath them?"

"Anything else, Sim?" she asked matter-of-factly, having no intentions of letting him die, not without the fight of their lives. "Got more to say before you go to meet those angels waiting on the crystal shores of paradise?"

"Yes," he answered. "I want ten fiddlers to play *Tallahassee* after you all sing Dixie, when they lower me down."

"Simeon you have pain and fever but you've not got the blood poisoning or any hemorrhaging. Those angels are going to wait a long time for you, because with God's help, and mine, you are going to live out your full allotment of years. Will you help us, me and God? It's the least you can do, now that He's brought you this far. What's wrong?" Susannah asked seeing him grimace.

"Susannah, I think I saw Terry Armstrong fall on the battlefield not twenty feet from me." She waited, then asked, "Fall how . . . alive or . . . ?"

"Hurt . . . bad. I don't . . . I don't know what

happened to him — or even if it was him," Simeon shrugged helplessly. "God, I want to go home to Carolina, Susannah," he said. "I want to see Mamma and Louly. That's what kept me going, when they'd given up on me, thinking of you all, and especially about . . . our baby." Now, it was Susannah's turn to yell like a Rebel because, in the midst of all their pain and loss, life was beginning again. Her friend, her brother's wife, was carrying his child and there would soon be at least one new Butler in the world. That was something to shout about.

Matron Ropes hugged Susannah as she was leaving the Union Hospital for the last time. "You know, Mrs. Armstrong dear, that I am an implacable Abolitionist. You and I are on opposite sides of this conflict but I must tell you, you are a noble young woman and a true nurse. You would make Miss Nightingale proud."

"Matron . . . ?" Susannah paused at the office door. "Dr. Haight mentioned a man who was carried in here yesterday, then transferred elsewhere. I know it's too much to hope, to find a brother and a husband on the same day but, I was wondering . . . ?"

"He seemed an older man so I doubt, from what you've told us, it was your dashing Terrence Armstrong. I would not have moved that man again, he was doing so poorly, but a Major from the War Department insisted he'd do better in more commodious surroundings. Lowly female nurse that I am, I had no say in the matter and the patient could not speak, not even to tell us his name."

"Where were they taking him?" Susannah asked. Hannah Ropes shook her head.

"I can't tell you that because I don't know. If I hear anything at all . . ."

"Call on me if you need me, dear Mrs. Ropes," Susannah said as the women clasped hands. Then, Susannah took her little brother home, not to Carolina, but to Lafayette Square, the best she could do for the moment. With three bedridden patients there, it was like her own small infirmary as she and Grace shuttled from room to room with trays and dressings and cheery words. Cheery was not what Susannah was feeling, aching so for Terry and worried sick over him, that her mind, during unoccupied moments, cast up dreadful images of him needing her and calling out for her in vain.

"I'll be indebted to you, Maggie Crandell, long as I live," Susannah told the girl once she had gotten Simeon comfortable and decently fed and went in to her room to fluff her pillows. "By the way," Susannah asked, "who were *you* looking for at Union Hospital?"

"Oh, no one in particular," Maggie sighed.

334

"Just anyone to fuss and worry over, and to comfort. I think I had an old beau in mind, Ken Lovell, but it didn't matter, really. I've been on my own half my life, I'd conjecture. I *need* to care for someone. I went to be a nurse but that ill-humored old frump Dix, turned me away. I was too pretty, she said. I know I'm not pretty at all. It was just the fever pinking my cheeks and putting a glimmer in my eyes. How *is* Mr. Armstrong?"

"Oh, I forgot to tell you, in all the excitement," Susannah said really surprised at herself. "It was my brother, not my husband who sent you to me."

Maggie looked confused and doubtful, but not until the next morning when she couldn't resist getting up out of her sickbed for a peek at the new patient, did anyone realize what had happened. Susannah was in the kitchen helping cook to string beans when they heard Maggie's hoarse squawk of dismay.

"Oh, my dear Lord and dog my cats! This ain't him. This ain't at all the man who sent me to get you, Susannah!"

Chapter Twenty-nine

Terry Armstrong *was* the man removed from the Union Hotel Hospital. Through Will Chauvenet's contacts, Susannah learned he had been taken either to the new, whitewashed Judiciary Square Hospital or to the Patent Office, which was where she actually found him.

In the lofty great hall of that building, with its marble floors and circular gallery, there was space for more than a thousand beds, though in those early days of the war, such a need to care for such a vast number of wounded was a shocking possibility.

Terry's bed was set between two gleaming glass display cases exhibiting working models of recent inventions, a printing press and some elaborate wind-utilizing object Susannah could not identify.

Terry was motionless. Blue veins were visible against the pale parchment of his eyelids. His full and beautiful boyish lips were waxen and his breathing very shallow. Susannah had, as a nurse, seen similar cases many times before, of eternity stretching out a hand for a young man whose lifeblood just barely pulsed in his veins, but who had so much to live for. If only she had told Terry *all* that was in her heart, said everything there was to say and not, by omission, lied to him, Susannah sorrowed, perhaps it would have been a help to him. But what was done could not be undone Susannah knew and, trying not to ruminate on past mistakes or reproach herself any more than she had already, she knew she had to reach Terry now, somehow. At once, she sent Jimmy flying off to summon her good friend, a young Army Surgeon, Dr. Bill Hammond. Quinlivin was then to go to Lafayette Square with the surrey to get linens and toweling and shirts and food, and any tempting fragrant delicacy the cook could whip up on the spot. The cook herself was to come later with more—hampers of meats, beef broth tea, tapioca custard, fresh bread, all she could carry for Terry and the men on his ward.

"I'm informed Major Armstrong has been unconscious most of the time since the Bull Run battle," Dr. Hammond told Susannah in a gentle voice. A dignified, gray-templed man though only in his mid-thirties, Hammond had been an Army doctor for some ten years before the War Between the States had begun. "In my experience, that's a long while, perhaps too long, to be insensible or raving, rarely lucid, hovering between life and death. Chances for a full recovery are . . . We'll do all we can, both of us, but be prepared, Susannah."

Terry's wounds were only middling-serious. One was the neat little hole of a Minie ball in the fleshy part of his shoulder, the other a messy scattering of gashes from grape shot across the back of his head. Found unconscious in his gray uniform, he had been kept in a Yankee field hospital for prisoners outside Alexandria. "I regret having to tell you this, Sue," Bill Hammond went on, "but Terry might have recovered well if some damn sawbones with a dirty knife and sponge had not operated to remove metal fragments from the scalp. Once infection set in, doctors held out no hope, but Terry Armstrong confounded them all by hanging onto his life. He hung on so long, against all predictions, that eventually they disposed of him and some other stubborn cases, at Union Hospital. There, a fellow name of Napoleon Baker, from the War Department, reclaimed his man."

"And now, Bill," Susannah said with determination, "I'm reclaiming him as *my man*."

She changed his dressings and sponged him repeatedly, head to toe, with cool water. There was no medical treatment to turn to. She could only pray, and barter with the fates, for his life. Watching him gasping for breath, his cheeks pur-

338

ple with fever, his blazing eyes like hot dark coals when they opened, rolling blind, Susannah would have been willing to give up almost anything in the world for Terry's life, even her own. But that choice was not hers to make.

She paced and paced and sponged him and paced some more and felt the chill hand of fear tighten round her heart and then recalled what matron Ropes always said:

"Susannah, *talk* to them. Always talk. Your voice may not belong to their mothers or their wives, but it's a feminine and musical voice, like those our poor boys yearn to hear again. That soft tranquil sound may be the best . . . the only . . . remedy or comfort we can give any of them." So, Susannah talked to Terry . . . and talked . . . and talked.

"Most every man here at the Patent Office and in hospitals south and north, was at Manassas and every man at Manassas was a hero. Live, Terry, please, if not for me, then to reap the rewards of your gallantry," she told him. There was no visible response. Her heart ached.

"Terry, my own true love, I'm here now. I'll send for Saidee and Venetia. Wait for them!"

Still, he did not stir and she went on talking about anything, everything—the girls first.

"Venetia has an admirer, a New York boy fighting with the Irish Sixty Ninth, Jimmy Quinlivin. He's coming for her, after the war.

339

And Baby Saidee has two good friends in Grace's little ones, Esther and Enoch. They all read together and talk endlessly and play euchre, or some card game they call that. I know it's a card shark's specialty, but they play for fireflies and have such a sweet good time."

Nothing from Terry, except a deep breath.

"Terry love, recall how Sam Houston was called traitor, as you and I have been for turning our backs on Dixie, for leaving the South? They called Sam a coward because he retreated from Santa Ana's great army. But they stopped calling Sam a yellowbelly after he and his men turned and caught the Mexicans off guard as he'd planned all along, *and* captured Santa Ana, too."

Nothing from Terry. Susannah wiped his brow and kissed his hand, and held it.

"Your ship's going to be waiting for you, love. Hull Number 203 is on the Mersey. She's waiting for you alone, for the touch of your hand. She's a faithful lover, like me, Terry. Don't you want to know if she's a spitfire, too, or docile and ladylike? Love, I have two bits of . . . important information to impart. I'll whisper because . . . well, because it's *private* news. You probably won't even hear me and, if you do, won't remember any of what I'm going to say, but I am saying it anyway!" She glanced about, actually blushing a little before she leaned to him, and spoke and brushed her lips to his. They *were* a fraction warmer, she tried to tell herself, but still they were too white, bloodless.

Then, Susannah told Terry about her childhood—picking wild berries, fishing in the pond at Colleton Plantation with strings and pins, Christmases in Charleston with all the cousins, Colletons and Butlers and others, gathered from the Low Country and Up Country.

"No matter what we were doing, Terry love, no matter which little boys were harmlessly tormenting which small girls—or which little girl was leading the others in a minor rebellion against older cousins and young uncles, we stopped and collected at the longcase clock in the library when it counted twelve noon. That clock is still there, Terry, counting off the minutes and hours and days, in Mamma's Charleston house. Do you remember it . . . remember the little hole made by a stray British bullet during the War of Revolution? It keeps ticking, Terry, all these years later. Its panels are inlaid with flowers and birds, remember? The clock is signed and dated Terry. Someone in the employ of Wm. Marquand made it in Fleet Street, in London, 1683. It was not made by Wm. Marquand himself because it was signed 'Wm. Marquand fecit.' I recall when my grandfather told me what that word meant. Terry, *he* lived to ninety-three and I want you to do the same, hear me now, suh? You would have liked my grandfather Colleton because . . ."

She talked and talked and when she ran out of relatives, having described every single one she had, including her father's Up Country fishermen brothers, she spoke in a lowered voice, in a more intimate tone, of what she and Terry had shared already, of their first time together . . . and other times . . . in the woods . . . and in fields and aboard ship . . . when they had pleasured each other beyond dreams.

"Terry, my own love, we were becoming true good friends, besides being lovers, and we've so much more to do together, more memories to create. Don't leave me!" When she said that, his hands moved as though he was reaching out for unreal things she could not see.

"Do you know the legend of the blue sailor, Terry love, the wildflower that grows along roadsides and trails? Louisa Alcott told it to me. She's a nurse I worked beside who has written an actual book, *Flower Fables*. Well . . . There was a young girl who waited and pined and longed so *hard* for her true love, gone to sea, never to return, that the gods took pity on her and changed her into a roadside plant with a lovely blue flower, the blue sailor. It's a wild chicory, darlin' and even *it* has a companion, Queen Anne's lace. The blue sailor and Queen Anne grow together, but Terry, if you don't awaken and live with me, the gods will be turning me into a lonely wallflower.

342

"All of us need you, Lafitte and Saidee and Venetia and me. Ben Speed is waiting for you, so's my papa, and Terry, this baby of ours is growing, already raising its little fist to knock on the door of it's little room, is yours and mine and I love that baby and you will, too, Terry, if you'll stay with us.

"Terry, I want you . . . I *need* you with me. Don't leave me, oh, don't!" She thought she saw his lips move just then, but she wasn't sure.

Susannah stayed beside Terry that night, and other nights, dozing, waking often, always with a start, and with hope, only to find him as he had been. But where there was life there was hope and she talked on and on, then read to him from the dime novels the men passed about the wards, first one of Bruin Adams' books about the American Revolution. But, she reasoned, Terry had had plenty of his own war, so she took up Anne Staples' *Malaiska: The Indian Wife of the White Hunter.*

One dark night, while reading, exhausted almost to the breaking point, she fell asleep. Her weary head just dropped to the side of the bed.

When she opened her eyes again, the room was awash in early sunlight that paled the gaslights, still burning. Cooler air caressed them and Terry was awake. He was pale, thin and gaunt, with a dark beard and dark circles beneath his eyes, *open* eyes, gray eyes full of love that caressed Susannah's face when she lifted her head and, speechless at last, reached for his hand.

"Susannah . . ." Terry smiled, "I didn't want to awaken you but now you're up, know what I need? A *good* cup of coffee."

She burst into tears.

Hannah Ropes, who had been calling in frequently, told Susannah to ask no questions — yet, about the battle or anything disturbing. Dr. Hammond warned Susannah not to upset the patient in any way at all because, with a head injury, one never knew what could cause a relapse. Bill Hammond would not even consider allowing Susannah to move Terry home, until he had been without any fever for at least a whole week.

"How *is* my favorite case?" she would ask each morning.

"Ah, my favorite nurse," Terry would smile every time she arrived at the Patent Office and, as the days passed, his voice grew stronger and his smile got broader until she saw the old boyish grin that set her heart to singing.

On his last day at the Patent Office, Terry's seventh without fever, she bathed him and trimmed his rich dark brown hair. He was gaunt, thin and feeble as a kitten, his long muscles atrophied from weeks of inaction. She shaved him, too, holding his head in her lap. She started with scissors, to get rid of the matted long ends of his beard, then took a straight razor to the well-defined plains of his face. The drawn, wasted man who emerged was a shock to her. Until she actually saw his face smooth and sheared, Susannah had not understood how close she had come to losing him forever. He read that in her eyes.

"I won't ask you right *now* to marry me again," he jested. "Because some girls don't like the long thin type of man. They prefer one with some poundage on him. Give me a few days?"

"I'll take you, sir, anyway at all. And I'll give you forever."

"But . . . will give you me a kiss? *That's* the question."

"Yes is the answer," she said looking around in mock trepidation, "a little peck or two can't hurt. Oh, Terry, let me hold you," she sighed after a very soft kiss, not one of passion but of a kind of love she had not felt before. He had been lost. She had found him. She could not look enough at him to satisfy her loving eyes with the sight of him. She could not be grateful enough.

"Uh, Terry, remember what I whispered in your ear a few days ago about marriage and . . . such?"

He looked puzzled.

"Whisper it again," he asked.

"Sir, I have been warned not to . . . to arouse or agitate the patient—you—in any way, so I'll whisper again, when the time is right," she grinned, implying seduction, a little disappointed she'd have to tell him all over again about their baby and such. But no matter, she thought, there's plenty of time now, for everything.

Not three weeks later, Pinkerton came to arrest Susannah and let Terry escape through a back window.

Chapter Thirty

On the evening Pinkerton arrived to put "Susie Shadow" as the lady had become known, under house arrest, Terry snatched up her notebook and left the Lafayette Square house by a rear window. He watched, crouched in the shrubbery, as the Federal operatives peeled his uproarious daughters off the front gate, then he lingered listening outside the parlor window.

Susannah gave him away, and he heard her. In less than no time, first thing, she sold him out, just like that and hearing her, he knew for a certainty that his suspicions about Susannah were founded in reality; she *had* been deceiving him, doubtless from the start. He took a quick look into her notebook while he listened and discovered encoded messages interspersed with her drawings and strategic notes. Terry was able to decipher the secret lines and discovered they were love poems. There was no doubt in his mind they had been written for Will Chauvenet. Susannah had no cause to disguise her so-called love from *him*.

Terry had first became dubious about that love, though he mistrusted his own instincts at the time, when he asked her to marry him in Galveston and, to his disappointment, she had flat out refused him, no ifs, ands or buts, just a vague maybe somewhere, someday.

He tried over the next months to ignore his suspicions and couldn't, not absolutely, not until she found him at the Patent Office and saved his life, no doubt about that, by nursing him back to health with what he took to be true love and total, selfless devotion.

And then, when finally he came home from the hospital, who should he find among the crowd of other recovering invalids harboring under his own roof but William Chauvenet. Had matters stood differently, Terry probably would have warmed to the man. But possessive of Susannah as he was, his misgivings festered and turned to mistrust. Jealousy, it was said, was the jaundice of the soul, the injured lover's hell, so when Chauvenet left the house on Lafayette Square, taking Maggie with him, Terry was glad to see the man go but, by then, irreparable damage had been done. It played out this way.

Though Terry's wounds were well-healed, he was weak from fever's ravages and before he could himself be up and about the city, he had

348

Susannah carrying sealed envelopes back and forth to the War Department. Also, he had visitors of an unsavory sort he would not have received at home, if there had been any choice, men with sly faces, shifty eyes and often upturned collars despite the warm weather. Some had southern-accented speech, others Down East Yankee or French or Irish or British accents. They came late at night after everyone but Terry and Susannah had retired for the evening. She looked polite but observant, frowned faintly and said little until an English seaman came calling at four one morning with a long tube under his arm. He and Terry were closeted alone in the library for an hour before the sailor was given a good meal and sent on his way, empty handed.

"Who *was* that man?" Susannah asked. "What a mysterious, shady looking lot of friends you have, love."

"In our business, mine *and* yours, one doesn't choose one's company," Terry said, rolling up the blueprints the man had left.

"Are those the plans for Hull 203?" Susannah asked. Terry nodded.

"Interim plans," he said. "She's a great ship, long and lean and shoal of draft. She'll be ready for her first test run in May and we'll be there to launch her." Susannah looked at him with what he perceived to be unsettling reserve.

"Perhaps 'we' but perhaps just you," she said.

Terry said nothing for a long pregnant moment as he took note of that remark.

"Do I detect a sign of azzling, as in 'azzling out?' he asked, his eyes narrowed.

"Not . . . precisely," Susannah answered, distracting his attention with a dazzling smile.

The denizens of Susannah's infirmary, as she came to call their house, gathered after suppers in the parlor to socialize, often joined by callers, among them Matron Ropes, Miss Alcott, a slip of a Yankee boy as Terry thought of Quinlivin, and a rotating crowd of politicians and military men that all seemed to him to be charmed by his lady. Business was quickly done, but after, Terry didn't say much. Mostly, he watched Susannah and Will and listened to the talk.

"The drummer beat the long roll for retreat and it echoed in my heart, thudding like the bullets hitting all around me," Simeon told them one evening, when he was ready to talk a bit about Bull Run. "I was really afraid it was the end. You see, during the time we recruits practiced drilling, all of the officers and volunteers, were undisciplined and real disorganized, except for those of us who had been to the academies or military schools. Our officers were elected, y'all know, and the electioneering was fierce. There was lots of cake and flattery passed out by the contestants and suddenly I found myself more popular and loved than I ever dreamed I'd be."

"West Point is a breeding ground for aristocrats," said Hannah Ropes. "All the Rebel command was trained there."

"The Yankee officers were also, Mrs. Ropes," Will reminded her. "Terry," he turned to the silent figure sunk deep into an armchair, "I'm told Galveston is a mere eight feet above sea level. Is that true?" Terry nodded, suspicious of Will and the question.

"Storms — hurricanes off the gulf — are pretty wild," Terry said. "There can be winds over a hundred miles an hour hurling flying debris, splintering timbers, twisting roofs. We often are cut off from mainland by high water and wild seas."

"There's a blockade of Galveston ordered," Will said. "With nothing but cotton-clads to defend the city, the Stars and Stripes will soon again be raised over the Customhouse there." Terry held his tongue. It was not easy. He looked at Susannah but she was fixedly gazing at Chauvenet and seemed not interested at all in *his* feelings.

Next evening, instead of sitting and seething in the parlor, watching Susannah fuss over Will almost as much as she did him, Terry went for a ride, a slow canter, his first since Bull Run and that, Terry mused, much to his satisfaction, surely left *her* surprised.

Terry was gone more than an hour and when he returned, the usual crowd was there in his parlor, but Susannah had heard him come in and she greeted him at the door. Rushed to him, actually, he was somewhat mollified to see.

"Oh Terry!" she sighed, "what were you thinking of, going off alone? I can see the exhaustion clear as day in your face." She took his riding crop and gloves, and relieved him of his Union military jacket.

"One day, I'm going to take you away from all this, darlin', on a real honeymoon, when you *really* marry me," he said, cupping her breasts in his hands and massaging them gently as she leaned back against him."

"That's delicious," she sighed, stepping up on a tuffet. Their eyes met, almost on a level, and she kissed his lips, her arms enfolding his neck.

"I feel like an old married lady, love, what with our house full of children and guests and days filled with work and both of us almost too tired to uh, well, do a whole lot of loving . . . later. "

"The important word is 'almost'," Terry, irked and jealous as he was, actually grinned before giving her a very complete caress. His hands went from full soft breasts, to narrow waist and then dropped below to press her to him hard while he

352

stole another kiss. It was a good-natured quick grapple and then they composed themselves. Smiling, probably a bit too sheepishly, they rejoined the crowd in the parlor, holding hands.

That same night, Terry took his first ride of another kind, astride Susannah's vibrant, needy, perfect body that was so warm and ready for his. He had pulled the pins from her hair and helped her undress, displacing layer upon layer of silk as if unfolding the petals of a rose. By the time he peeled off his own clothes, her flaming hair was fanned over the deep pillows, her lips were moist and parted, glistening in candlelight. She sighed with passion and kissed him deep and long and moved her long graceful legs to invite him inside her. As he probed, losing himself in her velvet softness, as it parted to him, accepted him, took him to the hilt, those legs enfolded his hips and they moved together, looking into each others eyes all the while the strength of their thrust and parry was building. They were still wide-eyed when they rode the peak of passion together, their matched desire and lust and yearning vented at last in a long sweet hot shudder of release.

"If you ever leave me," Terry said, "I'll call your name from the farthest reaches of the universe." He really loved her. He just could not help it, try as he might.

"How could I leave you, fool?" Susannah asked, *so* honest, *so* innocent, he felt he was seeing into the depths of her soul through her clear green eyes. He almost believed her. Next day, when he came upon her with Will, he knew he had been right not to.

Terry was glad to see Chauvenet go, but not the way Susannah was sending him off, bidding him a long loving goodbye on the veranda of his own house as Terry rode up. She was in his arms, kissing him just then. Terry dismounted and shook Will's hand reluctantly, wishing him all speed on his way.

"Where are you off to, sir?" Terry asked in a surly way. Will took no notice, simply answered the question.

"To master a ship, take her down to the Isthmus to pick up a cargo of California gold being brought overland from the Pacific to the Atlantic," Will explained. "And I'm taking little Maggie."

"Think that's safe?" Terry asked, viciously biting off the tip of a cigar that he then jammed between his teeth.

"Safe? It is my analysis of the situation, Terry, that the Confederacy is no threat on the open ocean and never will be. The sea air will be good for Mags, perhaps even would cure her consumption."

"I look forward to our next meeting,

Chauvenet, possibly on the high seas," Terry growled before leading his mount away muttering, "and I wish you a soldiers' wind all the way."

"Ours would have been a solid marriage, Will," Terry, heard his Susannah say to Will a half hour later. "You're not like a lot of other men, not an egoist or a strutting cock of the walk seducer. I know you'll take care of Maggie."

"Mags is like a daughter to me, Susannah. She and I need each other. We're both . . . alone," Will said with a really sorrowful look at Susannah. That's when Terry, his cigar a stump that he gnawed furiously, strode back onto the front steps and shook Will's hand goodbye—again.

"Still here, Chauvenet?" he asked. "You're going to miss the boat, man, if you don't get a move on." And when he and Susannah stood together waving their guests off, Terry was straightforwardly angry.

"You know, it's not agreeable for a man to come home to find his . . . lover in the arms of her former fiance, right on his own doorstep. Do you still think you could be happy married to *him?*" Terry demanded.

"I may yet be," Susannah snapped, truly vexed. "I do *not* like your dark, suspicious looks or your insinuating questions, nor you wishing them soldiers' wind, calm wind. Oh, damn! I didn't mean it about Will and me!" she called after Terry as he stalked away. Though he gave no sign, he did

hear her and she knew it. What she did not know
was that he didn't believe her at all.

"I saw your friend Beverly Bland today. He's a
Union prisoner. Mr. Baker is roughing him up
rather badly," Terry told Susannah over dinner. It
was the first word he had spoken to her all day,
since Will's departure. The girls, following the
adults' lead, were eating in silence. Simeon had
kept to his room.

"That Yankee, Baker, is said to be a cruel, ve-
nal man," Susannah answered.

Though Terry had not spoken to Susannah, he
had wanted her all day long. He had serious
trouble waiting for the cover of darkness before
he took her. It had felt to him all day that he was
listening for the sound of the sun going down.
He became more irritable, and more passionate
and yearning, as each hour passed. That was because he had decided it was pretty much over for
them, for him and Susannah. If she knew that
too, she didn't show it in bed that night. She was
warm and soft and lusty for him, the same as she
always was. She was quite the actress, Terry con-
cluded, but just on the off chance he was mistaken, he asked her one last time to marry her.

"When *will* you let me make an honest woman
of you Susannah?" he demanded. She was reclin-
ing on the bed beside him, with just a gauzy

sheet hardly shielding her perfect and lovely swells and declivities from his hot eyes, not defending them at all from his hot hands. He molded and shaped her figure memorizing every nuance and curve of her, and he mouthed and nibbled as he rested on one elbow beside her, sometimes tasting through supple fabric, sometimes diving beneath it. They enjoyed each other more than once, before the night ended. There was no satisfying Terry because it was going to be the last night, if she refused again to marry him. He had to own her, or leave her. There would be no middle ground, he vowed, not for Terry Armstrong and Susannah Butler. Not for *him* anyway.

Earlier that day, when he had dropped by to question Bland in his cell and was told by that cowardly cur she was again betrothed to Will Chauvenet, secretly though all of Charleston knew it, Terry was almost tempted to help Baker with his so-called questioning, but abusing defenseless men was not his style, nor was it right to blame the messenger for bad news. It was better for him to know sooner, rather than later, that the woman he loved was just another cheat.

So, Terry sulked, he had done it again, let himself fall for one more faithless female after he swore he never would love any one of them again. In a quiet rage of jealousy after she gave him away, he let Susannah and the damn diary

357

fall into Pinkerton's and worse, Napolean Baker's, ruthless clutches.

Then he went and broke her out of jail. He owed her that much at least, he convinced himself without much trouble, really.

Chapter Thirty-one

"Terry Armstrong a *Confederate* spy? Ha!" Alan Pinkerton barked a laugh at his prisoner, Susannah Butler. "The Potter Commission hears every accusation of disloyalty. Most of the time, they find something suspicious. With Armstrong it's different. They find nothing even worthy of investigation where Lieutenant . . . uh Captain . . . *Major* Armstrong is concerned. He's true blue through and through. Do you think I am deaf or just real dumb? Don't you think I heard him scrambling out the window when I was first interrogating you, ma'am? Don't you think I knew he was under the window, hearing every word you said to me?" Susannah stood tall and impassive, her expression contemptuous, her face pale as Pinkerton went on ranting at her. "You thought you were exposing Terry Armstrong as a Rebel spy, as you may recall. He did not appreciate your doing that, *Miss* Butler, nor your harboring your former lover, Chauvenet, under your eaves." Susannah appeared struck, hearing that, Pinkerton gloated, though she covered her hurt and confusion quickly. This was a woman who had some real social aplomb, he mused.

"I am surprised that, charlatan though he is, Lieutenant Armstrong would talk to you of such personal matters but as he has, I am forced to as well. Mr. Chauvenet was once my affianced, Pinkerton, never my lover, sir," she explained. "I still find it painful to believe Terry is a *real* Yankee but I did wonder, I'll admit, why I was not taken into custody as soon as I disclosed my espionage work in front of all those people at the Union Hospital. I also did ponder over how Terry escaped you at Lafayette Square, . . . almost as if he had been forewarned of your arrival, Mr. Pinkerton. Now I understand."

"Ha! He *was* alerted. Don't you realize I didn't put you under arrest until he grew strong and no longer needed your services as an errand girl? He was using you," Pinkerton smirked. "You have always been his cat's paw. You, the black woman who was standing out on the street for hours before I let her see you, even the children with her, were all part of his facade as a two-fold agent, *Miss* Butler."

The detective repeatedly emphasized the 'miss' once he had been informed that Susannah and Terry were not actually wed. He had secret aspirations regarding Miss Butler, and though he would never have considered marriage to a fallen woman, however magnificent she was, a liaison was a possibility he found tempting in this particular instance. But she wasn't falling into his arms as, in the situation, Pinkerton fully anticipated she would. Susannah Butler exhibited none of prisoner's or the humble remorse of the soiled dove who offered a crumb, nor did she exude the grateful perfume of the crushed flower. Pinkerton determined to be very stern with her, to bring her down a notch, knock her off her high horse.

"Just who, dear lady, do you suppose turned *this* over to me?" he asked and wagged her diary before her beautiful face. He was finding it a strain, trying to browbeat this woman. Firstly, he wanted her. Secondly, he could not frighten her. He would have to leave *that* to Nappy Baker, if she went on refusing to cooperate.

"So, that blackguard *did* give my personal diary to you, sir! Have you read in that book, Detective?" she asked, very impressive in her condition of high indignation. "If you have, and I blush to think so, that proves what I supposed from the start, that you, sir, are no gentleman."

Pinkerton blinked furiously and it took him a moment to find his voice that was now high-pitched and angry.

"That is the ultimate censure you southerners bring to bear, accusing a fellow of not being a gentleman. I have overheard on my forays south, myself disguised as a reb soldier among Confederate troops, a private of high social position out and

361

out refuse the order of an officer who held no claim to gentility. That is no way to conduct a war, Miss Butler, no way to win one. I have heard told the story of a high born private, chastised with the flat of an officer's sword for slouching on parade."

"Yes, yes, get to your point, sir," Susannah exhaled with boredom, further provoking the man's anger and discomfort.

"That private pulled out a bowie knife, ma'am, and stabbed the offending officer dead on the spot. Now, I am not going to put up with any more southern haughtiness from you, no matter how fetching a prisoner you are, no matter if men have always before done your bidding. You'll learn your proper place first of all or . . . I won't be responsible."

"Oh please, spare me your threats," Susannah yawned.

"Your husband, uh, rather your *paramour, Miss* Butler, placed this book, this evidence, in my hands, but as parts of it, the most import passages one would surmise, are written in cipher, I have got nowhere with understanding it." He opened to a page at random. "What's that say? 'Why sh456d 3 b65sh t4 488. 3. 64v2,' " he read out, not smoothly.

"It says, Mr. Pinkerton, 'Why should I blush to say I love.' Knowing that much will, if you are any good at all at sleuthing, enable you to break the code and peruse the entire book, my private diary, at your leisure. If you do, you are contemptible."

"Will it tell me names, Miss Butler, of other

agents in your circle?" he frowned. "I see you made sketches of the top secret Union ironclad vessel, *Monitor.* Who for?"

"Sir, the *Merrimack,* which has been renamed by the Confederacy *Virginia,* is pictured also. I'm a naval officer's daughter. I like the look of ships. You have already caught two absolute innocents in your wide flung net, Mr. Pinkerton, little Jimmy Quinlivin and Joe Dempsey, when they came to call on me. Neither one of them could be deceptive if he tried. Let them go free and I will consider putting some big game in your trap. Now, please call for Will Chauvenet, if he's still in Washington, as a witness. He loved me once and still does, I'm certain. He'll vouch for me now."

Chauvenet was an important man and Pinkerton hesitated, worrying what to do. Susannah turned her back on the detective and went to the window that faced on the prison yard quadrangle. Men, prisoners, were out there, whistling and cheering.

"They are playing a new thing called baseball, Miss Butler, which is like the old game of drop cat, only they use a ball. A Union officer of my acquaintance, stationed at Fort Moultrie in Charleston harbor, one Abner Doubleday from up in New York State, a village called Cooperstown, made up this new game. Men are playing it everywhere, in all the army camps, north and south, even in the prisons, as you see. I suppose it's better than bluff poker for pennies. I tried it."

"You, sir?" Susannah scoffed. "And? . . ."

"I could not hit the ball. Or catch it so . . ." Susannah cheered then and waved her handkerchief for someone who could hit and catch, and the prisoners cheered her in return, most of them fighting Johnny Rebs. There were also some Baltimore Secessionists being held in the Old Capitol, and workers at the arsenal or the Navy Yard or the White House who refused to take an oath of allegiance to the United States.

"I won't have this sort of fraternization between Susie Shadow and them traitors. Next thing, you'll be passing information south again. Miss Butler," Pinkerton said. "I'll be forced to throw you to the wolf, a man of singular cruelty who in no way resembles a gentleman, if you don't cooperate with me. Cooperate with me!" he implored. "I have brought you books, a looking glass and a decent straw mattress free of bedbugs, in all likelihood. Miss Butler, I'm enthralled with your pluck and beauty and cleverness. I myself might fight for southern womanhood had I such a southern woman as you to fight for. I beg you, on my knees . . ." the detective, red in the face and sweating, fell to his knees, "don't make me turn you over to Baker."

Susannah looked at him with revulsion as Napoleon Baker, a toothpick stuck between his lips, strode into the room.

"Get up, ignoramus. What have you gotten from our lovely spy?" Nappy asked.

" 'Why should I blush to say I love.' She decoded

that line for me, Nappy," Pinkerton bragged. "Now I can figure out the rest of it."

"Mrs. Armstrong, you may have taken advantage of this dimwitted sap and wrapped him about your finger, but I'm not the same sort of pushover. I quite enjoy extracting information from prisoners, male or female, though with the ladies, Mrs. Baker's creativity adds to the fun. I don't know which of us enjoys the process more, she or I. We are a most compatible couple."

Baker's thin mean mouth twitched with a smile as he approached Susannah and took her hand to lead her to the chair at the center of the cell, placing the looking glass on the table so that Susannah could see herself. "Very soft hands . . . and lovely hands. What a pity to ruin them. We try not to, so before we begin cracking the fingers joint by joint, we use toothpicks . . ." Baker took the one from his mouth, "inserted beneath the nails. Put your hands flat on the table, Madam, that or list for me all your spying accomplices in the north, particularly who it was who gave out details of the President's Cabinet meetings . . . who took a map of Manassas Junction to Beaugregard . . . who?"

"You don't really suppose I will make any of this easy for you Nappy, by doing as you ask without a struggle?" Susannah smiled.

Baker didn't answer as he laid out a row of ten toothpicks and another of matches parallel to it, beside a small pair of pliers. He removed his jacket, tossing it to Pinkerton.

"Do I have to stay, Nappy? I'll just go now, alright?"

"Stop where you are, you gutless worm. *You* are going to hold her for me until Gilda gets here. Start by helping her out of her dress. Blood stains are stubborn to remove and she'll need something to wear later, when it's over."

When half-eager, half-reluctant, Pinkerton tried to undo her top button, Susannah delivered a resounding slap to his face, leaving a clear red impression of her hand on his cheek. Baker roared with laughter and approached her himself.

"There is nothing like a real wild southern spitfire to get me . . . *warmed* to my work. Oh where, oh where is Gilda?" he snarled. "She's going to miss the best parts. Pinkerton run and see can you find my darling spouse. You sure ain't good for anything else, errand boy." Baker pulled up a chair opposite Susannah and sat staring at her. "I'll just wait. This is going to be too good for Gilda to miss," he smiled darkly as Pinkerton scurried to the door, unlocked it and flung it open to admit Gilda Baker with Terry following hot on her heels.

"Lieutenant Armstrong, here's the pleasant surprise I promised!" Gilda Baker cooed. "Fun and games with your trollop. Isn't our Terry looking his fit and handsome self again, Susie Shadow? I've been looking after him, in your absence."

"Lieutenant Armstrong," Susannah mimicked the woman, looking at him with daggers in her eyes, "aren't you looking dark and dissolute and mean? Have you come too, to assist the infamous Napoleon Baker to loosen my tongue?"

"*I'm* here to do that, assist my husband," Gilda said indignantly. Lieutenant Armstrong needn't trouble himself, just sit back and enjoy the show." Gilda tore off her gloves, tossing them aside.

At first, for just a quick moment, Pinkerton observed, Armstrong looked stabbed to the heart, because of seeing Miss Butler in jail, he presumed. But right off, Terry smiled, enviably cool and debonair.

"Well hello, Susannah, darlin'," he said to her pleasantly, conversationally. "I've orders to move you to a more secure, private location, for questioning."

"Don't address me in that overly-familiar tone, sir! I am a prisoner of war. I demand to be treated with all due formality, even by you. Especially by you, you base traitor!"

"Oh, isn't she a dilly!" Pinkerton observed as Terry got that dark look again.

"Hold your damn tongue and listen," he snarled. "Susannah, as soon as you were caught you tried to drag me down with you, accusing me to both sides of villainy. Well, know this: I *am* a damn Yankee alright and damn proud of it. Now, you're of no more use to me than yesterday's newspaper."

"Cur," she hissed.

"I may not be a gentleman but you are not the valiant southern woman I supposed you to be. Get your things together."

"You ain't taking her out of here until I say so," Baker slavered. "She's mine."

The knife flew so fast from Terry Armstrong's hand right past Baker's face, neither Susannah nor Pinkerton realized it had touched him until they saw the blood flow down his cheek.

"That's nothing, Baker, just a little claret spilled. Next time, I won't be as careful." Terry pulled his knife from the wall and wiped it clean on the shoulder of Baker's white shirt. "Now, I'm taking the prisoner. If you question her here with all this southern gentry listening in on her screams, you'll have a riot on your hands. Move out of my way, Baker."

So of course, Baker, mopping his cheek, moved.

"I am not going anywhere with this Yankee bastard," Susannah said. "I will not go with him! *I will not!* He will do outrageous things to me! Get my lawyer, my doctor . . . get Mr. Lincoln himself, damn it! The President respects *all* womanhood."

"Old Abe sent his own sister-in-law, a southerner, back down home when she wanted to go," Pinkerton told them, "with instructions to lock her up and throw away the key if she showed any sign of giving aid and comfort — or information — to the enemy. Well, don't you all look so mean at me," he shrugged. "It"s true. Now don't tell me *she's* going to start in fussing again." He held his head when Susannah did just that.

"This man played me false. He is a rake and a reprobate and . . ." Terry raised a hand as if to strike her. She didn't flinch. He didn't strike, just brought the hand to his furrowed brow. He must have scared her though, Pinkerton reasoned, because her fingers flew to her lips. She shut right up and stopped resisting. She gathered a few things and pulled her bonnet down low on her brow. He tied her hands behind her back and, docile as you please, she went with him. Neither one of them was heard from again for a long, *long* time.

Chapter Thirty-two

Susannah almost never used swear words, but she exploded, seeing Terry with that Baker woman and then being threatened by her. She was hurt to the quick and angry that Terry had escorted the dreadful woman, which is what Susannah thought then, when she herself was at a low point, feeling lost and betrayed and missing home and worrying about Simeon and the girls.

She knew they were all fine with Grace, but she loved those little girls — and their father — and that was the real problem. Susannah was distraught, trying to understand how she had gotten into such an impossible fix and she blamed herself for the whole debacle. Such things were not supposed to happen to *her*. She expected to be in control of her life. *She* was too smart and too sensible to betray the only man she would ever love. But that was just what she had done.

In that prison room, with those torturous instruments all spread out, two outlandish detectives leering at Susannah and that witch, Gilda, gloating,

Terry had tried to avoid looking into Susannah's defiant eyes. It was too painful for him, but he finally had to signal her with a wink that she had best shut her mouth and follow orders. She finally got the message, he knew, when he saw her left hand at her lips after his third or fourth try. After that, she finally got reasonable, for *her* anyway and went along more or less docilely.

Her wrists bound behind her, Susannah and Terry walked, not speaking to each other, past the military guards outside her cell and along the dank corridors, through doorways, around corners and down the steps of prison as the men in there cheered her every step of the way.

"We'll all meet again in Dixie, boys, God willing. Keep your spirits high!" she had said at the turn of each landing as they made their way through that pesthouse. Finally they passed out through the front gate onto the street where the guards, clanking and pacing, saluted Terry and Susannah. They stood beneath the stars and breathed the air of freedom for the first time in two long weeks. She started walking with Terry, but only a few steps before she turned back toward the prison to face the windows that were all boarded over with wooden slats.

With her neat, deep curtsey and a bowed head, she accepted a roar of admiration from the inmates and then answered their calls with the best Rebel yell Terry had ever heard. Like everything else about Susannah, her vocal cords were exceptional, top notch. He should have married when he had the chance, he berated himself, when she still wanted to marry him.

"Let's go," he said gruffly, stalking off, Susannah following.

"Where are you taking me?" she asked when they passed through Lafayette Square and she saw their house was dark.

"You aren't going to face a firing squad, Susie Shadow, if that's what you're worrying about," he said. After that, there was no sound but that of their footfalls for a long time as they went away from the heart of the city, toward the river. Susannah thought she heard Terry sigh once, but when she looked up at him, his face was closed.

"I'm not *taking* you anywhere. I stole you out of jail to send you home a heroine. You're being deported to Charleston," he said. "I owe you that."

"I never again will believe anything *you* say. I could not if I wanted to, which I don't," she announced. It was an untruth. She wanted to. And of course, she had long been deceitful with him, but now it was too late for her to say what was in her mind and body and soul. It was over, really over for them.

"Trust between a man and woman is never easily come by, even in the best circumstance. We've betrayed each other, Susannah."

"Why? Why did we, Terry? I love you. I have to say that," she said and he came close to giving himself away. But he didn't.

"That doesn't help now," he answered. He wouldn't look at her. He didn't know how he might react to her swimming eyes. He could hear the tears in her voice and that was hard enough.

Her heart broke. She started to cry, silently she thought but apparently that wasn't so because without a glance, he proffered his handkerchief. She couldn't accept it because her hands were still tied. He undid them. She took the handkerchief.

"You don't want me, Susannah," he said. "I can't really love you . . . or anyone."

"Who are you, damn it, inside—in truth? " she demanded. Whoever he really was, she really loved him. She *did* want him and now that she was losing him, she realized how well she *did* know the man, his soft gray eyes and soft voice and his softer heart and his loyalty and devotion to things he loved. She had seen him comfort his children, his every gesture signalling love. She had watched him with his mother, that demanding, lonely old woman, and to her, too, he revealed only love. He was strong with bullies and implacable with fools like *her,* to whom he had shown only love and she'd gone and ruined it all.

"Terry, you can't make your heart feel what it doesn't, but do you remember what I said to you, in the hospital about being married and . . . other things? If you don't recall anything, listen to me because I . . ." He placed his fingers on her lips to silence her.

"Too late for that now. I am what I am," he said, "and that's all I ever will be." I wouldn't ever ask for more, Susannah thought, but didn't say. Terry took her elbow and hurried her along so fast, she stumbled once or twice, but he caught her. Finally, when he could see the Potomac, and the truce boat with its stacks puffing, he did what he didn't want to do and had been trying to avoid — got close enough to touch Susannah, inhale her perfume, feel her hair against his cheek. He swept her up into his arms and began to run. There was no way he was going to let her miss that boat.

Setting her down at the gangway and stepping back without a word, a touch, or the kiss he longed for was one of the more difficult things Terry ever had to do in his life.

"If I know Lafitte, she'll be coming to claim her granddaughters before long," he said. He tipped his hat. He didn't even look at Susannah, who saw the girls were packed and waiting, ready to board with her, Saidee holding Mrs. Jefferson Davis' lost little dog on a tether. Simeon, learning to use his new crutch, was slowly propelling himself up the ramp, refusing offers of assistance from the crew. And Grace was there too, with Enoch and Esther.

"I came to say goodbye, dear Miss Susannah," Grace said with sadness, "because I won't be taking these babies of mine south. We'll meet again one day." Susannah hugged and kissed Grace and nodded — she could not speak and she wasn't at all sure Grace was right, that they would meet again. She turned to Terry one last time with still some ember of hope in her heart. She always was a dumb stubborn optimist but it did her no good this time. He kissed the girls goodbye and, before he strode away, he sort of smiled and said to Susannah,

"It's been a lively dance, darlin'. As we say in Texas, Susie Shadow, Adios."

Chapter Thirty-three

Benjamin Franklin Speed couldn't believe he had come all across the country from Texas with that termagant of a weathered Texas female, gaunt and stern, and handsome, too, he had to admit. Miz Armstrong had the same kind of dangerous appeal as a lean bobcat playing pussycat.

Lafitte — they were on first name terms — was a help to him sure, keeping that rowdy crew he was gathering, of seagoing outlaws, in line and sober enough to stay on their horses and ride. Even so, Ben really was glad to get to Charleston and deliver Miz Armstrong to Miz Butler's doorstep.

"You be back here prompt at midnight," she told the pack of would-be pirates that Ben had had to practically shanghai for Terrence. "Don't get so blind drunk you lose your way, hear me?"

"Yes'm," the men answered as one, sweeping off their hats and caps before turning tail and disappearing down the street. Then Lafitte Armstrong pounded on the Butler's front gate using her riding crop instead of the big iron knocker.

"I come for my little girls," she said to the startled black butler who answered her thundering rap. "Where the blazes are they?" she asked before Catherine Butler herself appeared, looking very reproachful and requiring to know what all was the noise about.

"What noise? I come for my girls, my Baby Saidee and Venetia," Lafitte said.

"Bless my soul! Can you really be Mrs. Armstrong, come all the way from Galveston, Texas!" Catherine Butler kind of clasped her hands and burbled, Ben noted, in that way southern ladies have, something like a purr. Then she embraced that Texas bobcat and drew her inside. "Ben," she said, noticing him standing there, "go round to the kitchen and tell cook I said feed you. What poor soul are you hunting down now?"

"He's not tracking anyone. He's with me," Lafitte announced. "I know this is high-toned Charleston, but where I come from, we let the hands into the ranch house."

So, Ben stepped inside a great house for the first time in his life and it was an education. It was cool and quiet in there, with flowers in bowls and rugs thicker than the best saddle blanket he'd ever had. The floors were shiny and the dark wood tables were too, and he liked watching the chiming clock with the little bullet hole in it. Even more, he especially liked watching and listening to those two ladies talking. They were a pair of what Ben thought was called

376

grand dames, and when those two got together with Mrs. McCord the day he drove them to her Up Country farm, it was a real episode. Just looking at the three women all at once was quite an occasion.

Plain-scrubbed, pious and resolute little Mrs. McCord, in a faded dress of homespun, offered her hand to imposing, big boned steely-haired Adella Lafitte Armstrong, who was all dressed up in her fringed suedes, leather boots and big prairie hat. And also, to Ben's particular pleasure, there was beautiful Catherine Butler looking on, with her porcelain skin and perfect hair, in her imported French silk fashion plate gown, very tight laced at the waist, with a skirt which looked to Ben as big as a cathedral bell.

Catherine Butler had come with a purpose to Mrs. McCord's and she announced it as soon as they all sat down under a tree in the shade of an oak, gone gold in the Indian summer sunlight.

"As you know, Mrs. McCord, I have lost my only daughter and I do not know the fate of my one son. The baby Louly is carrying, my grandchild, is very, *very* important to me. Let Louly come to me for her confinement, to be cared for by my doctor in Charleston."

"I never had any doctor help me deliver, thank you kindly, Miz Butler. I will not give up my girl and her baby to you, not for all your wealth and land and lofty ancestors." Mrs. McCord took a prim, resolute little sip of tea. "Louly is upset enough worrying if her Simeon is dead or alive or hurt, without you uprooting her. She needs her mamma now.

"Louly's brother, my third son Calvin, has a wife who also is expecting a young 'un, but *her* shadow will never cross my doorstep, she being a Yankee and a Philadelphia Methodist. When my son told her the only servants to be had in the south are black slaves, she said she would never come here, though I have never owned even one. My boy Cal has gone to fight for the Union. Why, for all I know, a ball fired from his musket may already have taken the life of one his brothers. I cannot bear to dwell on such things." Mrs. McCord had clearly said all she intended to say.

"There's more than one way to lose a son . . . a son who is in your heart . . . and then to have him come take away his two little girls who you raised. That," Lafitte said "is not tolerable. That's why I'm here. To get my little girls back." She stamped her foot like an irritated mare and it would not have surprised Ben if she'd snorted like one, too, she was that riled.

"I may have lost *both* my children, ladies. This baby of Louly's means everything to my husband and to me. The Commodore is not well. He has written from England to say he is pining so for his girl and boy, his health fails more each day. We have nothing else, Miz McCord." Catherine Butler, Ben knew, expected to have her way, whatever it was she wanted, but she was getting nowhere with Mrs. McCord.

"If Susannah was my daughter, long as she lived and breathed and walked this earth, I'd reach out and take her home to me, no matter what her crime. I would not abandon her even if she done murder — or turned Yankee." Catherine Butler became pale and her lips pursed. She brought one soft little jewelled hand to her brow.

"My daughter is dead to me, Mrs. McCord."

"I have heard that her letters come by the dozens on the truce boat like flurries of falling autumn leaves."

"What does she write about my son and my little girls?" Lafitte asked, getting more interested in the talk.

"I do not open my—that woman's—letters," Catherine insisted. "I send them right back on the next truce boat. I cast them at once into the stove, tear them into the sea. She has betrayed southern womanhood. I will not look upon her again, but I can do everything for Louly's baby . . . give him the world!"

"No, no, no," Mrs. McCord said, shaking her white head. "A child does not need the world, Catherine." She sat up as tall as she could, and appeared very determined.

"Then I shall have to come here when he is born Polly, and I will remain here until he is grown," Catherine Butler declared. "Please be good enough to show me the upstairs bedroom."

"You can't hardly call it a bedroom, Catherine. It's a attic, just a loft where all my boys used to sleep and will again, I pray. There's chinks between the logs."

"I do not care, Polly," Catherine replied. "There are things more important than physical luxuries."

"It's awful hot in summer, freezing in winter with only a small wood stove that must be fed all the night long. I have not got the fine jambalaya rice and turtle soup you are used to. Here it's mostly just potatoes, poke sallet, squirrel stew, and grits but . . ."

"Now, be calm, Miz McCord," Lafitte said to comfort the poor little woman who, it was very clear, was unhappy and apprehensive about having the elegant Mrs. Butler as a permanent house guest. "Now, who all is that arriving?" Lafitte had caught a glimpse of a small caravan moving up along the winding road, coming and going from sight as it navigated the curls and twists of the mountain road. Ben, with his acute eyes, had seen it a good ten minutes sooner than the women did. He knew there were people coming who meant a lot to each them in various ways. When they did see, he observed they stood really still with interest, before they started to walking out together down the mountain road to meet those climbing wagons.

"I guess someone down in town told the famous Confederate spy Susie Shadow where to find her mamma," Ben said.

"*Confederate* spy?" Lafitte asked.

"Well, why yes, you see . . . it went like this," Ben said, ready to elaborate, but by then, no one was left close by to hear him.

Chapter Thirty-four

Susannah was home again and, as Terry had promised, she was a heroine to one and all.

'For the first time ever in my life,' she told her diary, 'I swooned. That was when I saw my mamma, right there on McCord's Road. Just like a weak, fragile, silly female person, I folded right into Mamma's wide open arms. And that's how she knew, without my saying a word, I was carrying her grandchild. "Susannah dear," Mamma said when my eyes opened and I saw happy tears in hers, "life truly is either feast or famine. Now I've two grandchildren to wait for and dream on."

'It's so good to be home and Mamma, pleased as she is with the babies coming, is heartstruck at the change in Simeon's spirit. She needs me. So does he Simeon, even if he does have his Louly.

'Of course, my mamma was ready to take me back to her heart before she even knew about my baby, or heard my true story, most of it. There are some things best left unsaid, forever,' Susannah wrote on the first clean, crisp white bond page of her new book, a leather bound volume she had found slipped into her carpet bag.

'This above all: to thine own self be true,
And it must follow, as the night the day,

Thou canst not be false to any *man,*' was inscribed in Terry's strong hand on the back flyleaf. The implication was clear to Susannah: she had played *him* false and herself also. She and heaven both knew she never meant to, but Terry didn't, and so none of it mattered anymore. It was over for *them,* though not for Susannah and the child they had made together, who day by day was growing inside her, the true treasure she had been given by the man she loved and who she might never see again except perhaps in the eyes of his son. Or daughter.

The Armstrong girls chose to stay on with Susannah, a decision Lafitte accepted not with good grace, precisely, but with courtesy at least. She, too, remained in Charleston, as the Butlers guest, waiting for her son who she told Susannah, *would* come for his children one day, if not for his wife. Lafitte, Susannah told herself, gritting her teeth, was not an easy person to cherish.

Charleston was a celebrating city before the war and the citizens kept their spirits up through most of it, nearly to the end, with excursions — Fort Sumter was a popular one — and parties and dances. The annual St. Cecelia Ball, the most important of the season, *was* cancelled for the duration, though Mr. Pointsett, for whom the flower he bred was named, carried on with his Sunday breakfasts to which people still sought invitations as if for a royal audience.

Early in the war there was not terrible privation. The blockade was not efficient. Even when the Yankees got better at it with the addition of more Union ships, there was plenty of rice and produce from downstate, but not much salt. Some other things were in short supply, too. There was a lack of shoes and pins and needles, which were donated to the uniform factories along with pillowcases and bloomers, all needed for sandbags. By the time that a Nassau blockade runner from the Caribbean made port and an auction was held, the crush of people was overwhelming. No effort had to be made to even display merchandise attractively. The need for all sorts of things, from kitchen tools to lap robes, became so great, a whole shipload of goods was sold off in twenty or thirty minutes. Bolts of simple gingham for dresses was as highly prized as China silk once had been. The day Susannah secured a roll of checked fabric, the females at her house, young and not so young, even her mamma, were most excited.

"Teach me to sew?" Venetia asked Susannah, who was delighted. They worked together cutting, shaping, and pinning and they became good friends. It was during these busy, compatible sewing sessions that Venetia asked Susannah about something that had been troubling her for a long time.

"Susannah? Remember when we were reading from *What a Young Girl Ought to Know?*"

"I do. Why do you ask?" Susannah was tacking lace, taken from a worn petticoat, to the hem of Venetia's new dress while the girl gazed on her charming reflection in the glass. "Do you want to talk about the man and woman part? Did that unsettled you?"

"No, no. I grew up on a ranch you know, at the edge of the wilderness. I know all about bulls and cows and mares and cats and hens, that sort of thing. There was a 'Twilight Talk' about bad thoughts." Susannah sat back on her heels.

"Yes, I recall," she said. " 'As a man thinketh in his heart, so is he,' the Bible tells."

"It said it was wrong to think evil thoughts but . . . I can't always feel cheerful and content and kindly toward everyone. My thoughts are not always lovely and Dr. Wood-Allen wrote that bad ones will cause me to suffer bodily ill unless I say, 'I am not angry, I love my friend, I love everybody.' I don't love everybody. I can't. Now, will I lose my sweet face and grow ugly as the doctor says?" Susannah hugged Venetia and didn't laugh.

"Darling child, I must disagree with this expert doctor. You *can't* love everybody and you must get angry now and then and you will always have a perfectly sweet and beautiful face, even when you

384

have grown old and gray. Who are you angry with?" Susannah inquired when she saw Venetia smile with relief.

"My father. He always leaves us just when . . . just when . . ."

"Just when you think he really loves you and could never leave you in a million years? I know. He'll be back," Susannah said, not at all sure she was right.

Venetia became a wonderfully talented seamstress, so skilled she could rip apart an old hat, dye it and remake it as a brand new bonnet. She got quite a nice little business going with her two styles, the droop and the boulevard, trimming them with palmetto rosettes.

And as her brother or sister grew, Venetia's father was always in Susannah's heart and mind.

In November, Jeff Davis was elected president for a six year term even though he was spatting with General Beaugregard.

On December 11, 1861 a fire destroyed much of Charleston because most of the city's firemen had gone off to fight with the Confederate army.

On that cold winter evening, the girls and Susannah were out walking along the Ashley River wrapped in woolen cloaks and wearing warm felt bonnets, when they saw smoke. Their first thought, like everyone else's was "the enemy." It was not. Susannah thought it was fate giving them all a glimpse of what the future held. The Yankees would not start to bombard the city for about two years, but when they did, beautiful Charleston would be cut down, block by block, to rubble and ash. "Oh, we were going to die hard, we said. And we did," Susannah later wrote in her diary.

Drummond lights and fire barges lit the bays and there were gun boats in the harbor but the Yankees had nothing to do with the Charleston fire, not directly. The outer islands had been abandoned as too costly in lives to defend and Port Royal had fallen a month before the fire. General Lee happened to be in the city that December night, dining at the Mills House, and Charleston was crowded with refugees from the Sea Islands, one of whom it was theorized, kicked over a lantern in the barn where he was harboring and nature—wind—took charge from there.

The conflagration actually began at the Russell Sash and Blind Factory and soon, alarm bells began to ring. The wind picked up, the fire jumped East Bay and sparks were carried high into the air. Some structures were saved by bucket brigades and wet blankets. The Butler house was one, the Orphan House another. St. John's Cathedral burned and the steeple of the Circular Congregational Church fell, its bell shattering on the cobbles below. God, the people said, played no favorites.

By daylight, the scene's total desolation was apparent. Country planters began sending food into the city at once and Venetia, Susannah, Lafitte,

386

and Catherine worked in one of the soup kitchens set up to aid burned out citizens.

A few days later in December, Susannah, who was well along in her pregnancy, awoke one day shaking with chills and burning with fever and soon there was pain. Catherine, ghastly pale, sent at once for the doctor and the midwife and went to her daughter's bedside, feeling distraught and helpless, and terrified.

Susannah lost her baby and nearly her life. There had been no warning of anything gone wrong, but she delivered a tiny stillborn girl whose heart, white haired old Dr. Nelson told her, had probably ceased to beat some weeks before.

"You've lost a terrible lot of blood, Susannah, but your own body saved your life by dislodging that little lost soul. The infection would have been worse, insurmountable perhaps, in another few days. Now, you must get *your* strength back and when you do, and your young man comes home, why I predict there'll be other young ones for you, a houseful." The man meant well, Susannah knew, but she didn't want to hear any more of his zesty speech and turned her face away. She had no loving thoughts or feelings left in her.

"It was working so *hard* after the fire," the women, gathered to roll bandages for the troops, agreed.

"It was helping Louly to cope with Simeon, what with his downcast manner and quick temper," they said. "Oh what a change in that boy!"

"Catherine didn't help any, so preoccupied as she is with Simeon and demanding because of that," the women clucked.

"It's that Lafitte Armstrong, such a . . . a noisy woman, not a proper Charlestonian lady at all, not at all," it was commented.

"It was riding that wild little Arab horse . . ."

"It was a black cat . . ."

". . . or standing in the light of the full moon . . ."

"Ladies, ladies, please!" Louly implored. "We have all been dependent on Susannah, demanding her time and attention, but she has always had bottomless resources of energy and love. If that baby was sound, if she was meant to be born and *be* and meet her daddy some day why, she would have. There's just not a . . . well, not always a fathomable cause, not to us mere humans leastways, for everything that happens, now is there?"

The women all looked at Louly who was almost a mother herself, just weeks from becoming one. She was beautiful and glowing and they all agreed with her, even when she said *her* baby was going to be the salvation of its father, the one thing that would help Simeon Butler back to find his loving, open, and hopeful self again.

And then the women went on rolling cotton wool in silence for a time, each preoccupied with her own thoughts. There were many things about which they were no longer certain, ordinary every day happenings they could no longer rely upon in those troubled times.

"The way things are, you can't even be sure anymore, that the roosters are going to crow at dawn," Mrs. McCord said, thinking aloud. The others nodded, one and all.

Her physical health returned, but Susannah's heart was stone cold. She kept to herself, treading the Charleston Battery in all weathers, at all hours, like a sailor's wife pacing a widow's walk. Somewhere, though she didn't know it herself, the stubborn optimist deep inside her was still waiting for Terry to come back to her, and that's what would save her, sooner or later.

By the middle of January, Louly was gone, dead of the childbed fever, but she left a fine baby boy. When his wet nurse wasn't with him, he sucked on the sugar rags his grandmothers gave him and cooed. His father was more downcast than ever. Catherine Butler sighed. Polly McCord keened lullabies to the baby boy, tears running along the channels and lines that marked her face.

In March, the ironclads *Monitor* and *Merrimack* fought to a draw at Hampton Roads. And spring came again, fragrant and gentle and riotous. Susannah stopped gazing out to sea and removed herself from Charleston to Colleton Plantation where she took to the woods, to spend her days in a very beautiful dell just past the edge of the garden near the river. It was a tangle of vines over moss-covered stones. The ground was soft and the flowers in the hawthorne began to stir her heart and dreams again.

She didn't know if Terry was dead or alive, but she went there, to that one place, just to think of him and of what they had had together. And thinking, she came to know, that like Lafitte, though her own reasons were different, she never would take another man's name.

Nothing could compare to the way she loved that man who had walked away, out of her life, into eternity.

But Susannah was healing and, one night toward the end of April, she came to Terry's place in the woods with actual pleasure, to view the constellations through an elliptical space in the newly leafed trees. She looked straight up, her head thrown back. She heard the wind. In a wonderful vertiginous state of elation, she felt the earth shift. Everywhere about her, living things breathed in the darkness. She knew she would be all right even though she was alone.

And then, she was not alone.

"I've come to claim what's rightfully mine," Terry said from the darkness. Susannah couldn't move. He was an apparition and so . . . perfect, his eyes gleaming, his hair long, glintin, curling at his neck. His arms opened wide and enfolded her. His parted lips tasted, again and again before they devoured hers.

And he surely claimed what was his. They sank down together in that earth-scented mossy dell, their love-starved needy bodies touching, his fine, strong hands molding her, retaking what he'd already won. Before his body slid above hers and he moved into her, before she closed her eyes and gave herself to ecstasy and love, she saw a whole and perfect constellation, Cygnus the Swan, sailing above them.

Epilogue

"I came back to ignite to cold fire and claim the rights of the marriage bed. You've been withholding something from me that's rightfully mine. You *have* been, more or less, less rather than more . . . in a way, since the . . . since *our* wedding," Terry laughed. He and Susannah, had returned together to Charleston, and after a stroll, were making their way slowly, with frequent stops, up through Catherine's beautiful garden toward the townhouse. Their third detour had taken them to the summer cottage where it all had begun for them, a year before.

"A *cold* fire? How can you use such a word in connection with me, sir? The flame never died Terry, or even dimmed. But your feelings may be another matter. Tell me, what was it really brought you back to Carolina? Was it the girls, Terry, like your mamma said?" Susannah asked, running her hand through his dark hair as she arose from the cottage bed, her own hair in perfectly lovely disarray.

"I came for them *and* you *Mrs*. Armstrong. I ran into Colonel Wigfall in Richmond. *He* told me that he told *you* he would not mock the marriage service. *He* said *you* said you wanted to marry me, and then *he* said to you it was the best thing that could ever happen to *me*. He was right." Terry took the hand Susannah extended and stood, then drew her to him. "You should have told me, you really should have, that we were really married."

"*You* said it was up to me to work things out with the Reverend Wigfall. It was my decision, you insisted, because you didn't care. I cared a lot, love."

"So Wigfall told me."

"Lace me up, please, *Commander* Armstrong. Is that it now, the correct rank?"

"Delighted, Mrs. Armstrong. Turn your lovely back to me. Now, I asked you in Galveston to *really* marry me and you refused me and went on refusing me . . . Why wouldn't you marry me again, or at the least speak the truth, back then in Washington when I asked you once more?"

Because I wasn't . . . *sure* of your love, Terry and also . . . I didn't want to admit I'd deceived you. And besides, because of our baby, the marriage date had to be *right* . . . or else there was a chance of our child discovering one day she was . . ."

"A bastard? That's not what she would have been and if it was, I don't give a damn! Do you care, Susannah? Do you think she would have? I can't believe that of *you*, my free spirit, my wild lady love."

"There are some things that *matter*, Terry Armstrong, and one of them is knowing you're *loved* by certain special people in the world, by your lover, and by your mamma and daddy."

"That has nothing to do with calendar dates and weddings, darlin.' Love's love. You get it and give it out if you feel it, with or without a contract. It took me a long time, too long, to realize I didn't have to own you on a legal paper, like chattel, to . . . claim your heart and give you mine, to love you unconditionally, forever."

"You owned my heart unconditionally and forever, Lieutenant Armstrong, uh Commander, before you ever spoke a word to me," Susannah said and Terry's white hard sparkling grin flashed.

"I know that now, darlin' but still, I am real glad we got that piece of paper from Wigfall. Love's love as I said, but that piece of paper—it means this is forever by our own choice, in the eyes of God and man . . ."

"Could be," Susannah laughed.

". . . and in the eyes of your mamma and mine and . . . the girls and your daddy and . . ."

"We *were* really married."

". . . and then I heard you were betrothed again to Will."

"You sir, are not as shrewd as you led me to think." Susannah shook her head in disbelief. Terry shrugged and smiled sheepishly.

"There was Will Chauvenet, living in my own house, Susannah, and then, there you were, kissing Will and there was Beverly Bland telling me you were betrothed to Will, so . . ."

"You believed *him?"* Susannah demanded, her hands on her hips.

"Don't look at me like that, darlin' or I won't be responsible for my actions, hear? There were those coded love poems, in your diary, too."

"For you, fool. You were meant to read them. Only *you* were supposed to see the book, remember? That simple code wouldn't stymie anyone, except that detective Pinkerton. You just handed it over, gave it to the man, to the Yankees, with all my detailed drawings of the whole Confederate coast, from Texas on up."

"I changed everything, all the drawings, details, shore lines. I had to keep their confidence in Washington, by giving them some 'real' information. I am not as dumb as you're suggesting, Susie Shadow. Now, let me finish this lacing up, even if I'll soon have to undo it all again. If you agree, you and I are going to run the Yankee blockade tonight, together, before dawn. This gown, charming as it is, won't do, darlin'."

"I agree to follow you anywhere on earth, love, even past the Yankee blockade."

"To get to you, I came in through it, in the

Presto, loaded with seven barrels of whiskey. I'm a hero down at the harbor."

"You're a hero here, too, love. How did you do it?" Susannah asked.

"By keeping to the shallows. The blockade isn't working any too well, what with the mouth of the harbor twelve miles across and lumberous Union ships like the *Niagara* unable to sail out of the main ship channels. I took a shallow channel, close to shore. In a small boat like the *Presto,* you can do that. I found it challenging."

"A dangerous diversion. I hear all it takes is cold nerve and superb seamanship. You're made for the game, Terry." Susannah brushed out her copper curls.

"I met an English naval officer who was given leave specially to run this blockade. He said it was more exciting than fox hunting. That's your sport, if I'm not mistaken, ma'am?"

Terry and Susannah ran the Charleston blockade that night, hugging the shore, ducking their own troop's Drummond lights, their fast runner sliding past Yankees on watch in ships on the water and Yankee pickets on the offshore islands. The couple didn't stop until they gasped in the salt scent of the open ocean, saw the moon in the sea and stars in the sky and inhaled the fresh air of true freedom.

They were taken up by a British ship, standing by for them.

They reached England in time for the launching of Hull Number 203, on May 15, 1862, a dream brought to fruition by Terry and Susannah and many others, mostly by Commodore Butler's diplomacy, patience and caution. Hull 203 would not return to her moorings after a first "trial trip" down the Mersey. Barkentine rigged with vast sails and double screws, the *Alhambra,* as she was to be christened, would soon come to be known by Union merchants and whalers as the "Scourge of the Sea."

When the vessel made for the Azores on her first run, there to be armed and staffed, her Master and his wife, Commander and Mrs. Terrence Armstrong were aboard.

In the Azores, they found Simeon and Ben with the crew, waiting. Marcus Smart was harpooner in the whaler *Harriet Simms* which called at the Azores while the *Alhambra* was in port and so Susannah was able to learn that Grace and her young children were safe among friends in Ontario.

"The next time you see me coming, Smart, you better run," Ben half-grinned, half-grimaced. "That Yankee oil tub of yours is fair game for the *Alhambra*—and we've got guns."

"If you can catch the *Harriet* in that newfangled thing, steam and sails and what not, more power to you, Speed," Marcus laughed, punning, as the two men resolutely shook hands.

"We each must do now what we feel is right,"

Susannah said, "but you tell Grace, please, Marcus, whatever happens in this war, we'll all be together again after, not north or south, though maybe west where the sun sets . . . I must tell you . . ." she started to say and then, she fainted away in her distressed husband's arms.

"Terry, that's only the second time in my life I've swooned," Susannah smiled weakly when her eyes opened a few moments later.

"When was the first time, darlin'?" Terry asked placing a cool compress on her brow. He had carried her to their cabin. "Was it something serious?"

"Seriously wonderful! Oh Terry, the first time was when I was going to have your baby, so, now draw your own conclusion!"

"The *Alhambra*'s first voyage will take you to a warm, safe, neutral port where this ship and I can call on you regularly. My Susannah, from that very first day at Annapolis, I loved but I offered you glory instead. Now . . ."

"Now, you've given me love and glory, fighting together for Dixie, Terry Armstrong."

"And this darlin' is just the beginning," Terry vowed passionately as he took her in his arms.